TRIUMPH OF DECEIT

Published by

Librario Publishing Ltd.

ISBN: 1-904440-50-9

Copies can be ordered via the Internet
www.librario.com

or from:

Brough House, Milton Brodie, Kinloss
Moray IV36 2UA
Tel/Fax No 00 44 (0)1343 850 617

Printed and bound by
DigiSource UK Ltd, Livingston

TRIUMPH OF DECEIT

MURIEL ARNOLD

Librario

Acknowledgements

Once again I must thank the Editor-in-Chief and staff of *The Grantham Journal*, 46 High Street, Grantham for giving me access to their archives.

My sincere thanks go to the willing and helpful staff at Southampton Public Library, Civic Centre, Southampton, Grantham Public Library, Isaac Newton Centre, Grantham and the Biblioteca Municipal, Calle Astarloa, Bilbao, Spain.

Mr A Percival of the Glen River Riding School, Swinstead Road, Corby Glen, near Grantham, told me exactly what I needed to know about the price of a horse in 1920.

Thank you all.

Bibliography

Miguel Delibes, *El Camino*
  First Published in Great Britain 1963 by George G Harrap & Co Ltd

FUNDACION de los FERROCARRILES ESPAÑOLES
  El Ferrocarril en Cantabria
  Santander, 19 a 25 de Agosto de 1985

Michael Pointer and Malcolm G Knapp
  Bygone Grantham Vol. 3
  First published 1978 by Bygone Grantham

For Topsy, Gordon, and Monica

By the same author

THE RUN OF TIME

Chapter 1

August 1920

Bladon King had drunk too much. He always drank too much at the Rent Dinners, everyone in Ketsby knew that. It was his day for getting drunk. As landlord of The Pyewipe for more than twenty years he could hold his beer. The drinking bouts elevated him to a plateau where he would kick aside the problems gnawing away at his peace of mind: Hannah, Trynah, the double wedding.

So he enjoyed boozing with his fellow men, listening to the bragging about the size of their harvest or the size of their fat lambs. They had gone to find pleasure with the half-crown girls in Grantham or the lonely widows in the lonely cottages or back to their waspish wives. But he had decided to take Duke in the trap to Loston. He was now on his way home, cushioned in the load of straw, singing at the top of his voice.

Soon he was in Fosdyke Lane passing the gypsy caravans. Two stout horses were tethered to a fallen tree, their long manes hanging like curtains across their eyes, and a man with a halter rope stood at the head of a spotted Appaloosa mare. A stallion circled and snorted, nostrils flaring. Duke faltered in his stride, scenting the mare, and Bladon steadied him on the rein as they passed.

He glanced over his shoulder. The animals were coupling. "Should have more privacy!" he shouted to the men. "Take them to the back of the caravans, or into that field, but not here on the roadside. Horses are sensitive." There was no reply.

He flicked his whip in irritation as he trundled past the jumble of caravans. They were covered with old canvas and bits of oilcloth and the paintwork was peeling. Several little girls were collecting sticks in the ditch bunching them together like flowers. A mangy dog sat patiently at the bole of a horse chestnut tree. Two boys were swinging in its branches. A young woman was bent over a fire shaking a blackened pan, frying eggs. "Stolen from my hen huts in Copping Lane, I'll be bound," thought Bladon as he started to sing again.

But as Duke pounded along the singing faded to a low hum. The drink was now like a heavy balloon lodged somewhere near the waistband of his breeches, sapping his good humour, stealing his cheerfulness, and the anxieties began to sidle back into memory. There was Hannah to worry about, and there was the lame stallion. And Cadger Burrell; that gin trap was supposed to have taught him a lesson. It had cost him two fingers on his right hand but he was still thieving. Been at it for more than twenty years. Only last week Bladon had caught him stealing corn from his barn at Bunker's Hill.

"All things bright 'n beautiful..." His voice petered out and a loud belch rolled over the hedge and was lost in the trees.

As he passed the last caravan he saw three men with ropes huddled around a black mare. One of the men signalled for him to slow down. The mare was foaling. Long forelegs were visible. He steered Duke on to the grass at the side of the road to deaden the noise of his wheels.

"That's a day to remember," Bladon announced to the passing hawthorn bushes. "I can guarantee," giving another resounding belch, "I can guarantee... that you will never... you will never see such sight again. N..ev..er will you see such thing. Conception and birth, just yards apart. Creation. All things bright 'n beautiful, all creatures..." He scythed the air with his whip and bellowed, "Hey! Hey! Hey!" Duke tossed his head, enjoying the free rein as he streaked away with mane flying.

The gypsies had a new foal on the grass verge. The rent was paid. His twin daughters had managed to fall in love at the same time and they were going to have a double wedding. He didn't think it was such a good idea – all that lace and tears and crowds of relatives. One bride at a time was as much as he could cope with, but they were set on it.

Bladon's disapproval arose not so much from the double wedding but any wedding at all as far as Billie was concerned. She was planning to marry the son of Donner's Brewery. A good catch. But Bladon didn't want her to go. As for Becky, she hated her job at Newark and couldn't wait to get married. There were tears every time he visited her.

"Please take me home, father," Becky bit her lips. They were in the Copper Kettle Tea Room. It was deserted except for two elderly ladies sitting at a table in the corner. Both were dressed in shabby coats, both wore spectacles and both were resigned to some unknown desperation as they clutched their teacups and nodded their grey heads, staring into space.

"But it's for your own good, dear girl," he covered her hand resting on the blue check tablecloth. "The discipline of a good family..."

She pulled her hand away and fidgeted with a damp linen handkerchief.

"It's for your own good, Becky," he repeated, "don't you see? You have to do something. And you've never been interested in The Pyewipe, have you?" He gently raised her chin. "That doesn't matter in the least."

So she had gone to Newark to be parlourmaid in the house of Doctor Lister. But Bladon was sure that with her mind full of wedding plans she would settle until her big day. And her young man had good prospects, clerk in the Railway Office. His twins had chosen well.

Bladon's eyes were on Duke's glistening haunches as he laboured up the steep incline to Ketsby, a conceited little village sitting on top of a hill that enjoyed views in all directions. Ketsby knew what was going on for miles around. To the south, at the bottom of the hill, Grantham sprawled in a huge saucer of streets and houses dominated by the spire of St Wulfram's Church, needle sharp, piercing the sky. To the north, on a clear day you could see Lincoln Cathedral. Stretching away to the east and west were lazy little villages.

Suddenly Duke smelt home and with uncanny energy he

thundered over the rise and into the village pulling up outside the inn with a contented snuffle.

The Pyewipe was Bladon King's life, his joy and his agony. And as the years came and went he tossed everything into the melting pot. The good and bad, the happiness, the sadness, the disasters and the catastrophes. Getting married to Trynah Bishop had been good, so good. But returning to The Pyewipe that fateful day all those years ago had seemed like the end of the world.

It had been the day of Culbeck Spring Fair. When he got back she was gone. *Gone!* A note left on his pillow told him nothing. Married for six of the happiest months that had come his way for a long time. Where had she gone? Why had she gone? The brandy bottle had helped him through those first hours of shock as he sat brooding in the Private Room. Then he had heard the voices in the Tap Room. It was business as usual. His customers were here, supping his ale and yarning and smoking, and he was the landlord. He had a duty to them.

Standing in front of the fireplace his eyes skimmed across the rug at the hearth, the stained floorboards, the oak dining table, the settle with its pewter inlay. Trynah. Every item punctuated his memories. She's left me! An icy hand wrenched at his stomach. He was alone again. He grabbed the brandy bottle and replenished his glass.

The voices in the Tap Room had risen to a crescendo. Boisterous, good-natured voices. No, he was not alone. He staggered along the short corridor clutching the bottle in one hand and his goblet in the other, his shoulders bumping against the wall until he came to the Tap Room doorway. All eyes turned towards him and the chatter faded to a low hum.

"My wife's gone, left me," Bladon announced, waving the bottle in a wide arc. "Left me. Might's well hear it from me afore the scandalmongers get hold of it."

Barney Sedge was sitting in the corner, his quick dark eyes resting on Bladon's woebegone face. He was Bladon's right-hand man and had lived through all the catastrophes as if they had been his own.

Charlie Papple, the carrier, cleared his throat and was about to spit. Tom Favell leaned back on the bench. He was the baker, tall and thin and as pasty as the dough he handled everyday. He kept his eyes on the notice nailed to the beam across the low ceiling, which read 'Mind your head'.

Bladon leaned on the doorframe as he scanned the familiar faces. Bert Daubney, the glazier, always perspiring winter and summer, with cheeks like ripe tomatoes. Bob Willows, the carpenter, was studying his pipe. Joe Limon, the wheelwright, took off his cap, stroked his bald head and pulled the cap down to his eyebrows. Bladon edged the doorframe out of the way with his elbow.

"Come on, now, sit you down here a minute." Barney teased the bottle from Bladon's fingers and gently pushed on his shoulders until he sank into a seat next to Pegleg Pike. Curtis Pike had arrived from nowhere with his wooden leg, a bag of belongings and a keen intelligence that had earned him immediate respect as the sage of the village.

"How many times does a man have to lose a woman? Eh? How many times?" Bladon jumped to his feet, raised his right arm and smashed the goblet to the floor, the shards glinting as they came to rest under the trestle tables.

"Don't take on so," Charlie Papple moved to the serving hatch with his slow, clumsy gait, tripping on a stool. "She'll be back."

"If she's got any sense," Bert Daubney wiped his jacket sleeve across his forehead.

Bladon supported his back with both hands. "Well, now you know. So when the hens get cackling," he bent his body forward and swung from side to side, slowly, "you'll all be able to tell 'em that you know. And you can tell 'em all to shut their big mouths," he straightened up, smoothing his hands down his chest, "because you already know. How do you know?" Now he was shouting. "Because you got it straight from Bladon King. That poor bugger who runs The Pyewipe for you."

The Tap Room was silent. Mouths fell open, tankards rested on the trestle tables, pipes were dying on the smokers. "Now," he threw his arms wide and toppled forward but quickly regained his balance. "Everybody have drink on me. It's not Christmas, it's not my birthday, it's the day poor old Bladon got severed again! I'm alone again!"

The weeks and months and years went by with no sign of his wife, no news. So the memories boiled and simmered and stewed and he gave them a stir whenever the mood took him.

He clambered over the tailgate of the trap and led Duke round the corner of the inn through the double doors into the stable yard. He put one elbow on the shaft of the trap and surveyed the premises as if he were looking at them for the first time. The toilets were in the far corner, a neat little red brick building. Next to them were the pigsties and stables. Across the yard, on the opposite side was the coach house for the wagonettes, next to the double entrance gates, which were solid timber and kept the stable yard private from the lane outside. A flight of stone steps at the side of the coach house led to the Club Room above. Somebody had left a pile of flour sacks on the bottom step. Convinced that he was safely home and all was well, he backed the trap up to the open doors of the hay shed.

"Hannah!" He glanced across to the kitchen door but no one appeared. He loosened Duke's girth strap and led him to the drinking trough near the pigsty.

She was slumped across the kitchen table, her arms cradling her head. There was an empty glass near her elbow. He looked around the kitchen, where pots and pans were piled high in the sink, drying, and a saucepan murmured on the hob. He lifted the lid. She was making soup and it smelt good. The milk pails waiting by the door shone like silver and the floor had been swept. He could drop a heavy saucepan, that would wake her up. He could shake her, he could shout at her, he could curse at her, but he knew he would do none of these things. After Esther's death he had been a regular visitor to Hannah Cressey's cottage at Donsby on market days and Feast Days. A spree with Hannah put his world to rights until he found Trynah on the roadside with a sprained ankle, and eventually married her. But when his wife walked out on him he'd been glad of Hannah to siphon away the anguish, to fill the aching gap. Now she was housekeeping and mothering his twin girls and keeping him sane, but she had a fatal flaw. That was the trouble.

He stared down at the bowed head, his eyes fixed on the thick coil of auburn hair. He wanted to unpin it, caress it, bury his face in it, run his fingers through the silky hanks, but he resisted the temptation. He rummaged in her pinafore pockets and pulled out the little bottle of gin. Just as he had thought. Hannah sat up, trying to focus her bleary eyes.

"Oh... oh..." She got to her feet but lost her balance and flopped back into the chair.

"You've been at it again, Hannah. How many times have I told you?"

"Just had a little nip. Bad news. Louisa just lost her baby." Her elbows rested on the shiny oilcloth covering the kitchen table, her hands cradling her face. She looked up at him without moving her head. "Boy. Wouldn't have done no good. A poor thing. Well, we just had little drink to drown the sorrow..." She got up again gripping the edge of the table to steady herself. "Shall we go upstairs?"

He recognised the look, the desire, the hunger and he understood the power she had over him. With or without drink she could dominate him in one place only. In bed.

"It's nearly four o'clock. I have to go to Copping Lane to milk." His voice was harsh and he hated himself. He couldn't bear to see the disappointment in her eyes and she couldn't know about the ache in his groin. He tweaked her cheek. "We'll have an early night."

* * *

13

After Bladon had gone Hannah made some tea and took it to her bedroom. She had to sober up before the customers arrived. A pot of strong tea would do the trick. The gin had made her feel like a heavy old carthorse, lethargic and clumsy.

It had followed the usual pattern. A little drop of gin, then another little drink to keep the first one company. Then another one and she was there, laughing and joking, dismissing the follies of the world, jollying the twins along. She had tried. Tried hard to be a mother to them and they had responded. Billie, with her father's impulsiveness, always found time for a gesture that told Hannah all she needed to know. A bunch of violets picked in Munce's Wood, or a surprise cake for her birthday. And Becky, shy and hesitant, would embrace her spontaneously and hug her and kiss her and fill her heart with yearning.

She sat in front of the mirror, clutching the cup, sipping the tea, arguing with her eyes as if she were afraid of losing something. But there was nothing to lose. The bloom of youth had left her quite suddenly a long time ago. No slow, steady ageing process for her. It had happened overnight.

She could remember the days when she didn't need the comfort of the gin bottle. All she needed was Gilbert Cressey, that fine young man with his agreeable smile, his bright intelligence, his slim, energetic body, his very goodness of heart.

They had met one Ketsby Feast Day. He had stepped in front of her near the coconut shies and smiled. That was all. But from that first smile she knew that this was her man. Three months later they married. Then one day the policeman came to the door of their cottage to say that he had been knocked down by a train.

"How can that be? Gilbert is alert. He would've seen it coming." Hannah's suspicious eyes accused the policeman standing in front of her, who looked down his long nose and fiddled with the button of his tunic pocket.

"He was crossing the line at Hogtree Wood to take a short cut home." He raised his thick black eyebrows. "I don't know why he didn't hear the train or see it. It was broad daylight. No wind."

And those were the facts that changed Hannah's life and robbed her of her bloom, her youth. They wouldn't let her see him before they closed the coffin. "Just remember him as he was," they said. Hannah argued that she must see him but the doctor finally convinced her. She eyed the pall-bearers as they heaved the coffin on to their shoulders. Gilbert Cressey was as lean as a greyhound and the doctor had good reason to persuade her not to go to the funeral parlour. The coffin was packed with bags of sand.

And that's when she first made friends with the gin bottle. Then Bladon King was standing at her door, tapping his whip across the palm of his hand, blond and handsome, the finest horseman in the district with a nervous energy that could not be contained. She had known him before he married Esther. Before Esther died bringing the twin girls into the world. Now he was a widower, she was a widow, a perfect match in bed and out of bed. But he never asked the question, never proposed that they should marry. Then his visits dried up altogether. She had lived through too many disappointments to waste time on the fickleness of men. There could only be one reason for him to stay away.

News of the wedding of the year at Ketsby spread far and wide. Trynah Bishop, the cordwainer's daughter from Apsley, had won his heart and Hannah reached for the gin bottle. Six months later, one fine spring day Bladon King was at her door again, tapping his whip across the palm of his hand.

"Why, stranger! Come in." Hannah stepped aside and she caught that wholesome whiff of a horseman, something honest and earthy and a chord deep within her thrummed with desire.

He waited in the middle of the parlour looking around at the familiar scene: the dark green chenille cloth on the mahogany dining table, the solid oak dresser laden with plates and dishes, the grandfather clock, old and stiff with the years, the mantelpiece festooned with ornaments and the shiny brass log basket.

"Sit down, Bladon. Relax."

He propped his whip against the grandfather clock and sank into the green velvet chair near the fire, then his strong hands raked through the thick blond hair. It was a habit she knew well. He was nervous.

"Trynah's gone. She's left me." He spoke quickly, to get it over with, to remove the pain. "We went to Culbeck Fair, me and the kiddies. When I got back... she'd gone."

He got up and began to pace around the parlour, his fingers exploring the edge of the solid oak dresser, caressing the bobbles on the chenille cloth. "I found a note."

Hannah turned in her chair, watching his restless pacing. Nothing had robbed him of his vigour, his dynamism. "Did she say where she was going?"

"No. It was only a short letter. Said she couldn't explain." He paused near the grandfather clock, studying its face, then he turned. "Hannah, I need a housekeeper, my twin girls need a mother and I... and I..."

"Need a bedmate," she got up from her chair and swept into his arms.

"You can read me like a book, can't you? It was always the same." He folded his arms around her. "Confound you and your tantalising body."

"Well, at least you're honest."

"There's no point in beating about the bush," and he took her hands and put them to his lips. "I can't offer a wedding ring. Trynah is still my wife wherever she is, until... until..." he led her back to the fireside.

Her hands slid away and she sat perfectly still watching him as her thoughts plodded back through the years to when he was a widower and she was a widow. The rollicking times they had had on Market Days and Feast Days. He could have offered her a ring then, he could have proposed marriage to her. They had both been free. But he had put the ring on Trynah's finger, not hers. Now she had to listen to this excuse.

"Can you cope with the village gossips?"

"Huh!" Hannah tossed her head of glossy red hair, "if that's all I have to cope with life would be a bed of roses. I don't fritter my fat away worrying about the village tittle-tattle. They've always got a crow to pluck. Come now, you know me better than that, Bladon.

And so Hannah agreed to everything including the place in his bed. She enjoyed the conviviality at The Pyewipe, the drinking, the gossip, the laughter. She enjoyed people, and she enjoyed Bladon King without a ring on her finger. She gave up her cottage at Donsby, sold most of the furniture but insisted on bringing just one item that was dear to her.

It was a bronze statue of a young boy, naked, standing on a low pedestal. He was about four feet tall with his right hand on his hip, the left arm raised above his head. The expression on the child's face fascinated her. It was so perfect, so beautiful she couldn't part with him. It had belonged to her father who had been gardener at the Big House at Donsby.

Bladon was not so keen on this creature but he agreed and the boy stood naked and unashamed just inside the front door at the foot of the stairs in the inn.

At first the customers made sport with the statue, insulting him daily, and at Christmas and Easter the innocent little cherub came in for more indignities than it could ever have dreamt of in Hannah's garden. Tweed caps were placed at a cheeky angle on his head, walking sticks were hooked on to his arm, and scarves were draped around his private parts. When Billie and Becky were small they loved to climb through the space between his legs.

And so she came to The Pyewipe with only her boy statue at the bottom of the stairs to remind her of Donsby. She had visited the inn many times after a jolly market day at Grantham or Newark but she was surprised how big it was, with its long frontage on

High Street. She remembered the entrance door well. It had one deep step which customers tripped on as they went in and never saw when they came out.

Inside was a long corridor. At the end, on the left was the Private Room, the only place she and Bladon could call their own, away from the hurly burly of the Little Room. This was the bar where all drinks were dispensed and there was a serving hatch into the Tap Room with its bench seats backed up against the wall. Long trestle tables were placed in front of them. During the winter months a roaring fire kept the customers drinking. In summer the brass scuttle was filled with fresh flowers. Here the customers drank and swore and argued and shouted and sang and belched and never wanted to go home but she always gave them her time and a smile.

At the other end of the corridor, to the right, was the Back Room where the Council held their monthly meetings. The door was painted green and had a sliding panel at eye level. She could do without that monthly gathering of frowsty old cronies, chewing the hind leg off a donkey for two hours and achieving absolutely nothing, but it was an important booking for Bladon so she gave the Council members her time and her smile.

She was happy with Bladon. She gave him everything, almost. He was absolutely right for her but each time she suspected that a baby was on the way she dealt with it. She had no legal status here in his bed, he could throw her out. There was no ring on her finger for bairns so she did what the toffs did. She knew where the pennyroyal and wild horseradish grew. Those women of the gentry didn't have a baby every year because they did what she did. But they had the time and money to bear children and educate them. So no wedding ring, no son for Bladon. Besides, no one knew where Trynah was. No one had seen or heard of her since the day she left. She could walk back into their lives tomorrow.

Hannah threw the hairbrush on to the dressing table. And what if Trynah did walk back into the Pyewipe? But she tossed away the thought. She had given up worrying about the 'what ifs' a long time ago.

She faced the mirror, turning her head from side to side then she smiled. It was time to wash and change and get ready to meet the customers. She drained the empty teacup again. She was so thirsty she could drink the well dry. Pity about Louisa's baby.

Chapter 2

The clock on the mantelpiece did not need dusting. Nothing needed dusting. Dust was never allowed to settle but Becky had to dust everyday. The dining room, the hall and Doctor Lister's study. She saved the sitting room until last. There was the most to dust here. The mantelpiece over the marble fireplace was crammed. A pair of vases flanked the gilt bracket clock, which was too heavy to move so she dusted round it. And she dare not attempt to lift the gilt cherub candlesticks. She just tickled their arms and thighs and bottoms with the duster. The silver frames of the Lister family portrait photographs were easy. She stared at the sullen faces, wrinkled her nose and put out her tongue.

She would love to throw everything out of the window especially the waxed fruit under the glass dome. Luscious peaches, a bunch of grapes and apricots, which looked so real but they were just an aggravation. And the pot of peacock feathers was ridiculous. How could you dust feathers?

She wiped around the clock and didn't even notice the time. She hated cleaning, she hated Norcross House and she hated all the people in it, especially Doctor Lister. She shivered. He would turn up at the most unexpected moments, emerging from the shadows of this gloomy mansion, following her, talking to her, standing close to her. She didn't like the way he riveted his eyes on her. They were dead eyes that said nothing, did nothing but stare. She couldn't understand why he hovered around her. He gave her the creeps. She didn't like him however famous he might be.

From the mantelpiece she moved to the walnut pedestal table with its glassy surface, its vase of lemon roses standing in the pale porcelain bowl which she was terrified of dropping so she dusted round that as well. When she and Oliver were married she wouldn't spend her time dusting. She would spend her time loving him, that's why people got married.

She glanced around the mausoleum and saw that she had left the clock askew on the mantelpiece. Perhaps it was unfair to call the sitting room a mausoleum but that's what it looked like and that's what it felt like, and she had heard Mrs Lister and her gaggle of friends at tea time with their vicious tongues, mocking their guests, then greeting them the next day with their treacle smiles.

"They say her husband's gone off with the schoolteacher," said Mrs Jam Tart, blotting her bright red lips with the serviette. Becky was standing near the door as instructed by Mrs Lister, but she was listening and watching. Mrs Jam Tart was the wife of a solicitor and let slip all kinds of facts about her husband's clients. She was fat and ugly, but whereas most fat people were pretty, with an aura of good humour, mocking life with their extra, comfortable bulges, Mrs Jam Tart was vicious. Her lips and her eyes were cruel, small and angry. Becky couldn't remember her name, which sounded foreign, but she always took the last jam tart.

"Shouldn't think she's much to leave home for. The schoolteacher, I mean." Miss Wetherby took another buttered scone. She looked very much like the teacher they were talking about. Both were spinsters, as thin and dry as a bundle of sticks. Their sweethearts had not come back from Flanders and every pore in their bodies had shrivelled up.

Then there was Mrs Dunham, a widow. A rich widow. She wasn't as fat as Mrs Jam Tart but everything about her was round, her face, her big full breasts, her lumpy stomach and big round bum. Becky thought she was too old to use so much powder and lipstick. The powder was too white and sat in the creases on her face and the lipstick was too red. It streaked from her mouth in little rivulets. Mrs Dunham was on every committee and charity in Newark and knew everybody's business.

"She had a permanent wave. Took two hours and cost two guineas." Mrs Dunham pouted her shiny red lips and helped herself to another piece of fruit cake. "Looks like a helmet!"

They were hypocrites and they buried their friends and acquaintances alive, here in this room. It was all a sham and she longed for The Pyewipe and father and Billie and Hannah. They all called things by their proper names and did not pretend anything. But most of all she longed for Oliver. A great sigh moaned from deep within her.

It was only weeks now before the wedding but it seemed an eternity of dusting and sewing, and polishing silver and answering the doorbell and being at the beck and call of old Pycock, the footman. She didn't like him either. He had such awful smelling breath. She straightened the clock and with a final flick of the duster across the table she went out and closed the door.

"Ah, there you are, Becky." The voice startled her. It was Doctor Lister lurking in the doorway of his study, tall and thin and sinister. Yes, that's what he was, sinister. "Would you mind coming this way a moment?" He beckoned her to follow him.

She stood in the middle of the study, her heart racing. She knew she was alone in the house. Mrs Lister had gone visiting, Cook would not be here until six o'clock and she had heard Pycock leave half an hour ago to meet visitors at the station. Doctor Lister ambled to his important desk and sat down slowly. He shuffled some papers on the blotter. Becky waited.

"Do please sit down," he pointed to a seat near the fireplace. Those deep eyes were still on her as she sank into the velvet chair. He was fiddling with the papers on his desk as he babbled on about her future. "You will find married life very satisfying, you know. In fact, you will find it quite exciting, so different to what you have been used to."

He caressed a pencil with his long, bony fingers. She stared at his sleek, black hair, brushed straight back. Oliver had said beware of men with hair sleeked straight back, but he hadn't explained why.

"There will be babies. Do you like the idea of babies?" His sallow face wrinkled into a smile but it wasn't a smile at all. It was just a puckering of the skin on his face. Becky opened her mouth but no voice came. She swallowed hard and then she said, "Babies arrive because two people love each other."

"Quite so," Doctor Lister was now fiddling with something in his lap. Then he got up and went to the small table near the window. "Would you like a glass of wine?"

"No. No thank you." She remembered the last time she had drunk wine. It had been at Betty Marsden's wedding and she and Oliver had danced till they dropped. Wine had made them very happy but she had no desire to be happy with this horrible man. Becky stared at his tall, slightly stooped shoulders and the neat dark ridge of hair above his starched collar.

He turned from the table, glass in hand, and walked slowly across the study to the fireplace until he was standing over her. He put his glass of wine on the occasional table. She kept her head down, eyes glued to the faded red and blue pattern on the carpet, her heart thumping. He extended a hand and pulled her gently to her feet. As she rose from the chair she saw something sticking out of the front of his trousers. It was long and thick and tubular. It was flesh.

He opened his arms to embrace her and she could feel the heat of his body but she was too quick for him. She put both hands on his hard, flat chest and pushed him away with tremendous force. Then she darted underneath the outstretched arms, dashed across the room and wrenched the door open. The stairs came up to meet her flying feet and then she was at the top landing. She burst into her attic room, locked the door and stood with her back against it, staring at the ceiling. There was not a sound. He was not following her.

She dragged the heavy tapestry chair across the room and pushed its curved back against the door. Then she pulled her valise from the top of the cupboard and threw it on to the bed. This was it. She was going. Now. Away from this dreadful man.

Quickly she folded her skirt and dress and petticoats and pushed them into the valise. Then she surveyed the room. There was no trace of her anywhere. If she hurried she would get the train at half past four and by seven o'clock she would be home with father, with Billie and with Hannah. And soon she would be married to Oliver.

It was not until she was sitting in the corner seat of the compartment of the train that she realised the enormity of what she had done. She had run away from her place of work. She was supposed to give notice to leave employment.

As the train chugged past the fields and villages her agile mind leapt forward to combat the arguments that father would throw at her. He would be furious and he would try to send her back. Many times she had pleaded with him to take her away from Norcross House but he said it was important that she stay, to learn the ways of a refined professional family, to understand gracious living. And as he frequently reminded her, it would not be for much longer.

Well, she would not go back. She would stay at home and help Hannah and Billie. They could never find enough hours in the day to do all the jobs. She could wash pots and scrub floors, make beds and turn sheets. She could peel potatoes and shell peas. And she could dust.

But there wasn't much she could do to help Billie, who was always surrounded by cows and pigs and chickens and handsome young men. She had chosen Steven Donner. Becky didn't like him very much but Billie was head over heels in love with him. Becky was glad she had Oliver, who was much quieter, nicer. Not such a show off.

As the train whistled through Crookshaw Tunnel she thought of something else. Should she tell Oliver about Doctor Lister? Should she tell father? He would demand to know why she had left in such a hurry. She watched the spire of All Saints' Church slip behind the clump of beech trees at Millthorpe. The sun was tinting the grey stone church a gorgeous rosy hue. It was beautiful and she needed something beautiful today. This was a good omen for her. And she was nearly home. No, she would not tell them. It was too disgusting and she did not want to think about it ever again. She would make up a story. But she would never go back to Norcross House.

* * *

Not far from the village of Millthorpe and All Saints' church, Billie and Steven Donner were stretched full length on a pile of straw in the loft of the barn at Bunker's Hill. It stood a short distance from the cowsheds next to the crewyard, at the edge of a long field that swept down to the willow beds in the valley.

"It's the same colour as this straw. Did you know?" He was lying on his back sifting her hair through his fingers.

"That's a fine compliment. Who wants hair the colour of oat straw?" Billie was lying on her tummy, head sideways as she trailed a wisp of hay across his cheek.

"Stop it. That tickles." He bent over and kissed her. "How do you know what kind of straw it is?"

"Don't be stupid." She tweaked his ears. "Oat straw is different to wheat straw and barley straw is different again. You don't know much about farming, do you?"

"Should I?" He pulled down her head and kissed her.

"Well, I suppose not really. Except soon you're going to marry one." Billie raised herself on to one elbow and stared into his dark brown eyes, which looked almost black.

"No, I'm not. You're not a farmer. You're a pretty girl, too pretty to be crawling about a field pulling out weeds. Would you like another gasper?" Steven reached for a slim silver case from the inside pocket of his jacket.

"Yes please." She took the cigarette, rolled on to her back and puffed small, grey clouds of smoke into the air watching them as they crept away to the dark corners of the loft.

"Your father makes you work too hard." The cigarette dangled from his lips as he squinted against the cloud of smoke.

"No, he doesn't. I love the work. I love the animals." She teased out some strands of her blonde hair and put them against the end of her cigarette. There was a phut! and the smell of singeing.

"Don't do that. Please," Steven rolled on to her. "You'll spoil your hair," then he kissed her. "You know, I shan't allow you to work so hard when we're married."

"But I shall still help father when he needs me."

He pushed his head back so that he looked straight into her frosty blue eyes, and he knew they meant what they said. "Billie, my dearest. I am going to marry you, not your father."

"Yes, but..."

He silenced her by closing his lips over hers again. Then he rolled on to his back, pulled a long satisfying breath through his cigarette and stared at the tangle of cobwebs adorning the old wooden beams above him.

"Please don't be cross, Steven." Billie was aware of his mood. "It will all work out. You'll see. I shall be your wife and I shall help father when he needs me. Oh, I know he's got Hannah, but she's growing old. I'm young and strong," and she punched him in the chest. "Aren't I?"

"Right, young woman. This is it. You've asked for it." He rolled on top of her and began to fumble with her skirt. "I'm going to have you."

"Oh, no you don't, Steven Donner," and she brought her arm across his ear with a dull thump. He fell away.

"That hurt," he rubbed the side of his head.

"It was meant to. We agreed weeks ago that we would wait. You said that we should do things properly. And we don't have to wait much longer, do we?"

Steven was getting to his feet. "I must go."

"You needn't get all moody. You made the rules." Billie watched as he brushed straw from his trousers.

"Yes, but..."

"But nothing, Steven. We both agreed. In fact it was your idea. And now you want to spoil it." Billie crushed the butt of the cigarette on the sole of her boot. "Where's yours?"

"What?"

"Fag end."

"Here. I've nearly finished it."

"Whatever you do, make sure it's out. Race you down from the loft." She grabbed the thick wagon rope dangling from the beam above her, then she leapt into the air swinging on the end of the rope, squealing as she slithered down to the floor of the barn.

"Come on. Here's the rope." She coiled it and hurled it up to the loft. "Catch!"

"I'm coming down this way."

Billie watched as he came down the rickety wooden ladder backwards on all fours. "You look like a giant black insect," and she shrieked with laughter.

He straightened up as he reached the floor of the barn, his jaw set rigid.

"Oh, come on Steven, I'm only joking. But that's just what you looked like, honestly, with your long, thin legs and your long thin arms. It was funny... and I love your thick black hair, and your dark, dark eyes. And I love you, Steven." Her voice trailed off as she realised that a barrier had come between them. He was angry.

"Must go," he muttered as he flicked bits of straw from his jacket.

"Does your father know you were coming to see me?"

"No. I told him I was visiting a customer at Loston, at The White Horse."

"But, but – you haven't been." Billie shook the straw from her skirt.

"I shall say I've been and go tomorrow."

"What if he finds out?" Billie shook her head to get rid of the straw, wreathed her hair into a knot and jabbed a hairpin into it.

"He won't."

She turned away, disappointed. "How will you get home?"

"I'll cadge a lift from somebody. Must go."

"What about the dance on Saturday? It's in aid of the War Memorial Fund."

"Don't know," he called over his shoulder.

"When will I see you again?" Billie watched as he walked away from the barn. He hadn't kissed her and he hadn't said goodbye.

"Sunday." He reached for a stick in the hedgerow and slashed at the thick clumps of cow parsley as he strode along the rutted cart track. She waited until he got to the end of the lane but he didn't turn to wave.

"He's mad with me. And why did he lie to his father? He could just as easily have told him the truth. I didn't think he told lies." She grabbed the fork and went into the crewyard, where Lady was munching hay.

"You're very patient, old girl, and now you shall have a drink." Billie filled the bucket from the trough near the barn door. "You know, I think we'll call it a day. And I've upset Steven. Come on, old girl," and Billie climbed into the cart and coaxed the huge shire-horse on to the lane.

Lady was the slowest and clumsiest horse her father had ever had. She stumbled in the cart ruts, slipped on cobblestones and tripped on the tussocks in the meadows. She had two speeds, dead slow and stop but he wouldn't hear a word against her. Didn't buy her to win a race, he said. She was tireless and could haul tons and tons if you didn't push her. Father was right, of course. Billie stared at the massive back like a mahogany table dressed with bits of leather and buckles.

Steven had gone off in a hump. She wanted to do it just as much but they were not yet married and she'd seen what happens when you do it. Look at Louisa. She had said "yes" in Strawson's barn. And Tilly Daubney, the glazier's daughter had a baby. They said that Emma Turner went away to have a baby although the story was put about that she'd gone to be a governess somewhere. It's not as if she and Steven hadn't talked about it. He said they should wait. Now he's mardy because she wouldn't risk it. When they were married it would be different.

Billie's thoughts rumbled along with the cart as Lady slowly trudged her way through the dry ruts. Steven had said he would see her on Sunday but he hadn't said what time. She flicked the reins across Lady's haunches. He would turn up sooner or later. But last week he didn't turn up. She had waited two hours for him. They were going to Nottingham to a special jazz concert with cousin Lydia and her young man. She had put on her new red dress and red bead necklace and waited. He never did come. Said he had to help his father but he didn't explain what it was that made them miss the band from America. Lydia had swanked about what a good time she had had and everyone was raving about the concert, so it wasn't fair that he got so humpy with her. But he'll get over his bad mood. Besides she was getting used to them.

By the time she turned into the stable yard of The Pyewipe her disappointing afternoon had fizzled out. She was tired, dirty and hungry, but in spite of Steven's grumpiness she felt all aglow because he had visited her.

* * *

Steven's bad mood took no longer to dispel either. He got a lift back to Grantham on one of Donner's beer drays and hurried along Crane Street just a stone's throw from the Brewery.

He paused in front of the terraced house and scanned the neat little handkerchief of a garden bursting with dahlias and asters and lavender. Then he rattled on the door latch.

It was opened by a slim, young woman with a head of rich brown curls and eyes that smiled. Annie Lovitt had told him that she had waited faithfully for John Lovitt to come back from the trenches in France, but the war had been over two years and she was not waiting for anything, ever again.

Chapter 3

When Bladon returned from milking he found Hannah ready for the Pyewipe's customers. She was wearing a green rayon dress and the emerald brooch he had given her for coming to his bed all those years ago. Her hair was beautifully coiled in a coronet and the glaze had gone from her eyes. She looked like the elegant lady of the house, when only a few hours earlier she could hardly stand. He had to say one thing for her, she could always get herself together after a drinking session. But what troubled him was the frequency of the sessions. There was always an excuse: some relative had died, drown the sorrow, Louisa's baby had died, drown the sorrow, or the cat died, drown the sorrow.

He also suspected that flowing deep within those rivers of sorrow was the sadness that she had never given him a child. Somewhere he had a wife but it was too late to think about a son. Hannah would be fifty on her next birthday, and he would be fifty-one! As the thoughts stretched and stirred within their deep cave the images came to life and he began to feel again the hollowness, the despair that he had felt on the day Trynah left.

Nothing had erased that agony. The girls and Hannah could wrap it up and cushion him with their love but the torment would sear his mind without warning. When he was in the stable he would hear her call across the yard. In the bedroom he would see her brushing her sleek, black hair in the candlelight. It was still there, this aching, presenting itself with such smug reliance after all these years. But every time he allowed space for reflection he was done for. It took him days to pull out of the depression.

But he had Hannah, constant in her love but sustained more and more by the gin bottle. Was she childless because she was drinking or was she drinking because she was childless? They hadn't discussed the possibility of a baby when she agreed to come to The Pyewipe. Perhaps they should have done. There had been enough time for her and Gilbert to... A vigorous young man in the prime of life... yet there had been no child. But after losing Trynah he was only thinking of his loneliness, of Billie, and Becky. He had needed Hannah for them, for himself.

"Tomorrow I shall finish icing the wedding cakes," Hannah said, standing near the pantry door tying her pinafore strings. "Time's racing on. Vinny sent word that the dresses are ready for the final fitting."

"I shall be glad when it's all over." Bladon bit the loose skin on his thumb. "One wedding is bad enough but two takes some dealing with. All those aunts and uncles and cousins." He picked a pea pod from the shiny oilcloth on the kitchen table and inspected it. "As for the Donners, goodness knows what old ma Donner will look like," as he rolled the pea pod between his thumb and forefinger.

"Let her have her day. After all, she is losing her only son..."

"Huh! It'll be like a Feast Day gone wrong." Bladon went to the kitchen window and gazed across the stable yard.

"Don't worry. Just enjoy it."

He watched her scoop the pea pods into the pigswill bucket. "I'm going to miss Billie."

"I know you are." She put the plate of cold ham on the kitchen table.

"And she won't like living with the Donners. I know it's a big house and there's plenty of room, but I'm not keen on her starting married life under the same roof as that woman. Besides I don't think she'll take to town life." Bladon tossed the savaged pea pod into the bucket. "But it's no good interfering. She's set on it so she must have her way."

"I think Becky's made a good choice." Hannah carved the ham with smooth, deft strokes.

"She's quieter, different." Bladon was nagging at his thumb again. "Always was. She and Oliver make a good match, both long-headed. They'll be happy."

"And I should think he's got good prospects," she said as she put the bread on the table.

"Yes. The railways are here to stay, more's the pity. Less carriages and wagonettes, that means less horses. And we lost all those horses in France. They'll never be replaced, not now, with the railway. The market was quieter last week. Prices have slumped. Hello, what's that?" Bladon leaned into the kitchen window. There was a grinding of cartwheels and he saw Billie turn into the yard.

"How did you get on?" He was at her side, nuzzling Lady's velvet nose.

"Not bad. I haven't finished."

"You've been smoking again. I don't like you to smoke, Billie. Where did you get them from?"

She kissed him on the cheek. He slapped her on the bottom. "Off you go, I'll see to Lady."

* * *

Bladon was sitting in his usual place at the head of the dining table with Hannah and Billie on either side. The Private Room had come into its own again after he married Trynah. Since Esther's funeral a vase of flowers had stood on the polished dining table. The oak dresser had waited patiently with its array of china dinner plates to be placed in front of a family again. Trynah had unwittingly demolished the shrine that the Private Room had become since Esther's death.

She had brought the room back to life and united the family round the table once more. She had used the dinner service, the sparkling silver cruet and the crisp table linen had been taken out of mothballs. No more meals in the kitchen with the two girls bolting their food and dashing off to play.

Visitors had been welcomed, and when all was closed down at the inn at the end of the day they would sit here, by the fire, she in the settle with its medallion inlay and he in the leather arm chair opposite. She had given it back the dignity it deserved.

Bladon took some ham from the dish. It was people who had changed. Trynah had left him and Hannah hadn't felt the need to move anything around when she assumed the maternal mantle. The girls had grown up. The Pyewipe prospered. The customers kept coming, the wagonettes were hired, the Club Room was regularly booked and the milk was sold in the village. But his girls were about to leave him and he didn't know what he was going to do without Billie. The loud slamming of a door jolted him back to the table and today. Footsteps hurried through the kitchen and the door burst open.

"Becky!" Bladon's fork clattered to the floor.

"Father!" She flew into his arms clinging to his shoulders with both hands. "I've left Norcross House."

"You've what?" He held her at arm's length.

"I left. I hate it. And I hate everyone in it." She shook herself free and wandered around in a small circle. Then she stopped, covered her face with her hands and sobbed.

Now everyone was talking at once.

"I'll go and make you a nice cup of tea," Hannah grunted as she got out of the chair.

"Don't worry," Billie was at Becky's side, cradling her shoulders.

"Come on, now," and Bladon guided her to the settle. "We'll sort it out. Was someone rude to you?"

"I really don't want to talk about it." She sniffed into her handkerchief. "And whatever you say, father, I will never go back."

Her father strode across the room to the window, caressed the pleat of the dark red curtains and then marched back to the fireplace. "All right, Becky. Don't upset yourself. Everything will be all right." He knew his Becky and every one of her moods.

Something had happened. He wouldn't pursue the matter any further tonight, it could be sorted out tomorrow.

"Don't send me back, father." Becky's voice quivered. "Please don't send me back."

"No, no, Becky, don't worry. I won't send you back." He crouched at her side on the settle gently smoothing away the tears on her cheeks. "I must go and deal with the customers."

"It's all right, father." Billie was standing in front of them. "You go. We'll have some supper. Come on, Becky, you must eat a little."

It was one of the busiest nights at The Pyewipe for a long time but at last the chatter and singing crept away, the customers went home, the clearing up was done, the doors were locked and the clock was striking midnight when Bladon and Hannah slowly climbed the stairs to bed.

"What do you think happened to Becky?" Bladon pulled off his shirt.

"Don't know. Something bad for her to have walked out like that. She's brought everything with her you know. All her clothes." Hannah was at the dressing table picking at the hairpins until the thick rope of hair fell around her shoulders. "So she means what she says. She will not go back."

"I know."

"And you mustn't make her." She watched him through the looking glass. He was at the other side of the bed pulling off his socks.

"No, but I shall go and see Doctor Lister to find out what it's all about. I must get to the bottom of this. Becky's loyal and hard working. If she had reason to leave in such a hurry then I want to know why. I should think it was Cook or one of the servants. They can be swines."

Bladon rolled between the crisp sheets. "Mmm, I smell lavender." He yawned with a great roar, flinging his arms above his head. "In a day or two she'll have forgotten all about it once she gets her head full of the wedding." The bedroom was filled with another mighty roar. "What with one thing and another it's been quite a day. Come here, my beauty. We have unfinished business…"

"Wait a minute." She was sitting on the edge of the bed peeling off her stockings. As she flicked them on to the chair there was a loud banging at the front door.

"Blast and damn! Who can it be?" Bladon propped himself on his elbows, threw his head back and listened. The banging continued. He rolled out of bed and went to the front window. Down below he saw a dark figure on the doorstep. Dogs in the street started to bark and Gypsy in the stable yard joined in.

"It's the policeman! What on earth can he want at this hour? The whole village will be awakened by the bloody dogs." Pulling on his breeches and shirt he hurried down the stairs, and threw back the bolts on the door to stare into the bird-like face of Constable Leeson.

"Evenin' Bladon, sorry to disturb you." The tall, angular man stuck his fingers into his tunic pockets and looked down his thin, hooked nose.

"Come in, Henry, come on in." Bladon led him to the Private Room. "Sit down. What on earth's the matter?"

"I'm afraid there's a fire at Bunker's Hill." Constable Leeson put his helmet on the floor.

"What?" Bladon clutched his head with his hands.

"Your barn. Gone up like tinder. Not much of it left. The fire's almost out but I thought you should know about it tonight."

Hannah appeared in the doorway looking like an opera singer in a mauve satin housecoat, her long wavy hair cascading around her shoulders, hands clasped in front of her as if she were about to sing an aria.

"There's not a great deal I can do tonight," the constable cleared his throat, "but I'll speak to the Captain of the Fire Brigade tomorrow. He'll send someone to make an inspection."

"Thank you, thank you," Bladon paced the room head down, speaking to the patterned rug.

"Can I get you a drink?" Hannah stroked the pockets of her housecoat. "The kettle won't take long if you prefer something hot."

"Thank you ma'am. I won't stay." He picked up his helmet. "I'm after some poachers tonight, over at Munce's Wood. With that fire like a beacon on Bunker's Hill they won't be expecting me. So I'll bid you goodnight and I'll see you in the morning."

Bladon padded through to the kitchen, pulled on his top boots and reached for his whip from behind the door.

"Where are you going?" Hannah clutched her stomach.

"To Bunker's."

"But you can't do anything tonight." She hurried to his side. "And you're tired."

"I must make sure the fire's out. You go back to bed and whatever you do, don't mention a word of this to the girls."

He coaxed Penny out of the stable in whispers. She was a quiet filly and never made a fuss about anything. He decided not to saddle her up. It all took time and he didn't want the other horses disturbed at this hour.

Soon he was galloping bareback along the dry ruts in the lane leading to Bunker's Hill. The countryside had lost its greenness and was covered in a mystical silvery sheen of satin. Ahead he could see thin wisps of smoke drifting up into the clear night sky. He rode into the stack-yard, tied Penny to a gate and marched towards what was left of the barn.

The roof had gone, and the supporting pillars had crashed to the ground and were now charred heaps of wood. The ladder leading to the loft was a scorched skeleton, and the straw was a thick black carpet of ash. The barn was gutted.

"Bloody wars!" he screamed into the still night air clutching his hair. "It's ruined!" He marched across the yard to the empty cattle sheds. His legs were sluggish, his mouth was dry and his heart was racing. The fire hadn't spread, thank goodness. The other farm buildings were safe. He stared again at the silhouette of the gutted barn. "Roof gone. The building's no good without a bloody roof. Damn and blast." He turned to Penny waiting patiently at the gate. "There's nothing to be done here except build a new barn. Hup, girl."

* * *

"Everything happens to Bladon. Never known a man to have so much bad luck ladled out to him." Lavinia Pike was in the kitchen of her cottage in Church Lane at the bottom of High Street. Steam from the saucepan clouded the face of the black marble clock and veiled the little china ornament sitting on the mantelpiece. It was a miniature of the Clock Tower from Skegness.

She loved ornaments. They were lodged on every shelf and mantelpiece and alcove in the kitchen, the parlour and the bedrooms. They were dusted every day. Sometimes Curtis caught one with his elbow and it would crash to the floor. But she didn't get angry with him. She just bought another one.

She was at the old deal table rolling small balls of dough into dumplings. "He doesn't deserve it. Doubt if he's ever done anybody down in his life."

"It was ever thus, Vinny," and Curtis got up, hopped to the dresser and took an apple from the fruit bowl. "Depends on how the cards are dealt."

"Well, he's had a lousy hand, and no mistake." Vinny put the dumplings into the saucepan of broth. "But nothing ever got him down. Made of good stuff is Bladon King." If she had been a bit younger she would have accepted his proposal. Become the wife of the landlord of The Pyewipe. But Bladon had wanted more children, he had wanted a son. She had told him she was too old to be rocking the cradle so he had married her youngest sister, Trynah, who would have given him that son if only...

She fixed her dark blue eyes on the man she did marry. As perky as a pixie, now weathered and worn, his hair as thick as a thatch with the odd grey strand if you wanted to look closely. Instead of the dynamic Bladon King she had settled for Curtis Pike stumping about on a wooden leg. And she had no regrets.

He had arrived in Ketsby with endless traveller's tales to tell, but it wasn't the adventures that had captivated her. It was the man, tall and lean with a sharp, tense face and a determined set of the jaw, and decency about him. She marvelled that a being could retain such decency when it had cost him half a leg through no fault of his own. Now that tall, lean body was slightly bowed, collapsing, and his leg was getting more and more painful.

"Do you remember the day he brought you that bundle of asparagus? I was sitting here in this very kitchen when he called. Fair put the wind up me." Curtis was staring down at the red and yellow lino on the floor. "Might have known I had competition..." his voice petered out. "A man on two strong legs..."

Vinny was surprised that he had all but read her thoughts. She hurried to his side and pulled his head into her bosom, ruffling his curly hair.

"Now that will do, Curtis. When has that bit of wood had anything to do with our relationship? Huh! When have I ever taken that into account?" She framed his weathered face in her hands. "It wasn't your fault that you lost half a leg in South Africa. Can't say that I've ever heard you complain."

"Oh, I know I get a bit grumpy. This old leg lets me down..."

"And I'm just as irritable with me rheumatics. We're getting old, Curtis, rusting up. That's the trouble." She went to the hob and lifted the saucepan lid. "We never think when we're young that we're going to be old and crotchety, and thank goodness we don't."

He bit into the apple with a loud crack. "Do you think they'll come back to England, to Ketsby?"

"Don't know. If only..." She leaned over the sink and opened the kitchen window. "They never mention it, do they? That was the main hope when they left. But remember, Robbie will still be a wanted man."

"Yes, but most folk have forgotten about the Lees Farm tragedy." Curtis studied his half-eaten apple. "And, remember, Trynah never went to see him in Lincoln Prison. Not once..."

"Who can blame her for that?" Vinny wiped her hands down her pinafore. "She left that to you, to carry the messages. Do you remember how he always wanted to know what dress she had been wearing?"

"Yes, I remember," Curtis kept his eyes on the floor. "It could be safe for them to come back. Everyone knew he'd been hanged in Lincoln Prison and there was never any report about his escape in the papers."

"Huh! The authorities wanted to keep quiet about that, you could depend on it, not to alarm folks in their beds at night. Escaped prisoner! Why, Robbie wouldn't harm, anyone." She stared out of the window. "Except Redfern."

"But Redfern had it coming to him." Curtis studied his half-eaten apple. "Worried his father into the grave with his wenching and drinking. Never turned his hand to a day's work. It all fell to Robbie at the farm." He stood up, leaning on the kitchen table. "And then to... to violate Trynah... days before her wedding..."

The saucepan spluttered on the stove and the black marble clock on the mantelpiece paused to listen.

"But what wouldn't I give to see them again, and that son of theirs. Imagine it. They have a son." She stayed at the window, looking out across the garden, as the torture of her sister's departure knifed into her again. They had been in the kitchen of The Pyewipe delaying the moment of farewell.

"Now I'm going otherwise I shall fall to pieces. I'll wait for your letters, Trynah. They'll be safe with me. Write often..." and she walked across the yard and through the double gates. "Go with God. Keep faith," she called over her shoulder but she did not turn round. That had happened eighteen years ago. All the years of deceit, the years of secrets, the lies. She turned from the window.

"And think of Trynah. Think of the predicament she found herself in. That was the test of the mightiest. It's time we had another letter from her." She glanced at the black marble clock as if she were expecting the postman this minute. "At the time it seemed like the end of the world, leaving those two little girls. And here they are about to be married." Vinny swept a tear from her left eye. "Do you remember Bladon's drinking and ranting and raging? Poor man. I feared for his sanity in those weeks after she left, I really did... But we couldn't say a word, could we? Couldn't explain a thing, and still can't."

"No, it was dreadful but as you say he's made of good stuff. He weathered it all... and he's got Hannah."

"That's true," Vinny's mouth drooped. "But from what I heard in the shop, Hannah's problem is getting worse, but you know what they're like for gossip and Bertha Burrell is never happy unless she's plucking the feathers out of somebody's wings."

"True," Curtis went to the kitchen door and threw the apple core on to the garden.

"Less of this maudlin talk Curtis, it won't do. What's past is past. It's no good harping back. We know that Trynah's happy where she is and Bladon, well, he just got on with his life. Time for a cup of tea." She lifted the lid of the saucepan again and squinted through the steam. "I'm really sorry about the fire. They say the barn's nothing but a shell. Let's hope he's got some insurance to cover it," and Vinny poured boiling water into the fat, brown teapot.

"Depends how it started." Curtis moved his chair to the table.

She sat opposite him, cradling the teacup. "The girls are coming this afternoon for the final dress fittings. Then all we want is a fine day. He's going to miss having Billie around."

"Well, everyone knows she's the son he never had." Curtis pushed his empty teacup across the table.

"And she'll find it strange, living in town with that dreadful Mrs Donner." Vinny's mouth sagged. "Won't suit her. But they don't want advice from us old fogies. Bladon will still have Hannah."

"Well, she's not so young as she used to be, like the rest of us." He squinted at the clock on the mantelpiece. "Must be on my way. I've promised Bladon I'd help Barney clear up at the barn." He yanked on his tweed cap, gripped his walking stick and hobbled to the door. "I'm off."

His wife's eyes were on his back, lopsided now after years of leaning on a bit of wood. No, she had no regrets but he did aggravate her with his apple eating. She had never told him and would never tell him but she couldn't bear the sound of apples being crunched.

Chapter 4

Bladon steered Duke and the trap out of the stable yard of the inn and headed for the Great North Road and Newark. It was four days since the barn had burnt down. The Fire Inspector said the fire had started in the loft where he had stored the winter bedding straw. It could have been caused by a tramp dossing down for the night. Here today, gone tomorrow, and he'd never be caught. It was more work and more expense that he could have done without.

Soon he was in the leafy avenue lined with the smart, town houses and their fussy gardens and fussy railings and fussy wrought iron gates. He pulled up outside Norcross House with its bay windows and pretentious door, bold and darkly polished. He grabbed the brass lion's head and knocked three times. He had not made an appointment but the parlourmaid ushered him inside. She was younger than Becky, plump and confident with thick fair hair cut in the fashionable bob. He was surprised that Doctor Lister had found a replacement so quickly but with all this unemployment it was easy to find staff.

Doctor Lister was bent over his desk, writing. He looked up and Bladon met dark eyes under a ledge of thick black eyebrows. "Good afternoon, Mr King. Do come in. Sit down."

Bladon sat in the shabby velvet chair and studied this tall, swarthy man. He had only met him once before when Becky came for an interview. Doctor Lister was well known and had such a good reputation that Bladon had had no hesitation in urging Becky to take the position. Now she had walked out and arrived home in a high state of nervousness. He wanted to know why.

"I'm afraid your daughter has not quite come up to

expectations." Doctor Lister unrolled his long body and sat back in the chair.

"Oh, in what way?" Bladon's eyes went to the small table near the desk with its carafe of wine and crystal glasses then they swept around the study with its rows of books locked in glass cabinets, the fusty dark green curtains and the dismal pictures of storms on the walls. It was all so dark and brooding.

Doctor Lister fidgeted with a pencil, tapping it on the blotter. "She does not fit in with the rest of the staff. You see," he got up, came round to the front of his desk and perched on the edge, staring down at his long legs, "you see, she is of a quarrelsome nature."

"Becky! Quarrelsome!"

"With the other staff." He looked closely at the pencil, caressing it with his long fingers.

"I find that hard to believe," Bladon felt uneasy with this explanation.

"We can't have this sort of behaviour in the household so... she agreed that it would be best for her to go. Of course, she need not have left so hurriedly..."

"Whom did she quarrel with? May I talk to these people?"

"That would not be wise. Or necessary, Mr King."

"But... but... I know my daughter better than anyone can possibly know her. She is not of a quarrelsome nature." Bladon leaned sideways on the arm of the chair. "I really insist that I am allowed to clear this matter up with the person concerned."

"No need, I can assure you," Doctor Lister moved back to his desk and threw down the pencil. "I understand she is shortly to be married."

"That's right."

"Perhaps that has something to do with her attitude. It's a pity but I had no alternative but to relinquish her from my service." He pulled an envelope from the top drawer.

Bladon was being dismissed. He was not going to be given an

explanation by this learned man. Doctor Lister was holding out the envelope. "These are the wages due to her."

Bladon stared again into the deep-set eyes. They were lifeless and could have belonged to a blind man.

"Thank you." He found himself on the top step of Norcross House with the heavy door closing behind him.

All the way back to Ketsby he ruminated on the meeting. Becky was not the type of girl to argue. If she didn't like something she would go to her room and stay there rather than create a scene. But argue? Quarrel? Not Becky.

True, there had been tears every time he'd visited her and true, she had said she didn't like any of the people at Norcross House but he doubted if she would ever quarrel with anyone. He didn't know what to make of it all, but it dented his pride to have a daughter sacked.

He found Becky helping Hannah with the trimmings on the wedding cake. She knew he was going to Newark market but he had not told her that he was planning to visit Doctor Lister.

"Did you bring them?" Becky held a little silver bow at arm's length.

"Bring what?" He threw his whip behind the kitchen door.

"The sugared almonds. That stall near the Butter Hall always has them. You know where it is..."

"I'm sorry, Becky. I forgot. I got yarning and..."

"Never mind. Does this one go here, Hannah?" Becky pressed the little silver bow against the side of the cake.

Bladon had to decide what to do. If his daughter had been rude or quarrelsome he must know about it from her lips. There were always two sides to an argument.

"When you've finished pop into the Private Room, Becky. I have something for you. Sorry about the sugared almonds."

"I'll come now because we're going for dress fittings soon." She followed him along the corridor and flopped on to the oak settle.

"I haven't mentioned Doctor Lister since you arrived home Becky, and I don't want you to get upset but I just want to clear the whole thing up." He sat back in his leather chair and crossed his legs. "Tell me about the staff at Norcross House. What are they like?"

Becky's cheeks coloured. "Well, cook was very strict and everything had to be done at once and she got cross if it wasn't. The housemaid was as scared of her as I was. The gardener was kind but I didn't see a lot of him, only when he brought the flowers in. And Mr Pycock – he's the footman – he was not very nice."

"In what way wasn't he nice?"

"He... well, he has such awful smelling breath. And... and he used to stand too close to me."

"And what about the quarrels? Tell me about them."

"I didn't have any quarrels." Becky shook her head.

"Not with any of them?" asked Bladon as he uncrossed his legs and leaned forward.

"No. I didn't have much to do with any of them. Sometimes me and Martha – she's the housemaid – we went out together when we were off duty but that wasn't very often."

"Then if you didn't quarrel with anyone what happened to make you walk out?"

Becky smoothed the edge of the settle with her long, slender fingers, forwards and backwards. The clock ticked. Voices could be heard in the street. Two men were arguing.

"There was... there was an incident." Becky continued to stroke the edge of the settle. "Father, I don't want to talk about it so please... please don't ask me to tell you."Her lower lip was quivering.

"Today I called to see Doctor Lister."

"Oh!" She put her hands to her burning cheeks. "What did he say?"

"He said you were quarrelsome, and didn't fit in."

Slowly her hands slipped down her neck to her waist and then she smoothed down her skirt. "That's true." She swallowed hard. "I did not fit in and I'm glad I'm home. I'm sorry to let you down father, but..."

"Now that's an end to the matter. I shall never refer to it again." Bladon passed her the envelope. "He gave me this. It's your wages. Now off you go and try on the lovely dress that your aunt's making for you."

* * *

"You've both lost a bit of weight," Vinny turned from one to the other. "It's only natural before the wedding. I can soon put a tuck in."

They were in the parlour with its lace curtains veiling the window, protecting the modesty of her customers. Dark red velvet chairs stood around a polished table. Pincushions and a note pad for measurements were on the dresser, and a yard measure dangled between the knobs on the back of one of the chairs.

Billie and Becky stood side by side, twisting and turning in front of the long mirror. Curtis had bought it at an auction sale when Loston Manor and all the contents were sold. It was a boon for her customers. They loved to see what they looked like full length.

Vinny watched as they elbowed each other out of the way. This is where Trynah had stood being fitted for her wedding dress, in this very room, when she was to marry Robinson. A huge sigh escaped, emptying her lungs.

That gossamer wedding dress had languished in the trunk on the landing for years. But when she and Curtis decided to get married she had taken it out, wept for a long time and then took the scissors and cut up Trynah's wedding dress to make lavender bags for the Church Fete. Now her sister was miles away across the sea. If only she could be here today to see her little girls grown into such fine young women, about to be married.

"Well, there's one thing I can say for certain," and Vinny quickly wiped her cheeks. "You're both up to date with the fashion."

Billie stood with her back to the mirror, looking over her shoulder. "I love the headdress and veil."

"Pull it forward a little more Billie. That's the way." Vinny stood back, arms folded across her waist. "All right, I've just got to take up the slack under the arms. I'll bring them over on Friday ready for Saturday. The bridesmaids have collected theirs. Time for some tea, don't you think?" She plodded through to the kitchen, Billie and Becky following.

"And how are your young men?" Vinny passed the cups. "Nervous?"

"Oliver is as cool as a cucumber, but then he always is." Becky took a piece of fruit cake. "Never gets flustered about anything."

"Steven thinks it's all a lot of fuss," Billie munched on a biscuit.

"Of course it's a lot of fuss," said Vinny, cradling the teacup with both hands. "How many times does a girl get married? You're entitled to a lot of fuss on your big day. You must both enjoy every..." There was a knock at the front door. "Who on earth can that be?"

"We have to go, aunt Vinny, thanks for the tea," and with a whoop they were pushing each other out of the kitchen, banging the door, scurrying along the garden path, hair flying, arms waving.

Vinny shuffled along the passage to the front door. It was the postman. She took the envelope, squinting at the writing. It was from Trynah and Robbie. Thank goodness the girls didn't see it. They had no idea where their stepmother was, Bladon had no idea where his wife was and no one in the village knew either. And that was the way Vinny and Curtis had kept it over the years. Bertha Burrell was the biggest menace and never gave up. She would bring the mystery of Trynah's disappearance out for an airing whenever she could find someone to listen.

Vinny poured herself another cup of tea, reached for her looking glasses and hobbled into the parlour. The bunion on her left toe was painful again. She sank into the old tapestry chair, put her feet on the footstool and settled down to devour every word of the letter.

* * *

47

The girls galloped along Church Lane and pushed through the little gate into the churchyard.

"The dresses are lovely aren't they?" They were walking side by side along the narrow path between the gravestones.

"Yes, aunt Vinny is so clever." Billie skipped ahead of Becky. "Are you scared?"

"No. I'm not scared but I'm sure I shall be a bit nervous, won't you?"

"Yes, what if I lose my voice?" Billie grabbed a handful of cow parsley and wafted the small white flowers under Becky's nose.

"If you do it'll be the first time. Let's sit down here. I've got something to tell you." Becky hoisted herself on to the low grey stone wall. They sat side by side, with their legs dangling just inches away from an old tombstone, so old it was impossible to read the inscription. "It's about Doctor Lister. Father went to see him today. I expect that's why he forgot the sugared almonds. Doesn't matter. Anyway he said that Doctor Lister told him I was quarrelsome with the staff and that's why he had to relinquish my services."

"What! You arguing with the staff! I don't believe it."

"It makes me boil. Of course I haven't quarrelled with anyone but that's just Doctor Lister's story. I didn't tell father what really happened. I haven't told Oliver. In fact, I haven't told anyone but I want you to know. We haven't had a minute to ourselves what with wedding cakes and bouquets and baking."

"Well... why did you leave?" Billie threw her head back, half-smiling. "Come on, cough it up. Did the footman pinch your bottom?" She started to pluck the small white flowers from the stalk.

"No. Listen. Doctor Lister called me to his study. I knew I was the only one in the house and I was a bit scared. I don't like him, he gives me the creeps. And... and...well..."

"Do tell, Becky."

"Well, he was sitting at his desk and then he came round and

48

stood in front of me and do you know what he'd done? He'd undone his trouser buttons..."

Billie squealed with laughter. "What did you see?"

"It's nothing to laugh about, Billie, it was awful. A long thing with a sort of knob on the end, a bit like a toadstool. Can't really say what colour."

"What happened?"

"Well, he tried to grab me but I was too quick for him. I gave him a great big shove and ran to my room, packed my bag and caught the train home. So that's that." She kicked her shoes against the wall.

Billie shrieked and threw the white flowers high into the air. They fell like confetti all around them.

"Doctor Lister! *The* famous Doctor Lister!" And she whooped with laughter, wiping tears from her eyes. "Why he's nothing but a dirty old man."

"I know, but I don't think it's funny, Billie."

"Sorry." She put an arm around her sister's shoulder. "I didn't mean to make fun. It wasn't nice for you."

"Have you seen a man's thingy?"

"No. I haven't seen a man's doodah but I know girls who have and besides, I'm surrounded by the animals, all doing what nature created them to do. They're doing it all the time. But it's different with a famous Doctor. Fancy, with all his bridge parties and musical evenings! Perhaps he gets it out and plays with it when he sees someone he fancies."

Now it was Becky's turn to laugh. "Be serious for a minute. Tell me. Why do you think he did it? I mean his 'thing' is very private. Why show it to me?"

"Silly. He wanted to do it with you."

"What!"

"Course he did." Billie was shredding the stalk of the cow parsley.

"But what about Mrs Lister?"

"Oh, he wouldn't pay any attention to her. She would never know..." She threw the stalk into the long grass.

"If it had happened to you, Billie, what would you have done?"

"I would have done the same, I would have left, but I still think it's very funny. Fancy the high and mighty la-di-da Mrs Lister." Billie jumped down from the wall and strutted amongst the tombstones, one hand on her hip, the other cradling the back of her head. "Just imagine her receiving her guests – 'Oh, do come in. How nice to see you. I'm afraid my husband is busy at the moment playing with his diddle but he'll be here shortly," and Billie tossed her head in the air, exploding with laughter.

"Yes, that's just what she's like. I listen to her in the sitting room when I take the tea in. Thinks she's the cat's whiskers." Becky picked at the blades of grass. "But I've let father down. He thinks I was dismissed because I was quarrelsome, and I've told Oliver the same story. You'll promise never to tell anyone?"

"Promise," Billie reached over and hugged her. "Now I have a secret to tell, and you, too, must promise to keep it." She told Becky about Steven's surprise visit to Bunker's Hill and how they had smoked in the loft.

"I stubbed mine out on the sole of my boot, but he must have dropped his when we were fooling about. Now father's got the barn to rebuild. All that expense, it's awful. And I haven't dared confess to him. Curtis Pike thinks it was a tramp that caused the fire, dossing down for the night. I'm absolutely sure that it was Steven's cigarette. What am I to do?"

"Has father asked you?"

"No, but he knows I smoke sometimes."

"He'll think it was a tramp." Becky was kicking the wall with the heel of her shoes again.

"But he doesn't know Steven and I were in the loft that afternoon."

50

"Don't tell him." Becky got ready to jump down from the wall.

Billie stared at the gravestones. They looked like slabs of mouldy cattle cake stuck in the long grass. "All right. Then these are our two secrets, Becky. Promise, promise." And they clapped their right hands together and linked their little fingers as they used to when they were very small. "Father's got enough on his mind as it is, and I know he's worried about Hannah's drinking. Did you smell her breath this afternoon?"

"Yes. Why does she do it?"

"Because she likes it I suppose. Makes her feel happy. It doesn't matter. She's nice, I like Hannah."

"So do I. Come on, let's go."

They jumped off the wall and ran, hand in hand, along the footpath.

Chapter 5

Annie Lovitt put on her Sunday best dress although it wasn't Sunday. The dress was the colour of maize with a brown velvet bow at the neck and brown fringes on the hem. She rummaged in the drawer and found her long rope of amber beads. John had bought them for her at the mid-Lent Fair. Then she put on the hat. It was shiny, brown straw with yellow daisies scattered around the brim turned up at the front. He had bought this for her too. For Easter. Just before he went to the war.

She studied the reflection in the small looking glass perched on top of the chest of drawers and was pleased with what she saw. He would have been pleased too. He always liked her to look stylish.

"You're a good looker, Annie. Always remember that." His voice came from nowhere. Her hands went to her throat and a chilly anxiety made her gasp. He would never ever see her again, in her finery, in his hat and beads.

"How long will you be?" A man called from the room across the landing. The voice was as hoarse as a crow because he didn't use it much due to spending a lot of time alone in his bedroom.

"Coming." With one more glance in the mirror she tilted her hat to a sharper angle and crossed the landing. The room was small and square just like hers. The sun on the red gingham curtains drenched the walls with a rosy hue. In front of the window was an oblong oak table strewn with papers and a jam jar full of pencils next to a writing pad. A single bed, in one corner, was flush with the wall.

"My word, you do look a picture, our Annie," the plump little man jerked his body and bounced like a rubber ball along the bed and into the chair in front of the table. "It's not Sunday, is it?"

"No. It's Saturday." Annie watched her uncle rock himself into a comfortable position in the chair. "I have to go out. I shan't be long. Are you going to do some more writing?"

"Yes, I must finish the notes from my last travels, to the Doddington Fair." Wide brown eyes stared at her from below silky eyebrows set in a round, gentle face that gave the lie to the fact that his arms stopped six inches below his shoulders and he had no legs.

He had taught himself to read and write in fair copperplate with a pencil in his mouth. With only stumps on his arms, Annie had made special shirtsleeves so that his eating fork could be slipped into the little pocket and he was able to feed himself.

"Is there anything you want before I go?" She looked around the tidy bedroom. A cane-seated chair stood next to the bed and the floor was covered with yellow patterned linoleum. Annie kept it polished because if he did fall off the bed, or lose his balance, he could roll along the floor and support himself against the wall until help came.

"No, I don't think so. I shall stay up here until you come back. George said he wouldn't be long. He's getting that shaft mended. I shall be all right." He smiled his innocent smile. "My word, you do look posh, our Annie."

"Back soon," she said as she found the little pink stump partly hidden by the cuff of his sleeve and squeezed it, then she clumped down the stairs stepping past the pushchair, tripping on a wheel. She shoved it out of the way. Then she went to the larder and reached for the cocoa tin on the second shelf. She emptied it and stuffed the coins into her brown velvet Dorothy bag.

"I'm off," she called up the stairs and banged the door as she went out.

She hurried along High Street and was just in time for the Lington carrier as it pulled out of The Blue Ram.

"Will you put me down on Fonaby Road, please. Near the school." Annie ignored the chattering women in the cart. Their eyes were scorching her face, her dress, her hat but she stared beyond them as she rehearsed for the umpteenth time what she was going to say when she reached her destination.

She had lived with this idea for some weeks, pummelling and pounding her thoughts, night and day until she had teased out the truth. She had her father to think about. Well, William Day wasn't her father, he was her uncle, her dead mother's brother, but there was no need to go into all that today. He had to be looked after just as she would have looked after her father. And she had herself to think about. So here she was crunching on the gravel of the drive leading to Lynwood House.

The parlourmaid answered the door, a dark-haired girl, quite plump, with a spotty face.

"Good morning," Annie smiled and before she could say her piece, she was ushered into the drawing room. The parlourmaid assumed she was a wedding guest.

Annie had calculated the timing of her visit with great precision. This would put the Donners on the spot and this would make sure she would get satisfaction. She had told Steven about the problem but he refused to talk about it, as if it had nothing to do with him. It had everything to do with him.

She wandered to the French windows and looked out across an expanse of lawn. It was fringed with flowers of every colour and looked like the embroidered hem of a green velvet cloth. Such extravagance made her heart leap.

The door burst open and a flabby little man in a navy blue suit bustled in. "Good morning," he shuffled around her as if inspecting an item for sale, "and just what is your business young lady?"

Annie stood with hands clasped in front of her, as steady as a rock, her bag dangling from her left wrist. "Good morning, are you Mr Donner, father of Steven?"

"Yes, I am," he snuffled and cleared his throat. She thought he was going to spit. "And who are you?"

"A friend of his," Annie stared into floating, watery eyes. "A very good friend of his. But he refuses to discuss business with me."

"Business! Just what do you mean by that?"

"I mean..."

A large lady appeared in the doorway and barged across the room. "Are you ready, Basil?" She was like a sailing ship dressed with flags and flounces wafting in the draught from the open door. "Where's... and who is this?" Mrs Donner's voice echoed as if from a deep cavern. She, too, walked around Annie, sniffing.

"She says she's a friend of Steven's. She has some business with him..."

"Well, I'm afraid there's no question of anyone dealing with business today," she trilled. "Our son is to be married."

"Yes, I know," Annie held her ground. "And that's why I'm here."

"Whatever it is will have to wait. Come along, Basil, we shall be late." Mildred Donner pulled a white kid glove on to her podgy hand.

"Unless I get satisfaction there will not be a wedding." Annie studied Mrs Donner's hat. It was a huge concoction of what appeared to be pastries and cakes strung together with satin ribbons.

"The woman's mad." The hat shook with indignation. "Get her out of here. We must go. Where's Steven?"

Annie moved a step closer to her. "I'm expecting a baby and Steven is the father. He's refused to help me."

Mrs Donner sank into a tapestry chair, fanning herself with a lace handkerchief. Her husband turned from the window. "What proof have you?"

"He's the only man I've known since my husband went to France. He hasn't come back. Blown up, they said, but I didn't want to believe it. I've waited two years. John Lovitt is not coming back." Annie was shouting as she leaned toward Mr Donner, her clenched hands on her thighs. "He's not coming back!" She stepped away and took a deep breath. "Then Steven began to show an interest. I have no money, only what I earn and I have a disabled father to care for."

"And where do you work?"

"At the brewery, bottling."

Mr Donner started to pace around the room, his plump little hands wrestling with each other behind his back, his eyes following the pattern of the thick dark green carpet. There was the sound of muffled steps and Steven rushed in. He stopped dead in his tracks.

"Annie!" He moved closer. "What are you doing here?"

"Trying to get satisfaction for the business you started a couple of months ago."

His face drained as he turned to his mother to be rescued.

"Do you know this young woman?" Mr Donner was now standing in front of Steven, staring up at him, chewing on his thick, moist lips.

"Er – yes – er..."

"Course he knows me. Can't leave me alone. Told me he was a bachelor a dozen times, promised me the moon, he did. Now he doesn't want to know. Well, all I want is the means to care for this baby of his, that's all." Annie now felt strong and confident. "Well, here are my terms. Two hundred pounds."

"Two hundred pounds!" Mr Donner exploded, showering spittle in all directions. "Preposterous."

"Very well, I shall go directly to Ketsby Church. The marriage service provides for anyone with just impediment or cause for the marriage not to take place to speak now or forever hold his peace. I shall speak." Annie glared at Steven, then at Mrs Donner's crimson cheeks. "Good morning," and she swept past the stunned family. She almost bumped into the parlourmaid outside the door, who had been listening to every word.

"Just a moment, just a moment..." Mr Donner waddled after her. "Please come back, Miss..."

"Mrs. I'm a widow." Annie followed him into the drawing room.

"Please sit down, Miss..."

"Mrs. Mrs Lovitt." Annie followed him into the drawing room.

Steven was standing over his mother fumbling with a bottle of smelling salts.

"Get her to her bedroom," Mr Donner yelled at his son.

With the help of the parlourmaid Steven guided his mother upstairs and rolled her on to the bed. The hat toppled forward across her face. It looked like a squashed cake. He left the maid loosening his mother's corsets and hurried downstairs.

"I've prepared this," Mr Donner barked. "Have it despatched immediately." He tucked his thumb into his waistcoat pocket and pulled out a gold watch.

"But... but..." Steven read the message.

"Go to the Post Office and get it delivered to the vicar at Ketsby. Immediately." Basil Donner was waving his arms about. "If the Post Office is closed, hire a courier. And come straight back. Now, Miss..." his voice softened.

"Mrs."

"Now Mrs Lovitt. I'm sure we can come to some arrangement." He perched on the edge of his chair, wiping away the beads of perspiration on his waxy cheeks. "What about your parents?" He folded the handkerchief carefully and poked it into his top pocket.

"My mother died five years ago. My father is... my father is incapacitated." Annie was not going to tell him that her father was dead and that her uncle had no legs and only little stumps for arms. And she was not going to tell him that he had to be wheeled about in a pushchair, neither was she going to tell him that his brother travelled the length and breadth of Britain with him in a horse-drawn caravan visiting the showgrounds and fairs so that people could pay to look at him. She was not going to inform these money grabbers that what was missing in limbs was compensated for by a good brain. In spite of such gross disablement William Day was a handsome cut above Basil and Mildred Donner, for all their money.

"Two hundred pounds would seem to be a bit exorbitant, don't you think?" Mr Donner's voice was mellow. He had accurately assessed this young woman. She was dangerously astute.

"Cash in hand and then I'll go." Annie stood her ground near the French windows. "If not the carrier can get me to the church and the reason for the wedding to be cancelled will be known by all the congregation."

Basil Donner started pacing the carpet again, gently stroking his double chins. He turned and strode back to the window, pausing in front of her.

"Very well. I'll arrange for the money to be paid."

"No. No arrangements." Annie slapped the palm of one hand over the other. "Here and now."

"Sit down," he growled. "Wait here," and he shuffled out of the room.

Annie turned again to admire the large lawn stretching away to the fronds of the willow tree caressing the little stream at the bottom of the garden. One family with all this! Two hundred pounds wasn't enough. She should've asked for more. But she'd done her sums over and over again and decided to go for the two hundred. It would cover the costs and go a long way to help care for her uncle, and it should leave her with some savings. She might have known the Donners had money coming out of their ears – too late now. She heard the door open. Mr Donner had an envelope in his hand. She took it.

"With your permission," and she moved to the small walnut table and counted the notes. Satisfied that there were two hundred pounds she put the money back in the envelope and pushed it into her bag. "Good morning."

As she crunched along the drive she met Steven slouching along, head down. He didn't look up. As she passed him she swung her Dorothy bag under his nose, tossed her head and walked on.

* * *

Hannah Cressey adjusted the brim of her large flower-blown hat. Family and friends had been filing in for more than half an hour and the church was almost full but Steven and his best man hadn't arrived. Neither had Mr and Mrs Donner, and no one could fail to notice her grand entrances, be they at the Guildhall or the church fete, and certainly not at her only son's wedding.

Hannah had lived through too many of the King family traumas to be fazed by the late arrival of Billie's groom. The birth of the twins, the death of Esther, the arrival of Trynah then her disappearance; and now the Donners were holding everything up.

She leaned forward and peeped sideways across the pew. Oliver Bantoft, stiff and pale and nervous, was squinting through the thick lenses of the steel-rimmed spectacles perched on his long, thin nose. He'll never set Ketsby on fire but Becky would be all right with him. She was not so sure about Steven Donner. That family was a rum lot but it was none of her business. She filled her lungs with musty air and popped another peppermint into her mouth.

The church hummed with subdued expectancy. Every now and again there was the pitter-patter of feet on the flagged stones as someone was ushered to their seat. A child at the back started to howl. The mother tiptoed out of the church with the screaming bundle.

The organist, a wizened little bachelor, seemed to have taken root on the organ seat after playing there for fifty years. The tones of the organ encouraged the mounting anxiety as he waded into the Trumpet Voluntary once more.

He adjusted his mirror to get a better view of Mrs Tutty. She was sitting in the last pew near the door. He kept his eyes on her bright red hat, sprouting poppies. She would adjust it with both hands when the brides arrived. That would be the signal to him. But she was sitting motionless with her hands in her lap waiting like everyone else. He turned over the page and filled the church with a new thunderous swell. Double weddings were always the same, never on time. Double the number of people and you double your number of problems.

Now the congregation was coughing dry little coughs, blowing noses, rustling papers, fidgeting and turning at every sound in the doorway. A little girl kicked the pew in front of her, yawning with the boredom of it all.

Hannah looked over her shoulder. She could see the young bridesmaids flitting about like butterflies in the bright arch of the doorway ignoring the squat figure of Reverend Fryer gazing towards the clear, blue sky. The sun reigned and there was not a cloud to be seen.

* * *

On the forecourt of The Pyewipe Becky and Billy were being handed into the wagonette. Bladon followed and sat between them. Barney Sedge adjusted the white satin bow on the bridle, gave a final tweak to the ribbons on the door and heaved himself up on to the box grunting with the pain from his stiff hips. He spat over the side, sliced the air with his whip and they were on their short journey to St Sebastian's Church.

Bladon glanced at Billie and then at Becky, radiant in their finery. He reached under their bouquets to find their hands and held them firmly. This was a day never to be repeated, never to be forgotten and it reminded him of a day when he had claimed his bride. He and Trynah had ridden in this same wagonette. If only she could be here today. If only...

As they clopped towards the church the memories came back in a great wave of longing bringing vivid images of their first meeting in the little grey barn, then the day of their wedding, her crimson velvet bridal dress, her raven black hair. And then... she was gone. He had to swallow hard to get rid of a lump in his throat, squeezing the hands of the two brides for reassurance. They leaned over and kissed his cheeks unaware of the torment that had suddenly overwhelmed him.

As the wagonette drew up at the lych-gate he could see Reverend Fryer and the bridesmaids milling about in the church porch. Billie and Becky arranged themselves on either side and he walked them slowly along the broad path under the canopy of yew trees. The vicar hurried to greet them, his long, pale face rigid with anxiety.

"Will you excuse me, just one moment please," and he forced a toothy smile at Billie and Becky as he took Bladon's elbow and led him to a recess near one of the buttresses. "I'm very sorry Mr King. It's simply dreadful... I'm afraid... I'm afraid," and he pulled a piece of paper from his surplice pocket. "I've just received this."

Bladon read the telegram and then raised his head, squinting across the tombstones, the long grass, the gnarled old tree covered in ivy. In the meadow beyond the churchyard cows were meandering peacefully. Then he read the message again trying to control his twitching jaw.

Reverend Fryer cleared his throat. "Which is Miss Isabel? They look so alike, especially today."

"She's the one nearest to us."

The two girls were in the porch fiddling with their headdresses. "Leave it to me, I'll tell her. Give me a minute and then continue with the service for Becky and Oliver please."

"I'll be back in a moment girls." Bladon strode past the brides and bridesmaids and marched up the aisle to the front pews. He leaned over to whisper to Hannah. She followed him and joined the group in the porch. Then Bladon led Billie round the corner to a secluded footpath. He stopped in front of her, pulled back his shoulders and took a deep breath. "Steven isn't coming."

"What?" Billie put her hands to her head and knocked the headdress sideways. "Not coming! Why?"

He passed the piece of paper to her. With trembling hands she read the telegram. Her father's arms were around her.

"That's it then, isn't it?" Shaking herself free she put her clenched fists to her mouth, the bouquet hiding her face as she sobbed.

Bladon watched, helpless for a moment, then he guided her towards the church porch. "I must stay here for a while. Hannah will take you home."

"Of course," her voice was a whisper. "We mustn't spoil it for..." She started to pluck flowers from her bouquet.

"But I won't be long," he squeezed her hand.

Becky was now at her sister's side. "It *can't* be true..."

"Go along, Becky." Billie was fighting back the tears. "Go along, Oliver's waiting for you."

* * *

Billie watched as Becky took her father's arm and the retinue composed itself and disappeared into the dark cavern of the church. She retraced her steps along the pathway towards the lych-gate. Hannah was cradling her elbow as if she needed support but she felt as if she were walking on air. And she saw nothing of the day so full of blossoms, felt none of the warm sunshine, heard none of the birdsong. All she could hear was a distant humming, a tuneless, monotonous humming.

Barney had taken the wagonette to the green lane next to the church. He was sitting on the box, puffing away at his pipe, the blue smoke wreathing up into the branches of a yew tree.

"Will you take us home, please?" She saw Hannah wink at him. He read the cue and helped them into the wagonette.

Women peeped from behind their lace curtains, old men snatched off their caps as they leaned on their garden gates. Children stopped their hopscotch, their skipping, their squealing and frowned as they made their way back to The Pyewipe.

As soon as they pulled into the stable yard Billie flew indoors and thundered up the stairs to her room. She threw the bouquet on to the bed fired with an anger, a fury that could not be measured. She scowled at her reflection in the mirror. What a fool she felt standing there in so much meaningless frippery! She ripped off the veil, yanked off the wedding dress, the silk petticoat, the blue garter, the white stockings, throwing each discarded item across the bedroom floor.

She pulled on her jodhpurs, buttoned her check shirt and hurried down to the kitchen.

"Billie, will you have something to eat?" Hannah moved her glass to one side. "Or a cup of tea?"

"Nothing, thank you." She squeezed past knocking the large soufflé of a hat lopsided as she did so.

"Where are you going?" Hannah straightened her hat with both hands.

"Riding. Tell father not to worry, I'll be back later," and she stormed out of the kitchen and across the stable yard. She saddled up Penny with awesome speed, mounted and disappeared with scarf flying.

Hannah went to the larder, took the lid off the large preserving pan and pulled out a bottle of gin. "It's a right pickle and no mistake." She filled the glass. "But it'll be good for her to ride, stabilise the shock. But imagine what they're all going through in that church right now. Poor Bladon, he really doesn't deserve it. And as for that bastard, Steven, just what is his game?" Hannah sipped her gin slowly as she chatted to the deserted kitchen. "They're a rum lot, them Donners. Billie will come to realise she's had a lucky escape, specially from Mrs Donner. Should think she's at the back of this – she all but wipes the boy's arse for him. And he's twenty-four. She'd never let him go. Billie would just be the skivvy. There's money there, but old man Donner's as tight as a duck's arse." Hannah wiped her eyes with the back of her hand then emptied her glass. She must go and see how the women were getting on in the Club Room. "All those guests will be arriving in a few minutes and there are too many places set for the wedding breakfast. And there'll be a cart load of food left over."

* * *

Billie didn't ride back into the stable yard until dusk. She could hear the accordion and someone was pounding the piano. Voices shouting and singing, hands were clapping and feet were thumping on the solid wooden floor. There was much merrymaking and she wasn't there, neither was Steven.

As she rode across the fields, through the wood and along the lane the wind had been kind to her, carrying away her desolation, caressing her cheeks, flirting with her hair, and rejuvenating her but now for the first time since she left the church she felt a terrible emptiness. Oliver and Becky were man and wife and everyone was celebrating. But she was alone.

Suddenly a big hot ball in her throat choked her. Steven! How could be do such a thing? He said he loved her. He said he wanted to marry her and... now... what was in the telegram? Something about circumstances beyond his control. Nothing was beyond his control. He bossed everyone about. And a bit of a row in the hayloft hadn't been the end of the world, he'd just been in one of his moods.

She scanned the dark shapes of the wagonettes, the stables, the tackle shed, the pigsties and the toilets in the far corner. The orange moon, almost full, bathed the roof of the forage shed. Everything was the same, but she knew that nothing would ever be the same again.

Quickly she went back into the stable to unharness Penny, choking back the tears. It was quiet and dark and smelt of hay, a reliable, mature smell. The only sounds came from the deep, sonorous breathing of a tired horse.

She flopped across Penny's back tossing her head from side to side wiping tears away on Penny's rich coat. "What am I going to do?" Then she made her way across the yard.

"Is that you Billie?" a voice called from the Little Room.

"Father, what are you doing here?"

"Waiting for you." He was sitting in his favourite chair near the bar with his feet on a stool, clutching a brandy goblet.

"Where are the customers? The place is deserted." She flopped into a chair.

"Invited them to the Club Room." His hair was dishevelled and he had loosened his cravat. "For a little drink. What will you have?"

"Brandy, please."

"Did you enjoy your ride?" Bladon went behind the bar.

"Yes, especially coming back in the twilight. I went to Munce's Wood." Billie sipped her brandy. "Didn't see a soul." She was facing him across the small round table. "You don't have to worry about me father."

"I know." He twiddled the glass between his fingers. "You're made of the right stuff to ride this one out. It was a despicable thing to happen, Billie."

She held up the glass and squinted through the amber liquid. "Tell me, did Becky and Oliver have a good send off?"

"Yes. It all went very well. No one allowed their day to be spoilt. Left at five o'clock."

"I should've been here to see them off but I... I just couldn't face it." She got up and walked around the little tables, flicking the edge of each one, smoothing the back of the chairs. "Just couldn't face it. I'll send them a telegram on Monday, so that she won't worry about me. They'll have a wonderful time in Torquay." Her voice trailed off. "And I didn't see any of our guests, all those aunts and uncles and friends. It was rude of me but, honestly, father, I just couldn't be there amongst them, all happy..."

"Everyone understands, Billie. They all think you're very brave."

"Huh! Just made to look a fool." She kept her eyes on her father. "And what would cousin Lydia think? She was green with envy because I was marrying Steven."

"She's jealous of you." Bladon took his feet off the stool.

"Jealous!" Billie paused with the goblet in front of her lips.

"Yes. 'Course she is. Can't ride a horse," her father paused. "In fact, she can't, or won't do anything useful. No wonder she envies you."

"Well, goodness knows what she's thinking now. Laughing her head off." Billie scuffed the floor with her riding boots. "It's just awful. Too awful for words."

"Don't give her another thought," Bladon emptied his goblet. "Just keep on good terms. That's all."

"Yes, I suppose you're right. She likes being spiteful to me but always pretends to be friendly."

"What would you like to me to do?" he put his feet back on the stool.

"What about?"

"The Donners. I can go and see Steven. I'd like to whip the hide off him. Or I can go and see old man Donner and demand compensation for the expense incurred in arranging a wedding that never took place. What do you think?"

Billie fiddled with the ashtray holding one edge down with a finger, then releasing it with an irritating tap on the table. "I don't really want to do anything, only forget him. But why did he let it get to the very wedding day before calling it off?" She pushed the ashtray out of reach. "I saw him two days ago. We were a bit quarrelsome but he gave no hint that he never intended to marry me!"

"Oh there's more to this than meets the eye. Could be Mrs Donner. He's a bit of a mother's lad, you know."

"Yes. She's an awful woman but I was prepared to hold my own against her because of Steven. I thought... I thought I loved him."

"Give me your glass." Bladon went to the bar.

"It could have been a terrible disaster." Billie shivered. "For Becky and Oliver, I mean. The whole day could have been ruined. But it was held together thanks to you and Hannah."

"I'm here..." Hannah was leaning against the doorframe. Her

coiffure had disintegrated and skeins of thick red hair hung around her shoulders. She was grinning from ear to ear, waving an empty glass.

"Lovely party, Billie. You were the star," she burped, "Steven bastard. Shifty eyes, true, isn't it Bladon?" She left the security of the doorframe, bumping into the tables and chairs as she wove her way across the Little Room.

"There we are." Billie guided her to a seat. "I'm going to leave you in father's care now. It's been quite a day and I'm tired." She bent to kiss Hannah's hot, flushed cheek and then she moved to her father, squeezing his hand. "Goodnight."

Bladon watched her leave the room. "She's got some spunk, that girl." He looked at Hannah slumped in the chair. She sat awkwardly making her purple brocade dress seem too small for her. Her eyes floated around the room, her cheeks were shiny with perspiration, her lips were moist and loose. "You've done it again, Hannah. How many times have I told you?"

"Just a nip, for Billie. To drown the sorrow."

Bladon eased her out of the chair. "Come on, time for bed."

* * *

"Have you decided what you would like me to do about the Donners?" Bladon and Billie were in the tackle shed sorting out the harness. It was five days since the double wedding had become a single wedding and it was still the main topic of conversation rumbling around Ketsby in Barker's store, the butcher's, the baker's, The Wheatsheaf and, in whispers, at The Pyewipe. Most of the village had turned out to watch the two brides ride to the church and many of them had seen Billie King ride home in ominous splendour with Hannah Cressey.

"Father, I told you. I don't want you to do anything." Billie's voice was shrill.

"Young men don't propose to young ladies and then put them through this heartache." He looped the reins over a nail. 'Due to circumstances beyond his control.' Huh!"

"Oh, I know how you feel about it but nothing can pay for the anguish, father, the humiliation. Nothing. Did you lose a lot of money?"

Bladon turned to face her. "It's not so much a matter of money. It's a matter of principle, Billie."

"Well, as far as I am concerned it's all over and done with. I never want to see Steven again. And as for that mother of his, that bloated old battleaxe with the creaking corsets, forever knitting gossip with her tongue and that voice braying at everyone! Hannah says I've had a lucky escape. You know, I'm really beginning to think so, too. But Steven... how could he do such a thing?" She covered her face with her hands and shook her head. "How could he?"

"You know, all young men are not like Steven Donner." He put his arms around her shoulders. "I know how much it hurts you, Billie. But don't close your heart. In time you'll meet someone. Someone you can trust, someone you can't live without."

She wiped her face. "I must get on. Then I'm going to see Becky this afternoon, to hear all about her..." she choked again, covering her mouth with her hands. "Her honeymoon."

"Now, now," Bladon hung the reins over a nail. "All will be well. And I've decided I'm going to see Mr Donner to tell him that I shall no longer be buying beer from his brewery."

"But we need supplies!"

"There are plenty of other brewers. I shall go and talk to Bill Pizer. He runs a reliable outfit and I know him. Broke two shire horses for him in the spring, remember."

* * *

Becky and Oliver lived in the end cottage in a row of three at Ketsby Hill Foot, about half a mile away. Billie decided to walk but as she turned the corner at the church she saw Becky coming towards her.

"I told you I'd come and see *you*." They encircled each other, whirling round and round on the pavement.

"I know but I needed a bit of exercise after lazing around so much in Torquay. And it's such a glorious day. Shall we go to Bunker's Hill?" Becky suggested.

"Good idea. It's quiet there and we're away from everyone."

"I've been so concerned about you, Billie. I know what these gossiping old crones are like, specially Bertha Burrell."

They were soon on the green lane leading to Bunker's Hill. "Now I want to hear all about your honeymoon." Billie took Becky's elbow. "Let's go and sit on that log over there, under the sycamore tree. It'll be nice and cool and there's a lovely view down the field to the willow trees."

"All right," Becky kicked her legs out in front of her. "Where were we? Yes, the honeymoon. Not all it's cracked up to be, really."

"What do you mean?"

"Well, I didn't know what I was supposed to do, and we were so tired when we got to Torquay we just fell asleep in each other's arms the first night."

"Well, the girls that do it never really tell us much do they," Billie leaned back supporting herself on the log with both arms. "I mean, they don't explain to us. And we know they do it 'cos the boys brag about it."

"I know. Well, Oliver had got a book from somewhere, and, well, it soon got better. But at first it's awful, really awful Billie."

Billie was breaking a twig into small pieces. "I thought it was supposed to be exciting. That's why everyone wants to do it."

"It is. But at first I was nervous." Becky paused. A soft breeze played around them, teasing their loose, shiny hair, caressing their freckled faces. "Do you remember the day I ran away from Norcross House?"

"Yes, just before our, I mean, your wedding."

"I never told Oliver about Doctor Lister." Becky chewed on a blade of grass.

"Well, that was our secret, and it's all in the past."

"Yes, but it came back to me with Oliver in Torquay. He's been ever so good about that side of things. Didn't get cross with me at all."

"Why should he?" Billie threw the piece of twig into the grass.

"Well, I was scared. Thinking about that day in Doctor Lister's study." Becky held her sister's steady gaze. "And I'm telling you because you mustn't be put off. Steven's a rat for doing what he did," she cupped her chin with her hands.

"But Becky, I've had a lucky escape. Especially when you think of Mrs Donner. I thought I loved Steven. How quickly it dies. How quickly it evaporates, that feeling that I couldn't live without him. It's gone in a blink. I can't make any sense of it. I'll tell you something Becky, it'll be a long time before I trust anyone again."

"Now, that's exactly what I'm trying to say. You mustn't shut everyone out. They're not all like Steven Donner. Look at Oliver, kindness itself."

"You're lucky." Billie stood up, hands on hips. "I don't want you to worry about me. Father and Hannah worry about me, aunt Vinny worries about me, so does aunt Abby, and Lydia does in her own way. She's been inviting me to join her parties – jazz concerts and dances. And do you know we smoked Balkan Sobranie cigarettes at the dance last week? They're different colours and you choose the cigarette that matches the dress you're wearing. Also we drank cocktails. Father would have a fit if he knew. Where does she learn all these things?"

"Don't know. She doesn't have to work." Becky swept a strand of hair from her eyes. "At Flaxwell they have maids. So what does she do all day?"

"No idea. Do you think she does it, Becky?"

"Shouldn't think so. Imagine what uncle Robert would say to that! No! Shouldn't think so."

They each pursued their thoughts about Lydia for a while. The pigeons cooed in the trees. In the distance a dog barked. Above them, the leaves of the sycamore tree whispered to each other. Then the church clock struck four.

"Come on," Billie jumped to her feet. "I'm going to make us some tea, and then you can tell me about Torquay."

"It's a lovely place. It has palm trees! I thought you only got those in tropical islands, but Torquay has palm trees!"

As they got to the end of the lane a man on a bicycle swerved past them. It was Cadger Burrell.

"Bet he's going to steal something." Billie looked over her shoulder. Cadger Burrell was bent over the handlebars pedalling along the cart ruts, jacket flapping.

* * *

The breeze kept control of the burning sun, there wasn't much traffic and the drive to Grantham was balmy. Bladon was relishing his visit to Donner's Brewery. It would get just one more thing out of the way for Billie. She mustn't be reminded of that shit Steven every time they needed supplies. He didn't want to see anything to do with Donner's anywhere near The Pyewipe.

He drove the pony and trap through the double entrance doors of the brewery weaving between several beer drays waiting to be loaded. He wandered through the loading shed and then into the bottling area. It was a lofty, square shed with white walls and a network of narrow pipes criss-crossing the ceiling.

He passed a woman bent over the siphon-filling machine. She was passing the full bottles to a group of women standing round a circular table.

He could see the office in the far corner. It looked like one of his chicken huts with a long window giving on to the entire bottling shed. He could see the round, squat figure of Mr Donner crouched over his desk, and he was about to make his way when he felt a tug on his coat sleeve.

"Mr King. It is Mr King?" The voice was a gruff whisper. "From The Pyewipe?"

Bladon stared into sparkling hazel eyes that gave the pale face a liveliness, an easy courage.

The young woman glanced over first one shoulder, then the other and tugged his coat sleeve again. "This way, come this way," and she beckoned him along a passage between a stack of beer crates. "I just wanted to say, just wanted to... Well," her hands smoothed down the torn apron, "I just wanted to let you know how sorry I was for... about the wedding."

"How do you know about the wedding? And how do you know me?"

"A friend of mine lives in Ketsby. She knows you and described you to me."

"And you know my daughter?" Bladon frowned.

"No, I don't know her. But..." again she glanced over her shoulder. "It was my fault there was no wedding."

"Madam, you are talking in riddles." Bladon was trying to decide about this woman. She had not been drinking, there wasn't a hint of it on her breath. She was well-spoken. His eyes swept from the white cap covering most of her brown, curly hair to the long hessian apron tied round her waist with string. Her hands were red raw with the handling of the cold bottles, but she had a bearing, a demeanour that seemed out of place in Donner's Brewery. What circumstance could have brought her to work in this clatter with the nauseating smell of stale beer? She would have been more at home in a classroom or an office.

"My name's Annie Lovitt, and Steven Donner..." she whispered, "well, he did me wrong." And the whole story came tumbling out. "You see it was all my fault there was no wedding. I spoilt it for your daughter. I threatened the Donners when I knew he was getting married..."

"How long have you known him?"

"Over a year. Often came in here to look round. That's where he first saw me. Promised me the moon and all the time... he never told me he was engaged. Never." She was shaking her head. "Honest. I didn't know."

"Well, er..." Bladon stumbled for the words, "what about your future?"

"Oh, don't worry. I made sure they paid. Mind you I wish I'd asked for more when I saw their place." Annie Lovitt threw back her head and the bright eyes flashed. "I finish here on Saturday then I'm going to Nottingham, to visit a cousin. She's arranging things. Old man Donner will never know whether he's got a bastard heir to..." she waved her arm. "To this lot. I'll make him sweat. Must go, he'll be watching, he can see everything from that office. I'm sorry about Miss King. Really sorry."

Bladon watched as she scuttled back to her place at the filling table then made his way to the office.

Mr Donner was poring over a ledger when Bladon walked in. He looked up, opened his mouth but said nothing.

"Good morning. May I sit down?" and Bladon pulled out a rickety chair with a frayed cane seat.

"Ah! Mr King. Good morning. This is a surprise." Mr Donner grasped the arms of the chair as if to get up but decided to stay seated.

"You weren't expecting me then?" Bladon put his whip across the desk.

Basil Donner stretched his short thick neck and looked at Bladon from underneath his eyelids. "Well – er, well, I'm a very busy man."

"So am I." Bladon leaned forward on one elbow.

"What can I do for you?" Mr Donner picked up a pencil.

"You can cancel my contract for supplies from your Brewery as from today."

Donner's mouth opened and closed like a fish gasping for air. "But we value The Pyewipe. You're one of our most important customers..."

"Too late. Cancel it. And then you can explain what circumstances were beyond control to humiliate my daughter as you did."

Basil Donner cleared his throat. "He... hum... er, well, you see."

"No, I don't see. I want to know. That's why I'm here." He leaned back in the creaking chair.

"As I said, there were circumstances entirely beyond my control that made the marriage between my son and your daughter impossible."

"Very well. If you don't want to elaborate upon those circumstances I must take your word for it." Bladon pulled an invoice from his pocket. "You can pay this bill."

Basil Donner took the piece of paper. "But... this is an outrageous sum!"

"Outrageous! How dare you!" Bladon picked up his whip and tapped it across the palm of his left hand. "You're a fine one to talk about outrage. Quite apart from the emotional damage this has done to my daughter there was a wedding cake, wine, beer and half a ton of food not consumed. Not to mention the church expenses and the wagonettes."

Donner got to his feet and waddled around the desk. His foot caught the waste paper basket and it toppled over spilling litter across the floor. "I'll consider it. Perhaps we can come to an arrangement..."

"One hundred and eighty two pounds cash before I leave this office and the matter is closed." Bladon threw down his whip and went to the window. It commanded a view of the entire bottling shed. That woman was right. Every worker could be seen from this window. He gazed at the bleak shed, the racks of casks at the far end and the women in their white caps hovering around the filling tables. From the seclusion of this office he could hear the clamour and smell the sickly mixture of hops and malt.

"One hundred. To settle." The voice came from below his left shoulder.

"One hundred and eighty two pounds." Bladon pushed past him and returned to the uncomfortable cane chair. "I think you'd find action at Common Law for breach of promise much more expensive."

Basil Donner took short fussy paces across the office to the oak filing cabinet in the corner and pulled a Crawford's biscuit tin from the bottom drawer. He brought it to the desk and prised off the lid. The tin was packed with bank notes. Bladon watched as the greedy little hands counted the money and pushed it across the desk. He checked it and thrust it into his pocket.

"Good morning, Mr Donner," and with a flick of the wrist he threw the whip into the air, caught it and walked out of the office.

* * *

The jilting of Isabel King gave Ketsby an excitement that was lacking in the lazy summer months of a quiet village. The sun came up and stayed all day encouraging indolence and idleness. The whole village was buzzing with the news. On the street corners the women had their heads together and the postman heard a different version on every doorstep. Across the fields the men paused to scratch their heads and spit and wonder what it was all about.

In Barker's General Store the chatter bubbled and boiled. It suited Letty Barker. From behind that long, scuffed wooden counter she pursed her lips and listened. The shop was full of women eager to offer another scrap of tittle-tattle as they bought their packet of tea or reel of cotton.

Bertha Burrell was in her element. She had spent decades on her circuit of shops – the butcher's, the baker's, the General Store and the street corner, fomenting rumours, raking muck and scandal. It was her lifeblood.

"Serves Bladon King right," she announced as she clutched her ragged cardigan to her bony chest.

Letty watched as Bertha's sunken little eyes darted across the faces of the women, along the shelves laden with cocoa and custard powder, down to the large slab of cheese on the counter. The skin of her unlucky face was like parchment, yellow with age. The years had slowed her step, bent her body, dimmed her eyes but her relish for mischief making was as keen as ever. The woman had never learnt to smile in all the years Letty had known her.

"Too smart by 'alf he is." Bertha tapped the half crown on the solid oak counter.

"Ah, well, Bertha, you've always got an axe to grind with The Pyewipe," Mrs Tweddle shifted her lumpy bulk from one foot to the other. "You've been at it for years, ever since Cadger caught his fingers in that gin trap. It were his own fault." She put her long, angular nose in the air.

"No. It wasn't," Bertha pursed her thin lips.

"Yes, it were, he were stealing hay. I remember it well." A puff of air escaped from Mrs Tweddle's sulky mouth. Her corns were hurting and she wanted to get home. The Burrells were forever stealing and cadging and begging and borrowing. One night all her peas had been stripped clean from her garden. And Mrs Trolley was always complaining that her hens weren't laying like they should. "Two pound of sugar please and a quarter of tea."

"Think about poor Billie," Letty didn't want an argument this morning, or any morning. She was doing more business than usual which is all that mattered in these mean days of unemployment.

"That's who I'm sorry for." She poured the sugar on to the scales and selected a solid brass weight. Then she slid the sugar into the blue paper bag. "No bride deserves treatment like that. Besides, it had nothing to do with Mr. King. You can't blame him."

"Bladon King gets too big for his boots. Riding about Ketsby as if he owns it." Bertha would never forgive him for what he did to Cadger's hand.

"He don't go stealing other folk's property," Mrs Tweddle remarked and scooped up her packages. "In fact, he gives it away." She paused to glare into Bertha's doleful face. "No end of stuff left over from that wedding. Gave it all away, he did," and she plodded out of the shop banging the door behind her.

"Them Kings are fated, allus was. Niver known a family with so much bad luck." Hilda Dawson lodged her walking stick on the edge of the counter and fished in the bottom of her basket for her purse. "Why, I remember the to-do when Bladon married Trynah Bishop."

"There were nothing wrong wi' the marriage," piped up an old woman. She was swathed in a black woollen coat two sizes too big for her. She wore it all year round, summer and winter. "It's what happened six months later. That's the riddle, and still is." She gave a hollow, rasping cough. "A good husband, them two little bairns to care for, why should she walk out of the inn only months after getting married? A rum thing and no mistake."

Letty cut through the slab of cheese. It was true that over the years the Kings had provided much of the gossip for Ketsby. She had been six years old at the time of the catastrophe at Lees Farm but she remembered her mother talking about a rape and murder. She had not understood the word 'rape' and her mother had not been able to explain it to her but she knew the word 'murder' because a little girl at Nottingham had been strangled.

From time to time Bertha Burrell would try to light the fire again but her mother had taught her to change the subject if Bertha started. 'Sufficient unto the day is the evil thereof...' she would quote.

And now here was another catastrophe in the King family with everyone remembering fragments of the scandal. She heard the honking of a horn and the steady chug chug of an engine.

The women surged forward to the shop window pushing past the shiny new kettles and saucepans and frying pans dangling from the hooks on the wall. Bertha knocked over the cardboard display for custard powder as she scrambled to be first at the window. In doing so she brought down the sticky fly catcher swaying from a nail in the ceiling.

"It's Tin Lizzie," Bertha disentangled the fly-paper stuck in her hair.

They all stood on tiptoe craning their necks to see the only motor car in Ketsby spluttering and wheezing along High Street.

It was like a beige box on wheels with a black top and a dicky seat. The driver was a plump man wearing a tweed jacket and a tweed cap pulled forward over his eyes. His jaw was clenched in concentration as he leaned over the steering wheel.

"It's Doctor Robb," Letty rubbed her hands down her pinafore and went back behind the counter, "in that new fangled motor machine. Not safe."

"Any road on, as I were saying, Bladon King married Trynah and then she disappeared, nobody knows why. And now that young gel of his left in the lurch like that." Hilda Dawson took the walking stick, paused to stare at Bertha Burrell then hobbled out of the shop continuing her lament into the High Street. "Niver known so much bad luck in one family. Niver..."

"And then he took up with Hannah Cressey," Bertha snatched at another morsel and threw it to the shoppers.

"I think it was prudent of him to take a housekeeper." Letty reached for a packet of tea. "Heavens above, he had the twin girls, remember and the inn to run. You can't blame a man for that. He did the right thing."

"Why didn't 'e marry 'er?" Bertha sucked in her lips until her mouth was just a thin straight line.

"Only he can answer that, Bertha, and I'm sure you're just the one to ask him. That'll be two and fourpence please."

Bertha glared at Letty, paid for the tea and shuffled out of the shop. "Now, who's next?"

"I think it's me," the woman bundled up in a black coat piped up. "Half pound best butter please. Bertha Burrell's nothing but a menace. Never happy unless she's making trouble for somebody."

"Well, she got her come-uppance..."

The doorbell jangled and Bertha Burrell rushed in. Her pasty face was blushed, her mouth open as if in pain, the little eyes were like daggers.

"It's Hannah Cressey. Doctor Robb's there, but she's in a bad way."

* * *

Bladon was now urging Duke up the last bit of Ketsby Hill. It had deep banks on either side covered by a dense growth of hawthorn bushes menacing the innocent road. It was rumoured that highwaymen used to wait at the back of these bushes to attack the stagecoaches. It was a fact that every horse he had owned faltered at this steepest part and he didn't know whether it was fatigue or fear or a mixture of both.

He began to hum. 'All things bright 'n beautiful...' He was pleased he'd got justice from Basil Donner; spluttering and choking and waving his arms around, the bloody shyster. And now he knew why Steven had not turned up at the church. What a good job he had decided to go to Donner's Brewery! Another bloody shyster. like father, like son. Having a bit of slap and tickle on the side when all the time he was betrothed to his Billie! But for that young woman – what was her name – Annie something, he would never have known the truth, never known why he had to tell Billie that her fiancé wasn't coming to the church to marry her. It was nothing short of a scandal. And to think that Billie could now have been married to that prick. She had had a lucky escape. Now she would be staying with him at home. The thought made him glow.

And he had a new supplier. Bill Pizer would not let him down. He waved his whip as he passed the group of boys pelting stones at the clock on the church. He had been quite good at hitting it himself when he was their age.

Duke wheeled into Marratt's Lane, steered himself expertly through the double entrance gates and went straight to the drinking trough.

"Father! Father..." Billie came rushing from the kitchen. "It's Hannah. Come quickly. Oh, father..."

"Don't tell me she's been at it again..." He followed her through the kitchen and marched along the corridor. There was a mound of skirts and petticoats like a heap of discarded clothing at the foot of the stairs. It was Hannah curled around the plinth of her beloved statue. Her head was turned to one side and her eyes were closed, her lower lip slack as if she were in a deep sleep. One arm was stretched out across the floor, the other was underneath her.

"I've sent for Doctor Robb." Billie clutched her throat. "I didn't know what to do."

"Hannah! Hannah, can you hear me?" Bladon was crouching at her side, gently touching her shoulder.

There was no response. No recognition.

"We must move her," he looked around the corridor, "to somewhere more comfortable. But I'm afraid..."

In the stable yard Gypsy barked and hens cackled. Then heavy footsteps clumped through the kitchen. Doctor Robb came bustling along the corridor with tweed jacket flapping, his black bag at arm's length as if he were fighting his way through a crowd.

"What happened?" Doctor Robb fell to his knees.

"Don't know. I've just this minute got back from Grantham." Bladon stepped away from the bundle of skirts.

"I think she must have fallen down the stairs," Billie reached for the banister for support.

"Did you see her fall?" Doctor Robb was rummaging in his black bag.

"No. I was in the kitchen. I heard a heavy thump. That was all, there was no other sound. She didn't make any cry... I came to see what had happened and this... this is how I found her... I heard children playing in the street and got the Daubney children to fetch you."

Doctor Robb moved closer to the statue, narrowing his eyes as he scanned the bronze boy. "We must move her. Is there..."

"The Back Room", Bladon pointed along the corridor to a green door. "The Council hold their meetings there. Nothing booked for today."

"A large blanket please." Doctor Robb glanced at Billie, frozen in disbelief.

"Yes," she whispered and scampered up the stairs to the chest on the landing.

Doctor Robb flapped the blanket across the floor and slowly straightened Hannah's legs and arms.

"Lift her gently now. That's it, be careful." He stepped over the pool of blood and took the ends of the blanket at her head and Bladon scooped up the other end near her feet. Billie pushed open the green door.

The Back Room was full of chairs stacked in rows and there was a long trestle table near the window. The room smelt of rancid beer and stale tobacco and there was an empty glass on the window sill.

"On the table, Mr King. Slowly." Doctor Robb grunted as he raised the inert body and carefully stretched Hannah full length on her back.

He ripped open the collar of her blue dress and plunged his hand to her heart. Then he leaned over her face and opened her left eye. He saw the abrasion on the side of her head and the blood seeping through the thick hair on to the table. His fingers traced the indentation above her left ear.

"The statue," he pulled back his lips as he wiped his hands on a handkerchief.

"I'll get some hot water," Billie hurried out of the Back Room.

Doctor Robb pulled the stethoscope from his bag and listened, his eyes fixed on the buttons of her bodice.

Bladon gripped the edge of the table for support. The room was swimming. The empty glass on the window sill multiplied until he saw three glasses. Then he looked at Hannah. The expression on her face was much the same as when she'd had a good evening of drinking and singing and had tired after one too many and fallen asleep.

But her face was smooth, pale, her mouth was open and her green eyes had tilted out of sight. Large white orbs stared at the ceiling. There was no life there. No life! The room whirled around him and he had to push his thighs on to the edge of the table to prevent himself from falling. Hannah! *No, Hannah. Don't die!*

Outside children were squabbling, squealing, laughing, shrieking. He heard the contents of a bucket being emptied, swishing across the road. Then the street noises faded away and he heard it, that long, deep rattle, that terrifying departure of breath, that awful finality.

"I'm afraid…" Doctor Robb stepped away from the table, defeated. "I'm afraid…"

Billie pushed the door open with her left foot and steered her way to the table with the steaming bowl and a towel folded over one arm.

"Here's plenty of hot water. Shall I bring…" her voice faded. She looked first at her father, then at Doctor Robb and then at Hannah.

"Thank you. That won't be necessary, Miss King."

Chapter 6

Cantabria, Northern Spain. August 1920

"I'm surprised he's not back," Trynah leaned on the window sill of the kitchen and looked out across the courtyard expecting him to come riding through the wrought iron gates with his usual panache. Beyond the farm buildings she could see the goat paths winding through the fields up into the wooded hills but her eyes were drawn to the fountain in the middle of the courtyard showering its diamonds in the August sun. "Did he say where he was going?"

"Riding." Robinson Mann was sorting through the heap of tan fur at his feet.

"He seems to be disappearing quite regularly these days," remarked Trynah, smoothing a wisp of hair from her face. "Never says where he's going."

"He's getting to that age. He's a man now."

"So I've noticed," she turned from the window and surveyed the kitchen. It was much like the one she had walked out of at The Pyewipe, a long time ago. Not quite so big. But there were no little girls scampering in and out. Those little girls will now be young women. Oh! To see them again! But this was the price she'd paid. It had been exorbitant.

She glanced at Robbie squatting on the low milking stool in the doorway, handling the soft, limp bodies of the rabbits. He still beguiled her with his magic and his passion after all these years.

"Trouble is," Robbie came to the kitchen table and rummaged in the long drawer. "He hasn't got enough to do. Ah! here it is," and he pulled out a glinting knife. "We need more land, and I'm not going to give up. One day we'll get it. Daroca will give in, you'll see."

Trynah knew that Robbie never gave up. His tenacity had got him from Lincoln Prison to northern Spain and a small farm that gave them a living. It was eighteen years since the rendezvous at King's Cross. She remembered it as if it were yesterday.

Amidst the throng of people and the wheezing of trains Robbie had announced, "We're going to Cantabria, northern Spain, my lovely. It's as green and lush as Lincolnshire, believe me."

"Spain!" Trynah had been horrified.

"Don't worry. I'll explain everything before we get there." And he did.

Crossing the English Channel in that wretched ferry boat was dreadful. Her geography book showed the Channel as a slender blue ribbon separating England from France. Not so. All she saw was a vast grey ocean in turmoil as she gripped the boat rail with the wind tearing away her bonnet and streaking through her hair, biting her cheeks until she wept. Her head swam and her stomach had been turned inside out until it was hollow and raw. The awful seasickness had stayed with her long after they arrived at Los Rubios.

Then the train journey, which she had thought would never end. They had trundled across France for hours until at last they crossed the Spanish frontier at Irun, and after an overnight stay in a pension they were on their way to Santander.

The final lap of their gruelling journey took them south to Lavega. The train moved slowly, chuffing and snorting and belching cinders through the windows and the rattle of wheels on metal did nothing to calm her queasiness. The seats were rough plank benches that became harder as the day wore on.

A constant stream of passengers got on and off as the train shuddered to a stop at each little station, which was just a low, white building all alone by the side of the railway line.

An elderly couple grunted as they settled themselves into the seats in the corner watching them, listening to them, not understanding a word of their language. He was very thin, wearing a navy blue shiny serge suit. She was wearing a long black dress and her greying hair was scraped back and held in place by an ornate pink comb in the shape of a fan.

Next to them sat a sturdy fair-haired man. Trynah had not expected to see fair hair in Spain. She thought all Spaniards had dark hair. His wife was a lumpy lady, comfortable with life as it was. She opened her basket and was passing large chunks of bread and thick slices of dark red mouldy sausage to her husband and the two boys, who both had dark hair. Then to Trynah's surprise they all drank wine from a leather *porrón*. She knew it was wine in that leather bottle. She had seen an identical one in a picture in the Bridge Art Gallery in Lincoln. All were dressed in clean, mended clothes and they had an air of dignity and contentment about them.

The train puffed through the green valleys with thick woods lolling on the hillsides like large dark green cushions. It chugged past clusters of ramshackle farms and cottages with chickens and goats and cows and pigs roaming freely. The roads were not much more than cart tracks leading up the hillsides to more scattered cottages.

Then it was snaking around the foot of huge grey rocks towering above the broad river splashing over fallen boulders. She saw a heron, low and graceful, as it swooped over the tumbling water. The banks were lush with vegetation and she was amazed to see a clump of large white lilies growing wild on the embankment. Then they hurried along into yet another broad, green valley.

She sat opposite Robbie in the crowded compartment listening to the rest of his story, piecing together the missing parts of the jigsaw from that far-off day when they were planning their wedding at the Ring Dam before... They were together now, here in a bumpy, rattling train and she was being carried further and further away from Ketsby and all that she knew and held dear.

It had been such an agony to leave Bladon, such a good man, and Billie and Becky. But they were young. The wounds would heal quickly, but it was agony too to leave Abby, her dear ugly sister, and Vinny.

Now, with time and space separating them she wondered how she could have done such a cruel thing to all these good people. But she couldn't explain why she was doing it. It was too dangerous. Robbie was still a wanted man. She glanced at him sitting opposite, quite relaxed, the very reason she had done it. Robbie had proposed marriage and the wedding was less than two weeks away when Redfern, his ne'er do well brother, walked to the little grey barn. One sunny afternoon and... She pushed away the horror of it all.

Robbie leaned forward in his seat, fingers together to form a pyramid, elbows resting on his knees as he continued his story.

"Well, an inmate in the prison, Enrique Martinez, a Spanish sailor, was serving a life sentence for a crime he says he did not commit. He'd been drinking in a tavern in Boston but had left to go back to his ship when a drunken brawl developed. A man was stabbed and died. Someone identified Enrique as having been in the tavern that night. It was quite true but Enrique saw nothing of the brawl because he was back on board. Nobody believed him. I did. But what chance has a Spaniard in a British Court?" He lolled back in his seat and stared out of the window. "But he's a survivor. You know, it all depends on the will, that something deep down inside, that inner knowledge, inner confidence. That's what decides matters, especially in a prison. There's no way of assessing the endurance of the human spirit. Some go under. Some get stronger."

She watched him travelling through his thoughts, and waited. Then he leaned forward again.

"Well, he gave me the address of a man he knew in Spain. He also gave me his Spanish pocket dictionary. For some reason the prison authorities hadn't confiscated it. You look pale, my lovely. Are you feeling sick again?"

"I'm all right as long as I keep eating these. Here, have one."

The train had stopped at a station with an unpronounceable name and Trynah had leaned out of the window to get some fresh air. She felt sick and her head ached with the rattle and rumble of the train. She spotted a forlorn figure on the deserted platform. The bony little woman shuffled towards her carrying a basket of shiny red apples, much too heavy for her. Her weather-beaten face was witness to years of hard work and worry. Feeble, watery eyes seemed to stare at her from beyond the grave. The old lady held up an apple, beseeching her to buy. Trynah glanced at the apples again, so large and juicy. Yes, she would. After all, she hadn't eaten since Paris. Those apples had sustained her to Lavega and she was ever grateful to that old lady and her basket of apples.

"So when I got to Lavega I found this man, Carlos Daroca. He had a farm on the outskirts of the village and owned a lot of land in the district. He's not much of a farmer but he's rich and buying farms is a sort of hobby. I wrote down the name of Enrique Martinez and that was it. He could see that I was healthy and from farming stock and willingly rented Los Rubios to this foreigner."

"But didn't he want to know why you'd left England?"

"No," Robbie crunched into his apple.

"And you didn't speak Spanish then!"

"No. But the priest knew some English. He had studied in Madrid, disgraced himself somehow and had been sent to Lavega as penance. He was a great help. A lease was drawn up and I signed it. Everything was in order." He smiled at her. That winsome, one-sided smile that she had missed so much. "All I had to do then was work hard, make the farm pay, and then... I came back to England. To find you..."

Trynah remembered the moment, in the Club Room at the Pyewipe. Bladon and the children had gone to Culbeck Fair and she had decided to tidy the room before the next wedding. She was glad she did because it was a mess. The children played up there on wet days and it was littered with discarded clothing, old lace curtains, dusters and mops. She had walked up the three steps at the side of the stage and pulled back the cream curtains. Standing in front of her was Robbie, the man who had been hanged in Lincoln Prison six years ago. In the whole world there could never have been such a moment. Such disbelief. It was almost more than a soul could bear.

And here she was on a train having left her husband and two little stepdaughters and all her family and friends to be with the man she had promised to marry. She jumped out of her seat, cupped his face with both her hands and kissed him full on the lips. The chatter in the carriage died away to a low murmur and then there was a spontaneous cheering and clapping.

"Oh, dear," Trynah bowed her head. "Sorry, Robbie. I didn't mean to embarrass you."

"Nothing to be sorry about. You can do it again," He reached for her hand and squeezed it.

It was late afternoon when they stepped from the train at Lavega into its narrow streets and alleyways. Old men and women were stirring from their siesta, yawning and stretching and staring at the two foreigners. Young men and women deserted their crumpled siesta beds to drink coffee and return to the tempo of the day with a wary but friendly *'Buenas tardes'* for them as they walked by.

The houses were squat and of different sizes leaning on each other for support. Most of them had balconies and shuttered windows. Divided wooden doors had the top half open to catch any passing breeze. And everywhere she saw bright red geraniums; on the balconies, at the windows, in the courtyards. Children with boundless energy chased the scrawny dogs prowling around looking for something to eat.

"It's just a short walk. Do you think you can manage it?"

"Of course, the air will do us good. We need to stretch our legs. I've got quite stiff." She picked up her valise. "Robbie, your face is so dirty!"

"So is yours but I wasn't going to tell you. It's the cinders. Don't know what they'll think of us looking like tramps but we'll come clean again." He led her across the Plaza past the church, and into a narrow alleyway.

Coming towards them was a cart piled high with firewood drawn by two hollow-ribbed oxen with huge, scimitar horns. A handsome, dark-haired man with hessian sacks draped around his shoulders plodded along by the side of the cart.

"This way," Robbie turned into a lane. On the right was the school with its large, bare playground next to a row of dilapidated little houses. After a short distance the lane veered to the left and Robbie led her on to a narrow cart track across a field and she saw Los Rubios. In the failing light it looked quite magical, shrouded in a mist. They went through the double gates into a large courtyard. Trynah stopped in her tracks. "The fountain, Robbie, the fountain. How lovely!"

Cattle sheds flanked the courtyard on one side with stables and pigsties opposite and there, facing them was a confident, solid farmhouse with its tiled roof and walls of square grey stones. A porch sheltered the front entrance door, which looked as if it hadn't been opened for years. Trees nestled at each corner of the farmhouse, comforting it, protecting it.

Robbie dropped the bags at the door and led her along the path round the corner to the back of the house. "You see, fresh vegetables." And he pointed to the dense rows of cabbages, carrots, beans and plants that she had never seen before. "And there is the orchard, and at the bottom of the field, a river."

"Why, Robbie, it's wonderful." Just a short walk from the farmhouse and she would be at the river.

"And on the opposite side of the river, over there," Robbie pointed. "That's the large field I want."

Those first impressions of Los Rubios had never let her down. It was a lovely little farm. But everything was different. The wood-burning stoves, there was something fulfilling, a sort of sense of security from the smell of those burning logs. And the spicy food!

She had never seen or eaten peppers, and she had never tasted garlic. At first she couldn't relish these new tastes but she soon grew used to the different flavours. Besides they were able to grow many of the vegetables they had known in Lincolnshire.

The Spanish tobacco smelt like horse manure, and there was the reek of leather, the pungent smell of cheese being made and the tang of the whey coming from the dairy. The goats had a whiff of their own – mouldy excrement came to mind. In the sheds there was the mustiness of hay and cow dung. Even the air was different, not so damp as Lincolnshire. Her senses were overloaded by the new smells.

And there were new sounds. The tinkling bells echoing across the valley and up the hillsides as the goats and cows wandered along the pathways were such a novelty to her. She couldn't imagine the cows at Copping Lane with bells round their necks, or Mrs Rogers' goats jingling around that small paddock near The Pyewipe, or the creak of wooden ox carts labouring along the tracks. The tinny church bells were so different to the resonant force of tons of iron clanging in the English church belfries.

During those first weeks the magnitude of her betrayal overwhelmed her. When Robbie was across the fields she wept in her bedroom, longing for The Pyewipe and its stability, its certainty. The anguish of leaving her husband had haunted her for a long time but as the months slipped into years and life in Lavega established its own rhythm the distress had mellowed into a sea of memory that she dipped into every time a letter came from Vinny. Then she was back there in the inn with all its unpredictability, the customers singing, shouting, dancing, arguing, the clatter and banging. It was all so vivid. Her sister's letters quietly blanketed the aching gap.

Once or twice it had been on the tip of her tongue to bring up the possibility of going back but she didn't want to give Robbie the impression that she was unsettled. She was getting older, they were both getting older. But she wanted to see her sisters. She wanted to embrace Becky and Billie again. They could go back. It was a risk for Robbie but it would be just the thing for Richard who would be eighteen next birthday, just the right age to find an opening somewhere. He spoke fluent Spanish, too. But she never uttered a word to Robbie about her hankering. He had gone through enough.

"He killed his twin brother in the forage shed for what he did to me. And he stood on that hangman's trap door three times. Not once, not twice, but three times! That was more than any being could endure. The reward for that endurance was twenty years in prison." Trynah was speaking to the window, alone in the bedroom, looking beyond the courtyard and the fountain up to the beech wood. "But he escaped, here, to Spain. Established himself and then came back to England to find me. And I walked out on them all. Just like that."

Turning away she contemplated their flat, wide bed and felt a frisson, a thrill, just gazing at it. Yes, this is where she had found justification for all that deceit. She had promised to be his wife. Those promises had been realised in bed with Robbie. He had led her to those rarified uplands, to happiness and fulfilment and warmth and security in his arms. So she would keep these longings for the past buried.

The villagers looked much like the people in Grantham. Robust, many of them with blue eyes and fair hair. At first they had been suspicious of these foreigners who had arrived from nowhere struggling with their bad Spanish. It was Trynah's pregnancy and the arrival of their baby son that had really bestowed the seal of approval on them.

Taqui Ferrero delivered all the babies in Lavega but this was *otra cosa*, something else. She had never seen such a creature. "*Fijáte!* Look! Did you ever see such eyes, so blue. And that hair, like a halo!" Every woman and girl in Lavega knew about the little white baby with the clear eyes and sunshine hair. That little baby was now a reckless young man, handsome, blond and unaccountable.

"That stool's too low for you." Trynah carried a kitchen chair to him. "Here, rest your back. Lifting those heavy sacks. You really must get Richard to help you. All he does is ride off, never tells us where he's going. 'Out.' That's all he ever says."

"He's young. Leave him be." Robbie paused to study the slim blade of the knife. "I suppose we should have sent him to University."

"But we agreed at the time that Madrid was too far away and too costly." Trynah filled the saucepan with water. "He did well in college and he loves the farm... and he's happy, with lots of friends. For that we must be thankful."

"We need that land on the other side of the river but old man Daroca won't budge. Wants it for himself, he says. Can't blame him. Good land, plenty of water. But he does nothing with it. He's too busy making money in Madrid."

"He's stubborn and arrogant and rich. Not one of my favourite people." She didn't trust him with his flashing gold teeth and halitosis. And she didn't think he should leave his wife alone so much. Their farm was more isolated than Los Rubios. Heavens knows what she did with herself all day. "We mustn't upset him. Whatever happens we mustn't lose the tenancy."

"We're quite safe until renewal in December. And I'll get that field. But this is only playing at farming." Robbie lowered himself on to the stool. "The country's in a mess. Living conditions and wage levels have worsened. They send the Strike Committee to prison and the poor labourers have got no clout all. They can't fight the army and the civil authorities. They've no mechanization, they're even ploughing with oxen over at Tres Picos."

"What you say is true but we're here and we're lucky." She gazed across the courtyard to the cascade of water from the fountain sparkling in the sunlight. "But we really need to keep Richard occupied. More involved." She tossed the potatoes into the saucepan.

Robbie was snicking the tendons on the legs of the rabbits. His eyes met Trynah's. He stuck the knife into the block of wood and came to her, sliding his hands around her waist and burying his face in her hair.

"You smell of rabbits. Warm, furry rabbits have a special smell. Not unpleasant, a bit like a baby after a bath."

He kissed her cheek. "You stood by me, Trynah. Struggling with the language, the different food. You walked out of security and came all these miles for us to have a life together. Not many women have that sort of courage."

"There's no such thing as security, Robbie. Security is a coward's dream." She emptied the bowl of beans into the black pot. "You know, with good conduct you would just about have served your sentence. You would've been released this year."

"Huh! If I'd survived." Robbie gave an involuntary shudder. "Where can Richard have got to? He knows we're going to move the sheep from the hillside pasture this afternoon." He went back to the heap of rabbits near the kitchen door and counted them. "Nineteen. I'll go and get them gutted."

"Dinner will be about twenty minutes." She watched as he threaded the rabbits on to the long willow stick. Riba was sprawled under the beech tree but he picked up the scent and bounced around Robbie, barking and snapping at the rabbits.

"*Hombre! Hombre!*" the voice came from a thin little man hurrying across the courtyard. A gaggle of children were skipping and dancing all around him.

It was Pedro, Robbie's right hand man at Los Rubios. He had been the first person to arrive on their doorstep, lean and as wizened as a walnut with boundless energy.

His only daughter, Maria, lived with him. At twenty-nine she was plump and spotty with a mop of black curls above tolerant brown eyes and an eagerness to help that was difficult to appease. And she still kept an eye open for a wedding ring. There were not many opportunities in Lavega.

She had been the second person to arrive at the kitchen door

93

looking for work. She was soon helping Trynah with the baby, the cooking and cleaning, feeding chickens, feeding pigs, milking goats and then she would go home and look after her widowed father.

"*Qué pasa*, Pedro? What's the matter?" Robbie yanked the entrails from the rabbit and threw them to Riba.

"It's the sheep. They've broken through the hedge in Wood Field. The kids say they are all over the village."

"Confound the blasted sheep," and Robbie hurled the knife at the log of wood near the door.

Pedro stood in front of Robbie, his thin lips pulled back to show several blackened teeth, his bony rib cage heaving as he gasped for breath.

"Do you want me to come?" Trynah called from the kitchen.

"No, Pedro and I will go. If Richard turns up, send him to help."

Robbie and Pedro marched off along the lane towards the village followed by the children squealing and laughing as they scrambled in the ditches looking for sticks to drive the sheep. There were three in the school playground sniffing around, bewildered. The children prodded and poked and drove them out. Two more were in the doorway of the shoemaker, nosing amongst the dry slivers of leather. One big fat ewe darted into the grocer's shop next door followed by several shaggy lambs.

The women in the shop screamed as a pile of oranges was toppled. They charged past the sack of flour. It fell over and spewed its contents across the floor making a white powdery carpet for them to skip through. The lambs scudded after their mother, pushing into the kitchen and out into the patio at the back, leaving a trail of little black pellets on the shop floor. The ewe jumped the low wall and the lambs bounced after her.

The policeman was in El Paco's Bar with a glass of *tinto* at his elbow, picking his teeth. He heard the commotion, tossed back his wine, straightened his uniform jacket and caressed the buckle of the broad black belt across his paunch. He took a deep breath, gave a loud belch and decided to take control. He recruited more children playing in the street and after chasing and yelling in and out of alleyways the sheep were herded into the narrow lane at the back of the church.

"*Gracias*, Alberto!" Robbie called to the policeman as he wandered back to El Paco's. "Now, if we take them at a steady pace along the lane we can get them into the field near the river. Children, stay with Pedro and me. Once we get them started they'll be all right but don't rush them. Calmly now."

Beyond the bend in the lane Robbie could see a cloud of dust billowing above the low hedge. A galloping horse was thundering towards them.

"Watch out, somebody's coming!" Robbie yelled.

The horseman came at such speed that he found himself marooned in the middle of the flock. The frightened animals were trying to break through the hedges on either side of the lane. Others had turned tail and were bobbing back to the village.

A young man, as arrogant as a king surveying his troops, sat astride a fine black filly as it wheeled round and round amongst the sheep. He was lean and blond and his face was flushed pink.

"What the bloody hell... Richard! It's you!"

"Sorry. I was riding too fast. But I thought you weren't moving them till later."

The sheep were skipping along the lane chased by the children squealing at the tops of their voices. "Go and turn them back. We'll get the rest rounded up. Bring them to River Field." Robbie looked up at his son. "And where the hell have you been all the afternoon?"

"Riding. See you," and Richard cantered off towards the village.

* * *

Later that evening Pedro was sitting in his usual place in the corner of El Paco's Bar. It was a simple room with little wooden stools hiding under the small round tables. Benches lined the white walls, now yellowed with nicotine stain. On the wall at the back of the serving counter was a poster announcing the next football match in Serona, a market town three kilometres from Lavega.

On the side wall a large notice had peeled away and was rolling towards the floor so that you couldn't read its message. It gave details of the Fiesta de la Virgen de la Magdalena.

Paco stood behind the serving counter cluttered with bottles and jugs and carafes and dented tin ashtrays. He had one hand on the counter, the other supported his back, as he squinted through the wisps of smoke from the cigarette stuck to his bottom lip, watching the regulars drifting in to the smoky tavern.

Paco was short and fat and lazy and the successful administration of El Paco's Bar was due to the industry and dedication of his wife, Pila. She towered head and shoulders above her husband with a mass of rapidly greying hair swept back from her forehead like a mane. Smouldering dark eyes in a chiselled face distrusted everything they saw. No one argued with Pila. Her arms were as thick as tree trunks after years of heaving barrels and throwing out the drunks.

There was a small yard at the back of the bar where she kept a few hens in a hut in the corner. The belligerent cockerel got the same treatment as the drunks when it tried to peck her ankles. She chased it off with a frying pan. Her busiest time was Sundays, when the men got drunk to forget the previous six days of hard work, and came back the following Sunday to do exactly the same.

When the customers had gone and the glasses were washed and put away she and Paco would climb the narrow wooden stairs. There was a small living room above the bar, cupboards on the landing and one bedroom. To her chagrin she was childless.

"*Qué tal?*" Manolo, the shoemaker, picked up his glass and

ambled across to Pedro's table. After bending over boots for thirty years, pulling and tugging and shaping, he had perpetual backache and it made no difference whether he sat on a stool or a bench. Perversely, he chose the stool, his great buttocks bulging over the sides. The question was pure habit. Manolo had a pretty good idea of how things were in Lavega. A constant stream of requests for repairs to shoes and boots and saddles and harness every day made him the conduit for all the gossip. The customers deemed their problems safer in the seclusion of Manolo's little workshop than with all the chattering women in the grocery store.

"Not bad," Pedro watched Manolo slake his thirst. "Hombre's sheep gave us a rare run around this afternoon. It's just about worn me out."

"Ah! Sheep!" Manolo snorted into his glass. "Most stupid creatures the Lord ever created."

"Old Ma Perez is furious." Pedro explained. "Rampaged right through her shop, which was full of customers. Threatening to claim compensation for damage. Shit all over the place, oranges rolling around in it and a bag of flour knocked over."

Manolo sagged on the little stool, staring down at his dusty shoes. "Where was Ricardo?"

"You might well ask," Pedro kept his eyes on the bedraggled cigarette, willing it to stay alight. "He was riding."

"As usual." Manolo raised his head but it hung down again as if it were too heavy to be supported. "Do you still help old man Daroca?"

"Yes. Relies on me to keep an eye on things. You know what they're like up there. Nobody takes any notice of his missus. She wouldn't know the gob of a sheep from its arse." Pedro screwed up his wizened face and scratched his thick hair, still wavy, still dark with a few streaks of silver at the temples giving this dwarf of a man a remarkable air of distinction. "Can't think why he married such a woman. Years younger than him, you know."

"Ah, well, he likes to think he's God's gift to women." Manolo shrugged his shoulders. "These fancy city women are no good in a place like Lavega." He spat into the sawdust. "All we've got is sheep and goats and mules and floods. And the fiestas and Sundays give us all an excuse to get drunk. We need the good natural women here. Earthy, eh!" And Manolo nudged Pedro's elbow slopping wine down his patched trousers. "Señora Fancy Pants must be going mad up there at Dos Caminos."

Pedro kept his eyes on Manolo. "When I think of my Maria cooking and cleaning for Señora Hombre! Taking in washing, dressmaking, she's never got a minute to call her own. And there she is, Lady Daroca, with nothing more to do than twiddle her thumbs, paint her nails and ride horses."

"And horses are not the only thing she rides." Manolo guffawed. "Don't know how he came to get caught up with her."

"Oh, he didn't get caught. He knew what he was getting, and she jumped at it. Madrid is one thing, Lavega is another. She knew he had money." Pedro cleaned his ear with the long nail of his little finger. "A great persuader, money."

"No children, eh?" Manolo's eyebrows quizzed Pedro.

"Not yet." Pedro considered the dying ember of his cigarette.

"You can bet your life that old man Daroca wants a son. Who's going to inherit that lot when he goes? He'd better hurry up." Manolo emptied his glass. "She's no spring chicken."

"Who's no spring chicken?" A man waddled over to their table, his broad shoulders sloping away from a small round head sprouting bristly black hair. His thick arms hung away from his body as if they had been stuffed. It was Daniel who worked for Carlos Daroca.

For a shepherd he was remarkable portly. He walked miles and miles every day along the valley and across the fields and up the hills but no amount of walking melted the flabby cushion on his stomach. He knew every ditch and bush and on the hillside, amongst the trees, he had his little wooden hut, the shepherd's hut, where he could sleep undisturbed for hours. In the evenings he relaxed at El Paco's and went home with his winnings jangling in his pocket. Gambling was his passion and he would gamble with anyone who would take him on, from dominoes to the number of flies on the wall.

"We're talking about Señora Daroca, wasting away at Dos Caminos."

"Huh!" Daniel spat on the floor, "Needn't worry about her, and I wouldn't say she was wasting away." He reached for Pedro's scraggy cigarette and lit his own. "Far from it. When the cat's away... and there are lot of playthings at Serona." He gave Pedro a knowing wink. "Now, how much are we playing for tonight?" The dominoes fell across the table awash with beer and wine.

Pedro stood up and smoothed his hands down his chest. "Must be off." He didn't want to get caught up in Daniel's interminable game of dominoes, tonight or any night.

Chapter 7

She crossed the bedroom, threw open the shutters and stared into the courtyard below. Nothing moved. Not the dogs sprawled under the ash tree, nor the hens in dusty feathered heaps in the shade of the cattle shed, nor the goats dozing under the hedge. The workers were having their siesta and there would be no one around the farm-buildings for several hours.

The afternoon had slipped into carelessness. The heat weighed down imperceptibly until everything succumbed to the inertia, the suspension in time, the abdication of all things to the great eternal plan. No ambition here, no revolution, no violence, just Mother Nature quietly reciprocating, at ease with the Universe. The quick, dark eyes of Anita Daroca scanned the lane leading to the village. He would come galloping over the hill, down the field and clear the hedge near the clump of trees at the fork in the lane. She stood on tiptoe to get a better view beyond the courtyard. He was late.

She played with the carafe of wine on the bedside table, then held the glasses to the sunlight, one in each hand, squinting at them and then replaced them on the tray. She wandered to the bedroom door, turned and leaned on it. Her eyes slanted across the mahogany wardrobe dominating one side of the wall and she slid her long, manicured fingers across the polished surface.

It was crammed full of dresses. On the landing outside the bedroom was another wardrobe. It, too, was full of her clothes. Carlos bought her anything she wanted, dresses, jewels, horses. She only had to say. But all the clothes and jewels and horses in Spain did nothing to relieve the aching boredom of living at Lavega. How she longed for Madrid!

She slumped on to the pink brocade stool in front of the

dressing table and stared into the mirror. The reflection scowled back and she was shocked to see how old she looked.

"He will come," she smiled at the mirror and her face lived again, her eyes sparkled, her lips parted and with a defiant toss of her head the dark mane of hair fell over her shoulders. Then she heard a clatter of hooves in the courtyard. In her scramble to get to the window she knocked over the stool but was just in time to see the haunches of a black horse disappearing into the stable. She hurried back to the dressing table, and patted her hair. There was the rapid thump of footsteps on the back stairs. She moved to the window and turned to face the bedroom door, waiting for him to burst in.

"Sorry I'm late." Richard leaned slightly to one side as he steadied himself on the door jamb, smiling his broad, spontaneous smile. "I had to help father," and he tossed his riding crop on to the bed.

She kept her eyes on him as he peeled off his shirt and threw it on to a chair. His body was slender and supple and his skin was so pale it made her gasp. Even in her Madrid days she had never seen such an enticing figure.

She waited like a spider to lure him into her web again. He had been easy prey. Since the first time she had seen him riding in the woods above Dos Caminos over a year ago she knew that this man was different.

He was young. He was a good rider, bursting with reckless vigour. She had watched him stretch his horse over the widest streams and had seen him clear the huge boulders strewn about the hillsides without a scratch and put that horse to the highest fences. He had flown over them with invisible wings. He and his horse were just one dynamic thrust of energy, which left her with a craving that could not be assuaged.

Each time she visited the village she kept her antennae finely tuned for news of this young man's activities. According to the gossips he seemed to take little notice of the ripe young girls drooling over him. Anita was sure he was a virgin.

Her moves had been well calculated. She knew when Carlos planned to be away on business and for how long. Since the first fumbling encounter in the shepherd's hut she had led him through a new landscape pointing out the sights, the sounds, the smells, given him sensations that he had never dreamed of, bringing him to the promised land. He always came back for more.

"Wine?" she held out a glass as he pulled off his riding boots.

"Thank you." He was now naked before her, his gleaming body like white porcelain and his excitement could not be concealed.

"Put this on," she threw him a bathrobe. "I've told you, Ricardo, don't rush the fences."

"Of course, I want to rush the fences. How can I help it with you standing there? Wearing that... that slithery..." He put his glass on the table and embraced her, smothering her neck and hair with kisses, edging her backwards until she lost her balance and fell on to the bed.

"You learn very fast," she laughed as she freed herself and went back to the window.

"What time will he be back?"

"He's in Madrid for three days." Anita slowly untied the belt of the pale peach satin robe and it fell open. She, too, was naked. Slowly, with measured steps she moved towards him stretched full length on the bed, arms thrown above his head, his legs wide apart. He reached for her and within minutes he was spent, gasping for breath, his body limp and damp.

Anita cradled his head, smoothing his warm forehead with her cool fingers, clucking and cooing like a mother hen. His body became heavier, his breathing became deeper and she realised he was asleep.

She slid away from him, pulled on her robe and picked her way down the back stairs, stepping between the rusty pail and the old broom propped against the wall. The toilet was next to the kitchen and looked on to the courtyard. Several brown hens were chortling and pecking about in the doorway. "Psst," she clapped her hands and shooed them out of the way.

Peering out of the dusty, cracked window, she was alarmed to see a figure disappearing into the cowshed next to the stables. The goats and cows had to be milked and the hens needed feeding but she was not expecting anyone to stir for some time yet. With racing heart she kept her eyes riveted on the doorway.

A man emerged. She recognised Pedro Arganda. He often helped at Dos Caminos but she didn't know that he was expected here today. She made her way up the stairs. Richard was lying on his back gazing at the ceiling.

"Missed you. Come here." He caught her arm and pulled her on to the bed.

"I had to go downstairs. Have some more wine." She filled the glasses and sank on to the bed beside him.

"Can I smoke?" Richard raised himself on one elbow.

"No. He'll smell it. Tell me, does Pedro still work for your father?"

"You bet he does, don't know what we'd do without him. He's marvellous. So little and thin and bony you wonder where he gets all his energy from." Richard rolled onto his stomach. "Why do you ask?"

"Just wondered, that's all. He's a great help to Carlos, too." Anita put down her glass and turned to him. "Can you come again tomorrow?"

"Can I come again tomorrow? Anita, what are you asking?" He pulled her head down and kissed her. "Will the sun rise tomorrow?" He released her and flopped on to his back. "Of course I'll come."

"Then tomorrow afternoon we'll ride." Anita's fingers stroked the thick skein of long, dark hair. "Away over the back of Dos Caminos to the Mansilla Valley. We shall be away from everyone there, in our den amongst the trees. What do you think?"

"Wonderful idea. Same time?" Richard turned to face her. "What would happen if he knew?"

"He won't find out."

"But if he does..."

"He won't." She raised her voice almost to a shout. "Stop worrying."

Richard reached for his wine glass. "You must get very lonely up here with him away so much. But you've got me..." His fingers fondled her smooth, ripe breasts. "You're different. Not at all like..."

"Like what?"

"Like the local girls."

"Of course not, I'm from the city. That's where I met Carlos. In Madrid." She paused as memories paraded across the white bedroom wall. Madrid seemed so far away and yet it wasn't so far away really. She could easily visit if... But everything had changed because she had married a rich man. She knew life would be different but she had not expected to be such... such a prisoner. "And I'm happy here." The lie made her give a dry little cough.

She had fallen in love with Dos Caminos the first time she had been invited to visit. The weathered stones, the balconies, the shuttered windows. Its dignified rooms with lofty ceilings were full of beautiful old furniture, hand woven rugs, silver and the heavy curtains, she loved the heavy velvet curtains. Sensuous and secretive. It was all she ever dreamed of in Madrid, this permanence, this stability. And now here she was, bored with it all.

And outside, the regal entrance gates, so grand. The big, wide courtyard with its overflowing fountain, and all those sheds and stables and the smelly goats and cows. They didn't interest her in the least. But it was all property and it was all partly hers. She hated Dos Caminos.

"But there's nothing for you to do all day, is there?" Richard's fingers caressed her cheek.

She held his fingers then put them in her mouth and bit them. He was right but she resented his knowledge of her predicament. He wasn't supposed to know. He was here to amuse her, that's all. There was nothing for her to do here, at Dos Caminos, or in the village with the old women nodding their heads in the doorways, the pregnant mothers with scruffy children around their ankles, and the hopeful young women giggling in the Plaza craving for young men and babies. Boring. It was boring.

All the men went to El Paco's Bar, that shady little tavern in the Plaza. They spent hours there drinking and smoking and yarning and gambling and brawling and spitting in the sawdust. She could never go there.

"Oh, there's plenty to do. I help in the village, you know." Anita had taken off her wedding ring and was tossing it from the palm of one hand into the other. "The mothers invite me to the Saints Days and Carlos is very generous to them. They know that. But it's very different after Madrid. Be careful, don't spill wine on the sheet."

"Why don't you go with him?" Richard reached over and placed the glass on the floor.

"I don't want to go back to the city, not to..." she lied. How she craved to be back in Madrid with its sophisticated shops and beautiful clothes, its cafes and nightclubs, its music, the dancing, the handsome men. Time and again she had pleaded with Carlos to take her with him, just for a visit, but he always refused. She pushed the ring back on to her finger.

But she had found something to fill her days with excitement and her nights with longing. This young stud, eager to learn, with a healthy appetite to satisfy, was heaven sent. She knew that one day he would spread his wings and fly but so long as he was here in Lavega she could hold power over him. He couldn't get enough sex. As if reading her thoughts he rolled on to her, suffocating her with kisses and passion.

An hour later, she was sprawled across the bed, satiated, watching him pull on his breeches. He went to the dressing table and smoothed his ruffled blond hair. Then without so much as a glance at her he hurried down the back stairs.

Anita reached for her robe and moved to the balcony window.

She watched him walk across the courtyard. No, he didn't walk, he swaggered. She liked that. She thought only Spaniards swaggered but this young Englishman had the arrogance of many of her lovers. But he had a lot to learn. Never kissed her when he left, never said goodbye, never waved. No romance, none of the niceties that she expected from a lover. But he was not mature. He was a hungry young gallant. At the moment all he needed was the sex, the satisfaction. One day he would need love.

She watched as he led Brisa from the stable, leapt into the saddle and galloped through the wrought iron gates along the lane to the clump of trees. He cleared the hedge comfortably. She waited until he was out of sight then she began to tidy the bedroom.

She wanted more than this, more than this greedy fulfilment. These few hours were not enough. She wanted to be taken somewhere wearing her elegant dresses and jewels, painted and perfumed just like the old days. But here she was, stuck in this stinking, godforsaken valley.

This mood always swamped her after his visit, the paradox of accomplishment and dissatisfaction. She shook the pillows and plumped them up. Slowly the mood would dissipate. It always did and he would be here tomorrow. Perhaps they could go away, Santander for a weekend or something. She would have to plan it carefully... when Carlos was in Madrid.

She poured herself another glass of wine and sank on to the dressing table stool. Yes, that would be nice. She smiled into the mirror, pleased to see that her eyes shone and her skin glowed and she looked young and happy.

Pedro was sitting on a pile of old sacks just inside the open door of the harness shed opposite the stables. He had a jumble of leather reins on his lap and a skinny cigarette clung to the corner of his mouth. His right hand was swathed in a wad of old rags for polishing the harness.

There was a clatter of hooves in the courtyard. He glanced up and saw Richard leap into Brisa's saddle and vanish from view.

*　*　*

Fluffy white balls of cloud scudded across the sky as they rode with the wind in their faces. Anita set the pace, calling to him from time to time but he couldn't hear. The breeze snatched at the words and whisked them away over the hills.

It had been more difficult for Richard to get away today. His father had wanted him to stay and help muck out one of the cowsheds. He had been more persistent than usual and they had almost argued. But Richard knew that his father didn't like arguments and did everything to avoid them.

He had discovered at quite an early age that he was able to get his own way with his mother and father. He had never asked but guessed that it was something to do with the past, something to do with leaving England. It suited him, and gave him freedom to meet Anita or to go to Serona to raise a rumpus with his pals. Besides, clearing the cowshed wouldn't take long and he didn't feel at all guilty that he was riding in the hills with the woman he adored.

"This way. We'll go up here," she dismounted and led Pepita up the steep, winding pathway. Years ago saplings had grown in little grassy clearings and now the huge trunks and powerful roots had established themselves, swaying together to form a dense wooded hillside.

"Here we are. You remember it, no?" She turned, throwing both arms wide.

Someone had chosen this spot to build a little wooden hut tucked under the overhanging branches of a beech tree. There was a small window but it had no pane of glass. It was open to the wind and rain and sunshine and to all the creatures of the countryside. Magpies and pigeons sheltered in it, squirrels scampered around the roof, rabbits and dormice scuffled in and out and butterflies went in by mistake. Beech leaves blew in to make a curly brown carpet on the earth floor, and a thick old log of wood slouched near one wall.

"Yes, but we've come a different way." Richard dismounted.

"I know we have. Last time we rode from the other side of the valley," Anita threw the reins over Pepita's saddle.

Richard pushed on the sagging little door. It wouldn't move because it was hanging off its hinges. He tried again, lifting it to clear the bed of leaves. There was a flash of red as a squirrel darted up the wall and vanished through a hole in the roof.

"Yes, I remember it well," he pulled Anita into his arms. "It was here that I lost my virginity." He framed her face with his hands.

"You are not sorry, no?" She smiled her devastating smile.

"Of course not. Wait a minute. I've forgotten something." He disappeared and came back with the old tartan blanket from Brisa's saddle.

"You are improving." Anita watched as he spread the blanket on the earth floor. "Close the door. You will make a very good husband for someone, do you know that?"

"Husband!"

"Yes. One day you will meet a woman you cannot live without. She will drive you insane with desire, she will make you happy and she will make you cry. That will be love."

"But, I love you, Anita. Come here." He took her wrist and gently pulled her down to the ground.

"Well, I will allow you to think that but I can tell you my darling, that this is not love."

"Then what is it?"

"Infatuation. I know the difference. And one day you will, too."

He was not listening as he fumbled with the buttons on her blouse, then her jodhpurs. He threw aside the wisp of satin knickers and then he was kissing her, merging with her. They were united once more. Overhead the branches of the tree rasped on the roof of the little hut. The magpies chattered and the jays screeched as they flitted from tree to tree.

Far below, in the valley, the goats bleated disapproval and cowbells tolled their lament.

Daniel decided that he wasn't going to do any more shepherding today. He had walked all the way from the pastures at the back of Dos Caminos and up the hillside. It was hot and he was sweating and tired. He had eaten his bread and chorizo, drunk his wine and now he wanted to sleep.

Sitting on a sward of grass, he rested his back against the thick, gnarled trunk of an oak tree just a few yards from the roof of his little hut. From his vantage point he could look down and see everything that went on inside.

It was popular with lovers at all hours. They came from as far afield as Tres Picos and made their way on foot or on horseback, climbing the winding pathways. They thought they were the only people to exist up here, safe and secure in his shelter on the wooded hillside in Lavega. And they were, but that shepherd's hut belonged to him and they had no business in there. But he had a way of making them pay and there was never any trouble.

His head was lolling back on the tree trunk, his mouth fell open, his eyes were flickering and he was slipping into that familiar ocean of repose when he heard voices.

Leaning forward he looked down and saw two riders dismount in the clearing in front of the hut. He watched the young man struggle to open the broken door. Then the woman followed him inside leaving the horses to crop the grass under the trees.

He remembered them. They'd been here before. He sucked on a toothpick as he stroked his crotch, his beady little eyes glued to the heaving bodies on the bed of dried beech leaves on the floor of his hut.

They rode back to Dos Caminos with the sun slipping behind the distant hills, tingeing them with gold and wrapping a dark, green mantle over the valley. Anita was thinking about their visit to Santander or Bilbao.

"You know, we could go away somewhere."

"You mean, stay somewhere?" Richard held Brisa at a steady pace in line with Pepita.

"Yes," She tossed her head and the friendly wind took her hair, up and away, streaming behind her like a dark comet.

"But where can we go?"

"I'll think of somewhere."

"But... but... it all costs money. How can I ask my parents for money?"

"Don't worry about money. Carlos is generous. That's why I agreed to marry him."

"I'd have to arrange things at home. To be away, I mean."

"But you would like. No?"

"Of course. Where you are, that's where I want to be, and you know it," reaching over in the saddle and pulling her shoulders towards him so that he could kiss her cheek.

"*Bueno*, it's decided then." Anita spurred Pepita on and was quickly lost in a cloud of dust.

Soon they were riding through the ornate gates of Dos Caminos. They stabled the horses and she led him by the hand across the courtyard to the back of the house, past the little shack that was the toilet and up the back stairs into the bedroom.

"It's getting late," he whispered, "I must go. I've got to help..."

"Aw, just once more," she kissed him. Then she was unbuttoning his shirt, yanking off his breeches, stripping his willowy body. Within a minute they were naked again, together again. His breeches and shirt were strewn across the floor, her blouse was draped on the dressing table stool and her satin knickers had landed on a tall perfume bottle. The evening sun drenched the room and the two exhausted bodies sprawled as if lifeless across the bed.

Suddenly Anita sat bolt upright. "*Oye!* I hear something."

"It's nothing. Come here," Richard pulled her into his arms.

"Listen!" she whispered. "There's someone on the back stairs."

The door burst open. A short, thickset man filled the doorway. The podgy belly seemed to inflate with every breath he took, his arms hung by his side and his hands swelled into huge clenched fists until they were the size of hams. His jaw sagged and his mouth dropped open from below a tailored, jet-black moustache. His dark, greying hair and aquiline nose gave him a fading distinction. The whole scene was captured in time, fossilised, no one moving, no one saying a word.

"Carlos!" Anita pulled the sheet across her breasts.

"*De mierda!* Stay where you are!" He spoke through clenched teeth. "*Cojones!* You! Bring your horse into the courtyard and wait." Carlos Daroca turned, slammed the bedroom door and clumped down the stairs without another word.

"Hurry, Ricardo. Do whatever he says." Anita whispered. "He has a violent temper."

"What does he want?" He tripped on the bedside rug as he scrambled into his breeches, fastening his shirt with the wrong buttons.

"Go. Be quick. And do whatever he says."

He glanced at her. The colour had faded from her cheeks and she was biting into the sheet bunched under her chin.

"*Go*," she urged and he clattered down the stairs and hurried into the courtyard.

He quickly saddled Brisa and led her from the stable. Glancing around the deserted courtyard he was tempted to vault on to her back and streak away but Anita had said to do as he was told so he waited near the fountain. Then he heard footsteps behind him. Turning, he saw Carlos Daroca in his shirtsleeves. He was carrying a whip and Richard saw the long, flexible plaited thongs on the end of it. He froze. Suddenly Carlos cracked the whip in the air and Richard stepped back until he was against the wall of the stable.

"That's exactly what I wanted you to do," Carlos spat, his stocky little body bent forward, swaying from side to side as he stroked the whip. Then the leather thong scythed the air and Richard felt it score flesh from his shoulder to his thigh. He screamed and turned to the wall, burying his head in his arms to protect his face. The whip came across his back with unimaginable force. A streak of fire ripped through cotton shirt and flesh and he screamed again.

Now he was cornered between the stable and the cart shed. The dogs in their kennels near the front door started to bark, jumping about, straining at their chains. He could hear Brisa prancing and snorting around the fountain.

"Stop...stop..." Richard howled but the whip lashed his back again and again. If he turned it would come across his face and chest. His screams were like the shrill, piercing cry of a woman then they faded to deep, guttural groans as he succumbed to the torture.

Carlos grunted and sweated as he continued to flog but Richard no longer felt the red hot knives slicing his back. Liquid seared into his wounds making them smart and tingle. The pain was numbing his brain, his senses were slipping away and he felt strangely warm. Then he crumpled into a heap on the ground. He was staring at a bright green tuft of grass growing between the cobblestones a few inches from his nose. Then the cobblestones began to move as he was dragged by his feet across the courtyard.

The sky somersaulted as he was heaved into the air. He saw the roof of the stable and then he felt something warm and familiar beneath him. He recognised the smell. He was lying across Brisa's back looking down at the ground.

Carlos gave the horse a sharp lick of his whip and Brisa jolted forward with her cumbersome load. She headed out of the courtyard through the open gates and steadied to a trot in the lane. Richard was slumped across the saddle like a sack of potatoes. Grabbing the girth strap he held on but he was almost upside down staring at Brisa's legs. He began to feel dizzy.

"Good girl, Brisa," and he reached out with his left arm to

stroke her neck. "Steady Brisa," and she immediately slowed down. The jolting stopped and the pain in his back eased, then Brisa stood still, snorting with alarm, confused.

Nausea swept over him. He raised his head to vomit in a wide arc then slithered backwards and fell to the ground, rolling on to the weals on his back. A roar of pain exploded in his lungs. Everything went black.

Pedro was later than usual leaving Dos Caminos. He had been in the far corner of the field under the wood helping a cow to calve. He was tired and hungry and it was almost dark. As he plodded along the lane he doubted if the calf would survive the night. It had taken too long to deliver. The cow was in a bad way too and should never had been put to the bull again. She was still fertile but she had served her purpose for years at Dos Caminos. Her sinews had shrunk, lost their elasticity and could do no more. There was nothing left in her. She owed Don Carlos not a peseta, but Don Carlos never gave up. Another calf meant more money.

Every animal at Dos Caminos was kept until it could breed no more. By then it could hardly stand and was a bag of bones. But Don Carlos was greedy and cruel. Last year Pedro had put down a cow when he was away on a business trip. Couldn't get the calf out. Its head was presenting but the legs were folded back. The cow was exhausted and dying so he fetched the gun from Don Carlos's study, shot it and buried it in the field where it died. Ah, yes, Don Carlos fucked everything dry. Pedro spat into the cart rut.

Suddenly he was aware of something ahead, a dark form in the failing light. As he got nearer he could see that it was a horse grazing on the grass verge. "Brisa!"

Close by he saw a man's body curled up at the side of the cart track. Pedro put his left boot under the man's arm and rolled him on to his back. As the body unwound there was a long, shrill, piercing wail. It filled the night air, echoing around the hills.

"*Por Dios!* Ricardo! What happened? It's me, Pedro."

"Aahh! Pedro," Richard groaned as he rolled back on to his stomach, arms outstretched.

"Can you stand?"

"Don't know." Richard's head was to one side in the rutted cart track.

Pedro fished in his satchel for the water bottle. "Here...drink." He hauled him to his feet. "Steady now. Let's see if I can get you on to Brisa. Give me your left foot." He heaved Richard into the saddle. "Did she throw you?"

"No." Richard slumped forward, his head hung low. "No, I wasn't thrown."

"*Madre de Dios!* What happened?"

"Get me home, Pedro. I'll tell you later."

Pedro took Brisa's bridle and they set off at a steady walk. As they approached Lavega instead of taking the right hand fork in the lane that would lead to Los Rubios Pedro kept straight on to the village.

"*Vamos. A mi casa.* I'm taking you to my house," Pedro called over his shoulder. "You can't go home like this. You must be cleaned up first. *De acuerdo?*"

There was no reply as they clattered along a narrow alleyway, across the Plaza and into a small courtyard surrounded by humble single storey houses. A leafy tree in the centre of the courtyard gave the modest patio extravagance and dignity. The door of the house in the corner opened and Maria came out.

"Papa!" She put her clenched hands to her mouth. "What's the matter?"

Pedro tied Brisa to the tree trunk. "Help me get him off. Careful. Don't touch his back." Standing either side of Brisa they hooked their arms across Richard's stomach and slowly slid him off the back of the horse. "We need boiling water. And a clean sheet."

"Yes," Maria whispered. "Straight away."

Pedro put Richard face down on the little wooden settle in the living room. He placed a cushion under his chin and another one under his legs dangling over the other end of the settle.

Maria came in with an old sheet over her arm and placed the bowl of water on the deal table. Then she saw the bleeding back. "*Madre mía!*"

It had been scored with long incisions, criss-crossed from shoulder to waist. The shirt had been torn to shreds by the whip strokes and blood had dried in the little knots of material, forming a bizarre pattern on the white flesh.

"Get the brandy bottle, Maria. And a pair of scissors." Pedro tore a strip of sheet and rolled it into a swatch. Then he soaked it with brandy. "Bite on this. We'll be careful but I warn you. It will hurt... It will hurt." He met Maria's startled eyes in the yellow lamplight. They both crossed themselves.

Slowly and carefully he snipped at the remains of the bloody shirt. Tears were streaming down Richard's face as Pedro and Maria worked in the glow of the lamp, softening the dried blood on the knots of cotton shirt, bathing the deep wounds. From time to time there was a deep, hollow groan. Maria fetched more water and soon the back was clean and raw and swollen.

Pedro pulled the gag from Richard's mouth. "Lie there and rest awhile. We'll have some coffee."

Richard's eyes went to the wood fire in the hearth and the big black pan sitting on top of the logs. As he gazed at the dying embers he was sure the fire had been placed on his back and it was slowly burning every inch of his flesh.

"Sit up. Don't lean back whatever you do. Be careful." Pedro poured brandy into the mugs.

Richard gasped as he sipped. "Ah! Coffee has never tasted so good."

"Now we've got to get you home somehow," said Pedro, as he refilled the mugs.

"And I haven't got a shirt." Richard raised an eyebrow with a sidelong glance at Pedro.

"Bring him one of mine, Maria."

He winced with pain as they tried to put his arms into the sleeves then his head fell back and he slipped to the floor at their feet.

"He's passed out." Pedro stared at the crumpled body. "He can't go anywhere, he'll have to stay here tonight. Let's get him into my bed and I'll sleep there." He pointed his sharp little chin towards the wooden settle.

There was a musty, dry smell in the small bedroom sharpened by the whiff of camphor balls. Maria put them everywhere, under the bed, amongst the linen, even in her father's boots.

They put Richard face down on the bed and Pedro eased off his boots, then peeled off his breeches. Maria stared at the long white thighs then busied herself at the old oak chest looking for blankets.

"That's it." Pedro ran his hand through his hair. "But there's Brisa. She can't stay out there all night. I'll take her to Don Anselmo's stables. Shan't be long."

Maria waited until the clip clop of hooves had died away then she tiptoed into the back room to gaze at the young man stretched out on her father's bed. A sheet covered his legs but his back was bare, patterned with red, swollen lines, seeping blood. His eyes were closed and his breathing was steady. The brandy had worked.

She walked slowly around the bed. It was the first time there had been a handsome young man under their roof. The glow of the candlelight made his hair look like a golden halo. She had never seen a man undressed before, and she had never seen such skin. It was so creamy. She was now facing him. He was fast asleep, his head to one side, his mouth slightly open as if about to smile. Leaning over, she kissed him on the lips. She stepped away quickly and waited. He didn't move. "That God will take care of us all," she crossed herself again and backed out of the dimly lit room.

Maria was washing the coffee mugs when her father came in. "Papa, you sleep in my bed tonight. I'll sleep on the settle."

"*Mujer!* No." Pedro pulled off his boots. "Why?"

"Because you've had a busy day..."

"So have you. Did they pay you at the bakery?"

"Yes, they don't want me again till Friday. I can rest during the day. Go to bed. No argument."

"*Bueno,*" and Pedro scratched his head, yawned and shuffled into her bedroom.

She listened outside the door until she was satisfied that he had undressed. She heard the little grunts, there were a couple more bellowing yawns and then the creak of the bed.

She stood in front of the dying embers of the fire and untied her pinafore strings, then she pulled her faded brown cotton dress over her head. Next she peeled off her knickers and she was naked. She stroked her full breasts then her hands slid to her bulbous stomach. She sighed and pulled on the cambric shift. Leaving her clothes in a neat pile on the settle she tiptoed to the door of the bedroom and pushed on it. He was lying on his stomach, head turned away, almost buried in a pillow. Slowly she edged into bed and wriggled into a comfortable position on her back gazing up at the flaking ceiling. He murmured.

Slowly she tugged up her shift so that her bare right leg and thigh were touching his. She could now feel the heat from his body. Oh! How she had dreamed of such a thing. Feeling his skin, his closeness, his warmth. Hearing him breathe.

Since the day he was born she had been in awe of this pale creature with the yellow hair. Often she would take him to the woods above the valley to explore the pathways and climb the trees. It was during one of these outings that he'd proposed to her.

"When I grow up I shall marry you, Maria."

They were splashing about in a stream collecting stones to make a dam.

"That will be nice," she held her skirts above her knees. "And where will we live?"

"Here. In Lavega."

"That will be good," she ruffled his tangled hair. "But there will be many pretty girls to choose from when you grow up."

"Don't care. I shall marry you." His hands were full of small, smooth pebbles.

She had been eighteen years old. He had been seven. She was now twenty-eight with no *novio*, no boyfriend. There had been Alfredo from Tres Picos, an energetic, willowy boy, never still. They had been behind the rocks, near the stream when he kissed her, then he said,

"*Quítate las bragas*, Maria. Come on. Take down your knickers," and he grabbed her thighs.

"No." She pushed him away. She didn't go walking with him again.

Jose had asked her to take down her knickers at the back of the cinema and had got very forceful when she fought him off. So all the boys in the village knew that she wouldn't take down her knickers. Not for any of them. But she would do it for Ricardo. Here and now. She wasn't wearing any knickers, knew every inch of this young man by her side. She had bathed and dried that little *palo* between his legs and now... now... She caught her breath.

But he had long forgotten his proposal and treated her with contempt, almost as if she were invisible. So she had to watch him ride off to Serona to meet his pals and the girls who would take their knickers down for him.

Outside, she heard a dog bark. It was angry and it was running away from something. The only sound in the room was his steady breathing. Every once in a while it would race until he was gasping, then the rhythm steadied again.

"It'll be fever from the whipping," she told herself. Someone had done this terrible thing to him, someone in Serona perhaps. She turned her head and gently kissed his ear, so soft.

"*Ven aquí*," he murmured, "come here." He adjusted his weight. He was dreaming. Her eyelids began to droop. She must wake up before her father, who would thrash her if he found her here. She slipped her right hand inside the sheet and gently caressed his thigh, so silky, so smooth. Then she fell asleep knowing that Pila Paco's cockerels would wake her at five o'clock.

* * *

Carlos Daroca put the whip in its usual place on a bracket in the hall under the portrait of his father, then went through to the salon. He strode to the heavy polished sideboard, which stood on large carved balls in the shape of huge claws as if it were a powerful animal, ready to pounce.

It was a rich dark mahogany with ornately carved scrolls and fruits above a long, narrow mirror. He could see the reflection of his fingers as he poured himself a brandy.

Cradling the goblet he moved to the window sucking a tooth. It was gold and smooth and he loved sucking it. It was comforting. He stared into the courtyard. A few hens were still scratching about, pecking, looking, listening and pecking again.

So... his gorgeous Anita had deceived him. And with a youth who didn't look as if he had any balls. Yet he'd seen them together in the bedroom, their bedroom. But... it serves him right. Carlos had thought it would work out, bringing her here to Lavega.

And who else knew about this... about this young buck helping himself to his wife under his very nose? He snorted into his brandy goblet and answered his own question. Chances are no one knows. Anita was too astute for that. She wasn't going to foul her nest. She knew where she was well off.

Sooner or later she would come downstairs. Pouring another brandy, he then sank into the deep leather armchair by the side of the fireplace, swung one leg over the other and began to wag his foot. His eyes went to the richly patterned rug that covered most of the floor, swept across the red velvet chairs backed up to the walls, the mantelpiece laden with silver ornaments and vases and trinkets. Yes, she knows where she's well off.

When he had winkled her out of Madrid he had never suspected that she would be unfaithful to him. Not here in Lavega! There was only El Paco's Bar and she would never go there to find a man. And yet! His face began to feel hot, his glass was empty again so he went back to the sideboard.

Then he heard footsteps. Anita paused in the doorway. She was wearing his favourite dress, low cut, tight fitting, in green silk. She lowered her head and pouted her lips, then she tossed her chin in the air and her glossy hair skimmed bare shoulders. She had painted her face and nails and he caught a whiff of the perfume he had bought her last time he was in Madrid. She was dressed to go to a nightclub.

It totally disarmed him. She looked ravishing, simply asking for it. This woman knew her men. She had spent years manipulating them, tantalising them with her slim hips that swayed and squirmed like a snake, her exuberant breasts. Everything about her demanded. Demanded to be loved, demanded fulfilment, demanded a baby. Carlos drank quickly. He was sure that he could give her one. That was one of the reasons why he'd pulled her out of El Bigote in Madrid and brought her here. An heir for Dos Caminos. But his seed had been sown on barren land, and nothing had grown yet. He was fifty-four, she was thirty-five, there was still time.

He watched as she crossed to the sideboard and poured herself a brandy. The energy Carlos had spent on that whippersnapper in the courtyard had been renewed and he found himself fluctuating between anger and a deep desire for this beautiful woman.

"How long has this been going on?" he barked.

"What do you mean, how long?" She turned from the sideboard, head lowered, lips pouting. "I was out riding. Over in Mansilla Valley and so was he. Well... well..." She took little sips of brandy. "I invited him back here for a cool drink. He was thirsty." She shrugged her shoulders. "You can see he's nothing but a boy."

Carlos waited for her to continue to put her neck in a noose, but she didn't.

"Fumbling and puffing and squealing, like an excited puppy. Really, Carlos, it was nothing. Absolutely nothing. And besides," she took a cigarette from the silver box and paused. Carlos made no attempt to light it for her so she did so herself. "Besides, you leave me alone here in this wilderness, with stinking sheep, stinking goats, stinking chickens and gossiping old crones in the village." She thrust smoke towards the high ceiling. "So I decided to play a game."

"Anita, you've been playing games with men all your life. You should leave juveniles alone. You're too experienced and they're too innocent."

"You were cruel to do that." She flicked her cigarette at the cut glass ashtray. "To... to whip him like a dog."

"You're lucky I didn't whip you also. Who is he?"

"He lives on the outskirts of the village. They have a small farm. He's English, but he was born here."

"And speaks Spanish?" Carlos shifted his weight sideways in the chair.

"Fluent Spanish." Anita paused with her glass to her lips, her eyes locked on him.

"Ah! The Manns. Those people who rent Los Rubios. Always asking for the field on the other side of the river. Huh! Of course they want the River Field. Good fertile pasture." He got up, scratching his head. "Empire building, with a son to inherit. But you know I refused."

He crossed the room and stood in front of her. She was taller than he was, which irritated him beyond words but the irritation dissolved when they were in bed where it didn't matter how tall she was. "I refused, Anita, because one day my son will inherit, eh! Anita. Our son. Well?" He looked up into her blazing eyes. "You will not see him again," Carlos blew cigar smoke into her face.

"But if you do I'll break every bone in your body and he will never walk again. I'll feed his balls to the pigs." He turned away and poured more brandy. "*Comprendes?*"

"Yes," she whispered as she crushed out her cigarette.

Carlos could see that she was nervous and she was always nervous when she was lying. Well, tonight she would pay for her lies when he got her to bed. He listened to her frilly talk as she plied him with more drink. He knew what she was up to. She was hoping to get him so drunk as to be incapable of lovemaking.

At last they went upstairs. He paused in the doorway of the bedroom and saw again the slim, white body sprawled across the bed. His bed. Helping himself to his wife!

"*De mierda!*" His fury boiled over and he charged across to Anita standing near the window, calmly unfastening her dress. He tore it from her back.

"No, Carlos. Don't spoil it." But it was too late. The silk gave readily under his strength. Soon the dress was in shreds on the floor. He grabbed her and threw her on to the bed.

"You're hurting me, Carlos. Stop. Please stop!"

But he was like a mad bull.

"Get off, Carlos!" she screamed, long and loud, wailing. "Leave me alone!"

His heavy body squeezed all the breath out of her. She scored his back with her long fingernails but that only elevated his lust until with a deep groan he exploded, sagging like a balloon deflating. She shuddered with revulsion as she recalled the supple, smooth body that had tantalised her a few hours ago.

* * *

Maria heard the cockerels. They didn't sound so loud this morning. The wind must be in a different direction. She was still lying on her back, her thigh touching his. She hadn't slept much and hadn't wanted to sleep much. A couple of times he had roused, groaning and gasping. It alarmed her but she kept perfectly still and he soon slipped away into a troubled ocean again.

Quietly she slipped out of bed and glanced at him from the doorway. He had no idea that she had slept with him and he would never believe her if she told him. Perhaps, in the future, but not now. She quickly dressed and tidied away the settle. Soon the rich aroma of coffee filled the house.

Pedro wandered into the bedroom scratching his crotch. Richard was pulling on his breeches.

"*Qué tal?* How is it?" Pedro peered at the scarred back.

"Sore." Richard put his arms into the sleeves of Pedro's brown shirt as if it were made of tissue paper.

"Maria's made the coffee and you must eat a little. Then we'll go and fetch Brisa."

They set off across the Plaza, through the deserted streets, and were soon at Don Anselmo's house. It was an arrogant stone mansion with stables bordering one side of the gardens and lawns sweeping down to the river. Pedro heaved Richard into the saddle. He sat motionless as Brisa was led across the Plaza, through the narrow alleyways and into the main street. The smell of fresh bread from the bakery mingled with the reek of goats waiting to be milked in the back yard of Conchita Nobrega. Cockerels shrieked defiance and the hens joined in, clamouring for the daylight and freedom.

Soon they were clear of the village and making their way along the lane leading to Los Rubios.

"Pedro, do you know why I was at Dos Caminos?" His head was swimming with the light morning air. His body felt as heavy as lead, his back was on fire under the old brown shirt and he felt sick.

"Yes." Pedro flicked the end of Brisa's rein aross the palm of his hand keeping his eyes on the cart track.

"My parents don't know that I go there."

"No." Pedro glanced at Richard slumped forward in the saddle, his face ashen, his hands gripping the pommel. His filthy hair was tinted by the sun peeping over the hills, spilling across the valley, bathing everything with a soft pink light. He should've got Maria to wash it but the young one needed rest. "Of course they don't know."

And they would never have allowed him to visit her. But the boy is young and handsome and randy and Señora Daroca is a hungry woman. She regularly went to Serona when her husband was away. Pedro had seen her there. He went there himself for much the same reason except that he didn't have a wife. She had a husband, a rich husband.

"It's best they don't know." Pedro stopped on the lane. "No one need know. And Don Carlos won't be telling anyone. He doesn't want everyone to know you've been digging his potatoes. He's too proud."

"So what am I to tell them?"

"Leave it to me." Pedro spat into the hedgerow and wiped his nose with the back of his hand. "I'll explain everything. You were riding fast, Brisa tripped in a rabbit hole, threw you into a thorn bush and you rolled down on to boulders. I found you and took you home to clean you up. You were too shocked to get home last night. And that's an end to the story. Come on, let's go."

Chapter 8

"Well, he's never stayed out all night before," Trynah was slumped in a kitchen chair rapping a teaspoon on the coarse surface of the table. She raised her eyes to Robbie without moving her head. "It's half past nine. Where can he be?"

"It's not a bit of good worrying." He was standing near the window cutting a length of rope. "He'll turn up. Probably went to Serona with his pals. If he was too drunk to ride home one of them would've taken care of him. Please don't do that, Trynah."

Immediately the tapping stopped.

"He's a law unto himself these days." Robbie hacked through the stubborn rope. "Rode off yesterday afternoon and we haven't seen hide nor hair of him since. I asked him where he was going and all he said was 'riding'. 'Why the hurry then?' I said. 'You can ride after you've helped me move the sheep pens.' But he would have his way. Said he'd promised to meet someone."

"Did he say who?"

"No. That's the trouble. He never actually says who he meets. It's time we made him a bit more accountable." He continued to saw through the waggon rope, gripping it against his chest. "I suppose we should've been stricter with him, but in a place like Lavega! Well, what can the young ones do?" The rope came apart in his hands. "Ah, that's got it."

Riba jumped out of his basket and started to bark. Robbie glanced out of the window to see the hens scuttling across the yard in all directions.

"Well, I never..." Robbie threw down the rope. "Here he is, with Pedro leading Brisa." He charged across the courtyard. "What on earth?"

"Small accident," Pedro threw the rein across Brisa's neck. "Let's get him down. Be careful, he's hurt. Slide him backwards. That's it."

They arranged themselves on either side of Brisa and lowered Richard to the ground. He sagged between them as they staggered across the yard like three drunkards, edging past Trynah in the doorway. They placed him in a chair and he fell forward across the kitchen table burying his head in his outstretched arms.

Trynah poured coffee and Robbie reached to the top shelf of the sideboard for the brandy bottle.

"Sit down, Pedro." Robbie stood away from the table, his eyes on Richard's dirty hair. It was matted with soil and blood and sweat. "What happened?"

"Took a tumble." Richard mumbled from under his arms.

"Where?" Robbie marched round the table cradling the brandy bottle in his large square hands staring at Richard's arched back.

Pedro put down his cup, sucked on a front tooth, clicked his tongue, leaned forward on the table and told the story. "That's why I couldn't get him home last night."

"But you didn't send word." Robbie continued to prowl around the kitchen table.

"He needed rest after the shock." Pedro took greedy gulps of coffee.

"Well, where was he thrown?" Robbie continued his slow circuit of the table.

"Found him on the side of the road." Pedro shot a quick glance at Robbie. "He said he'd been riding through Mansilla Valley..."

"But that's a long way off. What on earth was he doing over there?" Robbie felt ill at ease with the explanation.

"Distance is nothing to him." Pedro finished his coffee and held out his cup to Trynah who refilled it. "He rides for miles."

"Yes, that's true." Trynah tied and untied the strings to her pinafore until they were in a tangled little knot. "All I can say is that he's lucky you found him. It's nothing short of a miracle.

Thank you for getting him home, Pedro, we're very grateful. Now let's get him up to bed. He's nearly asleep here. And just look at his hair, it's filthy..."

She put her arms around Richard's shoulders. He reared up from the table, screaming, arms flailing. "My back, my back!"

"Goodness gracious," Trynah stepped away clutching her throat. "Can you manage the stairs on your own then?"

Richard nodded and he slouched across the kitchen, along the passage and unlatched the door leading to the stairs. Trynah and Robbie followed. He flopped face down on to his bed and growled.

"Leave him to me, Robbie," Trynah fussed around the room like a broody hen. "I'll make him comfortable."

Back in the kitchen Robbie poured more brandy and offered the bottle to Pedro.

"No thanks. Must be getting on now." Pedro swept his dirty black beret from the stool and shuffled out of the kitchen.

Trynah came downstairs. "It's a mystery to me."

"He must have been riding too fast. He's always riding too fast but he won't be told. We've seen him take a lot of falls, but never one like this." Robbie scratched his hair with both hands. "Up on those hillsides there are boulders and gulleys everywhere. This terrain has been undisturbed for centuries. He should've been more careful. Lucky he didn't break his neck."

"We get back to the old problem, don't we?" Trynah sank sideways into the kitchen chair. "He hasn't got enough to do."

"No, but I'll change all that. From now on he'll do as he's told." His jaw twitched. "A little more work and a little less riding in future."

"Well, he's not going to be fit to do anything for a while. It's a mystery."

"What is this mystery you keeping talking about, Trynah?"

"Well, he didn't want to take that old shirt off. By the way, it's Pedro's shirt. Heavens knows what happened to his own. I persuaded him it would be better to get the air to his bruises."

Trynah got up and walked slowly round the table fingering the back of the chair, the edge of the sideboard. "I've never seen anything like the state of his back." She put her hands to her cheeks. "Oh, Robbie. It's a shocking mess." She hurried to his side, sobbing.

"Come now, Trynah. Don't distress yourself." He folded his arms around her, burying his face in her hair. "He's young and strong."

"Those are not abrasions caused by a fall." She wiped away the tears with the back of her hand. "They are weals."

"Weals!" Robbie echoed.

"Yes. Those marks on his back could only have been made by a whip."

"Are you sure?" His voice was a whisper.

"Yes," Trynah's lips trembled. "They're simply dreadful. His back is a mass of excoriations, and it's very swollen." She covered her eyes with the palms of her hands. "It made me wince. The pain must be unbearable. He's been whipped by somebody." She sobbed into her pinafore. "Oh, Robbie, I shudder to think what this is all about."

"Come now, Trynah. Don't upset yourself. He's home and safe." Robbie was at her side holding the quivering shoulders. "I'm going to see for myself."

Richard was stretched on the bed, on his stomach, fast asleep with a sheet covering his thighs and legs. His back and shoulders were just as Trynah had described. Robbie gagged at the pattern of the congealed blood on the wounds.

"You're right. The boy's been whipped."

"You know, when you think about it," she blew her nose, "when he goes riding he must go somewhere, meet someone."

"Yes," Robbie stared out of the kitchen window. "It had occurred to me."

"As long ago as last year I noticed the change in him. He's lost that youthful something, that innocence. You can tell by his eyes. Let's have some more coffee."

"Well, he's a man now, Trynah. Here, we need this." Robbie

reached for the brandy bottle again. "I just hope he hasn't got mixed up with the wrong people. And he's never shown much interest in the local girls. After all, he's grown up with them. Oh, I know Maria's always drooling over him..."

"Poor Maria. And he used to love being with her. She was so good to him as a boy, all those rambles and picnics." Trynah sniffed.

"We know he meets his pals in Serona. That's where the girls are. And we know they're a bit wild but..."

"Huh! Girls!" Trynah was walking slowly round the table again. "The wrong sort of girls. In those bars..."

"We can't stop him, he's a handsome young man. And, well, he's a novelty."

"Novelty?" She rolled her damp handkerchief into a ball.

"Yes, so tall and blond, and he can charm ducks off the pond. Of course the girls are buzzing around him."

"But who would want to whip him, Robbie? Who?"

"I don't know." He bit his bottom lip. "Pedro found him, took him home, dressed his wounds. If Pedro only had one eye he would've known that Richard had been whipped." Robbie wandered to the window again, turned and came back to the table. "So it's a pact of silence between them, isn't it? I doubt if we'll ever know what happened, but we can keep our ears and eyes open. You know how the villagers gossip."

There were hurried footsteps outside the kitchen. "Ah, here comes your helper. Good morning Maria."

* * *

Not a lot happened in Lavega from one year's end to the other. The women, the men, the children, the policeman, the postman, they all followed their routine and the goats, the horses, the sheep, the cows, the cats and dogs just ambled on doing much the same thing from day to day. But the news that young Ricardo had been thrown from a horse and suffered injury to his back kept the tongues wagging and the glasses full in El Paco's Bar. The regulars flocked in to devour the latest version of the unfolding story. Paco smiled and watched and listened. It was good for business.

"*Por Dios!* How could he have got such injuries," Manolo, the shoemaker, was leaning on the bar waiting for his glass of wine. "Must be stronger than he looks. He's got the milky skin and yellow hair of a woman."

"He's no *maricón*, no pansy." Pedro had built an invisible barrier to protect himself from the inquisition that was raging through the village. He was sticking to his story that he had found Ricardo, cleaned him up, and got him home after a fall from his horse.

Daniel, the shepherd, was less convinced. "I saw him riding in the woods with Señora Daroca." He drooped on the small stool near the open door, his round face glowing after an hour's drinking.

"They often ride," Pedro stretched out his short, skinny legs and leaned back on the wall, his thumbs in the pockets of his tatty old shirt.

Daniel chortled and spat over the head of the tom-cat preening in the doorway. "She's nothing but trouble here in Lavega."

"Huh! Not only Lavega." Andrew, the baker, was tall and thin, his pasty face dusty with the flour he handled every day. "She's always gallivanting off to Serona when the cat's away."

"Surely young Ricardo has more sense than to get mixed up with her. She'll eat him for breakfast." Manolo emptied his glass and banged it on the table. "Our womenfolk don't trust her and our womenfolk are never wrong."

"He's young and horny," Daniel glanced sideways at Manolo. "And she's sex mad."

"How would you know?" Manolo slapped him on the back with such force it nearly knocked him off the stool.

"Ah, remember the spectator sees most of the game." Daniel squinted against the thin blue curl of smoke creeping into his eyes.

"But that still doesn't explain how he was found half dead on the grass verge, does it?" Manolo pushed through the tables to the bar.

"I told you, he rides like a gaucho. Accidents happen." Pedro signalled to Paco. "Come on now, who's for another drink?"

* * *

Carlos Daroca acted quickly after whipping the hide off young Richard Mann. The respected landowner, the successful business man, the rich man, the husband of the beautiful woman from Madrid could not have his manliness threatened by that young buck.

He woke early the next morning with a headache because he had drunk too much brandy. And he still burnt at the memory of them on his bed. The audacity, the deceit, the ingratitude He gave Anita everything she wanted, everything she asked for. But he had to restore his reputation, his authority, his pride, his goodwill, for his own sake.

He knew for certain that Anita would not be telling anyone. And that young... that young fucker... Well, he was now branded for life. And he wasn't likely to be bragging about it either.

After a stroll across the top field to the wood he came back to the house and wandered through the rooms. The walk had cleared his headache. He had decided what to do.

Reaching for his gun from the wall of the study he went out into the courtyard to look for Pedro. He didn't need his gun but he liked to have it with him. It gave him confidence.

"Ah, there you are." Carlos found him in the harness shed.

"Good morning, Don Carlos."

"I want you to tidy up the courtyard," ordered Carlos, propping the gun against the wall and looking into the weathered face.

"Very good," Pedro kicked aside the old saddle. "What would you like me to do?"

"We're going to have a fiesta." Carlos raised his chin and

beamed his gold tooth at Pedro. "A big fiesta. It's a long time since we had a party. Come with me," and he stepped outside. "I want trestles for the food along this side of the courtyard. And over there, we'll have the band. Those musicians from Serona are very good. And we'll leave the centre area round the fountain clear for the dancing. Agreed? Eh?"

He was striding around the courtyard, which was littered with old buckets and heaps of straw. A cartwheel was propped against the cowshed door and a broken plough languished under the sycamore tree near the entrance gates.

"Get that door on the first stable mended. It's hanging off its hinges, and move the cart with the broken shaft into the corner. The children can play on it. Leave the rusty plough where it is. Put the flags and bunting in the usual place, up there, over the stables and barn. It worked out well last time." Last time was when he brought Anita to Dos Caminos, to present his wife to the villagers almost three years ago. "And if it rains we just move into the barn." Carlos flapped his short, thick arms in all directions. "What do you think, eh?"

"Very good. Shall I get the young Delgado lads to help? Same wages as last time?" Pedro was waiting for an answer. Carlos was sucking his tooth and staring at the old buckets and heaps of straw considering the expense.

"The barn will have to be swept out, and the trestle tables will need a scrub." Pedro continued. "They're propped against the wall in the barn. The hens perch on them and they're covered in hen shit."

"Yes. And move the pigs to the shed at the top of the paddock. Daniel's sure to get drunk and we don't want him fucking our pigs again. Señora Daroca will supervise all the food and crockery. And get Maria to help her, eh?"

Pedro shot a scathing glance at Don Carlos. Get Maria. Just like that. Maria was run off her feet doing things for people, minding babies, sewing, cooking, cleaning. Don Carlos had no idea how much work Maria did in the village. But Pedro had no choice but to ask her. "What day are you having the party?"

"A week tomorrow. Saturday, that'll be the eleventh of September. Agreed?" He smiled at Pedro, picked up his gun and stamped across the courtyard. He put the gun on its bracket in the study and called Anita.

"Come. Straight away." He sat in his large leather chair in front of his desk and waited. "Anita! I'm in the study."

He fidgeted with a sheaf of papers then he heard footsteps and she was standing at his side, one hand in the pocket of her jodhpurs.

"You wanted me, darling?" She smoothed the other hand across his shoulder.

"No time to ride, Anita. There's work to be done."

"Work! It can wait, can't it?"

"No, my dear," he picked up a pencil and tapped it on the blotter. "We're going to have a party. Sit down and take this." He handed her a notepad and pencil.

"A party!" She sank into the chair at the side of the desk. "What for?"

"Now, my dear, you're never the one to ask for a reason." He reached over and stroked the inside of her left thigh. "You like parties. It's next Saturday, a week tomorrow."

Anita frowned. "Well, who's coming?"

"All the workers, all the tenants. Everybody. Now, you'll need to make some notes because you're in charge of the arrangements. Ready." Carlos sucked on his gold tooth. "You'll need several large notices, one each for the general shop, the bakery, the dairy, the shoemaker and El Paco's Bar. We must make sure that everyone knows about it. Everyone, *comprendes*? And don't forget one for the church notice board, eh?" He reached for her thigh again. "And you'll be in charge of the food. The women in the village like to make things, you know who to talk to. Then there's the drink. I'll order it from Serona. We must have plenty of beer and plenty of wine. Don't worry about the musicians. I'll arrange for the same band that came for your party. Remember! It's going to be something they'll never forget. Given by Don Carlos Daroca and his beautiful wife, eh?" He leaned over and tweaked her left breast. "*Comprendes?* There's a lot to do. I don't want anything to go wrong. And don't worry about the expense."

He lolled back in his chair, beaming again.

"But... but..."

"But nothing, Anita." He watched her twisting her wedding ring. "Well, write it down my dear, the notices, the food, the linen for the trestle tables, the lanterns, the benches. Pedro will get those out for you. He and his gang will put up the flags and bunting..."

Carlos watched her scribbling frantically. And it was only a week away. She would have no time for that young man in his bed or anywhere else.

* * *

It was a week since Pedro had brought Richard home. Those first few days and nights had been a phantasmagoric nightmare. The pain felt like a heap of burning coals on his flayed back. He had to rest on his stomach and his neck got stiff. From time to time he heard the distant voices of his mother and father swirling around as if carried on some gentle breeze but he was never able to locate them. The voices were soft and comforting. Now those same soft voices were whispering again.

"I really think we should call the doctor." It was his mother's voice. "I'm worried about his temperature."

"Let's wait till morning, then we'll decide." His father was being prudent. A doctor would know exactly what had caused the lacerations. They decided against it.

His mother had bathed his back every day, put ointment on the wounds and made him drink some foul medicine that she had got from the pharmacist in the village.

The gashes began to heal and he could now wear a shirt. But he was unable to do physical work. Any exertion opened the wounds again, causing them to suppurate and bleed. The whiplashes extended to the inside of his thighs making it uncomfortable for him to sit astride a horse, so he kept Brisa in trim by exercising her on a lunging rein in the paddock every day.

But not once did his mother and father mention the 'accident'. He didn't think Pedro's explanation had been very convincing. They hadn't asked a single question. But he knew they'd do everything to avoid a row with him. They had never ever confronted him about any misdeed. It made him think of guilt of some kind, something in their past they didn't want to talk about.

And once again he wondered what had happened in England all those years ago to bring them to this remote valley in northern Spain. He'd heard them talk about Ketsby and Grantham and Lincolnshire, and family members and relatives, but they meant nothing to him. They were just names and he couldn't connect them with any image or face.

He'd never known any other way of life in this beautiful valley and he was perfectly happy with it. He longed to ride Brisa out of the courtyard, across the fields, over the hills, with the wind in his face, to Anita. He ached for her soft skin, her demanding body. But he had to be patient. And now he must be on guard. He must never cross the path of Carlos Daroca again which meant that he would never be in Anita's bedroom again. But she was clever, she was cunning, she would find a way for them to meet. She knew how to hoodwink that fat old sod of a husband. And she'd said she wanted to go away somewhere, together, away from the village.

They were all having coffee in the kitchen when Pedro brought the news of the forthcoming fiesta at Dos Caminos.

"Eight o'clock on Saturday night." Pedro studied his cigarette. "He wants everyone to join in."

Richard was surprised. Anita had told him that Carlos had little interest in the villagers. He was more concerned about his business associates and making money in Madrid. That's why she was alone so much. He had little concern for the people who lived in his grubby little hovels. Now he was giving a party for them.

"What do you think, Robbie?" Trynah refilled the coffee cups.

"I think we should all go." Robbie was sprawled at the kitchen table. "Time for celebration. It's a good idea. What do you say Richard?"

He was sitting forward on the stool clutching his cup of coffee. "I must go to Serona for new riding boots on Saturday but I should be back in time. Yes. We need a party. It's time to liven things up in Lavega." He glanced across at Pedro, who winked at him.

* * *

The day of the fiesta dawned with an overcast sky threatening rain but the brooding clouds rolled away over the hillsides leaving a sultry heaviness over the valley.

Pedro and his gang of lads had transformed the barn and the trestle tables were ready to be covered with the tablecloths. They would be brought from the linen cupboards in every house and cottage in the village.

Anita was exhausted before the festivities began. Two of the women who had promised to help prepare the food couldn't come at the last minute. Conchita had to go and visit her sick grandfather in the next village and Julita had to look after her sister's child, so Anita was in the kitchen slicing chorizo when she should have been painting her nails.

Pedro was supervising the hanging of the bunting when he heard a rattling of wheels on the cobbles and a raspy voice called out.

"*Holá*, Pedro. *Qué tal?*" It was Cucho, the knife sharpener, pedalling into the courtyard on his bicycle. He did the rounds of the villages and today was his day for sharpening the knives in

Lavega. The wiry little man jumped off the bicycle and positioned it near the fountain. Then he lifted the back wheel on to a stand and connected it to a pulley with a leather belt to the grinder mounted on the handlebars. "*Anda que*! You'll never believe it. The lorry's broken down."

Pedro took off his beret and whacked it across his thighs. "*Cojones!* Where is it?"

"About a kilometre away, near that barn in the fork in the road to Serona. The driver asked me to tell you." Cucho wiped his face with a dirty red handkerchief then stuffed it into his threadbare jacket pocket. "Is the Señora Hombre in?"

"Yes. In the kitchen." Pedro called to the young men up the ladders. "Come on down. Bloody beer lorry's broken down."

Then he went to the barn door. Three young men sweeping the floor emerged from a cloud of dust.

"Broken down!" The fat man leaned on his broom. "Well, we've got to have the booze. Can't have a party without the booze. What shall we do?"

"We need a horse and a big cart. Let's go and see Don Francisco. Come on, all of you. We need extra hands, too." Pedro turned on his heel and led the way out of the courtyard leaving Cucho on his bicycle near the fountain sharpening the knives with razor-like precision as he pedalled his way to infinity.

Don Francisco wasn't there but his wife told them they could harness up Rinco and take the dray, and they were soon bumping along the lanes.

They found the beer lorry exactly where Cucho had said. It was perched at an alarming angle in the ditch. The driver and his mate were sitting on a bed of dry leaves, each clutching a bottle, laughing and singing. They were quite drunk.

It took over an hour to load Don Francisco's dray because the men insisted on sampling the wine and beer.

"Salud!" Andrew's pasty face was rosy pink as he raised a bottle

of wine to his lips. He started to sing *"Allá en el Rancho Grande –
Allá donde vivía..."*

"Leave it alone!" Pedro shouted as they puffed and huffed and
heaved and shoved to get the barrels and casks moved from the old
lorry on to the dray. "There won't be a party if we don't get this to
Dos Caminos."

"Bugger Dos Caminos," Andrew yanked the cork off another
bottle. "Since when has old Daroca cared about us? Suddenly he
wants a party. Well, we're having one," and he tossed the empty
bottle at the trunk of an oak tree a few yards away.

"Leave it alone, will you!" Pedro was yelling at the men. "We've
nearly finished. You can drink all you want when we get there."

At last the dray rumbled into Dos Caminos with the drunken
men singing at the tops of their voices, swaying amongst the
bottles of wine and barrels of beer. Pedro was the only person sober.

A rusty old bus followed them into the courtyard. It was the
musicians. They tumbled out of the bus hugging their guitars and
drums, singing and slapping each other on the back. They had been
playing at a wedding all the afternoon and they, too, were quite drunk.

* * *

Carlos Daroca was near the fountain receiving the guests. He had
decided to wear his leather jacket, riding breeches and riding boots
although he hadn't been astride a horse for a long, long time.

Anita was at his side, smiling and fussing with the frills on the silk
blouse that she had decided to wear with her tan suede culottes. She
was nervous and in her anxiety she kept filling her wine glass.

The guests arrived in straggly groups. They came across the
fields, they came down the hillsides. They came in horse-drawn
carts. They came on horseback. They came on foot. They came.

The courtyard was milling with people. Old men and women
hobbled through the wrought iron gates, leaning on each other for

support. Young men were fooling about with their young ladies, tickling them, slapping their bottoms and squeezing their small, firm breasts when they thought no one was looking.

The adults were dancing and drinking, and the children were skipping around the fountain, splashing each other with water. Dogs were barking, and the cats had crept away to a quiet corner in the barn.

Robbie and Trynah decided not to wait for Richard. He hadn't said what time he'd be back from Serona so they set off for Dos Caminos. They could hear the hullabaloo long before they arrived at the open gates. They could see the lights, and could hear the music and laughter and screams of delight. It was going to be another good fiesta.

They elbowed their way through the boisterous crowd. "Come along. I can see our host and hostess over there." Robbie shook hands with Carlos Daroca. Anita was at his side, her arm linked in his.

"This is quite a party, Señor Daroca." Robbie glanced over his shoulder. "Very nice of you to invite us."

"Ah, good evening, Señor..."

"Mann," Anita supplied the name with dazzling satisfaction.

Carlos shot a searing glance at her. He could never remember names but this was one he would never forget. "Of course. How's everything at Los Rubios?"

"Fine," Robbie rubbed his hands together.

"Have some wine. Anita, where are the glasses?" Carlos raised his chin. "And what about your son, isn't he coming?"

"Oh yes, he'll be here shortly. He had to go to Serona."

Anita bowed her head and gave another dazzling smile as she passed the glasses to Robbie and Trynah.

"*Hombre*," Pedro was sitting at a trestle table with Maria at his side, waving a bottle of wine. "Move a bit Maria. That's right. Come on, sit down." Pedro patted the bench at his side. "Where's Ricardo?"

"He'll be here soon."

"It's going with a swing, isn't it! We should've been here earlier," Trynah whispered to Robbie. "We're never going to catch up with them but here goes. *Salud!*" They all clinked glasses as far along the table as their arms could reach.

Lanterns swayed from door lintels and the eaves of the cowsheds and stables. The flags and bunting fluttered and wafted in the night breeze. The lamps on the long trestle tables gave the damask cloths a pristine whiteness.

Small wicker baskets were piled high with chunks of bread. There were plates of chorizo, prawns, ham, pasta, hard-boiled eggs and dishes of olives and nuts. The women of Lavega had excelled themselves.

Robbie was dancing with Maria. Pedro took Trynah in his arms. Then she was in the grip of Carlos Daroca bouncing off his full, soft belly and turning her head from side to side to avoid the smell of garlic.

The wine flowed, the music blasted in great waves of sound, carrying across the fields and woods and hillsides. The courtyard was a riot of people swaying, clapping hands and stamping feet.

Anita was leaning on the door of the harness shed clutching an empty glass, her eyes fixed on the entrance gates bedecked with flags and bunting fluttering in the breeze. The wine had taken her to the peak of abandon but now she was wallowing around, waiting for Ricardo to come through those gates.

Carlos was in the study playing cards with Daniel. The brandy bottle was empty. Soon everyone would be too drunk to notice where she and Ricardo were.

Spots of rain began to fall but no one paid any attention. They assumed it was from the children splashing around the fountain.

"Oh, my goodness me," Trynah flopped on to the bench next to Maria, fanning herself. "I don't think I've danced so much since the day I got married." She drank some wine quickly realising that when she had danced at her wedding it had been with Bladon not Robbie. She was not married to Robbie, Bladon was her husband. They had danced in the Clubroom at The Pyewipe, on the night of their wedding, with Vinny, Abby and Kate and all the friends and family. Memories rushed in with the noise and music and wine and swept her above the merry throng in the courtyard. She was getting dizzy. Bladon. Robbie. The two men in her life.

"Come on, Maria, have some more," Trynah grabbed the bottle, missed it, reached again and slopped wine across the white damask cloth. "Oh dear," she giggled as she snatched at Maria's glass pushing the thoughts of Ketsby and Bladon back into the cave.

"Did you see Manolo, the shoemaker? He's asleep in the cattle trough. And it's full of water!" Maria shrieked as she beat time to the music with her head. Up, down, up, down. "When I went to the lavatory just now I saw old Ma Perez in the chicken hut with Andrew the baker. I think they're still there. And Paco", she squealed, "he's slumped against the dog kennel with a bottle." Her head continued its rhythmic nodding. "Did Ricardo say what time he'd be coming?" The memory of him lying on her father's bed had never left her. She dreamt of his smooth thighs most nights.

"No, but he'll be here soon," Trynah tossed back her wine keeping her eyes on Robbie, her man, not her husband. He and Pedro were near the fountain slapping each other on the back.

"Don't know what do without you," Robbie pushed a finger into the button of Pedro's waistcoat.

"*Hombre*!" Pedro's arm was across Robbie's shoulders. "It's life. I work, you pay me, that's it!"

"Couldn't do without you. Know that, Pedro." And they stood facing each other, holding each other's shoulders, swaying from side to side as the rain came pelting down lancing long silver needles across the courtyard.

Now everyone was pushing and jostling to get out of the rain, clutching their bottles of wine, kicking the empty ones out of the way. The neat, orderly barn was suddenly filled with the clamour of the music and singing, shouting and drinking.

The dancers were tireless and so was the band. The musicians were on a platform raised above the floor backing on to a pile of empty sacks. They'd been playing since two o'clock this afternoon and nothing was going to stop them now.

But something did stop them. A bedraggled figure appeared in the doorway, water streaming down his lean, sorrowful face. It was Rodrigo, groom for Don Anselmo, and he was looking for Don Carlos.

He shook the rain from his dripping black hair, craned his neck above the crowd and spotted him near the stage. He pushed his way through the dancers and whispered to Don Carlos. With a sudden roll of drums the barn was silenced and the eyes of the milling throng turned to the makeshift stage.

"I'm sorry," Rodrigo smoothed his hands down the wet shirt plastered to his chest, "but we need help in the village. The river's burst and the stables are flooding. Don Anselmo is away in Santander. We must move the horses. We need all the help we can get."

There were shrieks from the crowded barn and the villagers quickly sorted themselves into families again. They scurried out of the courtyard and headed towards the village, still singing and laughing with their heads bent into the driving rain, feet squelching through the muddy cart ruts.

When they got to the Plaza Rodrigo organised the men into groups.

"Shall we come with you?" Trynah's arm was linked in Maria's.

"No. There's nothing you can do," said Robbie, his tweed jacket saturated. "Besides it's dangerous. It's best you get off home and get dry, the pair of you."

"*Hombre's* right," Pedro wiped his face with his sleeve. "Nothing you can do. We'll go and help with the horses."

"All right, but be careful." Trynah and Maria strode off arm in arm, their wet skirts flapping around their ankles. They both turned and waved to the crowd of men huddled together in the Plaza. "See you soon."

Chapter 9

It was three kilometres to Serona and Richard usually gave Brisa full rein to get there, but not today. The weals on his back had healed well but there was none of the wild, carefree streaking across the countryside leaving everyone to stand and gape as he thundered past. Today he kept Brisa at a steady pace on the grass verges.

He had told his mother and father that he would join them at the fiesta but he'd already decided not to go. Anita would be there and he wanted to be in bed with her. There were staircases and corridors and lots of rooms in Dos Caminos all waiting for people who never came. It would be easy to disappear to one of them. But Carlos Daroca would be watching like a hawk. They wouldn't be able to do anything except gaze at each other and drink too much wine.

She had always fobbed him off about her husband. He remembered asking her when they were in the shepherd's hut, dressing, "What if he gets to know?" He buttoned his shirt.

"He won't." She stepped into her creamy satin knickers. "I know his every movement."

"Do you really?" Richard buckled his belt and moved towards her.

"Yes, I can do anything I want with him," and she held up the little finger of her right hand and made a circular movement. "Just like that. Don't worry."

So she had convinced him they were safe, but they weren't. Carlos Daroca was unpredictable, dangerous and cruel. Richard glanced at the sky. It was moody with sulky clouds over Tres Picos. Rain was coming. His thoughts drifted across the hedges to the fields and woods but try as he may he couldn't anchor on to anything substantial, anything that would give him direction, offer a solution to the problem, find a way for them to meet.

It was more than two weeks since his last visit to Serona and it had nearly ended in fisticuffs with Peludo. They had been in El Pollo Loco and, once again, Peludo had wanted the girl Richard was dancing with. Peludo was strong and sturdy and fascinated the girls with his thick mop of unruly curls. When he had a skinful of drink he was unstoppable on the dance floor. He had shoved Richard away and grabbed the startled girl.

"Peludo, I'm having none of your pushing in tonight," and Richard sent him flying across the polished dance floor. "Get off."

Chanza, fat and lazy, who liked food more than he liked girls, and Magro, always hungry for sex, saw the tussle and calmed things down. The manager had also seen what was going on and led them across the crowded, smoky room to the door. "*Que vayáis!*" He was waving his arms. He was angry. "*Y que no volváis. Comprendeis?*" They were banned. So no El Pollo Loco tonight.

Rain was falling steadily as Richard passed the straggling little hovels on the outskirts of Serona. Soon he was in narrow streets with the houses clinging to each other, needing each other. Old people, bundled up, shuffled along, children played in the gutters and dogs barked around Brisa's hooves. He made his way across the Plaza, turned left into Calle San Vicente and rode into the yard at Las Candelas.

"*Holá* Pepe!" Richard led Brisa into the deep obscurity of the stables. "How are things?"

"Not bad." Pepe was inspecting the shoe of a huge grey horse.

"Look after Brisa for me," Richard slapped her flanks. "I've got to buy new boots, then I'll meet some of my pals. And who knows what time I'll be back!"

"Enjoy yourself." Pepe swept the brush across the back of the horse. "Don't get too drunk."

"I won't, until later." And Richard crossed the Plaza and disappeared down an alleyway to a little kiosk next to a bakery. It was not much bigger than a wooden sentry box but this is where Mazo made and mended boots.

People were milling around the market stalls. A man wearing a woolly hat was wrapping the last bunch of *verdura* in newspaper. He handed it to the young woman with three children clinging to her damp skirt. The fishmonger's apron glistened with fish guts. He slid the last silver offerings on to the scales for the old woman.

Richard moved on, glad to be clear of the sour stench. But he felt uneasy as he left the clamour and noise of the market. He needed company. He wandered to the Plaza. His pals must be somewhere. Crowds of people were mixing and mingling in the moist night air. Near the steps of the Town Hall, an old woman turned her blank, watery eyes to the blank watery sky and bellowed, "*Dos iguales para hoy!*"

Every day her daughter pinned the slips of paper to the fringe of her black shawl and led her to this place. And every evening the daughter would come and collect her and take her home. She had been doing it for twenty years, since her drunken father had blinded her mother with a blow to the head.

Richard paused in front of the figure hunched on the stool. Nobody was buying the lottery tickets flapping about her bony chest. He studied the smooth face of the old lady. She would never know that she had no wrinkles. He thrust the pesetas into the ragged black mitten.

"*Gracias. Que Dios le pagará.* That God will bless you."

A group of youths were fooling about on the stone bench under a tree, tormenting a dog with a piece of bread. The chill weather had stripped the other benches of their usual occupants. Old men would normally sit there for hours, smoking their tobacco, leaning on their walking sticks, spitting on the cobblestones and watching the people go by, dreaming of the days when all had been right with the world. Tonight they had stayed indoors.

He glanced at the Town Hall clock. It was five minutes past ten. Music was coming from the opposite side of the Plaza. Las Pecas, the most popular nightspot in Serona, was coming to life. He no longer wanted to be alone and Chanza and Magro and Peludo would turn up sooner or later.

He pushed through the slatted door into a long, low room. Smoke hovered around the orange lights painting the faces of the clients with a sickly glow. The smell of stale beer and sweaty bodies wrenched at his stomach. Here the clients thrived in this fug and came again and again to get drunk, dance and fornicate.

Squashed into a small space in the far corner, three musicians were in a world of their own. Two guitarists looked at each other from time to time and then leaned forward to listen to their guitars. Pleased with what they heard they threw their heads into the air and smiled at the ceiling. A third man was beating a set of drums, his eyes in the middle distance, seeing nothing. All were determined to drown the voices and shrieks of the men and women sitting on stools, playing cards, drinking and singing. No one was dancing yet.

Richard went over to a group of men gathered round a table. A tiny monkey was sitting in a pool of beer, its alert black eyes swivelling from one ruddy face to the next. A piece of string round its neck led to the wrist of a woman sitting in the corner. She was trying to make it suck brandy from her finger. She saw Richard and quickly stuffed the monkey down the bodice of her red spotted dress. She scrambled to her feet and sidled up to him.

"Twenty-five pesetas." She pushed her knee into his thigh. "Upstairs and as long as you like, with eyes like yours. *Vamos*?" Her lilting voice broke into a cackle.

Richard stared into the woman's face. It was painted, exaggerated, with too much colour on the cheeks, too much lipstick. She had thick hair like a bunch of scorched hay and enormous brown eyes that blamed the world. She slipped her hand through his elbow and smiled, parting her lips to show stained, decaying teeth. The woman was older than he thought. His eyes went to the bewildered creature nestling among the frills and flounces between her proud breasts.

146

He removed her hand and went over to the bar. Next to him were a man and woman. Middle-aged lovers. He could tell they were in love by the way they looked at each other. Then the woman touched the man's cheek so gently. Richard stared straight ahead, watching them in the mirror that ran the length of the bar. It was nice to see older people in love.

Love was for everybody but most people thought it was only for the young. He was sure his father and mother were in love. They didn't argue and were nice to each other. The woman reached over and whispered to her man, who touched her knee, then they slipped off the stools and left hand in hand.

He emptied his glass and asked for more wine. He wanted Anita. How he wanted Anita. He lit another cigarette and glanced along the bar. A woman was sitting on a stool at the far end, leaning at an angle that profiled her slim waist. Young, much younger than Anita, she was pretty in an angular sort of way with long brown hair that she kept tossing about like a curtain swishing across her face and shoulders. There was something innocent about her and yet she was here for a purpose. New to the job perhaps? Their eyes met and she smiled, picked up her glass and came towards him, walking slowly, swaying her hips. Still smiling she levered herself on to the stool next to him.

The room upstairs was unkempt. The smell of stale tobacco mingled with cheap perfume. Everything about it was frowsy. Faded dark green curtains at the window kept out all light and air. The rug on the bare boards was patterned with dark stains. Two flimsy little chairs with cane seats either side of the washstand were indifferent to the activities taking place on the squeaky old bed.

She was shy at first but that was part of the act. She had been trained well and used her knowledge expertly. After he was spent he rolled on to his stomach and he heard the gasp, the intake of air and waited for the questions. But she didn't ask any. Her fingers were like feathers as they traced each line of the whip scars. So soothing, so relaxing, so... He closed his eyes and fell asleep.

Clients went in to Las Pecas on the ground floor and those who used the bedrooms left by rickety wooden stairs at the back of the premises. It was half past one when Richard rattled down the stairs into the pouring rain. He skipped along the pavement, splattering through the puddles, past the crowded bars and arrived puffing and out of breath at the stables at Las Candelas. Pepe was nowhere to be seen.

"Brisa, good girl. Sorry I was so long. There now," He anchored the brown paper parcel containing his new riding boots to the pommel of the saddle and wheeled into the street.

Soon the string of lights in Serona blinked and went out and the black, wet night closed in. He pulled the heavy torch from his satchel and held it at the side of Brisa's neck. The wind lashed around him, sobering him, clarifying his thoughts. He saw the shabby little bedroom again and he saw her face, pinched and hard for someone so young. She was poor otherwise she wouldn't have been doing what she did. She was thin, so different to Anita with her luscious, ripe body, her beautiful hair, her expensive clothes and that tantalising perfume.

The rain was whipping his face until he was sure it was bleeding. In the distance lightning ripped the dark satin of the night sky, then the thunder crashed. "Everything's all right, girl, easy now," and he stroked Brisa's neck. "Stay in the middle of the road." The thunder rolled away to another valley and Brisa walked on, calmer now, through the mud and ruts filled with water, past the sullen trees weeping into the ditches.

At last the barn in the corner of the field loomed up. It marked the fork in the lane from the main road to Lavega. Brisa faltered and slowed down. The water was up to her hocks. Richard flashed his torch around and realised there was no demarcation. No line of cart rut, no ditch. It was as if they were wading through a large lake. This was dangerous. Brisa couldn't see where she was stepping. He dismounted and led her by the bridle. "Steady now, Brisa."

Soon they were in shallower water and Richard mounted. Brisa quickened her step. There were lights ahead. Lavega at last.

The main street was like a river, swirling and eddying around the corners of sheds and houses and shops. A lantern had been hung in an alleyway near El Paco's Bar and he saw an old woman with a rusty bucket emptying water from the doorway of her mean little house. She looked like a bedraggled witch with her black dress flapping around her bony frame.

"River's burst its bank!" she called to Richard as she sloshed water across the street. It ran back into her doorway before she had time to straighten up. "What am I to do? I've got the little ones inside."

"Where are the men?" Richard shouted into the wind. "Can't they help?"

"They're at the party. Somebody's gone to tell them. They'll all be flooded out if they don't soon come."

"What time is it?" Richard pulled up close to her.

"Church clock struck three not long ago," and once again she filled the bucket with water and tossed it into the street. "There's been a commotion on the other side of the Plaza. Don't know what's going on." She wiped her face with the wet skirt. "It's no good. I can't do anymore. Be careful, young one," she called over her shoulder as she splashed through the water, back to the dark little house.

"Stay inside until they come!" Richard yelled. "This deluge doesn't know when to stop."

When he reached the bend in the lane leading to Los Rubios he could see a light in the kitchen. They were back from the party. He put his new riding boots on the ground near the manger while he unharnessed Brisa, drying her off with an old sack. Then he gave her a bucket of water, covered her with a blanket and hurried into the kitchen.

His mother was sitting at the table, hair dishevelled, her face ghostly.

"Thank goodness." She lolled back in the chair. "I'm at my wit's end, waiting, hic, waiting."

"But mother, why are you sitting in wet clothes? Why aren't you in bed? And where's father?"

"Should have been back ages ago," and she buried her face in her hands and began to sob.

Richard had never seen his mother cry before. It alarmed him. He moved to her side and put his arms around her. Then he smelt the drink on her breath. "Where is he?"

She fumbled for a handkerchief and blew her nose. "It came on to rain. Poured down. But we didn't stop dancing, hic. Moved into the barn. Then we got word, flooding in the village."

"But where's father?"

"Well, hic." She raised her head and covered her mouth with both hands to stop the hiccoughing.

"Let me get you some water."

She drank quickly. "Lovely party, pity you missed it. Crowds of people, everyone was there. Lots of food, lots of drink. The men went to help near the river, hic. You know, where they keep all those horses, in the stables. What's his name?"

"Don Anselmo. But where's father?" Richard mouthed the words slowly.

"Nothing the women could do so we had coffee then came home 'specting to find your father."

"Who's 'we' mother?"

"Me and Maria."

Richard paced the floor slowly, to the sink and back to the door. Then he paused in front of his mother hunched over the kitchen table. "I'd better go and see what's happening."

"You're wet through. You can't go like that."

"Mother, out there it's pouring rain. There's no point in putting dry clothes on. I'll light the lanterns and put them in the courtyard. Go to bed. Please."

150

He placed the lanterns high on the door lintels and went to the shed at the back of the stables, where the goats were huddled in one corner. Then he remembered the sheep in River Field. He hurried past the cattle sheds towards the orchard but stopped in his tracks, waving the lantern aloft. The orchard had become a lake with trees growing in it.

He returned to the house. His mother was stretched across the table, fast asleep. He yanked off his squelching boots. Then he remembered the new ones. They were in the stable. He would look for them in the morning. He peeled off his wet breeches and flung them over the clothes line in the washhouse next to the kitchen. He found corduroy trousers and a shirt drying on the line.

Suddenly his mother sat up. "What are you doing?"

"Putting on dry clothes. It's chaos out there, mother. The orchard is completely under water. I don't know what's happened to the sheep."

"I'll sit up for your father."

"Mother, it's nearly four o'clock. They must have moved the horses by now. He will have stayed with Pedro for the night. Go to bed. We'll sort things out later." Suddenly he was afraid. Where *was* father? He thought of the flooded orchard, River Field, the animals, the land, the buildings. "Soon it will be light enough to sort things out. Now, off to bed."

" I'm staying here until your father comes," and Trynah wiped her hands over her face. Her hair hung in damp strands like rats' tails, and her eyes were glassy. He'd never seen her look so old and tired. She looked a bit like a street vendor in Serona, without hope.

He sank into the chair and flopped across the table sinking his head across his outstretched arms. Soon he drifted into a dubious rest. The kitchen was warm with the faint whiff of newly baked bread, the stillness disturbed only by the gentle wheezing of Riba asleep in the log basket.

Richard felt something soft against his leg and murmured. He thought it was Anita. Then he heard a whimper. Consciousness slowly returned, drawing him out of a narrow black tunnel. He opened his eyes and saw the uneven grain of the kitchen table. Riba was rubbing against his legs. He wanted to go outside. Richard got to his feet and roared with the pain in his back. It woke his mother sprawled across the other end of the kitchen table.

"What happened?" She looked around her.

"Nothing, mother. I'm just stiff."

He went to the door. A crisp wind had blown the storm clouds away and a reluctant grey dawn was revealing a scowling, misty sky. The courtyard was awash. A sack of corn floated past the door of the cart shed. It turned and twisted in the muddy water and he became aware that it wasn't a sack of corn. It was a dead animal, a goat.

There were other bits and pieces eddying around. Dead hens and cockerels, some wedged in the spokes of the cartwheels, others circling slowly amongst the debris in the water. They looked so small and scraggy, no bigger than pigeons. Bundles of straw and branches of trees had become hooked on to doorframes and empty sacks were caught on the shaft of a cart. Buckets floated about aimlessly between piles of wood and empty barrels. And everywhere the bad smell of drains, the putrid smell of manure.

"Oh, my goodness! What's to become of us all?" His mother was by his side.

"Must check the livestock." Richard pulled on his boots. "Don't worry. We'll get order restored. When father comes we can... Hello, someone's coming along the lane now." He squinted at the group of people in the misty morning light. "It's Pedro and Maria. But I don't know who the other man is."

"Pedro, I'm so glad to see you." Trynah turned to Maria. "Thank goodness you're here. Good morning, Father Ignacio. Do come in." She led the way into the kitchen and pulled out the chairs. "Please sit down. Where's Robbie?"

Father Ignacio wandered around the kitchen but he didn't sit down. He seemed not to have heard the question. He took a deep breath and clasped his neatly manicured hands in front of the soft mound of flesh under his cassock. He looked as if he were about to pray.

"We're not sure," he said, pulling on the lobe of his right ear and staring at the kitchen floor.

"Not sure," Richard echoed.

Father Ignacio cleared his throat. "You see, you see..." he paused. "Last night Señor Mann and Pedro and the other men – well, we went to help with the flooded stables, to get the horses out. Down by the river..."

"Yes...Yes I know." Trynah's eyes were fixed on the black curly hair. It was like a cake frill around the back of his head. "But where's my husband?"

Father Ignacio glanced up, looking for help from the ceiling. "He – er – he's missing."

"Missing!" Richard jumped out of the chair so quickly it fell over.

"Yes. There was a great deal of commotion with the horses. They were highly excited and frightened. One broke loose and took off along the river bank. Señor Mann went after it to catch it." Father Ignacio continued his slow circuit of the kitchen, pausing at the dresser, staring at the chair in the corner. "He was some yards ahead of us, that is Pedro, Rodrigo and me. We were all hurrying along the bank. It was dark and the path was muddy. We saw Señor Mann miss his footing. He slipped and fell. Into the river." Father Ignacio sank into a chair at last and reached for the coffee mug.

"I tried to grab his arm," Pedro framed his head with his hands, talking to the kitchen table, "but I couldn't see properly." He raised his head and sat motionless as tears washed down his gaunt cheeks. He didn't move, for he had no energy for sobbing, for physical grief. He sat in the chair blinking the sorrow from his eyes. "If only... I could have grabbed his sleeve. If only..." Pedro spread both hands across the table. "He was swept away under my very nose."

"Please don't be upset, father." Maria's arms were around his shoulders. "He's blaming himself and he shouldn't."

Father Ignacio looked down his snub nose into his coffee cup. "The Civil Guard has been alerted all along the valley as far as Lesaya. He's a strong and powerful man, so we just have to wait for news."

An enormous silence filled the kitchen. One could almost hear the heartbeats of the men and women in rhythm with the clock on the mantelpiece as it continued its ruthless march of time.

"There must be something we can do," Trynah appealed to them all.

"Everything is being done, Madam. As I explained the Civil Guard will bring us news as soon as possible." Endless time filled every inch of the kitchen, silently, ominously, offering nothing whatever, neither hope nor sympathy. They were all captive in a huge space of nothingness.

"I'm afraid the storm has wreaked a terrible toll in the village." Father Ignacio drained his empty coffee cup again. "The water coming down from the slopes has created a bog near the bridge at Peinosa. We got news this morning that they've put a guard from the Municipal Offices near the bridge and they've arranged for a train to travel with a brigade of labourers and salvage material. It's a terrible business. Barns and sheds have been swept away, animals drowned." Father Ignacio cleared his throat. "Now I have to go and comfort Señora Garcia. Her husband was..." He paused. "Last night, near the railway tunnel. He was on his way home." He didn't say where from but he knew that Señor Garcia regularly visited a widow a mile away up the valley. "So if you'll excuse me. Rest assured, Señora Mann, everything is being done. As soon as we have news..." And Father Ignacio bowed his way out of the kitchen without finishing his sentence.

Pedro pushed back his chair. "Come on Ricardo. We'd better go and check the sheep."

There was not a sheep to be found in River Field. It was just a vast lake.

Pedro turned away. "They must have escaped to higher ground. They'll be under the wood."

"But they can't get to higher ground from there." Richard buttoned his jacket. "Not since we mended the fences."

They plodded along the lane, squelching in the muddy ruts past Los Rubios and up to Wood Field. There was not an animal to be seen.

"Do you think someone's rounded them up?" Richard raised his eyebrows to Pedro.

"No." Pedro leaned on the gate. "Nobody rounded them up. Everyone was at the fiesta last night. And then the men went to the stables."

Richard stared into Pedro's crumpled face. It was true. The old woman had said so as she ladled water from her hovel. No one had moved the sheep. "Well, then, what do you think has happened?"

The bright green pasture sparkled after the rain. The crisp wind stole down from the wood and into the valley to ripple the new pools and rivulets of water in the gutters and potholes.

"I don't know, but we'll find them somewhere. After flooding things turn up in the most unexpected places. But we haven't had a flood like this for thirty years. Come on, let's go back to Los Rubios. Robbie's probably turned up by now. This wind will help to dry us out."

Chapter 10

Two days later the body of Robinson Mann was recovered from the river. It had been carried by the flood waters to Mansilla, more than two kilometres away. Trynah had to go to Serona for the official identification.

"I shall take the nine o'clock bus." She was washing the breakfast plates. "Do you want to come with me?"

Richard was at her side looking out of the window. "I think I'll help Pedro in Wood Field."

"If you wish." Trynah put on her black dress and found a black scarf to cover her head. She was sorry that Richard didn't want to go with her but it was only natural. This was the first time he'd felt the brush of death's wings and he didn't know how to respond.

She was ushered into the office of the Registrar in the Town Hall. The small square room smelt musty as if death had seeped into the leather bound books on the shelves lining the walls. A tall man sat behind a desk poring over a battered ledger. His sallow face and lank hair seemed as weary of death as death itself and he appeared not to have a spoonful of breath in him.

"Good morning, Señora Mann." He took her hand. "I accompany you in your sorrow." She nodded. He produced a large bunch of keys from a drawer in his desk and indicated for her to follow. They went along a corridor, turned right and then left and the next door he opened gave on to a courtyard.

It surprised her. It was a blaze of colour. They walked along the pathway past bright red geraniums and clumps of cream lilies and bright green shrubs. It was full of life and beauty. Then he paused in front of another door, selected a key and they went inside.

The oblong room was bare except for a plain wooden coffin on a catafalque in the centre. The Registrar was at her side. He signalled for her to step forward.

She stared down at the corpse. The hair was thick and curly. The face was relaxed as if he were having a doze. His features were as noble in death as they had been in life. And he looked younger. She put her clenched fists to her mouth.

It was the second time she had mourned the death of Robinson Mann. Death by hanging in Lincoln Prison, a young man condemned to death for killing his twin brother.

Memories swirled around her in the cold, stark room, past the coffin, sweeping her back to Vinny in Burnett's Cafe. It was the place where all the bad news had been imparted in Trynah's life. It was here that she had to tell her sister that she was with child as a result of Redfern's violation.

"Are you sure?"

"Yes," Trynah bit her lip. "I've counted again and again. What am I going to do?"

"First of all you must decide whether you want to keep the baby..."

"No... no... no." Trynah was shaking her head.

Vinny stirred her tea. "When you've crossed that awesome frontier into the realms of childbirth you will not willingly give up the baby that cost you so much labour," she said, keeping her eyes on the teacup. "'Tis a wondrous thing, the birth of a child."

"But not without love and caring and... Robbie," Trynah's voice faltered. "He must never know about this." Tears were cascading down her cheeks. "How can I love this creature? This... this thing that wasn't invited by anyone's love? This child will have no father, no love, no future." She paused, tugging at the edge of the tablecloth. "I cannot dedicate my life to a creature conceived in such violence. And what about father? He will die of shock."

"He need not know. Indeed, he shall not know," Vinny tightened her lips.

"But I'll soon swell up and get fat. How can I keep it a secret?"

Trynah's secret was kept thanks to her sister. She made dresses with full skirts and a stunning cloak. And Vinny also arranged the confinement with her sister Abby who worked at the Blind Children's Home at Flaxwell. However, the baby lived for a few hours only.

Months later they were in Burnett's Cafe again. They always arranged to meet after Curtis visited Robbie in Lincoln Prison so that Vinny could give her the latest news. Trynah could never bring herself to see her beloved Robbie in prison. It was just too ghastly. So they met for tea at Burnett's.

"It's all over," Vinny reached across the damask table cloth and covered Trynah's hand.

"You mean..." she gasped.

"Yes," Vinny's voice was a whisper. "Robbie told him the date had been fixed for Friday, September..."

"No, no. I don't want to know the date. I don't want an anniversary of this dreadful deed."

Vinny reached for Trynah's cup and poured more tea. "Robbie had sworn Curtis to secrecy. Said neither of us must know until it was all over." Vinny stirred her tea slowly. "It's done with."

Now she touched the jagged laceration across Robbie's right temple. The tell-tale wound that had cost him his life. Then she kissed his forehead. It was as cold as marble. This courageous man, the man she loved so much that she had deserted a good, honest husband and two little stepdaughters and all her family. But now there was no mistake. He was dead. An icy wind crept around her and she shivered involuntarily in the heavy silence of this alien little room. Then she heard a movement at her shoulder. It was the Registrar. She had forgotten about him.

"Thank you," she turned and lowered her head. The tears ran freely as she followed him back across the courtyard blinking at the bright flowers, the shrubs and then along the corridors to his cluttered office.

He shuffled through papers, found the one he was looking for, signed it and passed it to her. It was the Death Certificate.

* * *

The church of The Virgen de la Magdalena in the Plaza was full to capacity for the funeral service of the Englishman. She and Robbie had always joined in the Feast days in the Catholic calendar but had remained Church of England Protestants. Señor Daroca had given permission for Robbie to be buried under his beloved beech trees at the top of Wood Field.

"Beech trees talk, you know Trynah." That's what he had said when they were courting at the Ring Dam at Apsley. "All trees chatter but it's the beech trees that captivate me so. Their leaves are crisper in the autumn, dark and rich, and they sigh and whisper..."

Father Ignacio was now leading the cortege along the lane past the track to Los Rubios. Don Anselmo's dray had been swept and scrubbed and draped in black cloths then the coffin had been placed on it. Rinco was now plodding up the incline towards the woods.

Trynah and Richard walked side by side. His face was pale and drawn, his jaw clamped rigid. Grief had aged him without warning, robbed him of his youthful aspect and given his face a hard maturity.

Pedro and Maria followed and behind them came the villagers headed by Carlos and Anita Daroca, heavily veiled.

As they reached the grave the mourners fanned out and Father Ignacio's thin voice piped into the wind. Then the dark earth that had not been disturbed for centuries was shovelled back into the grave.

Father Ignacio led the mourners down the hill to Los Rubios. Carlos and Anita Daroca excused themselves and left but Trynah was reassured to find the villagers joining in the bitter-sweet celebration. It was a compliment to Robbie that they were all here, eating, drinking and remembering. An army of willing helpers had prepared gazpacho, rice and salads, goat's cheese, ham, chorizo and bread. Beer and wine flowed.

"I accompany you in your sorrow," Señora Perez who kept the general store crossed herself and linked her plump little hand into Trynah's arm.

"We are so sorry," said the woman in the shabby brown dress, who was the mother of eight and had been a widow for as many years.

Trynah hadn't realised just how deep a niche Robbie had carved into the heart of this small village community since he arrived in search of a future for her all those years ago.

At last the villagers drifted away, back to their children and old folk, to their poverty and dignity and happiness. Maria helped her to clear up the food and dishes. Pedro had fed the horses and checked the goat pens. Richard had gone riding.

Now she sat alone in the kitchen listening to sounds she had failed to notice in the hustle and bustle of everyday life when Robbie was just a few steps away: the back door agitating in its warped frame, a branch of the young birch tree scraping against the window pane and the draught from the pantry window causing the fastener to jiggle against the milk ladle. Robbie was going to fix it but there had always been more pressing problems.

In the distance she could hear the creak of an ox cart rumbling along the track, the bleating of goats and the bellowing of the cows. In the birch tree outside the kitchen door the jays argued with their brash, rasping calls.

Her eyes filled with tears. A lump in her throat threatened to choke her. Robbie. Her man. They had lost and found each other. She covered her face with her hands and wailed, her loud keening filling the empty house, echoing up the stairs, through the rooms and back to the tidy, scrubbed kitchen, parading scenes that she had forgotten. The day he had come to her bedside after Redfern...

She had been staying with Vinny for the final fitting of her wedding dress. She could have said 'No' to him when they met on the footpath at Pippacott Wood. She could have said 'No' when he suggested they wander across the meadow to look at the little grey barn. Then it was too late. Redfern quickly overpowered her. She staggered back to Vinny's cottage and then Robbie was there, at her bedside, with eyes that no longer belonged to him.

He took her hands and pressed them to his lips. "Oh my God. I've ruined everything for you and me. I've killed Redfern. He was in the forage shed, singing. I grabbed the pitchfork... Trynah, I grabbed the pitchfork... and killed him."

Now the kettle on the hob was filling the kitchen with steam. She made the coffee and sank into the hard kitchen chair. She felt calmer now, almost serene. Someone was saying this is how it is and nothing can change it.

"So what the hangman's trapdoor failed to do in Lincoln Prison the floods of Lavega have achieved. It was a cheat." She sipped the coffee slowly speaking in a soft voice to Riba, curled up at her feet. "But if Robbie had not hit his head on the stonework of the bridge he would have survived. He had the physical strength. But unconscious in the raging waters of the river – impossible." She got up and Riba followed her to the sink.

And now there was the future. A bleak future, with no Robbie. Again that icy wind came from nowhere to freeze her heart, paralyse her stomach. She turned quickly from the window. There would be the empty chair at the table every meal time and familiar clothes hanging on pegs and nails, clothes that would never be worn again, the old tweed jacket, the shabby corduroy trousers and the battered old beret that had perched on his curly hair.

Restless, she wandered around the kitchen, touching the backs of the chairs, the edge of the dresser. Richard had gone riding. He didn't say where to but she was sure that he would never risk crossing the path of Señor Daroca again.

The village gossip. Oh yes! It had been watered and nurtured and grew by the day. Maria kept Trynah informed as they cooked and cleaned and sewed and knitted.

"The missus goes to Serona, you know. When Don Carlos is away," Maria was in the kitchen shelling peas. "Visits the taverns." And Maria knew who had whipped Ricardo. Her father had told her not to tell anyone, ever. No need to upset people, he had said. But Ricardo had been whipped because he had been to see La Señora Daroca. And Maria knew that La Señora would have taken her knickers down for him. But nobody knew that she, Maria Arganda, had slept with him until dawn. She had kissed him, she had stroked his smooth thighs, caressed his cheek. It was a night she would never forget and no one could take it away from her. Besides he would soon tire of La Señora and now, after the whipping... maybe he'd like her a little more.

"She used to live in Madrid, you know," Maria popped a handful of peas into her mouth. "Must find it lonely here after a big city."

"Yes, it must be very difficult for her here in Lavega," Trynah swept the pea pods into a bucket.

So thanks to Maria, Trynah was able to put the pieces of the jigsaw puzzle together. Neither she nor Robbie could ever have imagined who Richard was going to meet as he galloped out of Los Rubios in a cloud of dust. Anita Daroca! Shivers went down her spine. And she was at a loss to understand why he should be attracted to her. She must be old enough to be his mother.

Well, Richard would now have to act a lot more responsibly. All the sheep had been lost, three goats had drowned and many of the hens. Livestock must be bought. Crops must be sown. They had to earn a living.

In the suspended world of grief her desolation returned. She threw back her head and shrieked at the ceiling, tearing at her hair, walking around the kitchen. She threw open the kitchen door. The

162

fountain sparkled, the breeze was friendly, the day was fresh and promising better things but she hardly noticed as the anxieties jostled, confusing her senses until she just didn't know what to think. She sat down again and toyed with the empty coffee cup. Carlos Daroca. Something would have to be done about the renewal of the lease. But that man had almost killed her son. She saw again the ghastly scars on Richard's back as he lay sprawled on the bed. Daroca was a cruel man, selfish and greedy, and Richard would never be safe again. No, she couldn't possibly go and see Señor Daroca about the renewal of the lease and the extra land.

"So," she took the coffee cup to the sink. "There's nothing to be done. We shall just have to wait for him to bring the document for signature, won't we?" She spoke to Riba rubbing around her legs. "Good boy." He gave a plaintive little wail. "No, Robbie's not here," she leaned down to stroke his silky ears, choking back the tears.

There was a clattering of hooves as Richard came charging into the courtyard.

"Did you have a nice ride?"

He threw the whip behind the kitchen door. "Yes, I went to Tres Picos." It was a lie. He'd ridden to his father's grave under the beech trees at the top of Wood Field. He wanted to be sure that what had happened the other day was real – the priest, the people, the coffin, the grave.

Yes, this is the grave. This is the grave of my father. He stared down at the hump of bare earth. No flowers. Mother had insisted that the beech trees were all that were needed.

"I should have done more to help when you asked, but I made excuses. And you knew nothing about the way I deceived you and mother. All I wanted was to be with Anita and my pals in Serona." The wind rustled in the trees at the edge of the wood. "I should have done more to help you." He thrust one clenched hand into the other, biting his lips as he walked around the grave.

All was still and quiet except for a jingle of leather and metal.

Brisa was grazing near the hedge. Richard mounted quickly but he couldn't see very clearly. His eyes were awash with tears.

"That's a long way." She was about to ask if he'd gone with a friend but she stopped. She and Robbie should have been asking that question a long time ago. "What about something to eat?"

"I'm not hungry," and he strode out of the kitchen and across the courtyard, pausing at the fountain.

"He's working his way through the tunnel, Riba," she patted the sad little head resting in her lap. "We all have to. There are no short cuts."

Chapter 11

The wind was not in a hurry to leave the scene of devastation. It played around the valley for days picking at tufts of straw clinging to gate posts and door frames and roof tops, turning over the broken shards of timber, pushing the rubbish into little heaps at the corner of the streets and rattling the loose tiles. It was like the last guest at a party, not hungry but just scavenging around the debris, making a nuisance of itself.

"Must have been a rat's nest in here," the voice came from the cow shed. "All drowned."

It was the day after the funeral and Trynah and Richard were clearing up the litter at Los Rubios. They had wearied themselves during the previous day and by nightfall fatigue had carried them to sleep before grief could steal into their consciousness.

Pedro and Maria brought a small army of friends and soon their cheerful banter was ringing across the courtyard.

"Look at that. Two dead squirrels!" Pedro was in the pigsty.

Richard was up a ladder dragging tree branches from the roof of the stable.

"Are you there?" he called to Maria standing at the foot of the ladder.

"Yes," Maria's eyes were on his long, lean thighs.

"Be careful. This branch is heavy. I'll come down and help you with it." Since his 'accident' he'd noticed a difference in her. He'd always found her a bit *pesada,* heavy going, dull. Of course, he'd always been dashing away to see Anita. That's why he hadn't noticed her. But now there was something light-hearted about her, a liveliness. She had a sparkle and she smiled more often and dressed differently. She wasn't wearing her usual drab brown dress.

Today she wore a flowered skirt and pink blouse. Perhaps she's got a *novio,* a boyfriend.

Together they hauled the branch across the yard to the back of the goat shed and dumped it near the wall.

"It's going to be a big pile by the time we've finished," he said, turning to her. Yes, she did look different, vibrant.

"Yes," her voice was a whisper. The sounds from the helpers carried across the courtyard but all was quiet here, behind the shed.

"How are things with you Maria?" He didn't hear an answer. Suddenly she was clinging to him, both arms around him with his back to the wall. He could see the field stretching away to the wood. He could feel the warm body pressed against his and he devoured the soft lips and felt that dizzying sensation that Anita always provoked. Maria stepped away, smoothing her hands down her skirt then she waited with her hands behind her back staring at him.

"Coffee's ready!" a voice bellowed across the courtyard.

"*Bueno,* " Maria put her hands to her face. "Later, perhaps. No?" She held her head high, lips apart, challenging him with her glistening dark eyes.

Richard stared hard at her. "Yes, let's go," and he followed her to the courtyard startled by the desire this ripe, plump woman had elicited.

The children were tearing down the old sacks draped like curtains on the plough in the corner. Mud was shovelled into wheelbarrows and the cobbles brushed clean. The dead goats, hens, rats and squirrels were loaded into a cart and taken to the field next to the farmhouse. The bonfire blazed all day. Trynah and Maria made a huge paella for the helpers. They had eaten their fill, drunk wine and left, satisfied and happy that Los Rubios now looked normal.

"I'm going to check the bonfire." Richard was in the kitchen, and Maria was helping his mother with the pots. "Would you like to come with me Maria?" This afternoon, behind the goat shed, this woman had brought him to bursting point. He was certain that she'd made the first move. She'd grabbed him but it had all happened so quickly he couldn't be absolutely sure. Maria! Of all people! He wanted her and he knew that she wanted it as much as he did.

"Of course," Maria turned from the sink drying her hands.

"Off you two go then, before it gets dark." Trynah put the coffee pot on the sideboard.

They strode across the courtyard and into the field. Richard kicked through the mound of dark grey ashes, scattering them in a wide arc. "That's all right then." He looked into the dark, hungry eyes. "Let's go. To the barn? *De acuerdo?*"

"*Sí*," she clapped her hands and fell in at his side as they strode back to the farm buildings.

They were soon stretched out on a bed of soft hay on top of a pile of old, dry sacks in the corner of the barn. Immediately they were locked in each other's arms. Their lips met again. Maria was caressing his hair, his face, his back. Then he was fumbling with her skirt and petticoat. He found an expanse of smooth, naked thighs. She was not wearing knickers and he was fired to an uncontrollable frenzy. There was a shriek and then she was sobbing into his thick, blond hair.

He filled his lungs with the dry, musky aroma of the hay mingled with Maria's body odour. This woman was raw sex as Nature commanded, earthy, wholesome. No perfume, no lipstick. Not at all like...

Outside all was quiet as they lay there, the only sound a distant tinkle of bells as somebody herded their goats. "That was the first time, wasn't it?" He ruffled her thick, dark curls.

"Of course." She was staring up at the bits of hay caught in the rafters.

Richard pulled himself to his feet. "I'm sorry."

"I'm not." She got up and tucked her blouse into her skirt. "*Te amo*, Ricardo."

"*Vamos*," Richard quickly buttoned his trousers. He was not in love with her. That's not what this was all about. "Come on. It's getting late."

The flotsam and jetsam that had swirled around the sheds and ditches had been cleared away. The mud dried and Los Rubios was recognisable again, slipping easily into a routine, but Richard knew that life would never be the same. There was a huge void everywhere, in the farmhouse, in the kitchen, in the stables, in the fields. The familiar figure of his father was nowhere to be seen. No voice called across the courtyard and there was no steady footfall in the passages.

This void was blurred by the relief Maria had provided, on the hay in the barn. She had been a virgin. Now she wasn't. But she had been so willing. She had a habit of hanging about the yard and the sheds, which worried him. She would sidle up to him when she had a chance but he gave her no encouragement. He didn't want to be trapped again. And he did not love her. This unexpected turn of events had not swamped his craving for Anita but the vision of Carlos Daroca with that whip filled him with terror and he daren't go near Dos Caminos. So he drifted through the night hours, keeping Maria at bay, powerless to do anything about seeing Anita. She would have to make the first move.

It came early one morning, when he and Pedro were mucking out the stables.

"Got a message for you." Pedro jabbed the fork into the heap of manure. "Ride to the shepherd's hut. She'll wait for you there today, two o'clock."

"What!" Richard bounded across the stable grabbing Pedro's arms, whirling him round and round with horse muck flying in all directions. "Thank you, thank you. Ay, ay, ay!!"

"Calm it! Remember Señor Daroca..." Pedro wheeled the barrow towards the door. "And after last time... no telling what he'd do to you."

"What else did she say? Is she all right?"

"She didn't say anything else. Just to give you the message and to be sure that it was kept a secret."

Richard stared into Pedro's unassailable eyes and felt a pang of guilt about Maria, Pedro's daughter. Pedro would never believe that she had given herself to him in the barn. Now he had to find a pretext to get away. He had to tell his mother something. He couldn't just disappear on Brisa, not now. She was relying on him more and more since...

"I'm going to check our boundary fences this afternoon." He leaned back in the kitchen chair, hands clasped behind his head, watching her at the sink.

"Is Pedro going with you?" she asked as she glanced over her shoulder. "He knows them well."

"No. He's going to mend the chicken hut. The wind blew the roof off."

* * *

Trynah watched him gallop along the lane at such speed anyone would have thought his life depended upon it. She smiled. At last he seemed to have laid his grief to rest. He was cheerful and he was positive, taking much more interest in Los Rubios. She'd forgotten about the boundary fences with so much happening and was pleased he'd remembered them.

Half an hour later she was in the bedroom, the scent of lavender calming her troubled thoughts as she sorted the last pile of Robbie's clothes, the worn trousers, the patched jackets, the socks. They were strewn across her cold, forsaken bed, which was like a vast white ocean. Every night it carried her to deserted shores and stranded her there with no help in sight. She pined for him, for his nearness, for his strength, for his goodness.

She heard the sound of a horse and went to the window. A rider cantered into the courtyard and dismounted, pulling a leather satchel from the saddlebag. He tucked it under his arm and strode towards the front door.

Heart pounding, she hurried downstairs and struggled with the stiff bolts. The door was made of oak, strong and defiant, and was rarely opened. There were not many receptions at Los Rubios and most people came to the kitchen door. At last she managed to turn the old key and scrape back the bolt.

"Good afternoon, Señor Daroca. Do come in." The door screeched on its rusty hinges. Trynah led the way into the front room and offered Robbie's tub chair near the window. Carlos Daroca sank into it with a grunt.

"Phew!" He wiped the perspiration from his forehead with a crumpled handkerchief. "*Hace calor*, eh! It's hot. And after all those storms it's threatening thunder again." He clasped his hairy hands across his paunch, raised his chin and stared at her with fierce black eyes. "Well, how are you Señora Mann?" Before she could answer he asked another question. "How is everything at the farm now that..."

"Everything is fine," Trynah lowered herself into the chair near the occasional table, her heart still racing. "We're getting along. Of course, nothing is ever going to be the same again but we have to keep moving."

"Yes," Señor Daroca stroked his bristly black moustache with two fingers. Then he heaved his paunch sideways in the chair, linking one leg behind the other, studying this widow, unbelievably desirable in her grief. Mother Nature did that. Gave an aura, a lustre to attract a new partner.

"Ah, well," he stuttered, "you see, Señora Mann. Well, it's – er – it's like this. I mean to say," his voice choked in the back of his throat. "I came to see you about Los Rubios," and he pulled a sheaf of papers from his satchel. "This is the agreement entered into by your – er – your late husband. Of course, it's always been renewed on the due dates and as you know the current lease expires in December."

"That's right," she said meeting his steady glare. "I have the copy. May I offer you some refreshment while we finalise the renewal?" And before he could decline she was in the kitchen.

As she came in with the tray she recognised something in his eyes that she had not seen since she was in the little barn with Redfern. A wildness – something sinister, treacherous.

"But, Señora Mann. Don't you understand? The lease was signed by your husband, as the sole lessee. Robinson Mann is now..." He pushed out his lower lip, uncertain whether he could say the word. "I mean to say that I'm serving you with three months' notice to quit Los Rubios."

Trynah dropped a spoon. It hit the edge of the tray and fell to the floor. Her mouth opened but no voice came. She watched him shuffle through the papers and pull out a large document. With a flourish he placed it on the table next to the tray.

"I'm sure you'll want to make other arrangements as soon as possible." He drank noisily watching her over the brim of his cup.

She gripped the sides of the chair. "But... but... you mean... you mean we must leave! Leave here?"

"*Me lamento*, under the circumstances," he drained his coffee cup with a snort. "But that's how it is. I do not believe your son has the experience to farm in the manner of your husband. And besides I have plans for Los Rubios." He leaned back in the chair. His glare alarmed her. "I'll leave the document with you. As you will see you have until the thirty first of December to make alternative arrangements. A little more than three months!"

He hauled himself out of the chair. Then he tucked the satchel under his arm and threw back his head. His mouth was open and that gold tooth flashed at her. "I bid you good day."

Carlos Daroca marched towards his gelding waiting near the fountain. He stood on the upturned bucket and heaved himself into the saddle with a long hiss, flicked the rein and cantered out of the gates.

He'd done it. And it had been easy. There was no question about it, they had to go. And so did that young buck. Away from Lavega, out of Anita's reach. And a middle-aged widow with a wayward son did not have a very good prospect of getting another farm. So far as he was concerned he wouldn't be giving any landowner a reference on their behalf. He spat into the hedge.

Yes, he sucked contentedly on his gold tooth. This would get rid of that young fucker once and for all. He spent a fortune on Anita. He knew it would cost him to get her away from Madrid and all its temptations but he hadn't brought her here to fuck with this young foreigner. He'd brought her here to bring up his son. But... there was no sign of an heir yet.

Trynah sank back into the chair as the sound of hooves faded away. Her thoughts stampeded to every corner, every nook and cranny, the ceiling, the doors, the windows, the mantelpiece.

Leave Los Rubios after all these years! She went through the scene again, slowly, trying to recapture every word until she felt quite faint. It was all cut and dried! The documents had been prepared. There had been no discussion, Daroca had other plans for the farm.

She found herself at Robbie's desk in the alcove under the stairs. A pencil had been thrown across an invoice. A coffee cup stood on an old envelope and the ledger was open. It was as if he'd just gone to attend to a problem in the stackyard.

"Oh, Robbie, what am I to do? This is all you worked for. Years of dedicated labour to give me a home." And she was swept into that terrifying ocean of grief again sobbing for her man, for Richard, for Pedro, for Maria, for Los Rubios, for all the friends in Lavega. They were all part of the life that had grown from the desolation of walking out on her husband. Dear Bladon.

Remorselessly she was dragged through the anguish of that bright spring day when she had hurried out of The Pyewipe to the unknown. To rural Spain of all places! Robbie had made such a good life for her in Lavega. She tore at her thick hair. He's gone... he's gone... She fell forward cross the desk, cradling her head in her arms. "And we have to leave."

She didn't know how long she'd been stretched across the desk but she felt stiff when she straightened up. She stared at the wall in front of her. In fact, it wasn't a wall. It was the stairwell but Robbie loved having his desk here. He said it was like working in a cave. It was primordial.

A letter peeped out from a pile of invoices. She recognised Vinny's bold, square writing. The last letter which had arrived on the morning of Señor Daroca's fiesta and she had only read it once.

"... it threw us all into terrible confusion. No one knows why he should have changed his mind on the morning of the wedding. You can imagine the state we have all been in worrying for Billie but she has remarkable tenacity and continues as if nothing happened. One piece of good news is that Becky and Oliver are very happy. They are settled in their little terrace house at the bottom of Ketsby Hill. Curtis is as well as can be expected. His old leg bothers him a good deal but we both have much to be thankful for. We miss you and send our love as always. Awaiting your next letter with impatience. God bless and keep you all."

The letter slipped from her fingers and drifted to the floor. Once again she was swept back to the half-forgotten years: Vinny arranging the clandestine meetings with Robbie after coming face to face with him in The Pyewipe, herself in that little bedroom where Vinny had nursed her back to sanity after Redfern's outrage. She scooped up the letter and read it again and then in a flash she knew what to do. She reached for a piece of paper. "Dearest Vinny..." After she had finished the letter she started to make an inventory of what was left of the livestock. Richard and Pedro would check it and help with the list of farm implements: carts and wagons, swathe turner, plough. Then there were the feedstuffs, the wheat and oats and hay in the granary that had survived the flooding, always valuable at this time of the year before winter. They should make a good price. Next she listed the furniture in every room in the house. They couldn't take it with them. They would start completely afresh in England. Her energy soared and gave her undisputed confidence. Her plans were unstoppable.

Richard. He was as Spanish as the Spaniards. And he had never been to England, experienced the food or the weather. But he was young and adaptable. And Cantabria was not such a far cry from Lincolnshire with its rolling hills and fertile valleys. That's what Robbie had told her at King's Cross station. And there was plenty of space for Richard to ride. He would like Lincolnshire.

Her mood was so positive she had got the farm and household effects sold up and was mentally packed and ready for the journey home within a few hours of Señor Daroca's visit.

She left the alcove and went to the front window. Her eyes swept across the courtyard to the fountain and then up to the beech wood. The grave now wore a pale green veil of new grass. Her heart missed a beat and she collapsed into the chair, sobbing quietly.

* * *

"Come on, get dressed." Richard buttoned his shirt. "I didn't know it was so late. The sun's right over."

"Give me a pull up then," Anita held out her right hand. He took it and she pulled him down on top of her. "You see you can't leave me, can you?" She was stretched out on the tartan blanket lying flat on her back, legs wide apart. Her jodhpurs were draped across the log in the corner and Richard had hung her cream satin knickers on a little green twig near the broken window.

"You tricked me. I don't like being tricked." He scrambled to his feet. "Come on."

Realising the game was over for today, she stood up. "We can do this again, no?" She stepped into her knickers.

"You know we can always do this again and again. Whenever you say. Just give me the word. But always remember you've got a husband. And he has a whip."

"Yes. I've been thinking of something different. I told you about it." She yanked on her jodhpurs. "A weekend in Santander when he next goes to Madrid?"

Richard pulled on his riding boots. "Santander! You mean – to a hotel?"

"Why not?" She tucked her cream shirt into her jodhpurs. "And the Casino is opposite."

"But I'd have to get things organised with Pedro because of the work now that... And I haven't got any money."

"Don't worry, I have money. Remember my husband is rich."

"When do you think he'll be away again?"

She fastened the cuffs of her shirt. "Never can tell. Spends more and more time away doing business, making money."

"But you like money."

"Of course. But I like you just as much. Come here." She put both arms around his neck and kissed him.

"Anita. I must go. I'll leave first just in case anyone is watching." Richard took Brisa's reins. "Up that steep path through the chestnut wood and over the top."

Anita combed her hair with her fingers. "I go in the opposite direction. Down by the river. *Hasta pronto.*"

Richard urged Brisa along ducking his head as he brushed past the young trees on either side of the path, climbing all the time. He could see daylight as he approached the edge of the wood. Then he saw someone partly hidden near a thicket of ash saplings.

"*Holá,*" a stocky little man stepped on to the path, barring the way. Brisa came to a halt in front of him and snorted.

"What's the matter?" Richard had seen him before. The baggy grey trousers, the dirty green shirt seemed familiar but he couldn't place him.

"Get down," he spat sideways into the bushes.

"Let me pass." Richard touched the reins.

"I said, get down," and the man reached for Brisa's bridle.

"Who are you?" As soon as Richard stood in front of this man he remembered. He'd seen him wandering around the valleys and hills at Lavega. And he'd seen him in El Paco's Bar. It was Daroca's shepherd.

"*No importa.* I think we should have a serious chat. But friendly, you know." He gave a half smile and clicked his tongue several times.

"What on earth are you talking about? Please get out of my way."

"I'm talking about Señor Daroca. And I know where you've been." Daniel sucked every word slowly. "And Señor Daroca has a whip."

Richard took Brisa's bridle and made to lead her on.

"Oh, no," Daniel pulled back his lips showing discoloured, square teeth. "Now he would be very, very angry if he knew that you'd been fucking his wife this afternoon, wouldn't he?"

"Mind your own business. Let me pass." Richard yanked on the bridle.

"No. I'm a poor shepherd. You can keep me silent." A jay high in the trees gave a raucous, mocking call.

"What do you want?"

"Fifty thousand pesetas." Daniel's head went back, his lips parted and he clicked his tongue again.

"*What!*"

"Fifty thousand pesetas. Cash."

"And if I don't have fifty thousand pesetas?" Richard swallowed hard.

"Find it!" Daniel shouted. "*Comprende?* In one month. Here. At the same time. If not…" He clicked his tongue again, "Señor Daroca will fry your balls. Good day to you."

He stepped off the footpath. "Remember the whip! Here. Same time." He called over his shoulder and disappeared amongst the trees.

It was half past five when Richard rode into the courtyard, shaken by his encounter with Daniel. During the ride home he had calculated that fifty thousand pesetas was about five thousand pounds. He had less than ten thousand pesetas and mother had no money to spare, English or Spanish. It was needed to replace the lost animals and repair the flood damage. And old man Daroca might increase the rent in December. But Daniel meant business. As he put Brisa's saddle over the standing he got the answer. Anita. She had money, lots of it. She was always talking about it. He'd have to see her soon. That dreadful man meant what he said. The money must be paid.

He thundered into the kitchen. His mother was stirring the pan, her hair was a mess and he could see that she'd been crying again.

"Pedro asked me to tell you that he's fed the horses and gone home." Trynah took the cutlery from the drawer. "If you want him that's where he is. Did you find everything all right?"

Richard washed his hands at the sink. "What do you mean?"

"The boundary fences. I thought that's where you'd gone. To check. Is there any damage? You never know what goes on at the farther reaches of the fields and woods, especially those out of sight."

"No." Richard's voice faded. "Everything's fine. That smells good."

"It's *concida montañes*. Well, the ride has certainly brought colour to your cheeks. Come along now, supper's ready and I've got something to tell you." She placed the dishes on the table. "Whilst you were away I had a visitor."

"Oh. Who was that?"

"Señor Daroca."

Chapter 12

Lincolnshire. October 1920

Lavinia Pike was in the front parlour of her cottage in Church Lane putting the finishing touches to a winter skirt for Miss Dawson. It was cut on the bias and had been very troublesome but it was now ready and Vinny would be glad to see the back of it.

She heard the garden gate squeak. It needed a spot of grease and Curtis had promised to see to it. But his memory wasn't as good as it used to be and she didn't like to nag, so the gate squawked every time anyone came. It was the postman fighting against the cold east wind. She was at the door before the letter fell to the mat.

"Look! Look!" Vinny bustled into the kitchen. "It's from Trynah." She flopped into a chair, ripped open the envelope and began to read.

Curtis was sitting opposite leafing through the Grantham Journal spread out on the table, munching an apple.

"Oh, oh..." Her eyes raced across the pages. "Oh, my goodness, me." Her voice faded. "Oh, good gracious."

"What is it?" Curtis tossed the apple core into the grate and folded the newspaper.

"Here. Read it." Vinny passed a page to him. "Oh no. It's dreadful news. Robbie's dead." She passed him the last page. "He's drowned, Curtis." Her voice seemed not to be connected to her at all. "But Trynah's coming back! Coming back home. Oh, Curtis," and Vinny covered her face and choked with sobs.

"Come now, " as he hobbled around the table and gripped her shoulders. "Easy now."

She wiped her face with the pinafore. "Sit down, Curtis. I'm fine. It's just... it's..." and she put the kettle on the hob. She made tea and they sat at the kitchen table, reading the letter over and over again, passing the pages forwards and backwards until they knew every word.

"Bladon!" Curtis said the name calmly.

"Oh my Lord above! What does it all mean?" She clawed her face with her hands. "With him alone at the inn now that... since Hannah. Imagine if he gets to know. And what about Billie and Becky?"

"No need to tell him or anyone." Curtis shuffled the pages of the letter together and put them back in the envelope.

"Trynah's never mentioned him in her letters. Not once."

"No, and we've never said a word to her about him. And she knows nothing about Hannah. Being his house-keeper, I mean." She fanned herself with the edge of her pinafore. "It was a sort of unspoken pledge, wasn't it, as if The Pyewipe no longer exists. Suppose she had to wipe it out of existence considering what she'd done. If she'd asked, we would've told her. Never in all the years did she mention Bladon or The Pyewipe and now... Pity we drank all the brandy. Have some more tea, Curtis."

"I must get another bottle. Thank you." He pushed the cup and saucer across the table.

"Anyway, Trynah belongs here. And it's time we had her back. But... but... Bladon! What about him? What if he gets to know? Someone will see her and identify her."

"After eighteen years? Huh!" Curtis stirred his tea quickly. "Anyway, she's entitled to live anywhere she fancies. It's a free country."

"Let me read it again." Vinny's eyes skimmed over the pages. "She wants us to find a house to rent. She says there'll be money from the sale and she'll open a bank account when she gets here. Oh, my! And it's an ill wind that blows nobody any good." She glared at the black marble clock. "We shall have my dear sister back home, and we shall have her son. Fancy that! A nephew." She took the cups and saucers to the sink. "She says she'll telegraph us as soon as they're at Dover. About the fourteenth of October."

She squinted at the calendar dangling next to the toasting fork.

Then she groped in the top drawer of the dresser for a pencil and put a large ring around the date. "Heavens above. That's in ten days' time." Vinny clapped her hands. "We're going to be busy, Curtis. There's no time to lose." And she hurried to his side, leaned over and kissed him on the lips. "Oh, what joy. Trynah coming home, after all this time... with her son. Now, where's the Grantham Journal? Let's look for some accommodation. And we must tell Abby and Robert. They'll to want to come to the station. Not sure about Lydia. You know what she's like, a proper little madam if ever there was one. But Billie and Becky." Vinny was walking about the kitchen with quick little steps, to the window, back to the sideboard. "What are we to do about them? They were very fond of Trynah."

"True. But she walked out, deserted them."

"Time heals." She paused by the window and turned. "But if Billie knows Trynah's back she'll be sure to tell her father. Then stand by!"

"Leave it alone, Vinny," Curtis bowed his head, staring at the floor. "We're not telling anyone at The Pyewipe."

"I'll write to Robert and Abby today." Suddenly she froze in the middle of the kitchen. "But, Robbie. Robbie won't... be... here! She put her hands to her face shaking her head.

* * *

The next day Vinny and Curtis were leaning on the polished mahogany counter in the office of the Estate Agents on the corner of Elmer Street.

"Now Mr Pike..." the man with shiny black hair, shuffling through papers had not understood what they were asking for.

"No, it's not for us," Curtis explained. "We're looking for a house to rent on behalf of my wife's sister. She's arriving in England shortly."

The man scanned them over rimless spectacles, then puckering his lips he sifted the papers and passed over the details of four properties to let.

Two days later they were back at the Estate Agents and the skinny, nervous man was leading them up the two steps into a quiet sunlit office. A stocky, red-faced man got up from a big desk with nothing on it but a large blotter. He was wearing tweed plus fours and polished brown brogues. His square head, tufty eyebrows and shaggy moustache suggested that he ought to be in uniform.

Vinny was ushered to a seat next to Curtis. The room was impressive with an ornate fireplace and glass-fronted bookshelves on two sides of the room. Ledgers were stacked on a table in one corner, French windows gave on to a vast expanse of lawn fringed with flower beds and at the far end she could see a high wall. The garden was completely secluded. It was enchanting and she was only half listening to the Estate Agent explaining about tenants' rights and inventories and dilapidations.

Curtis signed the intention to lease a detached house on Fonaby Road in the name of Trynah King. They took the keys and spent the next two days making the echoing shell of a house look like a home.

"It's not a bit like our house at Apsley, nor The Pyewipe," Vinny stood in the middle of the front room, arms folded in front of her. "Perhaps as well. But she's sure to recognise some of my ornaments and vases. I'll bring flowers when we know the exact date. Trynah and Richard can make a fresh start here."

* * *

At Flaxwell the annual Autumn Fair for the School for Blind Children was in full swing. It was a cosseted, pampered red brick edifice. Cosseted because it was secluded and pampered because it suffered no interference from anyone or anything, hidden amongst the trees at the end of a curving entrance drive. It had a dozen tall windows looking out over wide manicured lawns at the front. Stables and outbuildings clustered around a large cobbled yard at the rear.

Every year Robert and Abigail Jacques and a multitude of helpers transformed the disused coach house for their fund raising event. This erstwhile country mansion had accommodated blind children for more than twenty years. Many of the children came as newborn babies, never knowing their parents. Others were abandoned on doorsteps, in buckets, in ragged bundles, under trees, or under carts in farmyards.

Robert Jacques, the principal, had met Abigail Bishop when visiting his cordwainer, George Bishop, who made all his boots in those days. She was one of three daughters and was only the second case of hypertelorism that he had seen. She was a classic case. An abnormally wide forehead forced the eye sockets to point in lateral directions. There was malformation of the nose but a perfectly formed mouth. She was a lively and exceptionally intelligent young woman, tall, with a regal bearing. She had intrigued him. He wanted to get to know her better, and he did. He suggested that they walk together so that he could build her confidence.

"You like to read, Abigail?"

"Yes, father has always encouraged us. Newspapers, and books." They were strolling along the green lane at the side of the church, her tall, willowy body leaning forward slightly. "I'm so thankful that dreadful Boer war is over. The horror of it all!" She paused under the canopy of trees and looked in both directions. The lane was quiet and deserted. He had noticed that she was totally relaxed when there was no one around. Of course it was that face. That's why she hid herself in the workshop helping her father make boots.

"It's sad Queen Victoria couldn't live for ever." She turned, tilting her head and smiling at him. It was a mannerism he grew to love. "And we now have a new king. Pity he's so old but he'll be wise, don't you think?"

"Yes. He's had little opportunity to prove himself but I think he will be good for us." The breadth of her knowledge astonished him given that she scarcely stepped across her doorway into the village.

"And the new Education Act is wonderful, isn't it?" Her face lit up. "Just think, all children will be able to learn to read and write now."

During these walks he had encouraged her to stop and talk to the children and chat with the villagers. She trusted him and she blossomed as he knew she would. He then offered her a position at Flaxwell, which she accepted. A year later, he proposed and they married. He was forty-two, she was twenty-three.

This year the theme for the annual Autumn Fair was Egypt. Lydia had reluctantly agreed to sell raffle tickets dressed as Cleopatra.

The coach house was hot and crowded and noisy and she would rather be in her room playing jazz records. Her father was chatting with the vicar near the largest pyramid. It was built of poles and straw and was beginning to look tatty. Bits fell off every time someone brushed past it. She waited until they had gone into the tearoom and then slipped away through the door at the rear, past the harness shed through the kitchen and along the corridor.

"Hello, Lydia!" Abby called. "How are you getting on with the tickets?"

Lydia went into the small office next to the deserted classroom. "I've sold quite a lot but I'm bored with it."

Abby looked up from the papers. "That's acceptable, my dear. You needn't sell any more if you don't want. You did so well last year with the Victory theme I thought you might like to do better this time. You look lovely in that gold and purple. It's most becoming. That's why people are buying tickets from you."

Lydia ignored the remark and wandered around the office, scrutinising the notices on the green baize board.

"Where's Billie? Can't she help you sell the tickets?"

"She's helping on the hoopla stall. Says she doesn't want to dress up. She rode over. Fancy riding all the way from Ketsby!" It peeved Lydia that Billie could ride. "She should've dressed up for the Fair. Everyone else does but oh, no, not cousin Billie."

"Well, you can go to the hoopla stall and sell your tickets there. You and Billie always get on well together."

"Of course we get on well together." Lydia watched as her mother shuffled the papers. "And I was sorry for her after the jilting by Steven Donner. I introduced her to all my young men."

"Yes, I know you did. That was a very nice gesture," Abby tapped the edges of the paper into a neat block on the polished desk, "helping her to meet more friends after what she went through. It must have been a terrible ordeal..."

"Now they're like bees round a honey pot." Lydia pouted. "Can't understand why. She always wears those horrid riding breeches, and she always smells of farmyard."

"Now, that's not a very kind thing to say," Abby's eyes blazed at Lydia, "and I'm sure there are enough young men for everyone. Please don't sulk Lydia, it doesn't suit you. By the way, this came today." Abby passed the letter to Lydia. "It's from aunt Vinny."

Lydia read it quickly. "Hmm. aunt Trynah? She's the one you've told me about, the one I've never met."

"Yes, my youngest sister. There's been an awful tragedy. Your uncle Robinson has died, so they're coming home from Spain."

"Who are 'they'?" Lydia rasped the letter against her fingernails.

"She and her son, Richard." Abby pushed the papers into a file. "Trynah and Robinson left us a long time ago."

"But why did they go to Spain?"

"It's a long story. I'll tell you all about it one day." Abby slotted the folder into the top drawer. "It'll be so exciting to see Trynah again after all this time."

The last time Abby had seen Trynah was when she visited The Pyewipe eighteen years ago. She had wanted to tell her sister that the ugliest woman in the world was carrying Robert's child. She had prayed that she would not give birth to another fish face.

"My dear Abby," Robert sat her on the velvet sofa in the drawing room, "hypertelorism is not congenital. It's caused by a fright, a severe shock. And the morning sickness will pass. All will be well, my dear." Robert had been right. Lydia was perfectly beautiful. And as this capricious young girl grew up Abby had taught her the cordwaining skills she had learned from her father.

"None of us have met Richard. I can't wait for them to arrive."

Lydia tossed the letter on to the desk. "Yes, someone new to meet. How old is he?"

"Seventeen. The same age as you."

"Ah, there you are Lydia. I thought you were selling raffle tickets." Robert Jacques strolled into the office and placed two leather bags full of cash on the desk. "From Mrs Higgs on the cake stall and Mrs Dodd on the hoopla."

"Hello, father. I got bored."

"You get bored too easily, Lydia. It's a most worthwhile job you're doing for the children. And you look charming in that dress. Do go and sell more tickets."

"Don't chide, Robert." Abby smiled up at him with her head on one side. "At her age she's entitled to get bored. If you don't want to help Billie on the hoopla stall why not do some cordwaining? You always find that satisfying. I did."

"If I go to my workroom everyone will come and gawp at me," complained Lydia, twirling the tassels on her gold braid belt.

"Of course they will." Abby went to the window. Some children were swinging on the low boughs of the yew tree. "No one makes shoes these days."

"Did anyone watch you working leather, mother?"

"No," she kept her eyes on the children playing in the tree.

"Well then, you don't know what it's like. And they all ask stupid questions." She leaned on the edge of the desk pulling at her tassels.

"That's because it's so unusual to find a lady cordwainer." Abby collected the pencils strewn across the desk and put them in the leather beaker. "In fact, there are few gentlemen shoemakers now. Boots and shoes have been made in factories for years."

"I don't care, I'm not going to do any shoe-making today. I'm going to my room." And Lydia swept out of the office with a rustle of silk and pattered up the broad red-carpeted stairs.

Robert sank into the chair at the side of the desk. "What can we do about her boredom?"

"Nothing. She'll grow out of it." Abby patted his hand. "Besides she isn't really bored, she just doesn't like helping at the Fair. There's never any boredom when she's doing something she likes."

"I suppose you're right." He leaned back in the chair, crossed his long legs and began to wag his foot.

"I don't think we shall see any more of her today." Abby returned to her desk and thumbed through the pile of invoices. "These are all ready."

"Thank you." His long fingers flicked the edges of the papers. "I'm afraid not. She'll be playing that infernal racket on the gramophone. By the way, do you know who she was with yesterday?"

"I think it was that young man with awful teeth, son of one of your governors. I can't remember his name. You know, the one that has a motor cycle."

"Ah yes. And I don't want her riding on that dreadful machine." Robert picked up a pencil and studied it. "They have these things called flapper brackets, a sort of pillion, and the rider hangs on behind. It's ridiculous and it's not safe..."

"Well, you know Lydia as well as I do. She will have her way." Abby put the file in the drawer. "But I'm quite concerned at the number of young men buzzing around her."

"Well, she's young and pretty. No need to be concerned, dear Abby."

"I suppose not. Now, what about some tea and then we must go back to the coach house for the lantern show."

* * *

A malicious east wind swept through Grantham station snatching at hats, tugging at coats and leaving an invisible icing on the faces of the passengers thronging the platform. It created shiny little globules on the end of their noses. It bit their ears and it made everyone cry abstract tears. It was relentless in its pursuit of discomfort.

The station was bustling with people arriving and people leaving. Several children were poking their fingers into a large wicker basket full of pigeons. Porters trundled up and down the platform. Whistles blew to split eardrums. Engines belched out smoke to choke the elderly.

Abigail, Robert and Lydia Jacques were already at the station when Vinny and Curtis arrived. It was almost two months since they had all met at the wedding of Becky and Oliver.

Vinny was surprised that Lydia had come. Her niece only did things that pleased her and Vinny didn't think long-lost relatives would be on the list. She was all dressed up in a beige wool coat and a hat that was too old for her, but she was turning every head on the platform.

Of course, Billie and Becky should be here too, and she felt a pang of guilt. They didn't know their stepmother was arriving in England today. The stepmother who had walked out of The Pyewipe without so much as a goodbye hug.

"This is quite exciting. Meeting an aunt I've never seen." Lydia bounced up and down in her shoes as if she were on springs. "I'm longing to hear all about Spain. Imagine Spain!" And she twirled around on the heels of her shoes, flapping her beige gloves across the palms of her hands.

"And there's someone else you've never met. In fact, none of us have ever met Richard." Robert Jacques stood tall and aloof looking down his long nose at the comings and goings on the platform.

Yes, thought Vinny, he's lost none of his seductive powers. As the spiteful wind sliced past her face it took her thoughts back through the years to her father's workshop, to Robert Jacques having his boots fitted. And she remembered how he used to linger at her side.

"Good morning to you, Lavinia. How charming you look this morning." This tall, handsome man was always saying things to make her heart beat faster until she had been consumed with an extravagantly foolish passion for him. She hadn't comprehended that this man with the pale eyes beguiled every woman in the village, from nine to ninety. She had never forgiven him.

He stretched his long neck and frowned as he peered along the railway track. "Ah! Here it comes." The big, black engine loomed into view, coughing and complaining as it rumbled to a halt. Doors flew open and the platform became a hustling, bustling mass. Slowly the passengers unravelled and filtered through the barrier.

At the far end of the platform a tall woman and an equally tall young man were talking to a porter.

"There they are!" Vinny shrieked as she waddled along as quickly as her legs could carry her. "Trynah!"

They were clamped in each other's arms, swaying and weeping. They disentangled and Vinny brushed away the tears with the back of her gloved hand. Then it was Abby's turn.

Trynah scanned the faces from the past. Vinny looked older. The years had furrowed her brow, burdened her jawline and saddened those unforgiving eyes. They had the same look Trynah remembered in father's workshop, after his funeral. And the unholy row between Abby and Vinny came screaming back into her consciousness and there it was, still etched in Vinny's face.

She turned to Curtis. The years had weathered him, twisted his once upright body and as her sister had said in her letters, that old leg was troublesome.

Abby had not changed much. A fulfilled woman who had learnt to live with so much scorn heaped upon her.

And Robert. Well, he too, seemed as arrogant and confident as ever. The years had passed over them kindly, leaving an imprint here, a disappointment and heartache there.

"And bless my soul, this must be Lydia," and Trynah swept her niece into her arms.

And so the reunion ran its course of hugs, and kisses, and squeals and tears and fluttering of white lace handkerchiefs. Trynah scanned the faces again and felt a deep pain. There was no Billie or Becky. And no Bladon!

Richard waited, balancing first on one foot and then the other, glancing up and down the platform, not quite knowing what to do as the group of relatives performed a ritual dance around him.

"Oh, I'm sorry, Richard," his mother was sniffling into her handkerchief. "Let me introduce you. This is my sister, your aunt Lavinia, we call her Vinny, and this is your uncle Curtis. This is my son, Richard."

Richard bowed his head slightly to Vinny who was wiping her plump cheeks. Then he shook hands with Curtis trying not to stare at a piece of wood protruding from his left trouser leg. "And this is my sister, your aunt Abigail. We call her Abby."

During the journey from London his mother had told him about her sister's facial deformity and now he understood why she had been so keen for him to know, to prepare him for the shock but he could never have imagined anything so horrible as this.

He stared into a face so ugly, it was frightening. The bridge of the nose formed a triangle of thick flesh on a wide forehead. The nostrils had been forced apart and were little balls of flesh. This monstrous face was topped by thick, black hair streaked with grey, and the eyes were in the wrong place, on the side, rather like a fish. The face was wrinkled and sagging. It didn't look human, but looked like a white rubbery mask.

"May I introduce my husband Robert?" Abby smiled, turning to the tall man at her side.

Richard took the bony hand and stared into a long, arrogant face with the strangest eyes he had ever seen, colourless and watery, spent of all life. His dark hair was going silver at the temples and there was a haughtiness about him that he didn't like. The strength of the old man's grip defied the frailty of his slightly bent body.

"And this is our daughter, Lydia." Robert Jacques stepped aside.

Richard was not prepared for the vision standing in front of him. She was tall and slender and supple. Her hair was jet black, glossy and fine, cut in a bob with a fringe. A little turned-up nose perched above rosebud lips, which she had painted bright red. And he was not prepared for the most unusual eyes he had ever seen. They were her father's eyes but the light and life had been transferred to his daughter. They were grey and sparkling. Her face was as perfect as her mother's was disfigured.

And he was not prepared for the soft hand that closed over his, or the smile that made the world sing. She seemed to be made of gossamer, floating, taking him with her to wherever they were going. Chords thrummed deep within him. Then everyone disintegrated until there were just the two of them on the platform at Grantham railway station gazing at each other.

* * *

The luncheon party had been arranged by Vinny and Curtis in a private room at The Angel and Royal Hotel.

The waiter hurriedly removed the two place settings that were not needed. Robert and Abby had excused themselves.

"I'm afraid we really do have to go." Robert tucked his long fingers inside the lapel of his coat.

"Yes," Abby was slightly flummoxed. "Do hope you'll understand, Vinny"

"Of course. Pity you can't stay for the party but its understandable." Vinny's mouth drooped. It wasn't at all understandable but she wasn't going to create a scene. For the first time in eighteen years they had their sister by their side with a handsome son none of them had ever met and they couldn't join the luncheon party! That old black ball of hatred and anger was alive and well deep in Vinny's stomach. Abby always managed to spoil everything, be at odds, be different.

Richard was placed between Lydia and Curtis. Waiters ushered in plates of food. The wine waiter hovered, filling glasses that were already almost full. The conversation soared and zoomed and shrieked with the recapitulation of long forgotten escapades.

"Do you remember that time..."

"Father was very angry..."

"And you came home wet through..."

The room bounced the happiness from the crimson walls, from the sombre oil paintings of cavaliers and kings. It twirled and swirled taking every memory, waltzing to the ceiling, the corners, pausing in front of the large ornate gilt-edged mirror.

"You know, Richard," Vinny's cheeks were flushed and shiny, her eyes glistened, and her speech was just ever so slightly slurred. "There's more to come. You have other cousins and friends to meet."

"Oh, yes." Curtis was drinking ale now. He found the wine too acid. "The Grantham girls are fair and fine. But don't cross them."

"*Claro que no,*" the wine had thrown Richard back into Spanish. "*Nunca haría tan cosa.*"

Lydia placed her hand on his wrist for a moment and then withdrew it. "Do tell me what you're saying."

He turned to gaze into those beautiful eyes. "I said I wouldn't do such a thing. I wouldn't dream of crossing a Grantham girl."

Lydia returned the gaze, lips parted, half smiling. "What language did you speak when you were in your house?"

"English mostly, wasn't it mother?"

"Yes. We spoke Spanish with our friends and helpers, but we spoke English at home."

"Is that why you don't have an accent?" Lydia was leaning on the table, hand cupping her cheek, studying this unusual young man.

"I don't know. About my accent, I mean." Richard turned away from the arresting stare. "Who else do I have to meet?"

"Well, there's Billie and Becky..." Vinny felt a light rap on her left ankle.

"All in good time," Curtis switched the subject quickly. "Tell me about this place. What did you say it was called? Ladruga... something."

"Lavega," Richard announced. "Well, there's a lot to tell. What do you want to know?"

Trynah cleared her throat. "I think it's time we vacated the premises." She could see the waiters hovering, fiddling with the white cloths over their arms. "You'll have plenty of opportunities to tell your cousin everything."

"Of course you will," and Lydia squeezed his arm.

Chapter 13

Motor cars, motor cycles and charabancs choked and spluttered as they chugged up Fonaby Hill. The garden was overlooked by the neighbours and there were rooftops everywhere. Everything was hustle and bustle after the tranquillity of Los Rubios, and Richard longed for the valley and rolling hills of Lavega.

"I want to ride again, mother." He stood by her side in the airy kitchen, looking across the garden. It was neat and orderly with rows of flowers. Little shrubs punctuated each corner. Not like Los Rubios where the flowers and plants grew wherever they decided, between the rows of potatoes where a careless bird had wiped its beak, or near the water butt, where there would be a clump of wallflowers and a burst of lilies in the hedge next to the chicken hut.

"Well, we're here now but we do need to live somewhere quieter than this. And that wretched dog next door will drive me mad with its barking. I've got details of a house to rent at Apsley." She took potatoes from the sack and put them on the kitchen table. "That's where I grew up, you know. It's my village. Would you like to come with me? I'm going to see it tomorrow. We'll take the carrier's cart."

"Don't think so. I want to find out what there is in Grantham. And I want to explore everywhere in time, Apsley, Ketsby, Flaxwell."

She took a saucepan from a hook. "Of course, it's all new to you, isn't it? I suppose we never appreciate what's under our noses. Grantham enjoyed great wealth from corn and malt and sheep."

"A thriving market town will be a novelty after sleepy Lavega." He picked up a potato.

"You can help to peel them if you like," Trynah offered him a knife.

He took it. "I miss Los Rubios." But his last rendezvous with

Anita had been terrible. At his suggestion they had ridden to Lesaya, a valley three kilometres from Lavega. There was a dilapidated shed crouching under brooding rocks with a broad river hurrying through the ravine. They were sitting on a boulder gazing at the little waterfalls splashing over the stones.

"All right. What is this big problem you have brought me here to discuss?" She tweaked his ear. "How can we have a big problem?"

Richard told her about Daniel in the woods.

"*Cojones*! Fifty thousand pesetas," and she sprang to her feet, whacking the riding crop against the boulder. Then she faced him, hands on hips. "This is too much. Carlos will get to know."

"But what could I do? Captive on that pathway..."

"You should not have dismounted." Now she was screaming at him with a voice he'd never heard before. "You should have ridden past him. Past that... that farting old shepherd."

It was the first time he'd seen her lose her temper. She could be sulky but now he saw the fury, the hatred boiling inside her.

"Anita, you don't understand..."

"No, I don't." She took a few steps towards the river bank tapping the whip quickly across her thigh. Then she turned. "And now you want me to find this money to give to... to... this stupid man. Just because... just because you were a coward."

"That's not fair, Anita." Richard strode towards her. "I am *not* a coward..."

"*Mierda!* You are a stupid, foolish coward." She spat each word slowly. They were now face to face, eyes burning into each other and then she did an alarming thing. She pressed her riding crop into his throat. "Well, *you* can find the money."

"Anita, I've told you." He pushed it away. "I haven't got any money..."

"Then get it from somewhere. Get it and settle it before you leave. *Comprendes?*" And she marched over to Pepita and mounted. She gave him one last scathing glance and galloped away.

He rode home slowly, his eyes on Brisa's mane, trying to decide what to do about Daniel. There wasn't any money to give him. It was as simple as that. He pushed the anxieties to the back of his mind. Tomorrow was the farm sale and all they wanted was a fine day.

The farmers and villagers came from miles around to look for a bargain. Richard watched as all the familiar pieces that had been his home were trundled away on carts and trolleys and old prams. And then there was the hurried departure from Los Rubios.

"It's unbearable, Richard." His mother was gazing at her fountain, still sparkling in the autumn light. "The empty yards and buildings. We must leave, there's nothing to stay for now. I shall go to Serona this afternoon and enquire about a passage to England. I can't stay a moment longer in this ghostly place."

When she got back he was surprised that she'd been able to make the arrangements so quickly.

"We leave next Tuesday for Santander."

And that was that. He didn't see Anita again and he did nothing about Daniel. Anita, the shepherd's hut and Daniel slipped beyond his horizon. It was all over with Anita.

It had been hard saying goodbye to Pedro, who had promised he would write with Lavega news as soon as they received an address in England. He didn't see Maria. Pedro said that she'd gone to visit an aunt at Peinosa.

"Say goodbye and good luck to her for me, will you Pedro?" And once again guilt swept through him as he stared at this solid little man who had been such a friend over the years.

The train journey had been an endless vista of towns and villages and countryside rolling past the window. His mother didn't chat much during the journey. Once or twice he saw her take out her handkerchief to dab her eyes. He hadn't done anything to comfort her. The compartment had been full and he hadn't wanted to draw attention to her sadness.

The overnight stay at the Spanish frontier had been a welcome rest. The incessant rattle of wheels on tracks had made his head ache. People coming and going, with luggage trunks, bags and bundles, everyone on the move. Such a restless world after Lavega.

Pangs of regret had overwhelmed him as he leaned on the boat rail gazing at the bewildering sea. Regret that they'd left Los Rubios. It was all that his father had worked for. He should've done more to help instead of spending so much time with his pals in Serona, and Anita. He'd spent a lot of time with her, riding and fucking. Yes, if he'd helped his father more perhaps it would all have turned out differently. No, he argued. Nobody could have stopped the flooding. No one could help his father in the river. And old man Daroca got rid of him and his mother at a stroke, the greasy old bastard. It was not a bit of good going over that again. And now here he was in Lincolnshire with its cold east winds, its damp air, its strange food and a lot of fresh-faced pretty girls.

He dropped the peeled potato into the saucepan.

* * *

Trynah had noticed that Richard didn't like to do things with her. Important things. He hadn't gone with her to Serona when Robbie had died, but he was young and he probably wanted to keep death at a distance. And she was disappointed that he didn't want to involve himself in choosing their new home. He'd set his mind on a riding school but it all cost money. The stock and furniture and implements at Lavega had made a good price but she knew he would never be happy until he had a horse. And he would have to get a job.

She glanced across the familiar countryside as the carrier's cart made its way down Brothybeck Copse and drew up outside The Fox and Hounds.

Turning into Church Lane she walked up Gomm's Hill. It was here she had fallen in the ditch and sprained her ankle. And it was here Bladon King had been passing in a pony and trap and had rescued her and married her a few months later.

She arrived at a bold, red brick house standing alone protected by a spinney of trees. There were double entrance gates and a trim little drive swept past the front door and out on to the road again past a narrow garden skirting a half-moon lawn. Clematis and rambler roses climbed an archway at the side of the house. At the back was a big, square yard with stables and sheds and beyond them, a vegetable garden and paddock. The nearest neighbour was half a mile away

Wind Cover House was spacious, a bit too spacious for two people but one day Richard would marry and there would be children. It was a far cry from Los Rubios. The house sat on top of a hill and not in a valley. There was no Pedro or Maria or... Robbie. But she must look to the future. Huh! That's what her sisters had said when she married Bladon all those years ago and here she was, staring future in the face again.

She stopped in her tracks on the garden path. Bladon! Just a few miles away. It was as if time had been suspended, waiting for her return, Bladon at The Pyewipe. Nonsense. Bladon didn't sit around waiting. He just got on with his life.

Vinny had never ever mentioned him in her letters and she had never asked about him. It would not have been fair to Robbie. Perhaps he had divorced her. Perhaps she had been pronounced dead or he had remarried. The magnitude of events clustered together filling her mind, rolling on like a huge boulder, destroying people and things in its path.

Anyway, it was all in the past. Almost everything that had given her life meaning was in the past, except Richard. He had his whole future ahead of him. She wandered back down Gomm's Hill and found herself in the main street of Apsley. It had changed little. She paused to gaze at their old house. Its solid walls looked as safe and secure as when she had lived there. The little wrought iron gate hung open as it always did. One of the hinges was rusted through. The japonica bush was now very dense and had grown to the level of the window sill. She and Vinny were often in trouble from father because they used to push each other into it breaking its prickly branches.

She longed to see the front parlour again with its large bay window and padded window seat. She wanted to see the homely fireplace, the red velvet drape and above it the big picture of the Monarch of the Glen that had been such a favourite with her father. He loved to lose himself on those windswept moors.

And mother. She always sat on the left hand side of the fireplace with the ornate little sewing table at her elbow.

And Vinny scampering down the broad stairs, squealing and giggling as she chased Trynah to the old gnarled apple tree at the bottom of the garden. There she would tell her about Robert Jacques who was due any minute for a boot fitting. Poor Vinny. She was sure Robert was in love with her but he turned every head in the village and the final blow came when he married their sister, Abby. Yes, this is how it all used to be.

Over the front door was a sign, 'General Store'. She pushed on it and a bell on a hook shaped like a question mark jangled on and on. Trynah paused just inside and waited until the bell stopped clanging. But there was no hall and there was no hallstand with its little bevelled mirror in which she used to glance before answering the door.

Her eyes skimmed across a long room and she realised that the wall between the front parlour and the workshop had been knocked down. A mahogany counter ran the full length of the room.

The front bay window was the same but the padded seat had gone. She and Vinny would sit there on a wet afternoon, kicking the wall with their boots until mother scolded them.

Shelves laden with jars of sweets and packets of tea and cocoa looked over the shoulder of a scraggy man with grizzly, colourless hair. He was serving a lady wearing a long brown coat, which was too big for her. Another lady whose face was muffled in the fur collar of her coat, was squinting at a packet of tea. The only thing Trynah recognised was the rack in the far corner where the boots ready for collection used to hang. Shiny, new saucepans and kettles now glinted from it.

Suddenly the customers and the grocer faded. The wall was rebuilt. It was the workshop. The old enamel clock dangled from the boot rack and she could see her father standing at his workbench staring out of the bare window that was never allowed curtains. She watched him turn and shuffle through the slivers of leather like a carpet of autumn leaves. He plumped up the cushion on the customer's chair. He was always doing that. Then she saw her sisters in the workshop, screaming and shouting at each other after father's funeral. And then she remembered opening the front door to Bladon who had come to win her hand.

"Is there anything I can get you?" The man gripped the edge of the counter with his spindly fingers. He raised his brow and the steel-rimmed spectacles were lifted a fraction up his long nose.

The two ladies had gone and she was alone in the shop. "Oh – er – yes. A quarter of mint humbugs please."

The apprehensive little man fixed his watery eyes on her and then turned to reach for the jar.

"I used to live here," Trynah proffered the information but the man was concentrating on the black and white sweets, checking the scales, trying to get the exact weight. Take one off, no, put it back. Then he slid the sweets into a bag and with an expert flick of the wrists handed it to her. "Anything else today?" His brows were furrowed again.

Yes, there was something else. She would like to see her parents and sisters, here in this house, to hear their voices, hear their laughter. That's what she would like most of all. She stared into the feeble eyes and a cold, inhospitable wind swept around her.

"Thank you. Nothing else." She handed him the coppers and hurried to the door. She felt relief as it closed behind her, the bell jangling on its hook again.

That was a mistake, she told herself as she strode towards the carrier's cart waiting outside The Fox and Hounds. Never go back. Times change. You just had to move with the changes. We must go forward. It was not the cordwainer's house, her father's house, which she had just visited. It was the General Store.

The journey home overwhelmed her with memories of journeys she had made in sadness and happiness as the carrier's cart clopped along the road past such familiar sights as the Ring Dam, where Robbie had proposed to her, Brothbybeck and Apsley Rise Wood. She was surprised to find herself at Fonaby Hill so quickly.

Richard charged into the kitchen as she was preparing supper.

"And what have you been up to?" Trynah noticed his flushed cheeks.

"Exploring. Smells good."

"It's *lebaniego*. Every time you come back you say you've been 'exploring'. But where?"

"You wouldn't understand, mother."

"What wouldn't I understand?" She placed the dishes on the table.

"It would only worry you. By the way, that girl who met us at the station, you know, the daughter of the ugly woman. What does she do?"

"The ugly woman is my sister, Richard. She was born like that. She's your aunt Abigail." Trynah glared at him. "Please be respectful. And Lydia is her daughter."

"Sorry I didn't mean to be..." He stopped eating and put down his knife and fork. "But she is ugly, isn't she?"

His mother saw his cheeks redden. "Yes, and she knows it. Pass the salt please. Lydia helps her mother and father with the blind children, and she has her own workshop."

"Workshop!"

"Making leather goods. She can make boots and shoes too. She's a cordwainer, like my father was. Whatever you've been up to this afternoon it's been good for your appetite. Would you like some more?"

"Yes, please. And I think I'll go and see Lydia's workshop."

"First things first. We must get our home settled. That house at Apsley is just what we need. It's a bit breezy at the top of the hill but nicely sheltered by trees. The Estate Agents are waiting for an answer." She placed the dish in front of him. "Now, just what've you been up to this afternoon?"

"If you really want to know I've been exploring the taverns. From the railway station to the market place."

Trynah froze with the dish in her hands. His roving eye and dynamic energy were going to get him into more trouble if he wasn't careful. Now she knew what had given him the sparkle, the appetite. Most of the taverns provided facilities upstairs for the half-crown girls. Yes, it's time they went to Gomm's Hill. Five miles from Grantham and very quiet.

Chapter 14

Richard agreed to view Wind Cover House with his mother. He liked it. There was no traffic here and although it was a bit isolated it was only a short walk down the hill to Apsley where there was a blacksmith, Mr Ross, and an inn.

It had been so difficult parting with Brisa but she would be well cared for at Las Candelas stables. He must have a horse then he would be free to visit his uncle and aunt at Flaxwell. Not that they had impressed him very much. Uncle Robert was a frail old man with eyes like dead tadpoles, and aunt Abigail – well, he'd never seen such a face in all his life. She gave him the shivers and yet there they were with a beautiful daughter, Lydia. That's why Flaxwell was at the top of his list.

Wind Cover House had been neglected and there was a lot of clearing up to do but relatives came to help. The names his mother and father had talked about in Lavega now had faces and bodies. There was aunt Vinny, plump and puffy, with a cloud of fair hair piled on top of her head. She would stare at him when she thought he wasn't looking, biting her bottom lip. Then she would wipe her brow and grumble about her rheumatics as she helped mother around the house. They didn't look much like sisters. Mother was thinner and more energetic and she had dark hair with a bit of grey. He watched and listened as they laughed and giggled and chattered like magpies sweeping and dusting and polishing everything in sight.

Then there was uncle Curtis stamping in and out of the sheds. His mother hadn't told him that he had an uncle with a wooden leg. It fascinated him and he longed to ask what had happened. Richard marvelled at his uncle's ability to lead such a normal life hobbling along on a bit of wood.

One day they had been disinfecting the stables and sheds. From time to time Curtis would pause, smack his lips together and ask questions. "Did everybody in your village have a horse?"

"Oh, no. Most of the people in the village are badly off." Richard leaned on the broom handle. "Most of Spain is poor. There was trouble all over the place. In the south there were land seizures by the peasants but they didn't affect us much in Lavega."

"Huh!" Curtis pulled two apples from his pocket and offered one to Richard. "Was there plenty of fresh milk?"

"Thank you. Yes. There was cow's milk and a lot of goat's milk and goat's cheese. It's strong and a bit smelly. But I like it."

"Did they grow wheat?"

"Yes, but it didn't fetch a very good price. Too much American wheat coming in. It was fertile arable land in the valley but we were surrounded by hills. Most of it was pasture for grazing." Richard came to the conclusion that uncle Curtis knew a lot and never complained about anything.

"Uncle Curtis, I need a horse." Richard pushed the wheelbarrow into the corner.

"Go and see Tom Ringrose. That's his farm just up the road, half a mile away." Curtis threw his apple core over the hedge. "Tell him I sent you. He's got a good eye for stock, knows what he's talking about."

The next morning Richard made his way to the neighbouring farm and found a sturdy man carting manure from the crewyard. There had been a sharp frost during the night and the muck looked like lumps of coal tinged with silver.

"Is it Mr Ringrose?" Richard introduced himself. "I need a good horse to ride and Mr Pike suggested you could give me some advice."

Tom Ringrose wiped his forehead with the sleeve of his threadbare jacket, pushed his lips forward and squinted at the pale face. "You're not from these parts, are yer?"

"Well, yes and no," Richard kicked the heap of manure at his feet. "My mother used to live in Apsley before..." He was going to say 'before my mother left Apsley, before my father drowned, before we had to leave Lavega, before I had to leave Anita'. His eyes came back to the ruddy, weathered face of Tom Ringrose. "Well, we're back. We've moved into Wind Cover House."

"Ah, I 'eard that new folk were coming. Been empty for months." Tom cleared his throat and spat over the crewyard wall. "You're a bit willowy for the country life but you seem to know what you're about." He stabbed his fork into the pile of manure. "Well, it's the Horse Fair at Armtree next week. That's where you want to be. Something for everybody there. Me and my missus allus go so if you like we can all go together in the trap. Bring your mother and father. It's a good day out for the family."

"My father's dead." Richard looked down at his boots then his eyes went to the tottering barn and the thick ivy gripping the stone walls of the pigsty.

"Oh... Oh!" Tom Ringrose took off his battered old felt hat and shook it for no reason at all. "I'm sorry." With one hand he put it back on his head and pulled it down to his eyebrows. "Bring your mother. She'll enjoy it."

When Richard returned he found his mother in the kitchen standing over a boiling saucepan.

"How nice! Inviting complete strangers like that. But people around here are kind and friendly. You'll like them Richard."

"So will you go mother?"

"Yes. But first of all I think we must get to know Mrs Ringrose. I'll invite her for tea."

Mrs Ringrose was a stout bloated woman with mauve cheeks and a mass of unruly faded curls, which seemed too heavy, causing her head to sink into her neck. She glared at everything with eyes that trusted no one and rarely smiled. But his mother was pleased to make a new friend and they both decided that they didn't want to go to the Horse Fair. They would make jam with the last of the blackberries instead.

* * *

A week later Tom Ringrose and Richard were trotting along the lanes with Bruno pulling the trap. It was a cold sharp morning with a frost crisping the grass verges. As they got closer to Armtree the road was crowded with ponies and traps, horses in boxes, charabancs full of families and villagers on foot. They followed the crowd into the field that sprawled away up a rolling hillside.

It was a seething mass of wagons and caravans and women and children and barking dogs. A horse-drawn dray carrying rolls of lino, carpets and shiny new pots and pans joined the party. Someone was cooking food. The smell of bacon and sausages wafted across the field. Richard had already eaten this mish-mash of an English breakfast only an hour ago but he could manage it all over again. It smelt so good.

Young men and old were yelling and shouting as they scrambled to find a good vantage place to picket their horses. Tom pulled up under a knotty oak tree halfway up the hill close to the dense hawthorn hedge. "Here we are. This will do. We're away from all that razzle-dazzle."

They wandered amongst the rows of horses tethered on rope halters held by stout men and skinny men in their frayed caps, faded jackets and threadbare trousers, who rested their backs against tree trunks and leaned against their caravans, while others stood in groups around their animals.

There were draught farm horses, slow and clumsy and contented, three year olds with undocked tails tripping over their first set of shoes, hunters with plaited manes and silken coats, thoroughbreds, half breeds and hollow skeletons destined for the knacker's yard.

"Surprised they bother to bring 'em. If the inspectors see 'em they'll be in big trouble." Tom moved on. "Now what about this beauty?"

Richard went to the head of the dapple grey. A stockily built man wearing a red spotted kerchief sidled up to them.

"How old?" Tom asked.

"Three years."

"How much?" Richard met eyes so small they looked like black pinheads.

"Four hundred guineas."

"Out of my reach," Richard patted the flanks and moved away. "Let's go and look over there."

The owner grabbed Richard's elbow pulling him back. "How much then?"

"I can't come anywhere near that price. Besides I'd need to try her first."

A short distance away three men were sitting on a ladder laid on its side, each with a rope leading to a horse. Richard spotted a chestnut gelding. "Look at him! I'd no idea there would be so many to choose from?" There were men and horses for as far as the eye could see. "I think we need some refreshment before deciding."

"Come on, there's a beer tent over there." Tom edged through the crowd of people.

They passed the brightly painted wagons of the Romany showmen with the hurdy-gurdy blasting out its raucous music. A gypsy fortune-teller in layers of frills, beads and bangles sat at the entrance to her tent. She reached for Richard's jacket. "Step inside."

There was bowling for a pig, and one enterprising man had nailed a dartboard to a tree – "Get a bull's eye and win a canary!" A man was handing out leaflets at the entrance to a small tent, and a large placard invited people to step inside to see 'The Living Wonder'.

"Come and see for yourself." He tossed a quiff of lank black hair out of his eyes. His navy blue serge jacket with gold epaulettes and the broad red stripe down his trousers gave him a military smartness. "It's a real live man. Only sixpence. You'll never believe it. Step this way."

Richard turned to Tom. "Shall we go and look?"

"If you like. No telling what's inside. Probably a stuffed turkey, they're up to all sorts of tricks. But I like his uniform."

A space had been roped off inside the tent and in the centre sitting on a brocade cushion on a chair was a man. Friendly eyes gazed at the people staring at him. He had no legs, not even stumps. His lower torso was in a black serge bag. A matching jacket had been made with short sleeves and little pink stubs of fingers could just be seen a few inches below his shoulders. To complete the incongruity a gold chain adorned his waistcoat and a white handkerchief peeped out of his breast pocket. The man was about three feet tall and looked like Humpty Dumpty.

"Good afternoon ladies and gentlemen," the freak's voice was quite normal. "Please take a leaflet. It tells you all about me. My name is William Day and as you will see I was born without legs and arms." He paused. There wasn't a murmur from the crowd watching.

"It bewildered my parents and doctor and several leading physicians. But nature having prevented me having limbs, has given me instead a good brain, which I can rely on." William Day slowly turned his head, addressing the sea of faces.

"I can dress and undress and I can feed myself. My daughter makes my shirts with tight fitting sleeves and my eating fork is slipped into this little pocket. Here, take a look if you wish." And his eyes went to the cuff of his right sleeve. "I can use carpenter's tools in my mouth." The round face creased into a smile to show serrated front teeth. "And I can read and I write with the pencil in my mouth." He paused as if expecting a denial from someone. "Thank you for coming to see me," and the little man smiled his benign smile.

Richard turned to Tom as they filed out of the tent. "It had to be seen to be believed, didn't it?"

"It were weird, especially when he spoke so ordinary. Poor sod. Fancy having to earn a living like that. But with no legs and precious little to call arms what else can he do? It's a rum 'un." Tom elbowed his way through the crowd. "Come on. Time for a drink."

As they approached the beer tent they saw a crowd of people in a clearing under the trees. An excitable young horse was bucking and rearing and lashing out. It had thrown its rider and was prancing round and round in triumph.

"Stay mounted, bareback for five minutes and the prize is yours!" the swarthy young man hollered at the circle of onlookers. His face was hard and solid as if chiselled from a block of mahogany. "Come along, now. Five pounds for the rider of this magnificent fiery steed. Who'll take my challenge? Ah! There we are. Come along, sir."

A man stepped forward. He was in his thirties and several pints of beer had given him confidence. The young gypsy held the horse and the challenger leapt on to its back, grabbing a fistful of mane. The horse went mad, bucking and rearing and kicking. Within seconds the man was sitting on the ground, his knees under his chin. He picked himself up, rubbed himself down and staggered away to the beer tent.

Someone else decided to have a go, a much older man. The crowd whistled and hissed. "No, no, granddad. Save your bones."

"I've bin dealing with 'osses all me life," he called over his shoulder to no one in particular. "I can master 'im."

Again the horse went crazy with the weight on his back. The old man couldn't maintain his grip. His wrists were not strong enough now and he fell to the ground, rolling away from the horse's hooves.

"I'll have a go." Richard pushed through the crowd.

"No. No. You'll never hold him." Tom grabbed Richard's shoulder. "He's been gingered up. You could break your neck. Let's go and find that beer."

"I'm going." Richard shook himself free and marched up to the swarthy young man. "Five pounds if I stay on the horse for five minutes. Is that it?"

"That's right. You stay on its back until I blow the whistle."

Richard paused at the side of the horse's head stroking his muzzle. "All right boy, all right," he whispered. Then he mounted the opposite way, facing the rump gripping the stifles on either side of the animal's flanks, lying across its back with his legs locked around the horse's shoulders. The crowd whistled and yelled and shouted at such daring.

The horse started careering around the small ring but Richard held tight. His legs were secure around the shoulders but it was much more difficult to keep his grip on the stifles. The hooves pounded below him kicking up the grass. He heard the horse snorting as it bucked and pranced and squealed beneath him, and he could hear the roars from the crowd. Then he heard the whistle. The five minutes was up. He slid from the horse and went to his head, patting his neck.

"Now who's next for the challenge?" The gypsy shouted to the crowd.

Richard tapped him on the shoulder. "Five pounds please. I won your challenge."

"No. You didn't win. You cheated. You didn't ride it in the usual way."

"I stayed on that horse's back for five minutes. Five pounds please." Richard felt his cheeks colouring.

Now the mob was yelling. "Give 'im the money! Give 'im the money!"

Then a lean, energetic man strode up to the gypsy.

"I watched this young man. He rode that horse for five minutes." The man was in his middle years, smartly dressed in a dark green riding jacket, jodhpurs and highly polished top boots. "That was your challenge. Give him the money." He tapped the gypsy's cravat with the tip of his whip.

"Bugger off." The gypsy pushed him away.

"You give him the money or I call the police. All these people are witnesses," stated the man, waving his whip in a wide curve.

The crowd roared. The gypsy pulled a five-pound note from his pocket, thrust it into Richard's hand and spat at his boots. Then he turned to the man wagging his whip across the palm of his hand.

"Now bugger off and mind your own bloody business in future. Fucking well interfering..."

Richard turned to his rescuer. "Thank you very much. Let me buy you a beer. Me and my friend here... Where is he? I've lost him. Ah, there he is."

Tom Ringrose emerged from a clump of bushes beyond the oak tree fastening his trouser buttons. "Well done, Richard, well done. That were some ride. You took a risk though, by guy. You took a risk. They're rum devils with 'osses – they put ginger up their arses, you know." Tom caught sight of the man following Richard. "Well, I'll go to Trent. Look who it is!" He slapped him on the back.

They all made their way to the beer tent. "You two know each other, then?" Richard pushed towards the serving table.

"Know each other?" Tom walloped his friend across the back again. "Known each other for years. Now this is the man to put you right with 'osses. What he doesn't know about them ain't worth knowing. This is Bladon King from Ketsby."

"How do ye do." Richard turned to the man with the whip. Beer, or would you like something else?"

"Beer."

The tent was full of noisy men slopping beer across the tables, down their jackets and down their breeches. They found a table in the far corner.

Tom turned to Bladon. "Richard and his mother have just moved to Wind Cover House, top of Gomm's Hill. Wants to buy an 'oss. He's seen a nice chestnut..."

"They think fancy prices here. Besides you need to ride it first," said Bladon as he took a long swig of his beer.

"That's what I said," Richard sat on the edge of his chair with his elbows on the table.

"Father," a lilting voice rang like a bell across the crowded, smoky beer tent. "There you are. I've been looking everywhere. You said..." A young woman stood over the table, hands on her hips. "You said you'd wait for me at the..."

"I'm sorry, but I knew you'd find me. Come and sit down. Let's get you a drink."

"Allow me," Richard jumped to his feet, knocking the table, spilling beer from the tankards. He stared into bright blue eyes that challenged him with a vague hint of mistrust. Then he scanned the trim figure in a cream shirt and dark blue jacket. His eyes came back to the smiling freckled face, the slightly parted lips, and the long, blonde hair. "What would you like?"

"Oh, let me introduce you. This is my daughter, Billie. And this is...What did you say your name was?"

Before dusk fell Bladon King, his daughter Billie, Tom Ringrose and Richard had tried five horses. Bladon had examined teeth, pummelled legs and tweaked flanks, checked for lumps and strains and he had ridden each one to listen for a roaring in the nostrils or a whistle in the lungs. The final choice was the chestnut Richard had seen earlier in the day.

"That was fun, choosing a horse." Billie smoothed a wisp of hair from her face. "You like riding?"

"Love it," answered Richard, standing close to her at the head of the chestnut gelding.

"So do I. It keeps me human."

"That's exactly how I feel about it. You seem to know as much about horses as your father."

She smiled and smoothed the wisp of hair from her face again. "Then you must come and ride over Bunker's Hill, at Ketsby, about three miles from here. That's where we live. And it's a good ride to Munce's Wood, too."

"I would like that. Once I get organised... with this beauty." He slapped the back of the handsome chestnut. "We're going to be great friends, aren't we?" Richard nuzzled the velvet nose. "And I shall call you Fiver."

"Why Fiver?" Billie had her head to one side, lips apart and he wanted to kiss them.

"Well, today I won five pounds on that wild horse owned by the gypsy. And today I found this magnificent creature, with your father's help. Lucky me."

The crowd was drifting away and only a few vendors hung about in the hope of a late sale to a gullible buyer. All the good horses had been sold hours ago.

Richard watched as Bladon King climbed into the trap and Billie scrambled after him. A horse drawn caravan pulled up alongside. The military man with gold epaulettes went into a tent and came out carrying a bundle, nursing it like a baby as he scrambled up the steps into the dark womb of the caravan. It was William Day, the Living Wonder.

Richard took the halter rope of his chestnut gelding and turned to Bladon. "Thank you very much for your help." Richard's eyes went to Billie sitting by her father's side. She smiled and smoothed that wisp of hair from her face again.

Bladon watched as the trap moved away.

"You know, Billie, that's a born horseman. It's a treat to see a young one riding horses instead of those infernal motorcycle machines. Wonder where he comes from?"

"Lives not far from Mr Ringrose. I've invited him over to ride." Billie glanced at her father. He was concentrating with the reins guiding Duke through the throng of people darting about from one side of the road to the other. "I can take him to Bunker's Hill and Munce's Wood. Do you mind, father?"

"Of course I don't mind. He seems a decent enough young

fellow." Bladon could not believe what he was hearing. Since Billie had been jilted by Steven Donner, her cousin Lydia had invited her to make up foursomes with young men in baggy trousers and suede shoes driving motor cars and motorcycles, who raced off to jazz concerts and War Memorial dances, smoking cigarettes and drinking some vulgar rubbish called cocktails. He was pleased that Billie was enjoying herself but it bothered him that he had never seen any of these young men astride a horse. But now she was going to ride with this young fellow who could handle a horse as well as himself.

"When is he coming?"

"I suggested next Wednesday afternoon. If that's acceptable with you."

"Of course," and Bladon started to sing through his teeth.

Trynah was in the kitchen when Richard and Tom turned into the drive. "I thought you'd got lost on the way." She went to the head of the chestnut gelding. "So you found him."

"Yes, he's magnificent. Have you ever seen such a colour?" Richard stroked the silky, tanned coat. "This is Fiver. Fiver, this is my mother."

"He's a beauty. You chose well, Richard."

"Well..." Richard hesitated. "I had some help. You see, we met this man, then on the way back we called for some hay. Mr Ringrose gave me some of his. That's why we're late."

"Well, come in both of you. Supper's ready. You must be starving."

"Thank ye kindly but I told the missus I wouldn't be long." Tom snatched off his Sunday best cap. "Just wanted to be sure we got home safely with the chestnut. So I'll be on my way. You know where I am if you need anything."

Over supper Richard gave an account of the day's events.

"And I won a wager. A gypsy had an unbroken gelding. It was

wild." Richard told the story. "The gypsy refused to pay me. But the crowd was on my side yelling and shouting and causing such a commotion. Talk about a fiesta at Lavega! It had nothing on Armtree Horse Fair. Then this man turns up and tells the gypsy that he must pay the wager or he would summon the police. That did it. The gypsy paid and we all went to the beer tent to celebrate. Then he helped me to choose a horse. There were dozens and dozens, mother, all shapes and sizes. You've never seen anything like it. Some were very expensive, but he knew exactly what to look for."

"Well, who was this man?" asked Trynah as she collected the dirty plates from the table.

"Mr King from Ketsby."

The plates slipped from her fingers crashing to the floor, scattering fragments of blue and white china to the farthest reaches of the kitchen walls.

"And to top the day's events his daughter turned up. Here, let me help you." Richard crouched on the floor next to his mother, gathering up the broken pieces. "She's a real beauty. And she's invited me to ride with her. My lucky day, eh, mother!"

"This man..." Trynah was sweeping the pieces into the dustpan. She sat back on her heels and stared at a leg of the kitchen table. "This man who helped you buy the horse. What was he like?"

"Oh, about fifty, perhaps. Thin rather than fat. You could tell he was a rider, something about him. Hair about the same colour as mine."

"We've got apple pie for pudding." Trynah's voice was a whisper. "Would you like some?"

Chapter 15

They thundered across the paddock at the back of The Pyewipe and on to the lane leading to Bunker's Hill. It was crisp with hoar frost and the breath from the horses wreathed into the cold air and evaporated.

Richard kept just half a length behind Billie. His eyes were on the slim waist, the curve of her back, the eager, forward thrust of her shoulders.

She wheeled left towards some farm buildings and soon they were in the stackyard, puffing and panting at the side of their horses.

"Let's water them," and she led Black to a trough near the cattle shed, then she was taking short, quick strides towards a sycamore tree. "Here we are."

They sat side by side on a fallen log. Her legs were stretched out in front of her, nonchalantly crossed, her shoulders back, breasts thrust forward as she supported herself on the log. She was wearing fine black leather gloves and with one little move he would be able to touch her hand.

A long field rolled down to the valley below with a white satin ribbon of water threading its way through the willow trees. With a stretch of imagination Richard could almost think he was back in Lavega. But this woman at his side was not Anita, she was younger, fresh, unused. And she was wary of him.

This was their second ride together. Last week they had galloped to the other side of the village to Munce's Wood. It was deep and dense and in the severity of a cold December afternoon it had majestic beauty.

"Do you like farming?" She picked up a twig and broke it into small pieces.

"*Claro que si.* It's all I've ever done but now... But it's different here."

"Tell me about it."

So he told her about Lavega, about the local school, the College at Serona then Los Rubios and the floods, his father's death, the loss of the livestock, the eviction and the return to England. But he did not mention Anita.

Last week they had only tiptoed around the pool of personal feelings, each longing to dive in, to explore, to know what had happened before this moment in time. Today he was more confident and so was she. He wanted to understand her wariness.

"I like to hear your bits of Spanish. But you won't be able to speak Spanish here will you?"

"Why not? Mother and I sometimes speak to each other in Spanish. And I can teach you, if you like."

"I would like that. Golly, you've done so much. Living in Spain. Speaking Spanish. What on earth are you going to do here? It'll be so boring."

"Lavega's a sleepy little place, like Ketsby. It could be boring. As I told you last week I would really like to start a riding school, but I've got to get a job. I'm not rich."

"Neither am I. But I don't ever want to be rich. I've seen the rich and I know what money does to people. They think it gives them power. Well, of course, it does but I think it also demeans and corrupts."

"That's a strange thing to say. What proof have you?" Richard had seen what money did at Dos Caminos. Carlos Daroca mangling and destroying lives with his cheque book, taking over any business he fancied, buying a sophisticated wife and dumping her in a remote valley. But Anita had been more than willing. She had confessed to him that she would do anything for money. She loved money. But it didn't make her happy. Gossip in Lavega said that she'd been a prostitute in Madrid but he didn't believe that.

"I don't have any proof, I just have my instinct to go by. And my experience." And Billie went on to tell him about Steven and the double wedding that didn't come off. It all came tumbling out.

"But... but that's terrible."

"Yes, it was ghastly." she kicked the turf with her boot. "Imagine it! Me standing there in all that finery and deserted... It was the humiliation really but once I'd got over that... Well, I realised I'd had a lucky escape. People were so kind to me." She tossed her head back and laughed at the sky. "His parents wanted a grandson, you see, to inherit the brewery fortune. Huh! Well, whilst he was courting me he was deceiving me. Of course, I had no idea. He fathered a child with a young widow who worked in the Brewery. Apparently she confronted him on the day of our wedding. That's why he didn't turn up." She was staring down the field.

"What a dreadful thing to happen." He wanted to take her in his arms, to feel her supple body. He wanted to love her, to make up for the hurt.

She got up quickly, rubbing her hands down her jacket. "Come on. Let's go. Father insists that you stay for tea this time."

"Thank you. Tell me," Richard hesitated, "tell me... is your father a widower?"

"I think so."

Richard followed her into the barn. It smelt of dead rats. "You mean you're not sure?"

"No, I'm not sure. We, that's Becky, my sister, my twin sister and me, well, we had a stepmother. Father loved her and so did we but she left when we were quite small. We missed her terribly after she had gone."

"Why did she leave?" They were standing in the gloom near the double doors. Richard reached for her gloved hand. The leather was smooth and silky and soft. She made no attempt to move away.

"Don't know. Nobody knows. Father doesn't talk about it." She put her other hand over his. "After she'd gone father had a housekeeper. She was such a nice person, and such fun. Always jolly. So good to me and Becky, but... but..." Billie stumbled on the words. "She died. It was an accident." Billie wandered across the dusty floor and paused near the corn bin. "You know... my father has had such terrible sadness in his life and yet he pretends he hasn't, if you know what I mean. You'd never guess, would you, that all these awful things had happened to him?

"No, frankly, I wouldn't." Richard moved to her side and caught a faint whiff of lavender. The heat of her body was exciting him and he wanted to touch her, embrace her.

"He buries himself in his work and uses up all his energy."

"Well, that's quite a good thing, really." Richard reached for her hand again and her fingers tightened a little. "Do you know what my father taught me? He told me never to preserve energy because there will always be more tomorrow. You know," he paused, "I was so lucky to meet your father... and you." He pulled her closer. This young woman was intoxicating him.

"Come on." She shook herself free. "We'll be late for tea. Race you!"

They cantered along the green lane towards Ketsby. Neither of them spoke but he was inquisitive about her father whose wife had disappeared. People in England seem to be more complicated than in Lavega. Perhaps his promised trip to Flaxwell would help him to get it all sorted out. Aunt Abby and uncle Robert would know the whole story. And Lydia. That's why he was going to Flaxwell, little to do with family history, little to do with his ugly aunt and strange husband, little to do with the leather workshop. He wanted to see Lydia Jacques again.

In Lavega there hadn't been a single girl to cause a murmur in his groins. Maria used to take him to the woods when he was a boy and he had idolised her. Then he got a taste of honey in Serona and forgot all about her until those last couple of weeks at Los Rubios. Her passion had taken him by surprise. She had been there all those years, under his nose, and had come to him without knickers!

And now here, in Lincolnshire, Billie King was taunting him to madness with her pretty face and freckles and the thought of Lydia Jacques dissolved him.

* * *

"So this young man wants to start a riding school, eh?" Bladon was sitting at the dining room table with Billie in a chair opposite. They were checking a pile of invoices. "That's a bit ambitious."

"I know. But he says he needs to earn money first and he hasn't got a job."

He sat back, tucked his thumb into his waistcoat pocket and studied Billie. "And you say he's been farming in Spain. Rum thing. Farming in Spain!" He got up, tugged at his waistcoat and started to pace the floor from the fireplace to the window. He paused and gazed on to the street. It was deserted except for Cadger Burrell's mangy old sheepdog sniffing along the gutter.

He returned to the table and shuffled the invoices. "Do you think he'd like a job here at The Pyewipe? It's only weeks to Christmas and we shall be rushed off our feet. We've always had Hannah but this year…" He saw again the crumpled body lying at the bottom of the stairs next to that wretched boy statue. It was a recurring image. If that statue had not been there Hannah would not have hit her head on it. And he still avoided going into the Back Room. One day he would, but not yet. Not until the image of Hannah on the trestle table had faded. Not until the ghosts had left.

"We don't know much about him." He pushed the invoices into the folder. "What do you say?"

"I like him, father," she replied as she reached for the wad of invoices from Pizer's Brewery. "He makes me laugh, and he tells me stories from Lavega. I like his outbursts of Spanish. I've no idea what he's saying… He's going to teach me Spanish." She leaned forward on the table, cupping her cheeks with her hands. "I think it's a good idea. Why don't you ask him?"

"I will. So long as you think you can get along with him. We don't want any upsets. You say he's got no father."

"No. He died in Spain. That's why they decided to sell up and return."

"And what about his mother?"

"Don't know anything about her. He's never mentioned her."

"Well, the best thing is for me to go and see them both. I want to talk to Tom Ringrose about that mare of his so it won't be out of my way. Now pass me those invoices Billie, no, not the ones in the folder. I've done them."

"Have we nearly finished?" Billie reached across the polished table and pulled the papers towards her.

"Won't be long." Bladon said, flicking through the bills. "Going somewhere?"

"I've promised to meet Becky for tea. We're going to that new cafe everyone's talking about. Lydia's supposed to be coming, too."

"Well then, you'd better get off. I can finish these on my own." He shuffled the papers together. "Give her my love. And find out if they need any potatoes. We've got a good crop. No need to be buying them."

Billie came to his side, bent over and kissed his cheek. "I'll go and change. I can't go like this. They say it's quite a posh place. 'Bye for now."

* * *

Bladon never allowed grass to grow under his feet and two days later he set off for Apsley. As he rode down the incline to Brothybeck Copse memories came flooding back. He turned in the saddle to gaze at the cordwainer's house he had visited to win the hand of Trynah.

A painted wooden sign over the front door read 'General Store'. He shrugged his shoulders and continued his way along Church Lane and up Gomm's Hill.

Tying Black to the gate at the side of Wind Cover House he went to the front door. He knocked and waited, then he knocked again. No one was there.

He wandered along the pathway through the archway at the side of the house and found himself in a large open yard.

"Hello, anyone at home?" He stood in the middle of the cobbled yard. No answer. He could see a vegetable garden. It was a sorry tangle of cow parsley and thistles. Beyond the garden was a paddock.

He decided to inspect the row of buildings. The first was a pigsty, empty. The large stable next to the forage shed was also empty. There was a washhouse and a dilapidated wooden shed next to it. He stood at the open stable door. The smell of disinfectant caught in his throat and he gave a dry cough. "Can't be too particular with animals."

He turned to look at the solid red brick house. There were no curtains at the kitchen window and he could see a clock on the wall.

"Nobody about," he said to the pigeon scratching amongst the cobbles. "Never mind. They seem to know what they're about. Clean sheds, good paddock. I'll give the boy a job," and with a flick of his whip across his left hand he strode back through the archway, mounted Black and rode away.

* * *

Trynah stood in the driveway. Richard was leading Fiver out of the stable. "And tell them we shall look forward to seeing them here when we get sorted out."

Richard sprang into the saddle. "I will. Now, tell me again. I can miss Grantham and go through the villages then take the Lincoln road..."

"That's right." Trynah patted Fiver's neck. "Flaxwell will be clearly sign-posted. Give them all my love." And he was gone.

She went up to the bedroom to sort out the linen chest. She was glad Richard was making an effort to get to know his relatives. He seems to be settling well. As she carried the clean sheets to the bed she thought she heard the sound of a horse. She went to the window. Standing on tiptoe she craned her neck but could only see the sleeve of a jacket as a man strode to the front door.

Who in the world would be riding to Wind Cover House to see her? No one had any business with her or Richard. They hadn't been here five minutes. There was another loud knock. Her heart was thumping. Probably a gypsy looking for work and things to steal. Or a vagrant. The countryside was full of the poor men back from the war with no job and a family to keep. But this man had come on a horse. Stolen perhaps.

Then she heard footsteps along the path at the side of the house. She kicked off her slippers and padded barefoot into Richard's bedroom at the back. Now she could see the man. He was standing in the middle of the yard with his back to her looking towards the vegetable garden and paddock. He didn't look like a gypsy or a vagrant. He was fair-haired, well-dressed, carrying a riding crop which he was tapping on his left palm. Then he turned to stare at the house. She stared back from behind the curtain.

"Aaah!" an icy cold wind squeezed her chest until she could no longer breathe. She leaned forward, gripping the window sill. Her legs gave way and she found herself squatting on the new, shiny lino. The echoes of his footsteps seemed to die away along a dark tunnel then a horse was riding through the same tunnel.

She wiped her brow, perspiring yet feeling cold. She heaved herself to her feet and flopped into the tapestry chair. She sat staring at the yellow rose wallpaper that Richard had chosen. Yellow for Spanish sunshine he'd said. Gradually strength returned to her legs, her thumping heart steadied. Gripping the banister she made her way downstairs very slowly. She found herself in the front room opening the sideboard cupboard, at the back of which was a bottle of whisky. She poured some into a glass and staggered to the easy chair by the fire, and saw again the flicking of the whip across the palm of his hand, the fair hair, the purposeful stride. There was no mistaking this man's identity. It was her husband, Bladon King.

Chapter 16

Richard cantered through village after village but at last he arrived at Flaxwell and was soon riding through the ornate gates, along the gravel drive to the big house hidden amongst the trees.

Lydia came running out to meet him. She was wearing a grey dress with long fringes that danced around her knees. "Hullo, I'd almost given you up."

"Sorry I'm late. Got a bit lost at Culbeck." His eyes were on the unusual rope of grey beads that cascaded between her gorgeous breasts. Everything about her was light and cloudy and grey and her eyes were greyest of all. A streak of lightning fired his body. "Can I put Fiver in there?" he asked, pointing to one of the stables.

"Of course. They're not used much these days." She danced from one foot to the other fingering the long string of beads. "It's motor cars and charabancs that bring people. Not many come in wagonettes now."

He led Fiver to the stable and unbuckled the saddle, then eased off the bridle and gave him oats.

"Horses are a bit smelly, aren't they?" Lydia was silhouetted in the doorway still twirling the beads.

"Do you think so?" Richard filled a bucket with water. "I don't notice."

"Come on, let me show you Flaxwell," and she led the way through the kitchen and along a corridor, whose walls were painted a dark, shiny green. "These are the dormitories," she tapped lightly on the doors as she passed, "and these are nurseries. Always full of babies." She turned left into another corridor. "And these are the classrooms, full of children."

Richard peered through a small, square glass panel at eye level.

"Most of them are blind or..." Lydia turned to him and grimaced.

He went back to the last classroom and peered at the children sitting bolt upright in their chairs, looking straight ahead listening intently to the tall, bony woman enunciating words slowly and carefully. "Oh! How awful. I didn't realise..."

They got to the end of the corridor and went through a door into a spacious carpeted hall with a sweeping staircase. Everywhere smelt of mothballs.

"There are some more dormitories up there, and our private accommodation." Lydia floated along in front of him, arms flung wide, the fringes of her dress rippling as she waggled her hips. "This way. Now I'm going to show you my workshop then we'll have lunch."

He followed her back through the kitchen and out into the yard. She pushed open a door into a small square building next to the coach house. There was a workbench in front of a window looking on to the stable yard. It was littered with small leather purses, belts, slivers of leather and tools.

"What's the bucket of water for?" Richard tapped it with the toe of his boot.

"That's for tempering the leather, to take the hardness out of it. It has to mull. Makes it easier to work with. Oh! I should have put these away," Lydia scooped up the awl and the moon knife and reached for a battered walnut box on the shelf. "Mother gets very cross if I don't look after my tools." She replaced each one in the compartments and secured the clasp.

"That's neat. Let me see." Richard examined the box of tools. "What are they for? All these things." He picked out an awl. "Ouch! It's very sharp."

"That's for piercing leather. Strictly speaking the tools are for making shoes and boots. This is a lady cordwainer's box. It belonged to my mother."

"Your mother made shoes?"

"Boots. Her father... my grandfather was also a cordwainer. But of course I never knew him. He taught her and she taught me."

"Can you make boots?"

"Of course! It's quite difficult. You need strong wrists. I've got strong wrists. And these are the tools you need. I haven't made any boots lately. I make these." She tossed an unfinished purse into the air. "For the Church bazaar, or our annual Fair. Whatever..."

"Will you make some boots for me? Riding boots?"

"If you like. I'll have to measure your feet and calves." She winked at him. "Come on, let's go. It's time for lunch. And then we can go for a walk." She led the way. "Or... or we can go upstairs and listen to some jazz. Father's in London today and he'll be very tired when he gets back. I've told him he's too old to keep going to London but he doesn't listen. And mother's got a meeting this afternoon. But I'm here." And with a toss of her silky hair she stopped and stood in front of him, lips apart, smiling. It made him quiver.

Lunch was served at a table in the bay window of the dining room looking over the lawns and naked trees. In spite of his early morning start Richard didn't eat very much. He was too aroused by this young woman. She never stopped talking. Her voice was like silver bells chiming and when she did pause for breath excitement continued to pour out of her. She was fluttering her eyelashes, smiling, taunting him until he hardly knew what to do with himself.

"Let's go upstairs," she suggested. Richard followed, his eyes on the fringes of her dress tickling her long sleek legs. They crossed the landing and went into a room. Everything about it was mature, established and it all seemed vaguely familiar. The smell of cigarette smoke lingered. He sifted through his memory but couldn't pin down the reason for the familiarity.

There was a roaring fire in the grate. The divan along one side of the wall was draped with a dark red blanket with a pyramid of small, square cushions at one end. In the window was a desk piled high with books. On a low table near the fire was a gramophone.

She bounced on to the divan and the fringes on the dress flipped above her knees. Her shoes fell off and she curled her feet beneath her. "No one comes here, only the maid to clean. Mother and father leave me alone. Besides, they're always busy."

Richard lowered himself on to the divan, his eyes roaming around the room. The deep red woollen rug and the heavy red curtains added to the warmth and sensuality. He had a sense of being closed in, wrapped in a blanket of intrigue, as if he were in a place from which he could not escape. His eyes went back to the curtains. Then he knew why it seemed familiar. It was a cleaner and smarter version of the room in Las Pecas where he had had the young prostitute on the night of the floods!

It was preposterous to compare a brothel in Serona with this room in such a prestigious establishment but Lydia had unwittingly created the same atmosphere.

"Now, I want to know all about Spain," She stroked her legs, gazing at him with those alarming grey eyes.

He was perched awkwardly on the edge of the divan. "What do you want to know?"

"Everything!" Smiling she reached for his hand pulling him towards her as she began to unbutton his shirt.

An hour and a half later he was buckling his leather belt. Lydia was pulling on her silk stockings. She twisted round to check that the seams were straight.

"Would you like some tea?"

"I really think I'd better be on my way, I'd like to be home before dark. I don't want to get lost again."

She opened her arms wide and stepped towards him. "Do you have to go?"

"Yes, I must. I really must," he unclasped her hands from behind his neck.

They walked down the stairs side by side.

"Is that you, Lydia?" a voice called.

"That's mother," Lydia whispered. "Yes, coming."

Abigail was sitting at the table in the window poring over a sheaf of papers.

"Hullo, Richard," she stood up. "I thought you would have been out walking on this bright, crisp day, but I can see that you're not dressed for that, Lydia. It's wonderful for December, isn't it?"

"We've been playing music on the gramophone," Lydia wandered to the window, "and I've shown Richard my workshop. He wants me to make him a pair of boots."

"I've never heard of a lady shoemaker and now I've met one. In fact, two." Richard glanced from Lydia to her mother. "I understand you were one once."

"Oh! That was a long time ago. There's little demand for custom-made shoes now but Lydia is kept busy with her few regular customers. Would you like some tea?" She put the sheaf of papers aside.

"Thank you. But I really must go."

Richard quickly harnessed Fiver and brought him into the stable yard.

"You will come again soon, won't you?" Lydia was fidgeting with her beads.

At the end of the drive he turned and saw that she was still waving.

He could remember nothing of the ride back to Apsley. The lanes were unfamiliar, the villages were new territory but Fiver seemed to recognise them all. As he galloped along the wind sharpened his thoughts. Robert Jacques was an eminent consultant, and Abigail, a clever and astute woman, everyone said so. Forget the ugliness. She was a match for anyone intellectually.

But Lydia! She had undressed him, seduced him and left him breathless. She was a young, unspoilt version of Anita. No, it wasn't quite right to say that. Anita was different, hungrier. But how many other young men did Lydia entice to her den to play the gramophone whilst her father was in London and her mother was at meetings? "You will come again." The voice rang in his head until he clattered through the archway at Wind Cover House and into the stable yard.

"I was beginning to worry about you," his mother was at the kitchen door. "It's dusk so early these days. Supper's ready."

"Good. I'm hungry." He glanced at his mother. She had been crying again.

"I'm glad the ride has sharpened your appetite." She brought the plates to the table. "By the way, I've written to Pedro. The letter's on the hall table. I've left it open so that you can give them your own news before I post it. We promised to let them have our address, didn't we? And we don't want to lose contact. What did you do today?"

"Lydia showed me the Home. It's terrible. All those poor children. Aunt Abigail was at a meeting but I saw her before I left. I didn't see uncle Robert. He was in London. And I saw Lydia's workshop. She's very clever with leather."

"Yes. Gets it from her mother and grandfather."

But Richard wasn't listening as he scraped his plate clean. All he could hear was Lydia's voice ringing out. "You will come again, won't you?"

Chapter 17

"I've got the job," Richard barged into the kitchen and threw his whip behind the door. "That smells good."

"Ready in about half an hour. What job?" Trynah took the lid off the dish and the kitchen was filled with the aroma of meat and thyme and garlic.

"I told you, mother. Didn't you listen? You know, Billie, her father keeps The Pyewipe. That's a funny name for a place isn't it? Pyewipe."

"It's another name for lapwing. Common in these parts." She glanced at Richard's bright, eager smile. She must tell him. He must know the truth. About Bladon, about her. She was afraid. Afraid his smile would evaporate and she would spoil it all. And yet...

"She said her father needed help in the stables, and well, just things generally." He leaned back in his chair and put his hands behind his head. "Asked me no end of questions, he did. Really it was to find out how much I knew about farming I think."

"So what is the arrangement?" His mother sank into the chair, her mind racing from Bladon to Richard to The Pyewipe. She could hardly believe what she was hearing.

"I work Monday to Friday, half-day Saturday. He knows I'll have to get to and from Ketsby, but that's no problem with Fiver." He rolled forward slapping his hands on his knees. "Mr King said he came to see you to talk about it, but there was no one in."

"I must have been in the village. Shopping." She swallowed the deceit.

"Isn't that great, mother? I've got a job. Now, I must take Fiver to the blacksmith. She lost a shoe coming home. Mr Ross says he can do it today. Shan't be long," and with a slap on the back of the chair, another on the kitchen door, he skipped across the yard to the stable.

She watched him from the kitchen window. She'd never seen him so excited. But he was going to work for her husband! She put 'her elbows on the table and covered her face with her hands and sobbed. Should she tell him? And what if Bladon found out that she was here, in Apsley?

Restless, she got up and walked slowly round the kitchen table wiping her eyes. What was she to do? Richard must be told. But Bladon! What was she to do about him? She glanced up at the enamel clock on the wall with its plain round face and clear black numbers. Vinny had given it to her. Vinny, of course. Yes, her sister had helped her through so many traumas. She'd know what to do about Bladon. She'd meet her for tea in Grantham. Yes, that's what she would do.

Half an hour later Richard rode into the yard, stabled Fiver and then he was in the kitchen.

"All done, then?" she asked as she shook out the red gingham cloth and put it on the table.

"Yes," He could see that his mother had been crying whilst he'd been at the blacksmith's. "He's very good, Mr Ross."

"Here we are then," and she placed the beef casserole and dish of vegetables on the table.

He noticed that she was just toying with her food pushing it around the plate. She wasn't eating. Then she stood up and circled the table, clasping and unclasping her hands.

"Mother, what on earth's the matter?" He put down his knife and fork and turned in his chair.

"There's something I have to tell you," she paused near the kitchen sink, grabbed the tea towel and stretched it into a long strip.

"Whatever it is can wait. Come and eat your supper." He watched as she slapped the tea towel from one hand to the other. "It will be cold."

Half an hour later they were sitting in the front room. The

curtains were closed and a blazing log fire made Wind Cover House seem a safe and comfortable place. The room was quiet and warm with the reassuring click of his mother's knitting needles and the occasional shuffle of logs as they collapsed into ashes in the hearth. Outside, the wind rampaged around the house, rattling buckets and window frames and whipping the bare trees.

She stopped knitting. "Mr King. Bladon King." She cleared her throat. "The landlord of The Pyewipe. You know, the man you met at Armtree, the man who helped you with Fiver... Well... He's... he's my husband."

A wind swept through him with such ferocity he felt as if he'd been pinned to the back of the chair. He got up quickly and walked to the door, turned and came back to stand over her chair but she didn't look up. "Mr King of The Pyewipe is your husband!" He was spitting the words on to the top of her head.

"Yes."

"Well then, mother." He collapsed into the chair and stretched his legs across the hearthrug. "Tell me how Mr King can be your husband."

"Before he and I were married... I was betrothed to someone else." She stretched the knitting and tucked it under her left arm. "I was to marry Robinson Mann. Two weeks before the wedding there was... there was an incident. A terrible incident, with his twin brother. Redfern."

"What kind of incident?" Richard was leaning forward in his chair, frowning.

"A serious, violent incident. And when Robbie learned about it he... he killed Redfern."

Richard sat bolt upright. "My father killed his twin brother!" he screamed, gripping the arms of the chair.

The knitting crumpled into Trynah's lap. "Robbie was condemned to death by hanging. In Lincoln Prison."

Richard started to prowl around the room again. He went to the sideboard, picked up the little cut glass dish, inspected it and replaced it on its crocheted mat. He went to the silver clock on the mantelpiece and stared into its face and then he sat in his chair and waited.

"Six years later I met Bladon King. We married on the fifth October 1901. One afternoon, in the spring of the following year, I was in the Club Room at The Pyewipe tidying up before a wedding when a man stepped from behind the curtains on the stage. It was Robinson."

Richard sprang out of the chair. "Mother, I need a drink. What will you have?"

"Elderberry wine, please."

He poured himself a whisky and sat down.

"So father wasn't hanged."

"No. With the help of an old lag in Lincoln Prison he escaped and fled to Spain. Another condemned prisoner, a Spaniard, gave Robbie a contact address, Señor Daroca in Lavega. And that's how he managed to lease Los Rubios. He worked hard to get things going and then came back to England to find me. At great risk, because he was still a wanted man." Trynah picked up her knitting again. "I then had to decide what to do."

Richard drained his glass and went to the sideboard to refill it. He turned to watch his mother fiddling with her knitting.

"And so you left your husband at The Pyewipe?"

"Yes." She did not look up. "Yes. I left my husband, my stepdaughters, my sisters, all my family and all my friends to be with the man I'd promised to marry."

Richard paced to the pale green curtains, touched them gently and then came back to the fireside. "Why couldn't you have told me all this before?"

"Because... because there seemed to be no need. We'd built a new life in Lavega. I didn't know Robbie would die. I didn't know that Señor Daroca would throw us out. We had nowhere to go. The only place I knew was England, Lincolnshire. Ketsby, and Apsley where I was born. Where I would find my family..."

"And your husband." Richard spat out the words.

"I did *not* know that I would find my husband. I've had no contact whatever with Bladon since the day... since the day I walked out of The Pyewipe. He didn't know where I was. I just left a note and disappeared. What else could I do? I couldn't tell him that Robbie was an escaped prisoner." Trynah's voice was shrill, tense. "On the run. Hiding in Spain! I couldn't tell anyone why I left. Robbie would've been caught and gaoled again."

Richard was watching the quick fingers dancing with the blue wool. "You deceived me for all those years at Los Rubios." He tore at his hair. "Did my father know?"

"Yes."

Richard locked his fists and clenched his teeth. "He knew you had a husband back in England!"

"Yes, Richard. He knew. But he left the decision entirely to me. I had to make the choice. To go with him or to stay in Ketsby." She looked up at him. "To leave a good husband, family, friends. Everyone and everything I knew and loved? Can you begin to imagine how a human being can arrive at such a decision?" Trynah was now shouting. "The anguish, the agony, the deception? No. Richard. You cannot. And I hope you're never in such a situation."

"So you were never married to my father?" He was striding around the room again, moving chairs, pushing the back of the sofa with his knees, pulling on the curtains. "In spite of the fact that you wore a ring!"

He punched the sideboard with such violence that it shook. "Really, mother, I think it's despicable. It was quite convenient for father to be drowned in Lavega, wasn't it?"

He picked up a dining chair and slammed it down with such force that one of its legs splintered. Then he stormed out of the room, through the kitchen and across the yard to the stables.

Chapter 18

"And he says he'll teach me Spanish," Billie lifted the teacup with both hands.

"That's exciting," Beckie reached for another macaroon.

"Don't you want that cream one?" Billie pushed the plate towards her.

They were at a window table in The Columbine. The walls were pale lemon with paintings of young girls in flimsy dresses dancing all around, arms outstretched, long wavy hair floating to the ceiling. In each corner, between the tables, was a large green shrub in a pot. The lights were pale lemon saucers, flush with the ceiling. The Columbine looked like a carefree summer day.

It was crowded. There were families with children on their best behaviour. There were old men and women with walking sticks hooked on to the back of their chairs, and there were women with baskets of shopping around their ankles. The room fizzed with novelty and newness.

"No thank you." Becky rubbed her tummy. "Got something to tell you."

"Ooh! What is it?" and Billie took the cream cake.

"First I want to hear all about – what did you say his name is?"

"Richard." Billie wiped cream from her bottom lip and sucked her finger. "I do like him, Becky. He tells me things about Spain. And he makes me laugh. Sometimes he forgets and runs into Spanish!"

"He's Spanish?"

"Yes and no."

"What on earth does that mean?"

"Well, he was born in Spain but his parents are British. Like us really," and Billie went on to relate how they had met at Armtree. "And now father's offered him a job."

"I'm so glad, Billie, after what..." She stopped. "Would you like more tea?"

"Yes please. He's so different to those young men Lydia introduces me to." She handed over her cup.

"Well, you know what a flirt she is. Never happy unless she's got some stupid young man wrapped round her little finger".

"I know she's met Richard. She told me so. But I mustn't be too critical of her. She's so kind to include me in her parties. Do you know what she said? She said always wear a hat and always get a young man with a car."

"You! In a hat!" Becky threw her head back and a peal of laughter rolled around the cafe. "That's really funny."

The family at the next table were gathering their bags and parcels together. She waited until they had gone then leaned across the table. "I think I'm going to have a baby," she whispered. "I've missed two. And I'm going to see Doctor Robb next Wednesday. Don't tell father yet, we don't want anyone to know until we're sure. It's our secret. Please don't tell anyone. And whatever you do, don't tell Lydia."

"Of course, I won't. That's wonderful! I'm so happy for you. I wonder what's happened to her. When I saw her on Wednesday she said she'd join us here. Probably got other things to do."

"Like flirting. Can I take the last one?" Becky reached for the macaroon.

"Of course."

* * *

"I thought it would be a change," said Vinny, peeling off her gloves and looking around the crowded cafe.

"The town's full. And I didn't expect Columbine's to be so

236

busy." Trynah pushed her shopping bag under the table with her toe. "I know you don't like coming into town on a Saturday but I was anxious to talk to you."

"It's hot in here. So many people! Everyone's raving about the place," her sister glanced around, pursing her lips. "Bit too bright for me."

"It is a bit," Trynah was sitting forward, twisting her wedding ring round and round her finger. "We're used to Burnett's cosiness. But I thought it less likely we'd see anyone we know here."

A waitress was at her elbow, poised with pad and pencil. She had a young, undeveloped body but her face was old before its time.

"Just tea for two, please. And cakes." Vinny smiled at the blank face but there was no response. "I quite like the little shrubs. Gives a garden effect. Well, now, how's everything at Wind Cover? Did you get the curtains up?"

"Yes, but... you'll never believe what I'm going to tell you..."

The waitress arrived with the tray. It was too heavy and she was awkward balancing its weight. Trynah waited until everything was on the table.

"What's bothering you? And leave that ring alone." Vinny inspected the cakes. "Doing too much at the house. I've told you I'll come and give you a hand."

Trynah leaned forward across the table. "It's Bladon," she whispered.

There was a loud clatter as a waitress on the opposite side of the room dropped her tray. It was the thin, unhappy girl who had just served them. Conversation was suspended, children were silent, pleased that they were not going to be in trouble for the mess on the carpet. There was a flurry of activity as other waitresses squatted to help clear up and then the chatter rose to a crescendo again.

"*She* won't last long," Vinny passed a cup of tea to her sister. "Now what about Bladon?"

"I've seen him."

"You've what?" Vinny spat out the words.

"He came to Wind Cover House last week." Trynah was sipping her tea quickly, her eyes on the green shrub in a few yards away. "There was no mistake. He was in the yard and turned to look at the house. He didn't see me, of course. I was hiding behind the curtains."

Vinny's cheeks coloured. "Lordy me. How on earth could he have known you were there?"

"He didn't know. Richard told me when he got home that he'd been offered a job at The Pyewipe. Said Mr King had ridden over to see me but that I wasn't at home. Oh, Vinny! Here we are again, in a bind. What am I to do?"

"Pass me your cup."

"What am I to do?" Trynah toyed with a piece of jam sponge. "Did you hear me?"

Vinny nodded. "There's a funny smell in here. Someone's bought fish in the market." She looked accusingly at the various bags of shopping at the feet of the people at the tables.

"Tell me. What am I to do? Richard knows. I just had to tell him." Her serviette was screwed up into a ball. "He was very, very upset. But what am I to do about Bladon?"

Vinny was concentrating on her chocolate eclair. Then she said, "He's your husband. You deserted him."

"But I never thought, never imagined Richard would meet him. And now he's working for him!" She paused. "And Billie. That's what's done it, Richard meeting Billie at Armtree Horse Fair."

"You know, Bladon was very angry when you disappeared," Vinny pointed out as she stirred her tea. "Ranting and raving. Getting drunk. Pestering the police. Then he seemed to settle down. Once or twice Billie and Becky asked me about you. They wondered where you were. I lied to them. Told them I didn't know where you were." She delved into a pocket for a hankie and dabbed her eyes. "Well, dear Trynah, this time I cannot advise you. I just cannot." She covered her sister's cool hand. "Do you remember what father used to say? "If you're not sure what to do, do nothing."

There was a loud shriek and all eyes went to a young woman as she sidled between the tables in a flurry of scarves and waving arms to get to the window table.

"Oh... Oh..." Vinny clutched her throat. "That's Lydia. And look. She's gone to join Billie and Becky."

Trynah turned slowly and peered round the shrub. She recollected Lydia immediately then her eyes were on Billie, her eager face bright with courage. Becky looked radiant. Trynah fell back in the chair. Her two little girls, now beautiful young women, with a lifetime lost in an abyss across a crowded cafe. "Oh, good gracious me," her voice faded and she reached for her teacup.

"Lydia will recognise us," her sister hissed. "Let's go. And remember what father said. Do nothing," and she swept the bill from the saucer.

* * *

"We'd given you up," Billie signalled to the waitress. "Thought you weren't coming."

"Well Rodney promised me a ride in his motor car and who could say 'no' to that?" Lydia flung off her coat. "So this is The Columbine!" She jerked her chair around. "Oh, look! Over there. That's aunt Vinny, and our new aunt Trynah. All the way fom Spain, with a delicious son. Have you met him?"

Billie's eyes went to the corner table. "You mean... you mean that lady over there, in the blue coat? With aunty Vinny..."

"Yes," Lydia peeled off her gloves. "Aunt Trynah. I love these," and she took the iced cherry tart. "Let's call them over. Find out where Richard is." She stood up.

But the two sisters were walking towards the exit.

"Oh, they've gone," Lydia sat down again. "Pity."

"Wait a minute." Billie leaned on the table with one elbow and fixed her eyes on Lydia. "Tell me again. That lady with aunt Vinny is... is aunt Trynah?"

"Yes. But I never knew her. Not until we went to the station to meet them. She's got a gorgeous son." Lydia popped a cherry into her mouth. "She's Richard's mother. His father died in Spain."

Billie turned to Becky who was waiting for her. They sat as rigid as statues, their eyes locked.

"More tea, Billie?" Lydia was poised with the teapot. "What about you, Becky?"

"No thanks. I really must be going." Billie picked up her brown paper package.

"Yes, so must I." Becky reached for her shopping bag.

"There's a dance at the Drill Hall on Saturday," Lydia licked her finger then wiped it on a serviette. "I think you should come Billie. It'll be fun. And Richard's coming, too."

"Thanks, I'll let you know." Billie scooped up the bill. "'Bye."

She took Becky's elbow and steered her across the street to the benches next to the statue of Sir Isaac Newton. "Let's sit here. We've got a minute before the bus. Phew! What did you make of that? Can't believe it."

"I feel quite faint." Becky held her tummy with both hands. "She's telling the truth you know."

"Yes. I think she is." Billie was tossing the package from one hand to the other. "But our mother! Our mother! I would've known her. Hasn't changed much. Her hair's a bit faded. Remember how raven black it used to be?"

"Yes, it was long and beautiful and I used to like twisting it." Becky scanned the throng of people coming and going on St Peter's Hill. "What are we going to do?

"About father, you mean? I don't know. He'll never believe it, will he?" Billie stared down at the package in her hands. "It happened when we got back from the outing. She wasn't there anymore. Do you remember? And she upset father a lot."

"No, I don't remember." Becky shook her head to confirm the denial. "But what are we going to do? Our mother is here. We've just seen her."

"Our stepmother, Becky. We never knew our proper mother." Billie was tossing the package from one hand to the other again.

"Yes, but she was always a good mother to us. I liked her but... Do you think we should tell him?" Becky watched the flower seller emptying the buckets of water into the gutter.

"Yes. We must tell him. If we don't and he gets to know he'll be very upset with us." Billie glanced up at the Guildhall clock. "Come on, or we'll miss the bus. I'll do it. As soon as I get home."

* * *

Bladon was slumped on a stool in the Clubroom in the alcove where he kept the harness. His head hung low, his fingers caressing the cork of the bottle on the floor near his left toe. His muddled thoughts were being marshalled by the brandy. They led him back into the Private Room where he had been two hours ago.

"I'm back, father," Billie breezed in waving a package. "That's the dubbin you wanted."

"Thank you," he threw aside the newspaper. "How's Becky?"

"Never looked better. We had tea at The Columbine. You know, that new place." She sank into the chair opposite, her legs spreadeagled. "Father, put the paper down. Listen to me, please. Our mother was in the cafe."

He looked over the top of the newspaper.

"Father, did you hear me?" She sat forward in the chair, elbows on her knees, cupping her cheeks with her hands. "Our mother. Your wife."

Bladon gripped the arms of the leather chair and stood up. The newspaper slid to the floor. "Now, Billie. What cock and bull story has someone given you?"

"No, father. It's true. We saw her. Becky and I saw her."

He stepped over the crumpled newspaper and paced the floor to the window.

"Lydia spotted them at a corner table."

"Who are 'they'?" He asked the window pane.

"Aunt Vinny and mother. Lydia said she'd met them at the station."

He came back to the fireplace and sat down, hands dangling between his knees staring at Billie. "How can this be?"

"Lydia was going to call them over but she was too late. They were already leaving the cash desk. Becky and I were at our wit's end wondering whether to tell you. In the end we decided you must know. Before the tittle-tattle gets around."

Bladon's thoughts had moved on to a place were there was no time. Only memory.

"Richard is her son, father,"

His face drained of all colour, his jaw was twitching.

"I'll make some tea." She jumped to her feet.

"No, Billie. Fetch the brandy bottle."

The bottle was now almost empty. It was half past nine and he should be in the Tap Room with the customers. But first he had to calm the storm raging through his head.

He studied the reins and halters dangling from hooks on the wall. Then he picked up the bottle, pulled aside the faded curtain and wandered across the solid wooden floorboards towards the stage at the far end. There was a feeling of loss in the Club Room, of desolation.

"Yes," he waved the bottle in a wide arc. "This is where it all happened. Here!" He stared at the chairs and benches. "The wedding breakfast!" He threw his head back and took a long swig from the bottle spilling brandy down the lapels of his jacket. Then, suddenly, in his mind the room was full of people, noisy people, singing, dancing, celebrating, glad that Bladon King had a wife after the brittle years of mourning Esther. He saw Billie and Becky, pretty little bridesmaids in their velvet dresses and then he saw Trynah, regal in a crimson gown trimmed with fur. They had danced. He looked down at the floor and started to waltz with the brandy bottle held at arm's length. The family and friends had cheered the happy couple. Six months later she had gone.

Bladon pointed the bottle at the chairs. "She disappeared," he hissed. The memories crept away to hide in the folds of the stage curtains, under the chairs and benches. The Clubroom was as empty and hollow as he felt.

He staggered up the steps at the side of the stage and sat down on the top one. Trynah! Back having tea with Vinny in a cafe in Grantham! Back from Spain. Of all the godforsaken places to go to. Trynah a widow, with a son.

"Aaagh" The groan was deep. A son. That's all he had ever wanted. He stood up quickly, wobbled and moved to the middle of the stage.

"That's all I ever wanted. A son!" Bladon bellowed across the Clubroom. "Not too much for a decent hard-working man to ask, is it?" a loud belch chasing the question around the room. He sat down on the top step again and he was back in the Private Room.

"She hasn't changed much." Billie came in with the brandy bottle. "Becky and I would have identified her again."

If they could recognise her, so would he. Why did she leave him? They had been so happy. Why did she go to Spain? Why couldn't she have told him, sent a message. Just something. He belched again. A long, low rolling rumble. Well, she's alive and well, she's back in Grantham. "And," Bladon stood up, "She's my wife," he announced to the empty, brooding room. "My wife!" he yelled.

He would go and find her. She could answer these questions that had tormented him through the years.

* * *

The next afternoon he was riding up Gomm's Hill to Wind Cover House. The brandy had played havoc with his system but the cold east wind was helping to clear his throbbing head, quieten the moody stomach. It sliced across his face, pinched his ears, sharpened his breathing and he was ready to find this wife of his.

He threw Black's rein over the wrought iron gates and went to the front door. Again, there was no reply so he wandered under the archway and into the cobbled yard.

A woman at the bottom of the garden was coming towards him, swinging a bucket, her head down as if looking for something on the overgrown path. He watched her come through the little gate. She still hadn't seen him. But he knew her. The girls had been right. She hadn't changed much. He cleared his throat. "Good afternoon, Mrs King."

"Oh! Oh! I was miles away." She swung the bucket on to her arm. Their eyes met and the whole world shuddered to a standstill.

"Trynah?"

She dropped the bucket. "Oh! Oh!"

He moved a step closer, frowning. "It is Trynah, isn't it? My wife?"

"Oh, my goodness," her voice was a whisper. "Bladon!"

The breeze whisked away the words leaving just the sound of the magpies gossiping and the rooks screeching as Bladon and Trynah were swept into another place, another time, another world.

"I feel quite faint. Let's go in." She led the way across the yard to the kitchen.

They stood facing each other at the deal table. His eyes were unforgiving, burning into her soul. Then she freed herself from them and quickly buried her head in her hands. The enamel clock ticked loudly reminding them of the here and now. "Let's sit down."

Bladon followed her into a light and airy room. It had cream walls and pale green curtains at a deep bay window. A pale green vase had been placed next to a copper jug.

"What happened to that chair?" he pointed to the splintered leg.

"Just a small accident." Trynah was standing near the fireplace. "I keep meaning to get it mended."

A simple oak sideboard against the opposite wall was beset with silver trinkets and dishes. She had always been fond of trinkets. The room had a comfortable, used look about it. She had a knack for that, too. She'd done the same to the Private Room after her arrival at The Pyewipe.

They sat opposite each other in front of the fire. Something deep within him gnawed at the uncertainty of the situation. He was sitting opposite the woman he had last seen in the stableyard on the morning of the Spring Fair at Culbeck. She had made up her mind that she didn't want to go to the Fair.

"That's fine, my dear. You'll get a rest from the kiddies. It'll do you good to have a bit of peace."

When he got back she had gone. That was eighteen years ago and now, here she was, sitting in front of him.

"Let's get something to drink," her voice was trembling.

"Brandy please," Bladon sensed a slumbering violence deep within him. An anger that here she was, pouring drinks for a husband she hadn't set eyes on for years. The fury rumbled. But he couldn't take his eyes off her. She had gained some weight. Not much. Lines of sadness were etched around her mouth but she had energy, vitality. It was still there. And he felt a murmuring in his groin.

He took the glass. "I didn't know where you were. I couldn't find you."

A deep silence haunted the room, searching for the lost years. But it seemed they had never existed and that they had seen each other only last week.

"You disappeared. Left me a note." He got up and started to pace the floor. "I used to rage and fume and get drunk, night after night. That's what I did, Trynah." He was shouting as he marched back to the window, nursing his glass. "You gave no explanation. You sent no message. I didn't know whether you were alive or dead." He paused. "I vowed revenge." And suddenly that revenge engulfed him. He drained his glass and hurled it across the room. It smashed into the wall next to the sideboard. He stood, fists clenched staring at the shards of splintered glass glinting in the wintry sunshine.

His wife sat in her chair, motionless.

"I vowed punishment." Now his voice was low, soft. Then he returned to his chair leaning forward, his elbows on his knees. "Why did you leave me, Trynah, why?"

She was at the sideboard reaching for another glass. She handed the brandy to him and her unsteady legs took her back to her chair.

"I'll explain," she sat very still, her hands folded in her lap, blinking at him slowly as she told him the whole story. From the day she left The Pyewipe to the day she arrived at Grantham station. "Nothing can be undone, can it?"

"No," Bladon got to his feet, cradling his glass, calmer now. "Your note was brief, saying that you had had to make a calamitous decision that would be beyond my comprehension. But you didn't explain anything!" Bladon shouted at her. "Now I understand why. You couldn't have told me that Robbie had escaped from prison." He stood in the middle of the room, "and if I'd come through what Robinson Mann had come through I would've moved heaven and earth to get you. Three times with a noose round his neck. Huh!" He moved closer to her, crouched in the chair. "Tell me, were you and Robinson married?"

"No," she twisted the gold band on her finger. She didn't look up. "This is the only ring I've ever worn. You put it there. Robbie and I were never married. No one ever questioned us. Not even... Not even at the inquest when Robbie was drowned. And you, Bladon," she raised her head, "what about you? Did you divorce me?"

"Perish the thought," he sat down staring into the fire, the brandy goblet dangling between his fingers. There was a long silence. Only the clock shaped like a silver star offered any record of these passing moments. Its soft tick could scarcely be heard. He cleared his throat and was about to tell her about Hannah but once again the anger surged through him. He jumped to his feet, hurling the glass at the same spot on the wall. The fragments joined the little pile of glinting crystal.

He strode to the door and paused. She was hunched in the chair eyes on the floor. Then he hurried to the archway, mounted Black and wheeled him round. Trynah was standing on the path, supporting herself with one arm on the wall. Without another word, he rode away.

* * *

Nothing seemed familiar as Bladon rode along the lanes and through the villages. It was as if he were seeing the countryside for the first time. It disturbed him.

Back there in Wind Cover House was his wife. It beggared belief. After her disappearance he'd often wondered where she was and why she'd left. But a living, breathing Robinson Mann was a good enough reason. After all, he had been her first choice. She had been betrothed to him. So Bladon shouldn't have got so angry with her. He was sorry he'd smashed those glasses. It all needed sorting and he must talk to his daughters.

He was soon through Grantham and on North Parade. He pulled up at the row of terraced houses and looped Black's reins on the gate. A fussy little terrier barged out of the garden next door and came yapping around his heels.

"Father, this is a surprise," Becky was at the open door. "Go away, Tinker. He's a nuisance. Always barking."

"I'm glad I caught you. Can you come up to The Pyewipe as soon as possible?"

"Yes, but won't you come in for a cup of tea?" She caught the whiff of brandy.

"No, I can't stay. What about tonight?"

She noticed his flushed face, his agitation with the reins. "Why... er ... yes."

"Bring Oliver as well, it's a family matter. Sorry I can't stay. I'll see you later."

Soon he was at Ketsby Hill. Black slowed down as he passed the spindly hawthorn bushes and then there was the sudden spurt over the rise, past the church and into the stable yard. He dismounted, confused and detached from the world he knew so well. Trynah back! His wife, just a few miles away. He had to talk to his family, and quickly.

Oliver couldn't come but Becky was punctual. They were in the Private Room, sitting round the dining table.

"Well, what's to be done?" Bladon leaned back, tucking his thumbs into his waistcoat pockets. "Your mother has turned up and I've given you the story exactly as she gave it to me. I am quite sure it's true."

"I think it's wonderful news that we have our mother back." Becky was fingering the silver bracelet on her wrist, a present from Oliver. "It must have been just as terrible for her as it was for us."

"I agree," said Billie, her elbows on the table, running her fingers through her hair. "But it was a cruel thing to do to father."

"And she could've stayed and looked after you both," said Bladon, inspecting a scratch on the back of his hand. "We have to look at every aspect. And remember what happened in the... What did you say the name of that new cafe was?"

"The Columbine." Billie was twisting her hair into a silky hank.

"You saw her. Lydia saw her. We're going to be in a dreadful stew if we don't do something. Bertha Burrell will grow another head..."

"I don't think there's any question about what we should do." Billie was now stroking the polished surface of the table. "I think she should be invited back here, to return to her home with Richard, for Christmas."

Bladon stood up and wandered about, nudging the chairs,

moving an ashtray, stroking the back of the old settle. This magnanimous attitude of the girls surprised him. He'd expected dissent, anger and resentment.

"I agree. And father..." Becky half-turned in the chair. "There's more good news for you tonight. Oliver's sorry he couldn't be here but he insists I tell you. We're expecting a baby!"

"Oh, my dear Becky." He gently pulled her to her feet, embracing her, kissing the top of her head. "This is wonderful news. It calls for a celebration drink."

"Not for me father." She stepped away, smoothing down her dress.

"Nor me, thank you." Billie put her arm across Becky's shoulders. "I still have to finish in the stables."

"All right, we'll wait until Christmas. It's all settled then? Trynah comes back." Bladon was running his hands through his hair. "Is that what you want?"

"Yes, of course," the girls chorused.

"If you're sure then I'll go and see her again." He walked away, stroking his chin, staring at the rug. "I owe her an apology. I got angry with her, very angry." He glanced at his daughters. "But remember, she may not want to come back."

"You must invite her and see what she says." Becky reached for her coat. "And don't forget. We will now have Richard as a family member. I think Billie's lucky," she winked at her father, "I must go."

* * *

The next morning Richard and Billie were working in the barn in Beck's Close. He was pacing up and down hands deep in his pockets, shuffling through the hay littering the floor.

"I think you're being too hard on your mother," Billie declared, perched on the edge of the manger. "What would you have done if you'd gone through all that for someone you love? She was in an impossible situation."

249

He paused in front of her. The thin morning sun shafted through the dirty window, bathing her face in a golden calm. He wanted to grab her, hold her close. He'd been deceived. His mother and his employer were man and wife. And his father was dead in Lavega. He needed comforting.

"I haven't spoken to her since she told me." Richard kicked the manger and moved on. "It was such a shock to learn that my father and mother were not married. I mean, if they were not married that means I'm..."

"Does it matter? It means that your mother and father loved each other very much. Clearly your father could not have stayed in England." Billie leaned back against the hay rack over the manger. "And your mother loved him enough to leave, to desert us and all her family to move to some foreign country where they didn't even speak the language. And all that strange food! I think you should be proud of them."

"But it's the..."

"It's the shock. I know. It's been a shock for all of us. Imagine! After all these years, Becky and I couldn't believe our eyes when we saw her in The Columbine with aunt Vinny. But I think you owe your mother an apology. She must be breaking her heart. The truth is that my father and your mother are man and wife." She pulled a strand of hay from the manger and teased it into a knot. "Love is a very powerful thing but no one seems to know how to deal with it."

Richard was striding the length of the small barn again. Anita had not been in love with him. She had said that one day he would know the difference between infatuation and love. She had been right. He knew that he was in love with Billie.

"Mother and father worked very hard at Los Rubios. But I didn't know anything about these hideous events they left behind in England. They never told me anything about their past." He waved his arms about. "Living in Lavega was all I knew. I realise now I should have helped on the farm more. Look at what you do for your father." He kicked the wall and turned. "I let them down badly. Used to clear off to meet my pals in Serona." He was now standing in front of her. But he was not going to tell her about the drinking, the nights with the local girls. And he was not going to tell her about the hours he'd spent with Anita, at Dos Caminos and in the shepherd's hut.

"How could they have told you? There was no point. They did what they thought was the best thing."

"Even though it left you all wondering what on earth had happened to her?" Richard paused and then continued his striding.

"Father was worried. He told the police. I remember he used to go out looking for her day after day. And at night he drank a lot. No one had seen her except that old gossipy woman. She told people at the time that she saw mother on the carrier's cart going to Grantham. But she's such a mischief-maker no one believed her." Billie had twisted the hay into the shape of a little man.

"Everyone knew Robinson Mann and that he was to marry Trynah. It was widely known he killed his brother and everyone presumed that he'd been hanged for it in Lincoln Prison. Father thought she'd lost her memory. I was quite young, so I don't remember much about it." Billie jumped from her perch on the manger and tapped the end of his nose with the little hay man. "So I think you should buy her a present on the way home and say you're sorry. Not many women are made of that sort of stuff, you know." She moved to the dirty little window and stared across the meadow. "When are you going to see Lydia again?"

"What makes you think I'm going to see her again?" Richard thrust his hands deep into his pockets and stared at her back. The change of subject had caught him by surprise.

"She told me you'd ridden over especially to see her." She turned away from the window.

"I went to see aunt Abigail and uncle Robert, that's why I went to Flaxwell." He hadn't known that Billie and Lydia saw so much of each other but he supposed it was only natural, being cousins. He was nervous about Lydia. He knew she'd do everything to ensnare him again. Billie was suspicious. In Lavega he had had just his friends but here, there were cousins and aunts and uncles all over the place.

"I just want to be with you, Billie, honestly." He moved closer to her and caught the lingering perfume of lavender again. He wanted this woman here and now on this pile of hay. But Billie wasn't Anita in the shepherd's hut, and she wasn't Lydia either, in her den. They knew exactly what they wanted and got it. Billie was different. She wouldn't understand the frenetic desire for sex.

"You're not going to say, are you?" and she cupped his face and kissed him on the cheek.

Richard clamped her into his arms, his head buried in the thick golden hair. "Oh, Billie," and he raised her chin and kissed her lips.

"Hey!" She ruffled his hair. "We've got work to do. Father wants the barn cleared out ready for the new winter fodder. We should have finished by now and look...we haven't even started. Come on."

When they got back to The Pyewipe Richard went to look for Bladon. He was in the Private Room, sitting at his desk sorting a pile of papers.

"May I speak to you, please?" He hovered in the doorway.

"Come in." Bladon left his desk near the window and came over to the fireside pointing to the oak settle. "Sit down."

Richard sat on the edge of the long hard seat. This was the second time he had been in this room. It now had more meaning. His mother knew this room well, as this is where she would have spent the evenings. His eyes went to the large vase of bronze chrysanthemums on the polished dining table. Mother would have had flowers in here, too.

"Well, what's on your mind, young man?" queried Bladon, leaning back in the leather chair.

Richard cleared his throat. "Mother told me about..." He was stammering, choking on words that would not flow. "She told me... About you and her. Being married, I mean." He looked down at his hands. "I got very angry and stormed out. I haven't spoken to her since she told me. But I wasn't angry with you. I was furious because I thought she was married to my father, in Lavega."

"That's understandable." Bladon leaned forward. "If your father had not died so tragically I don't suppose you would ever have known that your mother was my wife. Your father provided you with a good home, and a good horse. What did you call your horse?"

"Brisa."

"What does it mean?"

"Breeze."

"Nice name." Bladon was silent for a moment, head back, studying this young man. "Your father did all the things a father does for his son. There's no need to be so upset. We live in a strange and mysterious world, Richard, and we discover things that make us happy and we discover things that make us sad and some things make us angry."

"Yes," Richard's voice was a whisper. "And now that I've had time to think about it all, I see how much I must have upset mother and I wondered if you would let me take time off this afternoon. I want to buy her a present before the shops close."

"Have you and Billie sorted out the barn in Beck's Close?"

"Yes. It's all ready."

"Well, then I see no reason why you shouldn't leave early." Bladon sucked in his bottom lip. "As for the other matter, of course it was a shock. It's been a week of shocks for us all, hasn't it?" He rose, strode to the window and turned. "Off you go then. And buy something nice for your mother. Take Billie with you."

Richard and Billie hurried into Chambers on High Street and paused in the hushed elegance of the spacious emporium. Gowns and coats were draped on dummy women with no heads or legs. A few smartly dressed ladies were wandering from one counter to the other leaving their trail of perfume in the air. Others were sitting in chairs doing nothing.

"I'm not used to buying presents, Billie." He'd never purchased his mother or his father a present and he'd never bought Anita anything.

"Come on, let's look over there," Billie tugged the edge of his jacket and led him to a glass counter displaying shawls and lengths of material. Leather gloves looked like large leaves on a skeletal tree.

"May we look at some scarves please?" Billie smiled at the saleswoman. She was round and plump, and her dress was too small for her. Every movement demanded a little more than she could give. She grunted as she reached for the drawer and put it on the counter.

She flicked the scarves into the air with her chubby fingers. They were like rainbows floating over the polished counter.

"Oh, I wasn't aware there would be so many different ones," remarked Richard as he turned to Billie.

"I like this one," said Billie as she flicked a scarf into the air, "but you must decide," and she moved away to look at some linen handkerchiefs.

The saleswoman continued to pluck the delicate cobwebs until the counter was covered with gauzy clouds in shades of blue and beige and red and green and grey.

"Richard!" A voice rang out. Turning, he found himself face to face with Lydia. She was wearing a mauve coat with a brown fur collar. A large feather waved from the back of her hat.

"What are you doing here?" She asked, raising her pencilled eyebrows.

"I'm looking for a present..."

"For me?" She winked.

"For my mother."

"Oh!" She leaned on the counter pushing a little closer to him. She picked up a blue and grey scarf and started to tease it through her fingers. The nearness of this confident young woman unsettled him. She knew she could reduce him to a floor cloth in her little den. He looked over his shoulder and saw Billie bent over a glass showcase.

"I miss you." She lowered her eyelashes and looked sideways. "What's keeping you so busy?"

"Well, I have a job now."

"A job. You have to work!"

"Of course."

"With horses." She flicked a scarf across her cheek.

"Yes."

"They're smelly, always farting. But I don't mind really." She turned pressing her back on to the edge of the counter, her fingers caressing the fur on the lapel of her coat. "When are you coming to see me again?"

"I don't know. As I said, I have to work." Richard glanced across the shop. Billie was still at the display case with her back to him.

"Well you mustn't leave me alone too long. Come the day after tomorrow, on Thursday. If you don't I'll come and find you." She leaned closer and he caught a whiff of her perfume. "I want to see those scars on your back again, and next time, next time," she wagged a finger at him, "I won't let you go until you tell me how you got them." She threw back her head and laughed at the ceiling.

"Hello Lydia," Billie was at Richard's elbow. "Got what?"

"Oh, hello." Her eyes swept over Billie's riding jacket and scruffy jodhpurs. "It's a private joke. What are you doing here?"

"Shopping." '

"Is Richard buying you a present?"

"Why not?" Billie met Lydia's eyes. They were angry eyes and her lips were tight and she was not smiling. Billie recognised the mood. It was her jealous mood.

Lydia tugged on the collar of her coat. "Must go, see you. And don't forget, Richard." Lydia clasped her small leather bag under her arm and headed for the door in a flurry of swirling coat.

The saleswoman cleared her throat. "Have you decided which scarf you would like?"

"Yes. This one please." It was the one Billie had chosen. The saleswoman folded the scarves and grunted again as she replaced the drawer in the mahogany cabinet. Then she wrapped the scarf in tissue paper and handed him the package.

"What did she mean about the private joke?" Billie stopped on the pavement. "And what is it she doesn't want you to forget?"

"I don't know what she's talking about." Richard was not going to explain to Billie that his back was scarred for life. "You know what she's like, always beating up a froth about something. She loves attention."

"Yes, that's true. Sorry."

He was striding along the pavement and Billie had to hurry to keep up with him. He was angry with Lydia for taunting him about his back and he was angry with Billie because she didn't understand his feelings for her and he was furious with himself but he didn't know why. Soon they were at The Blue Cow. He swung into the saddle and led the way out of the stables. They had to stop in the archway as a motor car swerved and just missed a group of children playing in the road.

The driver of the car was wearing a dark green cap perched on top of lank, black hair. At his side was a young woman wearing a mauve coat with a fur collar. Her hat was swathed in a long white scarf tied under her chin. It was Lydia. The young driver honked his horn and leaned over the side of the car door. "Get out the way, you blasted urchins."

"Now perhaps you'll believe me," stated Richard as he waved his whip after the car. "I must go. See you tomorrow," he wheeled Fiver into the street. "And thanks for helping with the present."

Richard kept Fiver at a steady pace across Apsley Rise towards Brothybeck Copse. He was pleased that Billie had seen Lydia with that young man in a car. She must now believe what he was trying to tell her. Anita and Lydia – they were both reckless with the immortal longings of the human race. Billie, however, didn't demand anything. He pictured her in the barn with the sun shafting across her face, gilding those freckles. And he felt her warm body, her soft lips and knew there was nothing prodigal about Billie. She was lovely, and different. She was not going to be easy to win over but he was sure he could. He was going to marry her.

* * *

Bladon arrived at Wind Cover House just after eleven o'clock. It was a cold, clear morning and the ride had clarified his thoughts and given his world a glow again. He was glad the girls had been so positive about their stepmother coming back to The Pyewipe, especially Billie. She knew all about the pain of desertion. Since the Steven Donner affair she'd kept all suitors at a safe distance but he'd noticed the thaw with Richard. Billie was coming to life again. He'd heard her singing in the Club Room.

Trynah was in the hall, holding a vase of white chrysanthemums. "Come this way." That's all she said as she led him into the front room and placed the vase in the window. He walked round the back of the sofa. Then he stood with his back to the roaring fire and surveyed the room. "It looks as if you've lived here for years."

"It was in poor shape when we moved in but it didn't take long. Curtis and Vinny were a great help." She sat on the edge of the chair.

"You're more up to date than we are at The Pyewipe. Nothing much has changed there since..." Bladon sank into the armchair at the side of the blazing fire.

"Since I walked out," Trynah looked down at her hands.

There was a stiffness about the atmosphere. She was wary. And he must have frightened her with the broken goblets. He watched her and the more he saw her the more he wanted her. She had changed so little. The tilt of the head and the smile were exactly as he remembered. She was wearing a smooth dress that wrapped across her thighs. It was light blue and a string of black beads hung below her waist. And her hair was different. He used to unpin it in the bedroom and it would fall like a dark silk curtain around her shoulders. Now it was short and neat and in spite of the wisps of silver it made her look younger. She had moved with the times.

He cleared his throat. "I owe you an apology, I broke your crystal goblets. And you didn't flinch."

Trynah bit her bottom lip. "It wasn't the first crystal you've smashed against a wall. Do you remember? In the Little Room, after..."

"Yes, I do." He looked at her without moving his head. "And you were just as unflinching then. Please accept my apologies. I'll make sure they are replaced."

She sat in silence, which disturbed him. The silver clock ticked its silver minutes but nothing happened. They both needed rescuing from the void. The only sound came from gritty, grinding wheels on the road as a cart trundled past.

"I'll come to the point. Will you... er... will you come back to the inn? After all, we are man and wife. I'd like you by my side," and that blanket of silence enveloped them again. "As it used to be..."

"Bladon! Things can never be as they used to be." She twirled the beads. "So much has happened. So much..."

"Well?" he watched her fingers caressing the necklace. They were scratched and scarred by pulling weeds. Outside in the spinney the crows were cawing, in the distance a dog barked.

"Yes, Bladon, I will be your wife again."

He shot out of the chair, pulled her to her feet and folded his arms around her. "My Trynah," he whispered in her hair.

She stepped away. "But what about Billie and Becky? Remember, I deserted them when they were at their most vulnerable. It was such a cruel thing to do."

"I've already spoken to them. They think you should come

home." He stroked her sleek short hair then framed her face with his hands. "To The Pyewipe."

"Oh, my goodness. To see all these people again." She grasped her throat but was unable to fight back the tears. "How I missed them. No one will ever know how much I missed them."

"We'll have a family party, after Christmas," promised Bladon, lifting her chin. "There, I'm rushing the fences again. Always rushing the fences."

"Yes." Her voice was a whisper. "You always tended to rush the fences, dear Bladon."

Chapter 19

It was half past three in the afternoon on Christmas Eve and it was cold. The bright golden sun had tried to warm the day but it had given up and was now fainting over the roof of the coach house. The wind was thin and icy, tormenting Billie and Richard. They had just put away the tackle and were standing at the bottom of the Club Room steps. Events had moved so quickly since his mother had told him that Bladon King was her husband. She had agreed that they should spend Christmas together and tonight they would all be under the same roof at The Pyewipe. But he wasn't so sure about this dance Lydia and Billie had been talking about.

"You'll enjoy it." Billie was trying to keep her hands warm under her armpits.

"But I've never been to a dance in England," explained Richard, clenching his teeth against the cold wind

"Well, now's your chance." Billie buried her chin deep into the woollen muffler.

"And I don't know any of the dances." He thrust his hands deeper into the pockets of his breeches. "I've never heard of the Jog Trot."

"Don't worry, you'll soon learn. Just enjoy yourself. There'll be a good crowd tonight."

He would really like to be somewhere with Billie, just the two of them on their own. Yes, he'd go but he couldn't be persuaded to go in Rodney Moate's motor car when he came to pick up Billie. He was a dark-haired, clumsy young man with a sparse black moustache, which looked as if it had been pencilled on his upper lip.

"There's plenty of room. We've had seven in it." Rodney sleeked back his hair and grinned. His widely spaced teeth gave him a demonic look. Richard thought there was something a bit evil about the small black eyes and that grimace.

"Thanks, but I'll ride. See you there."

"Bloody wars! Riding to a dance on a horse!" Rodney threw back his head and guffawed. He sounded exactly like Consuelo Nobrega's donkey in Lavega.

"Come on Billie, in you get," and he opened the door for her. "Different but dangerous I would say. And what about later...don't think you'll find a row of chicks lining up to ride home on the back of a horse," and he guffawed and snorted again as he revved the engine. Richard watched the motor disappear, spluttering and coughing, down Ketsby High Street.

Well, what's so strange about riding a horse to a dance? After all, he'd always ridden to Serona to meet his pals for a night out. He'd take Fiver and leave him at The Blue Cow. Mr King and he and Billie always used Mr Copeland's stables when they went to Grantham.

Richard had no difficulty in finding the Drill Hall. The man hunched in the corner seat of the Tap Room in The Blue Cow had directed him. 'Sandon Road is where you want to be. You'll see the Barracks. Go through the arch and it's the long building in front of you, across the parade ground'.

He peeled off his coat and left it at the cloakroom just inside the door. He found himself swept along by young men pushing through to the dance hall to join the willowy girls in their gaudy dresses with tassels and fringes, twirling ropes of beads impatiently, adjusting the bandeaux and ribbons and bows decorating their bobbed hair. They brought a splash of colour to this huge shed with its lofty ceiling strutted together with metal rods. Soldiers' boots had pulverised and pounded the floor until the hall reeked of dust and decrepitude. Streamers and bunches of holly and mistletoe dangled from hooks on the walls and there was a Christmas tree in one corner, close to the bar.

Sets of tables and chairs were placed along the half-timbered walls. In the middle of the dance floor was a pyramid of what appeared to be dried leaves with a bunch of holly perched on top. Richard had no idea why it had been put there. Couples were dancing around it in a clockwise manner.

Five musicians on the stage filled the hall with screeching trumpets, braying saxophones, and a beating drum with a piano hurrying along behind.

Then he saw Lydia and Billie surrounded by a group of young men near the makeshift bar of trestle tables covered with white damask cloths. It, too, was decorated with bunches of holly.

"Here he is!" Rodney slapped Richard on the back. "Jolly good show. Where's your horse? In the cloakroom?" And Consuelo's donkey honked and snorted again.

Lydia grabbed Richard and whisked him on to the floor. Her dress was made of some kind of silver and it glistened with every movement. She seemed to have grown an extra pair of arms and legs. They were flailing all around him until he felt dizzy.

"I don't know how to do it," he looked down at her frenzied feet.

"Oh, yes you do," she whispered and her face came close to his. He thought she was going to kiss him but she stepped away, smiling. The music stopped and she collapsed into a chair near the bar. She took the cigarette offered by Rodney then delved into her clutch bag and produced an ivory cigarette holder.

The music blasted off again and Billie was swept away by Rodney, leaving Richard and Lydia together again.

She crushed her cigarette in the glass ashtray and snatched at his arm, dragging him into the middle of the dance floor.

"Will you take me home tonight? You can stay. In my den."

"But...but... What about Rodney?" Richard glanced across the dance floor. Billie and Rodney were shimmying around the pyramid in the centre of the floor, the bobbles on the hem of her dark red velvet dress firing him with an insatiable desire.

"Nothing to do with Rodney," shrugged Lydia. "He can take Billie home."

"But... I rode here..."

"You what!" Lydia froze on the dance floor, hands on hips. "On that farting horse!" Her voice softened. "Leave it where it is and drive me home, to our den. Remember, you've promised to show me your back?"

"I can't leave it where it is..."

"Well, that was stupid of you. How can you take me home on a horse?" And she flounced off the dance floor. Richard just stood there for a moment, abandoned. Then he elbowed his way through the frenetic dancers and made his way to the gents' toilet. It was a dreadful place, dimly lit with dark green walls and a strong smell of urine.

He stood in front of the mirror and didn't like what he saw. He was hot and flustered and the awful lighting made his hair look dingy. He wasn't enjoying himself. This place was like a derelict barn trying to be clever, trying to give fun and intimacy. He just didn't fit in with these friends of Billie and Lydia. And if Rodney what's his name referred to Fiver again he would surely take him outside. He decided to go back and find Billie. He wanted to get her away from this dump and take her home.

"Where's Billie?" he asked Lydia. Her arms and one leg were entwined around a tall, thin man with oily, black hair. Richard recalled him. It was the man who had been driving the car when he and Billie left Chambers.

"Gone," the tall, thin man answered the question.

"Excuse me." Richard made his way to the cloakroom, pulled on his coat and stepped out into the street. It was full of young people dancing and yelling and swinging round and round the lamp-posts at the crossroads. He had had his share of beer but it hadn't lightened him. Instead he felt heavy and sober and sad as he made his way to The Blue Cow without Billie. She was somewhere else, with another.

* * *

It was late before the merrymaking died away at The Pyewipe but at last the hubbub faded to a murmur and peace descended on every room. The silence was punctuated by the dripping taps in the kitchen, the voices of revellers in the street and, in the distance, the haunting call of a tawny owl.

Bladon and Trynah were in the bedroom. He was standing next to a small octagonal table pouring claret into the two glasses as he had done on their wedding night. He watched as she undressed in the candlelight, as he had also done before.

After all these years she was still swathed in modesty and he loved her all the more for it. They slipped into bed and effortlessly found their way to the sunny uplands they had deserted long ago. They were together again, young again, happy again.

"Are you still awake?" asked Trynah, running her fingers through his hair.

"Yes, and I'm not going to sleep for a long time. I want tonight to last for ever." He nuzzled her soft shoulder. "You know... you know when you disappeared I decided that your first child had returned from somewhere and that you'd deserted me to go and look after it."

"My child!" Trynah raised herself on to her left elbow.

"Yes," he said as he turned to look at her. "When you miscarried just before Christmas. Remember? Doctor Robb told me it was not your first pregnancy. Well, this knocked me sideways. I wanted to ask you about it. Where was this baby? Who was the father? But I decided it was too cruel." He pulled her close and cradled her head. "So I didn't ask you any questions. And then... when you disappeared I decided that perhaps your child had turned up or the father had come back and that was why you left."

Trynah caressed his cheek. "Doctor Robb was right. It was not my first pregnancy. That was the result of the rape by Redfern." She flopped back on to the pillow. "The baby was born in the Home at Flaxwell," she ran her fingers over his eyes, his nose, "and died during the night." Her fingers continued to trace his lips, his cheeks. "The baby died," Trynah swallowed hard, "the baby died because... because I got out of bed, took my pillow and went next door to where the baby was sleeping in a cot. I placed the pillow across the baby's face. It didn't move, Bladon. It didn't move." She gasped with the memory. "Then I took the pillow and went back to bed and prayed for forgiveness."

A silver arrow from the moon shafted through a gap in the curtains, across the floor and on to the bed. She kept her eyes on the arrow a few inches away. "That baby wasn't created by anybody's love. It had no father, no love, no future. I just could not dedicate my life to a creature conceived in such violence, so I..." The silence in the room was disturbed by the scream of a vixen not far away. She tried to control the sobs but they were choking her. "That was my first pregnancy. I decided that if you asked I would tell you what happened to me in the barn at Beck's Close. But... but you never asked a single question."

Her husband's arms were around her. "Hush now. Those questions haunted me but I decided you'd gone through enough." His lips brushed her smooth shoulders. "It's something we all have to endure alone, this distressing poverty of guilt, of death. And I had to get on with my life, you had to work through your own nightmares. And now, now! Here you are, back in my arms. Everything will be well now, dear Trynah, you'll see. Let's leave the past and gather up the shattered dreams. We can make a go of what's left to us."

* * *

Christmas at The Pyewipe was much as Trynah remembered but it was subdued.

"There didn't seem to be as many people as usual." She was on her knees in front of the fireplace in the Private Room arranging holly in a large brass coal-scuttle. "Just want to finish this, I should've done it last night but it got late..."

"No, well, many of my regulars didn't come back and those that did can't find proper jobs." Bladon got up from his desk and flung his arms wide. "Soldiers of our victorious army stand in their khaki greatcoats on street corners with begging cups." There was a pause. "Remember Bill Otter the blacksmith? He lost fingers from both hands. Can't grip anything. Well, he goes to Newark Market hawking boot laces. Would you ever believe it? And John Rycroft the cattle dealer? Lost an eye and half his face. He does the same at Sleaford, selling soap and scrubbing brushes. His missus fixed him up with a little tray on a string round his shoulders. Huh! Kitchener needed them and they went." He came over to the fireplace and stood over.

"You know, the war has gouged great holes in family life. Leaving aching gaps that can never be filled. Ketsby will never be the same again." He picked up a shiny, green holly leaf. "Do you remember Josh Valder and Toby Gibbs?"

"Yes, I do," Trynah pushed the last few sprigs of holly in place. "Who could forget those two, they were into everything. They brought Miss Kirk's donkey into the Tap Room on Christmas Eve. Through my kitchen! And you got the whip to them."

Bladon dropped the holly leaf into the fire grate. "Yes. Such rips. Remember the night they knocked the policeman's helmet off and trampled on it? Drunk as lords they were. You never knew what they were going to get up to next. Well, without batting an eyelid they hurried off to join the army. Singing at the tops of their voices along Westgate. Off to France on the great adventure, to one of the biggest slaughters in history. They didn't come back. And I can tell you Ketsby's a sadder place without 'em. But that's war for you. Such a waste."

Bladon gazed at the scuttle full of holly. "That looks nice." He helped her to her feet and pulled her into his arms. "But I have you." He cupped her face in his hands. "Oh, Trynah. You can't imagine... you can never know what it means to me. You, back here after all these years."

* * *

It was a crisp afternoon with an ivory sun too weak to shine. There was no wind and the frost crackled underfoot as Richard and Billie galloped to Bunker's Hill after Christmas dinner. They had chatted about everything except the dance. Neither of them had discussed it at breakfast nor during Christmas dinner nor whilst saddling up. They had pushed it to the perimeter of their minds but now it could not be pushed anywhere.

"Let's sit under the sycamore tree again," Richard led the way and they sat side by side in awkward silence.

Billie broke the ice with a question, which was not at all what he was expecting. She was staring across the valley, eyes half closed then she turned to him.

"You still haven't told me what Lydia meant about the private joke. You know, that day we were in Chambers?" She reached for a twig.

"Oh, it's nothing. I don't know what she's talking about."

"Well, it must be something because she said so." Billie was tapping the twig on her boot.

He felt his face colouring. He couldn't and wouldn't tell her about the scars on his back. She would know one day. When they were married she would see them. But Lydia was a worry. She might tell Billie that she'd seen his scars. How could he explain to her what had happened in the courtyard at Dos Caminos, or in Lydia's den? No, he couldn't. It would ruin everything. "I looked for you last night but couldn't find you. Then they told me you'd left with Rodney."

"Yes," she was scratching her boot with a twig. "I wanted to tell you that he was giving me a lift home, but it was impossible to find anyone in that crowd."

"Ridiculous wasn't it," Richard dug his heel into the turf, "both looking for each other." He stared at her serene profile, so calm and dignified and resigned to something but he didn't know what. Anita had been so demanding, so possessive. Lydia was just the same. 'I missed you. I wanted...'"

"Oh, look!" she pointed, 'Down there, near the willow trees. It's a fox."

'In broad daylight,' he shaded his eyes. "It's hungry. Did you hear what I said?'

"Yes, I missed you, too. And I like you," she ruffled his hair. "Lydia likes you."

He decided to change the subject. Lydia was becoming a menace and he didn't know what to do about her. "One day I'd like to ride all the way down to the bottom of this field." He pointed to the willow trees with their pale green fronds wafting in the breeze. The fox had gone.

"Yes. It's secluded down there, a nice place to think. All calm and quiet." She stared straight ahead. "You're not going to tell me, are you?"

"Tell you what?"

"About your secret with Lydia." She turned to look at him but he couldn't meet her eyes.

"Forget Lydia." There was a dreadful hollowness in his stomach. He wanted to be happy with Billie and yet Lydia pushed herself on to the scene every time. He reached for her hand. "Come on. Let's go."

* * *

The next day Richard rode over to Wind Cover House to check that everything was in order and to collect the mail. It gave him time to think about Billie. She's going to ask again, about Lydia. Lydia was a pest and he didn't know what to do about her. If only he could talk to someone about it. But who? He couldn't tell his mother or stepfather. He wandered across the yard and along the overgrown path in the vegetable garden. He paused to gaze across the paddock then he turned towards the house, the empty stables, the empty sheds, all so quiet and forlorn. Then he remembered uncle Curtis. They had worked together here, in these sheds. He knew things. Seemed interested. Yes, he could talk to Curtis, privately. He hurried back indoors, scooped up the letters and stuffed them in his satchel.

On the way home he debated with himself how he was going to tell his uncle about Anita, about Daroca and about the whipping, and Lydia's den. He would have to tell him everything. It was all such a muddle.

"Look, mother. We've got a letter from Pedro." He threw his whip behind the kitchen door. "This'll brush up our Spanish."

He read the spidery writing. "Maria's gone to stay with that aunt she talked about." He gazed across the stableyard. Maria. He'd forgotten about the dark, simmering, awkward sex in the barn. But she didn't like aunt Rosita. She had never said why and now she's gone to stay with her at Peinosa. "Señor Daroca didn't lose much time did he? He's turned Los Rubios into a Country Club. The farmhouse is a nightclub and the stables are the restaurant. How could they get rid of the stink? El Paco's Bar has been extended. Oh, my goodness. Daniel, the shepherd!" He passed another page across the table to his mother.

"Found in a hut in Mansilla Valley with severe wounds. Extensive excoriation of the skin was consistent with injuries caused by a flogging instrument. Oh! My God! And with fifty thousand pesetas in his leather satchel. Where on earth could he get such money from?"

"He was a gambler." Richard pictured the hut, the carpet of beech leaves, Anita lying on her back, naked, legs wide apart, demanding, and Daniel on the path in the wood.

269

"Whatever next," Trynah flicked through the pages again, "in sleepy little Lavega. That Country Club will be attracting the wrong sort of people."

It was all a world away. A world that he couldn't relate to, from here in Ketsby. Last night he had spent hours tossing and turning as images came across the dark of his mind. Anita. One more time! Don't go! Then the young woman in that dingy room at Las Pecas was with him, pushing Anita out of the way. Lydia joined in, swathed in her chiffon. Maria was in the shed, laughing. Dawn came and he dragged himself out of bed with a headache. He must find uncle Curtis, and never again would be possessed by these women with their insatiable appetites. Never. He'd found Billie and he was going to marry her.

* * *

"He's moodier." Bladon was sitting on the edge of the bed staring down at his bare feet.

"Well, he's got a lot to think about. I'm glad he's taking life more seriously. It's about time. He had a pretty free rein in Lavega," said Trynah, peeling off her stockings.

"He's probably anxious about his income," said Bladon rolling into bed. "He seems determined to get the riding school going. Come here."

Billie, too, was puzzled by Richard's mood swings. She decided to find out. They were in the shed at Copping Lane.

"Is something bothering you, Richard?"

"No. What should be bothering me?"

"Well." She pushed the hurdle out of the way and moved to his side. "You're so damn secretive, and so serious. You don't seem so... Well, I don't know what it is. You don't seem so happy. And we used to be."

He took her in his arms. "It's just that.... well, there's a lot to think about with the riding school. And you..." He buried his face in her hair.

"Yes, but you don't talk about it now. You never tell me anything. You never smile. You never speak any Spanish." Billie hesitated. "Is it because you no longer want to be near me?"

"Oh, no," he held her closer, swaying with her in his arms. "No, Billie. It's just that... I suppose I'm thinking about all the things that can go wrong."

"Well, there's no need to be so tight-lipped. Can't we talk about the things that might go wrong?" She stepped away. "I think you're working too hard. There's a film at the picture house, 'Up Romance Road'. Let's go tomorrow. What do you think?"

"Yes, fine, but not tomorrow. I'm meeting my uncle in Grantham. We need new wire netting for fencing. He's going to help me choose. I don't understand the gauges and tensions but he does." He pulled her into his arms again, whispering into her hair. "We'll go the day after tomorrow."

Uncle Curtis hadn't been a bit surprised when Richard caught him outside the General Store. And he hadn't asked any questions.

"Right you are, young man. What about eleven o'clock in The Granby tomorrow? See you there."

All so matter of fact. His uncle would understand.

Billie was going to Copping Lane to help her father clear the ditches, which meant that Lydia wouldn't find her today. Lydia had nothing to do and was always on the lookout for someone to waste time with.

"I shan't be long, then I'll come and help you," he called over his shoulder as he urged Fiver out of the stableyard.

"Right, then we can go to the flicks tomorrow," she waved from the kitchen door, "and I'll take you to The Columbine for tea."

There was no one about when he stabled Fiver at The Blue Cow. The Christmas tree in the entrance looked tatty and neglected. In the market place a skinny black and white dog wandered amongst the piles of rubbish and boxes and sprigs of unsold holly but found nothing edible. Christmas seemed older than a few days.

He'd practised what he was going to say to Curtis many times but it didn't seem to come out in the right order. It got jumbled up, stuttering in his head.

"Richard, cooee!"

He turned. Lydia was hurrying towards him.

"Wait," she said as she swept up in front of him with a waft of cold perfumed air. Smiling, she pulled her turban hat down over one ear. "Where are you going?"

His eyes swept over her velvet coat that looked so soft he could scarcely save himself from touching her.

"I've got... I'm going to see a friend. Just up there," he pointed with his chin.

"Well, don't go. Come with me." And she linked her arm in his.

He pulled away. "I'm sorry. I must go..."

"Well, I know you're not meeting Billie!" She tossed her head back, lips parted.

"How do you know?"

"She's meeting Rodney. I think she's quite keen on him."

"Don't believe you."

She thrust her painted lips close to his face. "You know him. You met him at the dance."

Richard looked beyond Lydia's turban hat across the deserted market place. Billie. Meeting Rodney. That braying donkey of a prat! He'd seen her not an hour ago.

"Is that true?"

"Would I lie to you? Now, come." She hooked her arm into his again. "Let's go and have some coffee and then we'll go back to my den. Play music... and I want to see your scars again... If you don't, then I'll tell everyone I've seen them..."

"Lydia. I must go." He was walking away backwards.

"Shall we meet later then?" She kept advancing with slow steps clutching her coat around her.

"I can't, I'm busy. Must go."

The Tap Room of The Granby had an air of contempt about it, a smug superiority for having survived the onslaught of the past few days. It was quiet and unoccupied apart from Curtis Pike. A tankard of ale stood on the deal table in front of him, his head rested on the back of the settle, his eyes were on the flames cavorting around the logs in the fireplace and his thoughts were on young Richard. He'd stopped him yesterday on High Street and said he wanted advice. Wench trouble, no doubt. All the girls in the neighbourhood will be swooning for him. Poor sod.

It was five past eleven when the tall, young streak strode into the Tap Room.

"Sorry I'm late," Richard hurried across the room.

"That's all right, no problem. Many folk about?" he asked.

"No, but I bumped into someone I knew." Richard smoothed his hands down his chest. "Can I get you another drink?"

"No thank you." Curtis watched him go to the bar.

Richard plonked his tankard on the table and sat down next to Curtis. They drank in painful silence. The only noise came from the crackle of the logs in the hearth. The silence didn't know what to do with itself.

Curtis came to the point. "Well, what's on your mind, young man?"

Richard toyed with his tankard, his fingers caressing the handle, then the sides and then he put his hand flat across the top of it. "The trouble is..." He took another long swig and the story tumbled out. "And I want to marry Billie."

"And you're afraid that Lydia is going to spill the beans, and tell everyone about your back?"

"Yes," Richard stared down at his boots. "I just don't know what to do."

"Are the scars bad?" Curtis half-turned, fixing his inscrutable eyes on Richard.

There was a pause. "Yes, very bad. I'll show them to you if you like. We can go to the conveniences."

"No need." Curtis put his arm along the back of the settle. "Draw them here, on the table, with your finger. That'll give me an idea."

Richard moved the beer mats. "This is my back. See." And he traced with the first finger of his right hand, criss-crossing the blank table with imaginary lines. "And the scars go like this. From my shoulder all the way down... I told mother and father that I'd been thrown, hit a boulder and fell into bushes. They believed me."

"Jesus!" Curtis drank quickly. "What a bastard! And you survived that?"

"Yes."

"Well, I can see what's worrying you. It's Lydia isn't it?"

"Yes, I'm afraid she'll tell Billie before I can... before she can see them for herself."

Curtis put his chin in the air, pursed his lips and looked through the bottom of his eyes. "Well, you'd best get back to The Pyewipe and propose to Billie, and tell everybody. That'll put an end to it. Lydia will then have to go on to pastures new, won't she?"

"Thank you, uncle." Richard shook hands with this rugged man with a wooden leg. "Thank you."

"Off you go now. Don't delay. Now I'm going to see a man about a dog."

Richard couldn't remember walking back to The Blue Cow. He couldn't remember mounting Fiver, or remember clattering down Watergate and out of town. He was so encouraged by uncle Curtis. He hadn't reprimanded him for his behaviour. He hadn't criticised him or blamed him. He'd just listened.

Recognition returned as he rode up the hill into Ketsby. The forecourt of the inn was deserted but he rode on scattering hens, frightening children as they played on the roadside, startling the old women with their heads together sorting the gossip. He ignored the entrance to the lane and urged Fiver to take the five-bar gate into the turnip field. He cleared it with tremendous vigour.

They pounded on towards Bunker's Hill, thundering towards the buildings but he made no attempt to rein Fiver. He would take him right through the stackyard, over the fallen tree trunk and ride down the field to the willow trees to the stream. Billie had said it was quiet down there. He had to get this thing right and he needed time to think it through properly. Say the right words. Then he'd go back to The Pyewipe and propose to Billie. Just like his uncle had said. Then he would have to speak to his mother and stepfather.

But Richard didn't know that Bladon and Curtis had hauled the chain harrows out of the shed near the barn. They were ready for Lady to drag over the ploughed ten-acre field to break down the clods of earth before sowing. They had turned the harrows upside down to oil them and the rows of metal tines in their square metal frame were like long pointed teeth reaching for the sky.

Richard saw the harrows partly buried in the long grass as he and Fiver came round the corner of the barn. He yanked on the rein but Fiver was travelling too fast to avoid them. The horse galloped on to the harrows, impaling his legs on to the metal tines, squealing with pain as he fell. Richard was catapulted out of the saddle and flew through the air like a scarecrow blown away in the wind. He landed in a crumpled heap at the bole of the sycamore tree.

Cadger Burrell was in the barn stealing corn from the bin. He had cycled to Bunker's Hill, left his bike propped against the back wall and had gone to shoot rabbits. He had seven.

Now he needed a bit of corn for his hens. He was ladling some into a bag when he heard the screams. He stood anchored to the dusty floor clutching the rusty old bowl to his chest. Then he picked up his twelve bore gun, peered round the door then edged along the wall to the corner of the barn.

He saw the horse's crumpled legs locked in the harrows but it was losing strength, sinking and rolling on to the metal tines.

Cadger moved forward slowly. The chestnut gelding struggled and groaned but could not get free. He moved a step closer until he was staring at the wild eyes, the flaring nostrils, the frothing mouth. Then he raised his gun and took aim. One loud shot rang out across the valley. The horse looked up as if to see who did it and then fell back, motionless.

Cadger was sweating. He wiped his forehead with his coat sleeve and glanced around. Then he saw the rider curled up near a log under the tree, looking for all the world as if he were having a doze. He leaned into the ashen face and recognised the new man at The Pyewipe.

"Can you 'ear me?" He saw the eyelids flicker.

Cadger was on all fours crawling around the body. He put his head to the man's chest, then he felt for the pulse in his left wrist. It was faint but it was there. He hurried to the barn and came back with an armful of old sacks. He rolled one into a cushion and pushed it under his head and then he spread the others over the body.

"Don't move. Whatever you do, don't try to get up. I'm going for help. Can you 'ear me?" The eyelids flickered again like drowsy moths. "Stay still."

Cadger had never pedalled so hard in his life. He had to find Bladon King, the man who had set a gin trap in the hay shed and mutilated his hand all those years ago. The man he had not spoken to since that very day. The man he hated.

But he lived off Bladon. He took his eggs from the chicken huts, he helped himself to milk, he shot rabbits, hares, and pheasants. He dug up swedes, turnips, carrots and potatoes. He stole firewood, he took pig meal from his bin and he helped himself to hay. Yes, he still stole hay. He stole anything that belonged to Bladon King. Cadger had another word for stealing. Compensation.

But this young man must be helped. He had no choice but to find that arrogant bastard and speak to him.

The rutted lane from Bunker's Hill made for rough riding and the rabbits weighed heavily in the sack on his back. He puffed and panted and sweated and was soon on the tarmac road. Then he picked up speed. Children were playing, dogs were barking, old women were tittle-tattling but he sped past them all and swerved into the stable yard of The Pyewipe.

He propped his bike against the wall of the Club Room and found Bladon in the tackle shed sorting through a bundle of reins. Cadger stood in the doorway. He spat sideways, wiped his mouth with the back of his hand and then blurted out his story to the man he hadn't spoken to for twenty years.

"Didn't see no blood. Covered him with old sacks but you'll need the doctor. And transport. He were alive when I left but I 'ad to shoot the 'oss," Cadger said as he spat at Bladon King's polished top boots and walked away.

Chapter 20

"Mek me a cup of tea, missus," and Cadger threw the sack on to the kitchen floor next to bucket of waste near the sink. It needed emptying. Potato peelings, food remnants, slops and washing up water combined to fill the little kitchen with a rancid, rotten stench. A bundle of clothes crouched on the floor next to an old packing case he had found outside Barker's Store. A dirty towel was draped on the sink. Small circles had been rubbed into the kitchen windows to give a view of the little garden. He swiped off his cap and flopped into a chair at the old deal table.

Bertha had her back to him and didn't look round. "Wait a minute. Can't yer see I'm busy?" She stirred the saucepan. "You and yer tea. You'll have to wait."

"Mek some tea!" Cadger banged both fists on the table. The salt pot rattled against a jar of pickles.

"Oohh! Got out of bed the wrong side this morning, eh! Well, you needn't start throwing your weight about here." She waggled the spoon at him. "I've got summat else to do besides making tea for you every hour."

Cadger jumped to his feet, glared across the table then he picked up the salt pot and hurled it at her. It missed and fell behind the old stove.

"Mek me some tea, woman, are yer deaf?" Cadger was shouting, his thin lips slicing back into his thin cheeks.

Bertha's pasty face sagged. "What's the matter?"

"Just shot an 'oss." He sank into the chair and held his head with his hands.

"Where?"

Cadger told the story.

"My word, that'll take the wind out of their sails, won't it?"

278

Bertha rubbed her hands down her torn pinafore. "My word. What a to-do." She watched the old black kettle jiggle its lid. "And as for Bladon King – well, he 'ad it coming to him."

"Shut up Bertha!" Cadger shouted at her again.

"Well, there's been summat going on there, at The Pyewipe, I mean. I can tell you," she waggled the spoon at him again. "That there wife of his. She's back."

"Don't talk so wet," Cadger ladled sugar into his mug of tea.

"It's true, I'm telling you. After all these years. I told everybody at the time. Saw her go, I did, on the carrier's cart. With me own eyes, but nobody believed me." She sat in the chair opposite her husband, elbows on the table watching him drink his tea. "And this new man. Where's he come from? Does anybody know?" Bertha threw the question into the steam-filled kitchen.

Cadger ignored her. "I got seven rabbits. Keep one. The rest are spoken for." He pushed his mug across the table for more tea. "I should go and see if they want any help." He picked up his large, flat cap, and pulled it down to his eyebrows.

"You do no such thing," she said, leaning into his face. "Wouldn't cross the road to help Bladon King. That arse-hole. You stay out of it, do you 'ear?" She went to the stove and lifted the lid of the saucepan. "Dinner's about ready."

She rescued some stray lank hair and pushed it under the woolly hat then she put two enamel dishes on the table and ladled the mutton stew into them. "They'll get no sympathy from me. Not after what they did to you."

Cadger wasn't listening. He never listened after the first sentence.

"Too big for his boots, I've said so time and again..."

Probably get Charlie Papple to help with the 'oss.

"Nobody knew anything about her..."

Doctor Robb would know what to do about the young man.

"... and you keep out of the way, do you hear? Don't you dare go near them!"

He was slouched over the dish of stew poking it about with his spoon. "I'll go to Beck's Close and see what I can find. There'll be nobody down there with all this going on."

"And I shall go to Barker's." Bertha dunked a piece of bread in the stew and sucked on it. "They'll want to know."

* * *

News got to the butcher's shop first. Someone lit the fuse and now the gossip was raging through the village. Even the blacksmith was up to date. They fetched him to help with the dead horse. But Barker's was invigorated after a slack morning.

"He's Italian," Hilda Dawson tapped a florin on the wooden counter. "Heard him speaking foreign."

"Well, he don't look like an Italian," argued Annie Cobley who lived in Dog Kennel Yard, "they have black hair."

"Now what would you know about Italy, Annie? You've never been." Mrs Tweddle put her shopping bag on the other arm.

"Neither have you," Annie sniffed. "But he don't look like his mother. She's English enough. Anyway they ain't been here five minutes, have they?"

"Saw Bladon King bring her in the pony and trap one day last week. When would it be? Monday. No, I were busy with the washing." Hilda tapped her florin on the counter, impatient to be served. "Anyway I were in the butcher's and saw them. They had a lot of luggage."

"Well, this new man's been working here a fortnight or more." Annie Cobley knew everything. "He rides about with Billie King. Saw them at Bunker's Hill."

"Well, he ain't going to be riding anywhere for a while now." Mrs Tweddle clasped her hands in front of her.

Letty listened as she always did and she held her tongue as her mother had taught her.

"What happened then?" asked Hilda, shifting from one foot to the other.

"Seems he were riding when his horse fell into a trap," Mrs Tweddle sniffed, punctuating her facts.

"A trap?" Hilda turned to look over her shoulder at the towering figure of Mrs Tweddle.

"Yes. They reckon the gypsies had set it. They plague the life out of Bladon. He's always chasing them away."

"Not surprised." Annie Cobley rummaged in the bottom of her bag for her purse. "They just about clear him out every time they come."

"The horse threw him. Somebody went and told Bladon. I saw him and Doctor Robb in that motor, tearing up High Street."

The door flew open, the bell jangled and Bertha Burrell stood there in her woolly hat and shabby brown coat. "They've got him to hospital," she announced, "the young man."

"What happened?" Letty decided it was time to get to the truth.

"He rode into some harrows. Didn't see 'em."

"Where?"

"At Bunker's Hill. The 'oss is dead."

* * *

It was half past five when Bladon handed Trynah and Billie into the trap, passed them a travel rug and urged Duke on his way.

"Father, you should've told me before."

"But Billie, I didn't know where you were. Once we'd got him to hospital I went to Copping Lane but there was no sign of you. Barney said he thought you'd gone down to see Becky..."

"And I was at Vinny's," explained Trynah, pulling her coat collar around her. "We were all there but nobody knew where to find us. Ridiculous, really."

"Is he badly hurt?" Billie pulled the rug around her knees.

281

"Doctor Robb wasn't sure of the injuries." Bladon's eyes were on Duke's haunches as he trotted down the hill towards Manthorpe Road. "Too early to say."

"But will he be all right?" Billie pushed her hands under the travel rug.

"Of course he will." Trynah found Billie's hand and squeezed it. "He's young and strong, and he knows how to fall from a horse. He's taken a lot of falls. In Lavega." She was whisked back to the day that Pedro brought him home after the whipping. And she saw again the bloody mess on his back and heard again his groans during those long and anxious nights.

"He's in good hands, Billie," reassured Bladon, his jaw twitching. He wanted to urge Duke on but Duke had done a tidy bit of work today so he must make his own pace.

They turned right into Manthorpe Road and were soon driving past the garden to the entrance doors of the hospital.

Trynah and Billie waited until Bladon had taken care of Duke then they hurried to the reception desk. A thin, energetic nurse appeared from nowhere.

"Good afternoon. This way please." she walked quickly along broad white corridors and paused in front of a white door.

"Ten minutes," she said, opening the door and then disappearing.

Billie hesitated a moment, taking in the clean, bare room. It had that distinct hospital smell of disinfectant, a mixture of Sanitas fluid and carbolic soap. Then her eyes went to Richard. The sheets, the pillows, the walls, the ceiling seemed to absorb everything except his head. She rushed to his bedside and crouched down. Bladon, hands slotted into his breeches pockets, stared at him from the foot of the bed.

"How do you feel?" Trynah moved closer to Billie.

"Bit of a headache, but not too bad," he replied in a weak voice. "Good of you all to come."

Bladon winked at Trynah and they quietly slipped out of the room.

Billie scanned his left arm cradled in the calico sling. "Sorry I couldn't get here sooner," and she sank into the chair beside the bed.

"Don't worry. They probably wouldn't have let you in. All sorts of people have trooped in and out and I've been trundled up and down corridors and into rooms full of shiny instruments."

"Is it terribly painful?"

"It's a bit better now. I've got a dislocated collarbone and some bruises."

"Well, what happened?"

"I rode to Bunker's Hill..."

"But what were you doing at Bunker's Hill? I thought you'd gone to Grantham with uncle Curtis..."

"Yes, I did. But when I got back I wanted to go down to the willow trees. I wasn't to know those harrows were there, and I needed to think..."

"What about?"

"About what I was going to say to you when I next saw you. You see, I'd decided..." His closed his eyes taking in a deep breath, the sanitised air tingling in his nostrils. "I decided to ask you to marry me but I wanted to get it right. So that's why I went to Bunker's. To practise, to make sure I said it right." He caressed her fingers. "I bumped into Lydia in Westgate and she told me you were seeing Rodney today. You told me..."

"She's a liar." Billie stood up. "I haven't seen Rodney. When you didn't come to Copping Lane I decided to go and see Becky."

He lifted her hand to his lips again. "I believe you. Billie. Will you marry me when I've got rid of this?" His eyes went to his left arm. "Of course, I must speak to mother and father but I need to know..."

There was a silence in the empty, still room – a big, white ghostly silence. Billie stared at the dusty blond hair. It needed washing. His eyes were a brilliant blue, his cheeks were tinged with a pastel pink. She leaned over and kissed his slightly open mouth. "Yes. I will marry you."

"Lean a bit closer, Billie," He ran his fingers through her hair. "Say it again, please."

"Yes, I'll marry you. But now you must rest. And I'm going to call mother and father. They're both very worried about you. It was nice of them to leave us together, wasn't it?"

Richard closed his eyes and a long, soft sigh escaped. "Leave me something of yours. Something I can touch and feel."

"Well," Billie opened her coat and inspected her thick jumper, her corduroy trousers. "I don't have anything really. Only my watch..."

"Put it on my wrist," he held up his right arm, "and you must wear mine. It's in that drawer there."

Billie rummaged in the bedside locker and fastened the watch around her wrist. "It's a bit big..."

"Wear it until I can buy you a ring, Billie. Kiss me again, please."

She paused at the doorway for one last glance. He looked so vulnerable lying there and she wanted to dash back to his bedside, to hold him and hug him but she resisted.

Richard turned his head to the window and smiled at the dark green bushes silhouetted against a vast, grey wintry sky. He'd said it. It had been easy. And she'd accepted. He ran his hand through his hair, which felt sticky. Uncle Curtis had been right. 'Get back to The Pyewipe and propose to her,' he had said. But he'd done it from a hospital bed.

His thoughts darted through the events of the day. Everything had moved so quickly since riding to Bunker's. Then there were some blanks but he remembered the pain after his shoulder had been pulled and manipulated. The sharp pains reminded him of that day in Lavega and Carlos Daroca.

"I notice this isn't the first fall you've had, Mr Mann." He was in another white room and Doctor Mills was studying his back, but said nothing about the whip scars. "The bruises will fade. Fortunately the skin is not broken." He looked over his horn-rimmed spectacles, furrowed his deep bushy eyebrows and said, "You must rest the injured shoulder for at least two weeks. No riding. Everything will be fine."

Yes, Richard's eyes swept around the stark room. He smiled. Everything will be fine. He was going to marry Billie. Lydia couldn't torment him ever again.

Billie made her way along the corridor passing nurses in rustling starched aprons pushing trolleys laden with linen, the click, click of their heels tapping on the highly polished floors. Men in spotless white coats hurried by clutching papers to their chests, their eyes on their shoes. Everything seemed urgent, almost dangerous. Somewhere, not far away, a metal dish clattered to the floor. Then Billie was back in the reception area. It was deserted. She felt exhilarated yet restless. Restless because he was in pain. She could tell it was worse than he admitted by the little grimaces when they chatted, but she was exhilarated because he had asked her to marry him. Clapping her hands in front of her she went to the window and smiled at the lonely little garden. It was surrounded by an evergreen hedge waiting for spring, for colour. A blackbird alighted on a bare branch of the apple tree and cleaned its beak. Yes, she would marry Richard.

She heard the swish of the entrance doors and then there was a commotion at the reception desk. Voices were raised, a telephone rang, a door banged.

"Well, I know he's here." She recognised the voice. It was Lydia. A tall, thin young man was by her side. He had been at the dance but Billie couldn't remember his name.

"Billie! I went to find you. Aunt Vinny said you were here. Is it true?" Lydia was wearing a purple velvet coat and a turban hat and smelt as beautiful as she looked. "Oh, this is George."

"Hello," Billie stared at the young man with black hair flopping over his forehead. A cold, thin hand enclosed hers.

"Is what true?" Billie engaged the mischievous eyes.

"Richard. He's got a broken leg." Lydia gripped her clutch bag. "Have you seen him?"

"Yes I've seen him. He's got a dislocated shoulder. Mother and father are with him at the moment." Billie looked at George and then at Lydia and then decided. It was time something was done about Lydia and her lies. Perhaps the reception area of a hospital wasn't the best place but Billie couldn't stop herself. She felt confident and she was happy. The words gushed up and came tumbling out.

"Why did you tell Richard I was seeing Rodney today?" Billie was surprised her voice was so calm.

"Oh, don't be silly." Lydia tapped the little leather clutch bag. "How could I have told him? I haven't seen him since the dance."

"You saw him this morning, in Grantham." Billie's eyes seared Lydia's face and she saw the cheeks redden.

Lydia grabbed George's arm. "Come along. Let's go and see darling Richard. I wonder what the time is?"

"I have the time," Billie pulled back the sleeve of her coat. "It's exactly ten minutes to seven."

"That's Richard's watch!" Lydia remembered it from the day in the den. "What are you doing with it?"

"He's asked me to wear it." Billie smiled.

"Why?" Lydia stepped away.

"Until he can give me a ring."

"*A ring!*" Lydia pulled on Billie's sleeve to look more closely at the watch.

"Yes, he's proposed to me." Billie tossed her head back. "We're going to be married."

"You're what?" Lydia slammed her clutch bag across her knees.

There were footsteps along the corridor and Bladon and Trynah came through the swing doors arm in arm.

Lydia stared at them and at Billie, then with a toss of her head, she turned to the nurse at the desk. "Can we go and see Mr Mann now?"

"No more visitors today. Sorry."

Cover Design: The Digital Canvas Company

Layout: S. Fairgrieve

Font: Adobe Garamond (11pt)

Copies of this book can be ordered via the Internet:

www.librario.com

or from:

Librario Publishing Ltd
Brough House
Milton Brodie
Kinloss
Moray IV36 2UA
Tel / Fax No 01343 850 617